Wakefield Press

OPEN DAY

Most of Dr Leslie Kilmartin's professional life has been in Australian universities. He began as a teacher and researcher, but in mid-career stumbled into higher education management, initially as a dean and then as a pro vice-chancellor. Later, he spent a decade-and-a-half as a human relations consultant headhunting senior staff for universities.

Open Day is thus a well-informed if somewhat surreal account of the murky, bizarre micro-culture that thrives in the upper echelons of the modern university. Happily, Batman University doesn't really exist, and the characters (with one exception) are fictional. Among the targets of this rollicking yarn are university governors, managers and the ubiquitous marketers.

Leslie Kilmartin is the author of a family history biography, *The Elusive Captain William Cromarty*, and an historical novel, *The Cromartys of Port Stephens*.

OPEN DAY

LESLIE KILMARTIN

Wakefield
Press

Wakefield Press
16 Rose Street
Mile End
South Australia 5031
www.wakefieldpress.com.au

First published 2023

Copyright © Leslie Kilmartin, 2023

All rights reserved. This book is copyright. Apart from
any fair dealing for the purposes of private study, research,
criticism or review, as permitted under the Copyright Act,
no part may be reproduced without written permission.
Enquiries should be addressed to the publisher.

Cover by Design by Committee
Cover illustration by Josh Durham
Typeset by Michael Deves, Wakefield Press

ISBN 978 1 92304 203 2

A catalogue record for this book
is available from the National
Library of Australia

Wakefield Press thanks
Coriole Vineyards for
continued support

Contents

Are university Open Days scary?
No! They are there to make you feel comfortable
about the choices you make for university.

The Complete University Guide (UK)

Come as you are,
leave as you want to be.

University of Melbourne Open Day, 2019

Breaking News

Professor Sally Sloane reached for the off button on the car radio as soon as she heard 'breaking news'. She'd been enjoying the Sunday afternoon classical music and resented being dragged back into the awful reality of the world. Her finger was still hovering over the button when she heard the words 'There has been a mass shooting at a university Open Day in Melbourne'. There was only one university having an Open Day that day. It was hers. And that had even won a rare dispensation from the surviving COVID rules about assembly.

She braked suddenly and pulled into the emergency lane of the freeway, earning herself a blast from the Audi that had been tailgating her. She waved a perfunctory apology, brought the car to a halt and turned up the volume.

'What else can you tell us, Polly?'

'Jane, Batman University was conducting its annual Open Day; and we're not sure what happened but we've been told that there's been a shooting. I'm here at Robert Gordon General Hospital where the victims have been brought. We're expecting to have a statement from hospital authorities soon.'

'Do you have any information about the reasons for the shooting?'

'Police are very tightlipped, Jane, but we believe an ISIS flag and two rifles have been found on top of the main admin building.'

'So, it's terrorism, Polly?'

'It certainly looks that way, Jane.'

'Maybe, but there was also a racially charged event on campus.'

'It's apparently unrelated, Jane. Their Open Day coincides with Invasion Day for the local Indigenous community. The statue of the infamous John Batman, now located on the campus, was defaced, torn down and thrown into the creek.'

'So, it's not all bad news,' Sally muttered.

'Indigenous actors had performed a play about Aboriginal oppression in front of the statue. At the end of the play, a large black sheet was draped over the statue and a sign hung around it saying "Dead White Man".'

'An eventful Open Day for Batman University, Polly?'

'Certainly, Jane. A great deal of publicity but the kind no university wants. There's enough trouble already about breaching the COVID rules.'

'Thanks, Polly. Now, back to Sunday Classics and a charming little piece by Rameau.'

Sally felt numb. As Deputy Chairman of the university's Board, she should attend the Open Day, but had deliberately absented herself after deciding to allow the new Chairman, Reg O'Toole, whatever glory went with being in the spotlight. Sally Sloane was a retired university Vice-Chancellor and had had quite enough of academic ceremonies, meetings and, yes, even Open Days. She'd chosen, instead, the company of some women friends and a movie that Sunday afternoon.

Now she was regretting that decision. Not that her presence could have changed anything. But it was more a matter of optics. Would the Open Day committee wonder why she wasn't there? Or the senior staff? Or Batman's new President, Nicholas Razer? Hardly. That sybaritic prick couldn't care less. She loathed and distrusted him but that shouldn't have kept her away; the fact was, it had.

But what now? She should call Nicholas right away. And Reg. The first Open Day at Batman University for both of them. She needed the full story about what had happened but both calls went to voicemail, so she messaged them to return her call as soon as possible.

They never did.

Chapter 1

Back to a Beginning: Batman University Gets a New President

Kurt Kropp's executive search firm, GoodKropp, was widely acknowledged as the 'go to' recruiting firm for senior appointments in Australian universities. Over two decades, Kropp had won a reputation as the kingmaker for senior appointments in higher education. An assiduous networker, he'd nurtured professional contacts at the most senior levels throughout universities in the Anglosphere.

He could call any university President in the land to get an off-the-record appraisal of an academic on his or her staff. Executive Deans, Vice Presidents, research directors, HR directors, chief finance officers and many more sought him out, confided in him. A quiet word to Kropp could make or break a career.

Kropp was at his desk perusing his list of Presidents of Australian universities to see whose turn it was to be schmoozed when his EA buzzed him.

'Kurt, call for you from Professor Sally Sloane from Batman University. Are you in?'

'Sally Sloane, eh?' Kropp raised his eyebrows, intrigued. They went back a long way to the days when university Presidents were known as Vice-Chancellors. He'd headhunted her for Western Metro University when they were searching for a new Vice-Chancellor. Years later, he'd been a special guest at her retirement dinner when she publicly acknowledged her debt to him. They were once very close. Indeed, close enough for the scuttlebutt to have been spot on. When Sally heard that Kropp had been indiscreet about their affair, she ended it angrily and abruptly.

'Put her through.' He smiled to himself as he moved to his couch.

'Sally, long time.'

'Good morning, Kurt.' Kropp wasn't surprised by her formality, but he was sure he could break down that coolness.

'Are you enjoying your retirement?' he asked.

'I doubt my responsibilities at Batman University would qualify as retirement,' she replied dismissively.

'So, you're still on the Council?'

'Board,' she said, savouring the chance to correct him. 'The Council's now a Board. I'm acting Chairman. The sole survivor from the former council after the government reforms. And, to add to my woes, I'm also acting President. That's why I'm calling.'

Kropp's spirits suddenly rose. A call from a university President was rarely bad for business. Even if Sally Sloane had been a little frosty, he understood she was capable of putting personal feelings aside. Such a professional.

'I want to appoint a new President, and fast.'

Oh, lordy, happy days, thought Kropp, punching his spare fist in the air.

'Despite our personal history,' Sally continued, 'I want you to do the search. The Board has the Minister's approval to spend whatever it takes.'

'So, the usual commission?' Kropp tried to conceal his elation.

'The usual,' said Sally, deadpan.

'Any names you'd like us to contact?'

'There's one I am very keen on. An Indigenous woman. I'll email her details.'

Kropp was curious, but said nothing. He prided himself on

knowing most of the aspiring Presidents, and couldn't think of any senior Indigenous women he'd consider suitable for the role.

'We'll put advertisements in all the usual places, providing your name and contact details.'

'Good. Once I've had a look at the position description, we'll need to meet for a briefing. What about dinner later this week?'

'That ship has sailed, Kurt. Let's meet for coffee.'

'Now you've hurt my feelings.'

'I'm not sure people with your condition have feelings, Kurt.'

'You're heaping hurt upon hurt.'

'One other thing, I want to be sure you'll personally do the work. No flicking this to some buxom underling.'

'I wouldn't dream of that, Sally. I'll be leading this one.'

'We can meet for coffee next Friday, 10 am.'

'OK. I'll sign you in at the club,' Kropp said as he made a diary entry.

'We'll meet at the Professional Women's Club,' Sally countered.

'My membership's lapsed.'

'Goodbye, Kurt.'

ooOOoo

Kropp had become accustomed to receiving calls from senior academics about university appointments within days of a post being advertised. Not all calls were self-interested. Not on the face of it. Some were disguised as off-the-record offers of assistance. It was one such call that Kropp's EA took.

'Kurt, call for you about the Batman President position.'

'Who is it?' Kropp was peeved that, once again, his new EA had neglected to get the caller's name, which put him at a disadvantage.

'He wouldn't say.'

Another Deep Throat, thought Kropp. Why are there so many

pussies these days? Surely they know I don't leak names. Bad for business.

He pressed the speaker button. 'Kurt Kropp.'

'Mr Kropp,' the caller said anxiously, 'I saw your ad for the President at Batman and I'd like to suggest someone.

'A colleague of yours?' Kropp probed.

'Not exactly. A man in a related field though.'

Bad start, thought Kropp. They all want women Presidents these days.

'Go on, please.' Anticipating he was about to waste time on an anonymous informant, Kropp moved to the window to check the weather moving in from the west.

'Well, Nicholas Razer's an academic psychologist with a formidable academic record in neuropsychology. He spent a study leave here at Sandstone a little while ago as visiting research professor at the Cephallus Institute.'

'Cephallus? I don't know it,' Kropp admitted.

'It's a spin-off from the Brain Institute. Cephallus deals with men's psychosexual health. They do research and have clinics. It's a growth area.'

In more ways than one, thought Kropp.

'They get lots of research dollars and plenty of endowments from wealthy men with everything from performance anxiety to erectile dysfunction.'

'And the name …?'

'It's a contraction of "cephalic" and "phallus".'

Ah, yes, thought Kropp. More a matter of what's between your ears than what's between your legs.

'You just have to remember to put the emphasis on the second syllable.' The anonymous source sniggered. 'I attended some of Professor Razer's seminars and also met him socially a few times. He's a larger-than-life sort of person.'

'Any experience in management?' asked Kropp, knowing that high-flying academics rarely have much management experience.

'He was elected Chairman of his academic Board in the UK so has had some management experience but not, of course, at the most senior level. No disrespect, but we're talking about Batman. I wouldn't be surprised if he could persuade the Sandstone President to be a referee. They've done joint research projects and published together in prestigious neuropsych journals.'

'Why would he be interested in coming to Australia? And to Batman?'

Kropp heard the caller inhale.

'He loved his time here. He's extremely ambitious and confident. I reckon he'd imagine he could turn Batman around and then … well, what I mean is, I don't think Batman would have him for more than a few years.'

That's a bloody sight longer than most of his predecessors, thought Kropp.

'And whether you follow up or not, please don't mention my name!'

'You didn't give it, Professor Naylor.' Kropp had been googling the university website while they spoke.

The caller fell silent, and Kropp imagined him squirming with embarrassment.

'You're Richard Naylor, Head of Ed Psych at Sandstone. Don't worry, it's not in my interests to blow your cover. Why don't you tell me more about Professor Razer.'

'Now I feel silly.'

'Don't.'

'In for a penny,' he sighed. 'There are some push factors – a nasty divorce from wife number two and there's another woman in the picture. Wife number three.'

Kropp frowned. He knew what was coming: spousal employment.

'Batman may have to find her a role. She works in the international office at the same university. She's Thai.'

'I'll look into that,' said Razer. They're desperate, he thought to himself, maybe they'll come across if they want him badly enough.

'Another issue is that Razer's somewhat persona non grata in his own university. Seems he goes away overseas quite often and some of his colleagues are resentful. And suspicious about where he goes and under whose auspices.'

'Suspicious of what?' asked Kropp, assuming envy rather than suspicion.

'There's a lot of speculation. Some believe he's conducting or supervising research on some sinister aspects of brainwashing or the like.'

God, is that all? That could kill any chance, thought Kropp as he saw the briefly promising prospect of a suitable candidate suddenly fly out the window.

'There's another consideration which you might at first blush consider a negative. But I think it might be just what Batman needs in a President.'

'And that is?'

'Let's just say he'd score high on any conventional test of psychopathy. And narcissism.'

Essential qualifications for being a university President, thought Kropp, without looking up from Razer's bio, which he'd found online. Nicholas Razer was indeed a high flyer. His record at his elite university hadn't been updated for about twelve months but it was stellar. His academic qualifications were from first-rate universities in the UK and the US, his publication record was superior, his competitive research grants impressive. He'd recently been President of the International Neuropsychology Association and visiting professor at a number of prestigious universities, including the year at Sandstone. A series of public lectures on men's psychosexual health on BBC television had enjoyed high viewer ratings.

'Has his personality caused any problems?' inquired Kropp, trawling through the university bio.

'None that I know of. In fact, he can be charming and he's a brilliant raconteur. His colleagues at Cephallus liked him and would love to have him back in this part of the world. If being out at Batman could be considered being "in this part of the world". I'm just trying to help.'

Are you? thought Kropp, or are you just interference?

'One more thing,' the caller went on. 'You'll need to know that Nicholas isn't currently using his university email account or phone number. The EA to the head of Cephallus could give you his contact details.'

Nicholas Razer and Batman University? Kropp wondered as he phoned the Cephallus Institute.

ooOOoo

Time was short. The closing date for applications was almost upon them. Kropp pressed a button on his desk phone and called a UK mobile phone number. It was approaching 5 pm in eastern Australia.

'Nicholas Razer,' a polished Oxbridge voice answered. Bingo! thought Kropp, it's rarely as easy as that.

'Good morning. Professor Razer, my name is Kurt Kropp and I'm calling you on behalf of the Board of one of Australia's newer universities, Batman University in Melbourne. May I have a few moments of your time?'

Over a long career, Razer had developed a nose for detecting calls from headhunters. What's more, he'd been expecting this call.

'How can I help you, Mr Kropp?'

'Our firm has been engaged by the Board of Batman University to identify senior academics who might be interested in applying for the post of President of the University. Your name's been suggested to us as a potential candidate. Would you be interested in learning more about the role?'

'Oh, I don't know about that,' said Razer with confected reluctance. 'I love Australia and would be glad to work there again. As you probably already know, I spent some time at Sandstone not so long ago. Loved the people, the city, the climate. But, I'm fairly much anchored here for now.'

'Perhaps if I can explain a little more about the university and what the Board is looking for?'

'By all means, but I doubt I'll be enticed to apply.'

Kropp felt he might have a struggle on his hands, and it was one he wanted to win. He pulled out all stops. He sang the praises of the university, its new and revitalised Board, its committed staff and aspiring students. He painted a picture of the beautiful rustic region in which it was located, the rolling hills, serried rows of vines producing the best wine in the country. He mentioned the research budget available to the President and the generous travel and study leave negotiable for the right candidate.

'I've got to hand it to you, Kurt. You paint a very attractive picture.'

Even the cynical Kropp was susceptible to flattery. And, importantly, they seemed already to be on first name terms. Brilliant!

'My CV's up to date, so how about I dash off a brief letter of application and email it to you? Say, this weekend?'

'That would be marvellous, Nicholas. And I'll send you the information kit right away.' In his excitement, Kropp had stood and was punching the air. He little guessed that Razer was very interested indeed in having a period of time out of the UK. An undistinguished, peri-urban university on the other side of the world and near to Asia would be ideal for him, personally and professionally.

oOoOOoo

Kropp was so elated at having the certainty of an application from Nicholas Razer that he called Sally Sloane on her mobile immediately.

'Sally, I think I have a very interesting candidate for the President's role,' he began.

'Name?' she demanded.

Kropp had barely started his spiel to excite Sally's interest before she had Razer's university bio on her screen.

'He's promised to send me an application. This weekend. I think he'd be good for Batman,' said Kropp confidently. He knew it was going to be difficult to get any applicants, and certainly not such a well qualified one.

'Maybe it's more a matter of Batman being good for him,' Sally mused, scrolling still through Razer's CV.

'How d'you mean?' Kropp asked, somewhat deflated.

'I'm looking at his CV online. Doesn't add up. Why would a high-flying academic like Razer want to come to Batman? Sounds fishy to me.'

'We'll do the referee checks on all that,' Kropp said, hoping Sally wasn't about to veto what might turn out to be Kropp's best and only find.

'When could he start?' Sally asked.

Hah! thought Kropp. Her own plan to get the Batman University monkey off her back might yet prevail.

'Early in the year,' Kropp lied.

'Which year?' Sally asked.

'Really, Sally, 2022. Next year.'

'That's soon and that only adds to my suspicions. How come he's so available? I can tell you, Kurt, I have reservations about your Nicholas Razer.'

Our Nicholas Razer, I hope, thought Kropp.

'But we're struggling to find anyone, Sally,' Kropp pleaded. 'You must know that.'

'That's how things always are with BU,' Sally acknowledged. 'I'll reserve judgement. How's progress on Gladys Cherbourg?'

'Thanks for suggesting her. She's proving difficult. Indigenous professor in Townsville. She's not crazy about the idea of moving to Melbourne.'

'She's a north Queensland woman, born and bred. She'll be hard to budge,' acknowledged Sally.

'I've persuaded her to send her CV as a registration of interest. But she's holding out on providing a full application. She's agreed to a campus visit. I'll organise it. We'll turn it on for her.'

'I can tell you she won't be susceptible to duchessing,' warned Sally.

'I think if we're lucky, then, we'll have just two applications,' said Kropp.

Chapter 2

The Wisdom of the Marketer

Jamie Jamieson regarded himself as one of the best marketers in the Australian higher education system. He'd learned his trade in a regional water authority, and had brought his marketing insights and expertise to Batman University. He'd served at Batman rather longer than he'd hoped, but he'd settled in comfortably and lost none of his passion for what he regarded as the noble profession of marketing.

Among his many and varied responsibilities at Batman was the role of Convenor of the Open Day committee. His grand plans for Open Day 2021 had been thwarted by COVID when the campus was closed most of the year. But every cloud has a silver lining, he consoled himself: memories of his disastrous 2020 Open Day had hopefully now faded. He'd had to concede that Open Day hadn't lived up to his high standards. He reasoned his Open Day committee had been too big, too lazy and unable to grasp his innovative ideas.

He was determined never to concede control of the committee again, and he'd persuaded the powers that be to let him rule over a smaller committee to plan the 2022 Open Day. He was determined to impose his stamp on the committee and, indeed, on the day itself. Open Day 2022 was going to be one for the ages, he resolved as he made his way to the first Open Day committee meeting for the year.

To add drama to his arrival, he delayed a few minutes until the members were seated.

'Good morning, playmates,' he gushed as he breezed into the meeting room, taking his place at the head of the table. 'It's my absolute pleasure to welcome you all to the 2022 Batman University Open Day committee.'

'Jamie, we're not your playmates,' grumbled Dr Marilyn Worthy from Arts. 'Please don't infantilise us and trivialise our work.'

Jamie was taken aback at this fierce rebuke. He'd been told the handpicked committee would be like putty in his hands.

'Just a bit of fun, Marilyn. Yeah?' he said defensively. 'I want this committee to be the funnest committee any of us ever worked on. And we want to plan the funnest Open Day Batman has ever mounted.'

'By the way, Jamie,' she continued, 'there's no such word as "funnest".'

'I made it up,' Jamie smiled proudly. 'Don't you think it adds to the language?'

'No more than a word such as "baddest", which, suddenly seems rather apt.'

'Let's not play semantics with words, Marilyn. Yeah?'

Strike one, he thought. Put her in her place.

Jamie opened his iPad and checked the agenda.

'Now, you're all new appointees to this small but vital committee. So, I want to extend a special welcome to you. We have a bit of ground to make up after the 2020 Open Day which, to be honest, wasn't our best ever. I'm afraid the dates didn't smile on us that day.'

'I think you mean the gods, Jamie. The gods didn't smile on us.'

'No, I meant the dates, Marilyn. 2020, as in "20:20 vision". We lacked 20:20 vision and that's why it turned out the way it did. That's what I meant.'

'It was shambles,' declared Dr Arso Kikavic from Science. 'Numbers down. Your people, Jamie, forgot to send notices to schools. You hadn't produced enough pre-enrolment forms or programs.'

'I think you're being hypercritical, Arso,' said Jamie.

'I am not hypocrite!'

'No, I said hypercritical. You know, overly critical.'

'Overly critical? I took my daughter to Open Days at other universities. Batman's was embarrassing.'

'And that's why we're going to do better next year, Arso,' replied Jamie.

'My opinion, it's not possible. As Australians like to say, you trying to make silk pouch out of pig's arse.'

'That's a very negative view, Arso,' said Jamie.

'But I'm wrong? Don't think so.'

'I've heard on the grapevine,' Jamie lowered his voice to share a confidence, 'that the headhunters are about to identify some amazing candidates for our new President. Our role is to put on an Open Day that will really impress him.'

'Him, Jamie?'

'Him, her. Whatever, Marilyn, All I'm saying is Batman will be entering a new era. So, our Open Day has to be like no other. Yeah?'

'And how can we do that?' inquired Kon Economopoulos from Business.

'Good question, Kon. It's one I've been unleashing all my creative juices over. I've searched the internet for examples of Open Day excellence. I've looked for world's best practice.'

'And world's best jargon, Jamie?'

'I think what you call "jargon" are actually marketing innovations, Marilyn,' retorted Jamie. 'Let's get back to basics. When I say "Open Day", what comes into your minds? Let's drill down a bit on the concept. Two apparently simple words but pregnant with meaning. What about the word "open"? What comes into your mind when I say "open"? Anyone?'

'With the last Open Day in mind,' said Kon, 'how about open wound?'

'Or,' sniggered Arso Kikavic, 'bearing in mind our entry standards for some soft programs, how about open slather?'

'If you're referring to Arts, that's a pretty cheap shot coming from someone in Science,' objected Marilyn Worthy.

'Please, colleagues, can we stick to the task,' pleaded Jamie. 'Let me start the ball rolling. There's a clue right in front us. Open, open … what?'

Nobody spoke.

'OK, here's a clue. "Open" is a noun, a verb, an adjective and a … what?'

'Got it!' exclaimed Declan McGee, the student representative. 'An adverb!'

'Not there yet, Declan. No, "open" is an attitude. Yeah?'

'Not an adverb?' Declan's disappointment was obvious as he frowned and ran a hand through his long, dishevelled red hair.

'So let's look around. Yeah? It's open sandwiches, of course. Nobody seemed to notice I've ordered open sandwiches. Not ones with lids.'

'And, so …?'

'Don't you see, Marilyn? It's a metaphor for Open Day. Yeah? We take the lid off Batman University and reveal what's in the Batman sandwich. What its filling is and what the filling means to the bread. Their interaction. There's a dialectic going on there. We have to let people see what we're inviting them to consume. It's the attitude. Our attitude. We have to be open, in every sense of that simple four-letter word. I believe in metaphors.'

'Jamie,' ventured Marilyn, 'I think … oh, forget it.'

'Now, we've seen the importance of openness. Of being open. So, drilling down further on the concept of Open Day. Where to next?' Jamie threw out the challenge. No-one responded.

'Don't you see? It's the word … or is it a concept? – "day".'

'What's wrong with the word "day", Jamie?' inquired Declan McGee, the sociology student whose interest was suddenly aroused by deconstruction of the language.

'Only three letters compared with four for "open"?' asked Arso.

Jamie ignored the intended trivialisation.

'The problem, Declan, glad you asked, is that the concept of "day" is too narrow. It's too restrictive, too limiting. It strangles our thinking.'

'You mean we should have open at night, Jamie? Or day *and* night?' said Kon. 'Sounds weird to me.'

'No, you're not following me, Kon. We love "day". But "day" can't do it all alone. It's becoming an unbearable burden for poor old "day". We've got to find ways to give "day" some support.'

'Jamie, this is becoming a little Dada,' said Marilyn.

'Dada? Not sure I'm following you, Marilyn. But stay with me. We're on the edge of a marketing breakthrough. A genuine conceptual innovation to put Batman University ahead of the pack. Even internationally.'

Marilyn Worthy sighed.

'C'mon, help me out here, gang,' Jamie urged. 'I want us to workshop our way to a whole new marketing concept. It won't be easy but you'll have an exhilarating ride. Yeah? Now, what allies can we offer to our friend "day"? Anyone?'

'Look, Jamie, in the Business School,' said Kon, 'the marketing lecturers are sprouting jargon all the time. But I'm not sure I get your drift.'

'Kon, no disrespect to your colleagues, but that's why they're marketing lecturers and I'm a marketing practitioner. I unthink, therefore I am.'

Still no-one took up Jamie's challenge.

'OK, I can see it's a bit beyond you all. Yeah? How about we augment our signage in ways that differentiate us from our competitors.'

'Differentiate us?' scoffed Kikavic. 'How about better teaching and more research?'

'You're not thinking like a marketer, Arso. Nothing wrong with teaching and research, of course. No-one's saying that. But to get into the public's inner mind, into both the left and the right brain, we need powerful marketing. Yeah? I call it Jamie's Brain and Heart marketing.'

Jamie looked in vain around his committee and concluded they were never going to make the mental leap he was seeking.

'OK, let me help you here.'

'Please, Jamie, get to it,' pleaded Marilyn.

'Yeah, this is awesome,' enthused Declan.

'Right. Instead of just the two naked and lonely words "Open Day", we're going to have a marketing campaign which in cinemas, on TV, in brochures, Facebook, all the social media, on all our platforms, is going to leave the tired old words "Open Day" behind in the dust.'

'Please, Jamie, I have a lecture soon,' Arso said.

'We're going to have a range of products rolled out in each and every marketing outlet that enlarges and enhances the phrase "Open Day".'

'You sound like Moses descending from the mountain with a couple of tablets to change the course of human history,' observed Marilyn.

'That's actually not such a bad metaphor, Marilyn.'

Marilyn let it go.

'From now on,' Jamie continued, 'Batman's signage is not just going to be "Open Day", we're going to dazzle our targeted customers by varying the stimulus in different outlets at different times. The public is going to see concepts such as "Open Day, Open Minds" or "Open

Day, Open Doors" or "Open Day, Open Eyes". Yeah? The marketing possibilities are endless! And little old Batman University will have a world-first marketing tool. Batman University will be on the map.'

Jamie sat back and looked around at his committee triumphantly.

Chapter 3

Red Studies at Batman University

Sally Sloane hated sitting at the President's desk. She'd reluctantly agreed to the Minister's entreaties to fill in as acting President and told him unambiguously that she would not be interested in staying in that role. Furthermore, she intended stepping down as acting Chairman of the Board as soon as a new appointee could be found. The Minister pleaded with her, but she was not for turning.

Her simmering resentment at being drawn back into the tedious business of running a university led Sally to make the smallest protest: rather than sit at the President's desk, she would operate from his conference table. Purely symbolic, but it made her feel better. While poring over the alarming budget papers for the upcoming executive meeting her mobile phone rang.

'Sal, Reg O'Toole.'

Reg was the only person she allowed to shorten her name. What was the use of complaining? He did the same to everyone.

'Hello, Reg. To what do I owe the pleasure?'

'Y'know I asked you about giving a shitload of money to Sandstone a couple of years ago. To fund a professor and Centre for Celtic Studies.'

'I recall it well. I told you how much any university would welcome such a large grant.'

In fact, Sally had hinted to Reg, a working class boy made good, that her own Western Metro University would be a more deserving beneficiary of his generosity. But Reg knew a gift to Sandstone would reap greater rewards for him and his business interests.

'Yeah, well, Sandstone have really stuffed up. They took over a year to make an appointment and within months of arriving, bloody professor O'Hare packed his bags and pissed off back to Dublin.'

Sally expressed her surprise but she'd heard scuttlebutt that O'Hare was not having an easy time settling in. It was rumoured that O'Hare's colleagues in History didn't regard him as a real historian.

'They tried to bury the story,' he scoffed. 'Like a family trying to forget the death of an alcoholic uncle.'

'They'll find a replacement, of course.'

'They might, but not with O'Toole money. They've done their dash with me. They wanted to put the Centre in some other department in Sandstone but I told them to get stuffed. I demanded they return the grant.'

'Good luck with that,' said Sally, who knew how tightly universities cling to grants.

'I gave them no option. Had a call from the Dean. Then some research boffin and then the President himself.'

'It's pretty hard to wrench money from universities.'

'Having a bit of influence around town helps.'

'I'm sure it does.'

'Anyway, I wanted to speak with you about what to do with the grant. I want to stick it up Sandstone and give the money to Batman.'

'All of it?' asked Sally incredulously. 'BU's never had such a generous grant.'

'There's one catch, Sal. Sandstone didn't want it to be called Celtic Studies. Have to come up with another name. Has to include the Irish thing, y'know, in my dad's honour. Any ideas?'

'Leave it with me. I'll get back to you soon.'

'Sooner the better. Universities take a bloody long time to get anything done, if Sandstone was any guide.'

'I'll give Kurt Kropp a call, too.'

'The headhunter bloke?'

'That's him.'

'But he's the one who found O'Hare for Sandstone,' Reg protested. 'I was on the selection panel. Thought he was up himself.'

'He is, but he's the best in the business. Remember, Reg, the headhunter's role is to assemble a group of applicants. They don't make the final choice; that's up to the professorial selection committee. O'Hare was Sandstone's choice.'

O'Toole grunted.

'By the way, I've started the search for a new President.'

'I heard about the last dud. Here's hoping the new bloke gives Batman a shake-up, whoever he is.'

'Or whoever *she* is, Reg?'

'That seems to be the modern thing,' conceded O'Toole. 'I hope whatever it is, they give Batman a good shake up. You know my thoughts on universities.'

'I do, indeed, Reg. And despite your views, you've been generous to Batman over the years. And you're going to be very generous once more.'

'I'm trying to give something back to the community, Sal. Batman University is one of my favourite charities in the outer east.'

Sally joined Reg in laughing at his weak joke.

'By the way,' Reg wheezed, 'what's happening about the Chairman of the Board? How come you're still doing it?'

'The Minister's waiting for the government to announce the new regulations for the governing bodies of universities. Fact is, given the obligations and responsibilities expected of the new Boards, it won't be easy to find a suitable person. However, our chat's given me an idea.'

Reg fell silent and Sally hoped he was imagining a new public honour.

'Don't even think about it,' he warned.

Sally smiled, figuring she knew him better than he knew himself.

'Thanks, Reg, I'll get back to you soon about the O'Toole Chair.'

The call ended, Sally checked her contacts list for the mobile number of the Minister of Higher Education. She knew he'd welcome what she had to suggest.

'Hello, Sally.'

'Hello, Simon. Got a moment?'

'Sure, for my favourite ex-herder of academic cats.'

Simon was an ingratiating politician to his core and it irritated her.

'Do you have a nomination for Chair of the Batman Board yet? And, just in case …'

'You've reconsidered, Sally? That's great news.'

'Let me finish that thought, Simon. I'm going to make an exit from the BU Board as soon as you can find a new chair. But I have a name you might like to consider. I think he'd be ideal.'

'Did you say "he"? Bad start, Sally.'

'I know the Premier wants a female but most women are far too smart to take on roles like that.'

'Didn't stop you, Sally.'

'Your man is Reg O'Toole. Not sure why you hadn't thought of him yourself. He's in the Party, lives in Robert Gordon, is active in the community and has no experience with higher education.'

'So far, so good,' said the Minister.

'Best of all, he's very wealthy. And he's about to award a multi-million dollar grant to Batman. One that any university would be delighted to receive.'

'And pissed off to lose, I understand.'

'You heard?'

'That's my job, Sally. To hear things.'

'What do you think about Reg for Batman?'

'I think it's the best idea I've come up with in a while. Leave it with me.'

oooOoo

Sally Sloane allowed a few days to pass before contacting Reg O'Toole again.

'Hello, Reg, it's Sally.'

'I thought I might hear from you. Would you happen to know anything about a call I had from Simon bloody Brady?'

'The Minister?'

'Don't play dumb, Sal.'

'Actually, I was calling about the O'Toole Chair, Reg,' said Sally, avoiding the question.

'I'll take that as a "yes".'

'I think I've got an idea and a name for the O'Toole Chair. It might sound a bit odd at first but I can assure you, it's very academically respectable. And it retains the Celtic connection.'

'Yes?'

'I'm suggesting the O'Toole professorship in Red Studies. I think it's a little bit edgy and has great potential.'

'Red Studies? "Red" as in "communist"? No way I'm going to fund any lefty thing like that.'

'I can assure you it has good academic connotations. And it's nothing to do with the people's flag.'

'What then?'

'There's an emerging field of teaching and research known as Red Studies. I recently read a book on the topic. About 12 or 14 per cent of the Irish population, like you and your father, are redheads.'

'More like used to be in our case,' Reg wheezed again. 'Bald as a pair of grey-skirted eggs these days.'

'In Australia,' Sally went on, 'people think of redheads as Irish. But, there's Jewish redheads, eastern European redheads, even redheads in the Middle East and the Pacific. Red Studies would give Batman an international marketing advantage and take the whole O'Toole professor concept way above what Sandstone could ever have done.'

'You really think so?' Reg asked, his interest piqued.

'I'm very confident that, with the proper marketing, we'll be on a winner. I envisage a Centre for Red Studies, led by a professor. That would give BU the opportunity to attract students and researchers from all over the world.'

'You're the expert, Sal. I'm just an old Irish farmer. What would I know?'

'You're the richest old Irish farmer I know, Reg. Maybe you know a lot.'

'I know one thing, Sal. I'm going to be the Chairman of the Board at Batman bloody University.'

'That's wonderful news, Reg. Congratulations. I'll give you any support I can from the sidelines.'

'You can forget the sidelines. I've told Simon I'll accept as long as you stay on as deputy and you stay another three years.'

Sally Sloane sighed deeply. She was longing for a real retirement.

'I guess so, Reg. But, back to Red Studies. It won't be easy to find suitable candidates, but I think we should try to have someone in the role by Open Day.'

'When's that?'

'Late July.'

'Sounds optimistic. I can't believe how long it takes to make university appointments. In any of my businesses, I can get people

I want in a few weeks, if not days. I make the decision, there's no bullshit committees – pardon my French – slowing things down.'

'Universities deal with taxpayers' money, Reg. And there are stringent quality controls over appointments, especially senior ones. If a university makes a bad appointment, it can be very costly and difficult to reverse.'

Batman's former Vice-Chancellor and at least three of the Deans sprang to Sally's mind.

'I could have told you that,' Reg admitted ruefully,' but, when I know the sort of man I want, I just go out and get him.'

'Or her, Reg?'

Chapter 4

Roddy in Confidence

Roddy Rodman left the final meeting of the search committee with a precious morsel of information. Professor Sally Sloane had sworn the members to secrecy as to the name of the incoming President of Batman University until she, as Acting Chairman of the University's Governing Board, had issued a press release. Respected for his discretion and loyalty to his superiors, Roddy Rodman had served as secretary to the committee. But, strictly speaking, was he a member, and did the cone of silence apply to him?

Roddy struggled with this fundamental ethical question as he left the meeting with his characteristic poker face and languid gait. It wasn't until he heard the stairwell door on Level 12 of the O'Toole Building slam behind him that he quickened his pace down to level ten where the university's large and growing marketing department was based.

As head of marketing, Jamie Jamieson observed an open-door policy. Open door, open mind, he believed. Roddy entered, brushing the door with a knuckle, closed it behind him and sank into one of Jamie's soft armchairs. He said nothing but crossed his legs, smiled smugly, cocked his head slightly and raised his eyebrows.

Jamie had his mind on pressing matters but recognised that expression. 'Spit it out,' he demanded.

'Hmmm?' Roddy kept a straight face. He loved teasing Jamie.

'Haven't got time for games now, Roddy,' Jamie said, gathering a slim file. 'I'm on my way to chair a meeting of the Open Day committee. Mustn't be late for a very important date.'

'Thought you might like to know the name of the new President,' Roddy said nonchalantly.

'You know?'

'Just left the final meeting of the search committee.' Roddy examined his fingernails. 'Sally Sloane in the chair, two other Board members, Betty Allsop and Prudence Wills. And Kurt Kropp, the headhunter.'

'Save that for the minutes. Who is it?'

Roddy leaned forward and lowered his voice.

'His name ...'

'His name? I thought it was going to be that Indigenous woman.'

'His name, in strictest confidence, fanfare,' said Roddy, drumming the fingers of one hand on the desk, 'is Professor Nicholas Razer from the UK. He's a Scot, a psychologist and a very high flyer.'

'Sounds unlikely. The high flyer bit, I mean. I'll google him.'

Roddy rose and moved to look over Jamie's shoulder at his desktop screen.

'Oooo! An expert in men's psychosexual health. I'm starting to like him already!' Jamie enthused. 'But the mug shot. That's a bit disappointing, isn't it? Not exactly a pretty face, is it?'

'Don't judge a book. He starts in the new year.'

Chapter 5

When Razer met Sally

'Good morning, Chair,' Nicholas Razer rose and offered his hand to greet Sally Sloane. 'I think you're familiar with this office.'

'Good morning, President Razer.' Sally smiled and accepted his hand. 'And remember, I'm Acting Chair, not Chair,' she said with an expression of mock rebuke. She wrong-footed Razer by ignoring his gesture to sit at the chair opposite his desk, and instead sat at the top of the meeting table. He moved to sit opposite her, aware of the distance between them. Was that a deliberate tactic of hers, he wondered.

'How are you settling in after your first week?' Sally began as Razer eased his large frame into his chair.

'Everyone's been very welcoming,' he smiled, still smarting from having been directed where to sit in his own office.

'And Sinn?' Sally inquired solicitously. 'Have I got the name right? I'm looking forward to meeting her.'

'Oh, yes, absolutely loving it here. Looking forward to working in the International Office.'

Sally hoped she wouldn't regret having made an executive decision to create a role for Razer's wife.

'Thanks for agreeing to a quick take up.'

'I'd come to the end of a couple of major projects,' Razer lied, 'and the timing suited me.'

'Nicholas,' she said putting her hands flat on the table. 'I wanted the opportunity to give you some background that might be useful.'

'I'm all ears,' offered Razer, hoping she'd be brief. He was confident he'd be on top of the main issues at Batman quickly and without anyone's advice.

'You no doubt read in the Higher Education Supplement about our separation from your predecessor, Malcolm Richardson,' Sally began.

Razer feigned discomfort at the mention. 'I heard he assaulted a Dean at a university senior staff retreat.'

'Goodenough, the Dean of Engineering, had had a lot to drink and he was needling Richardson about various injustices and slights he felt. Richardson was a drunk, an aggressive type, and he took offence at Goodenough's barbs. Eventually, Richardson chested him and Goodenough pushed back. So Richardson took a swing at him and it ended up with Goodenough sitting on his backside on the floor.'

'All a bit unseemly, eh?' observed Razer.

'The Dean of Engineering is a bit of a hothead. When he threatened to lay charges against Richardson, the game was up. Richardson's resignation was received within a few days. He was with us less than two years.'

'And the Dean of Engineering?'

'Still here, and still prickly. He's likely to cause more problems, including for you. Keep an eye on him.'

Razer nodded.

'This was the last straw for the Minister. He wanted major changes to corporatise universities, and BU gave him an opportunity. He sacked all eighteen Council members except me. He appointed a Board of six with me as acting President. Without staff or student membership. The Vice-Chancellor would now be known as President. Soon enough, he did the same with all the State universities.'

'Very sensible move, if I may say so,' Razer agreed.

Yes, thought Sally, an ego as big as yours would love being called President.

'I thought I'd tell you about the Board as you'll have to have a good relationship with them. First, I'm the only one who knows anything about higher education. I'll help you out when I can. Especially with Reg O'Toole, the Chairman-designate whose appointment will be announced soon. I imagine you'll find him a rather unlikely chair of a university governing Board. He'll take some handling.'

'Do go on,' said Razer who, as a professor of psychology, harboured no doubts about his people-management talents.

'Reg is a born and bred local. Self-made man, university dropout. Knows nothing about higher education but that won't prevent him from having strong views about it. Very rich, very canny, very influential. Don't let his manner suggest he's a simpleton.'

Razer nodded affirmatively.

'Betty Allsop was a headmistress in the private school system. Came out of retirement to head up Dame Pattie College, a private girls' school in the outer east. Frankly, she's a fish out of water. She knows about education of young ladies from privileged backgrounds.'

Should be easy to handle, thought Razer.

'Then there's young Prudence Wills. A lawyer in her father's firm out here. The Minister wanted her father but he sidestepped and suggested his daughter instead. She's pure Generation Z and still learning her trade as a suburban lawyer.'

Hopefully easy on the eyes, thought Razer.

'Pieter Schiesser is from the Outer Eastern Development Authority where he heads the city planning department. Vast experience as a city planner in the former East Germany. Irrelevant here, of course. He speaks with a heavy accent and is a rather bureaucratic, wooden character. Specialises in minutiae, you know the type.'

Don't mention the war, thought Razer.

'Next, the mandatory ethnic. Mario Tempeste made his money out of gelato shops. He's active in community and ethnic affairs and retirement and nursing homes where he had a bit of trouble with COVID deaths. He's always looking for business opportunities at Batman and is the only one who can't see any potential conflicts of interest.'

'Must be on our guard there,' Razer assured Sally.

'And that's who's who in the zoo,' smiled Sally, giving a single gentle clap of her hands. 'Apart from me of course, and I'm sure you've looked me up on Google Scholar.'

Razer smiled but admitted nothing.

'It's not like any university governing body I know,' he observed. In fact, Razer knew very little about university governing Boards.

'No retired judges, no captains of industry, no higher education experts apart from myself,' Sally went on. 'You'll find this Board pretty malleable. And I'll be there to help out.'

'I'm very grateful for all that, Sally,' said Razer. Sally knew he was dissembling and decided to prick the prick's ego. Kurt Kropp hadn't satisfactorily established why Nicholas Razer would want to leave the UK for Australia; why he'd left the relative comfort and security of an elite UK institution to become head of a small, struggling Australian university. He struck her as a 'man with a past'. She'd known a few of them over her long academic career.

'You know, Nicholas, the selection panel was very impressed with your application.'

'Thank you for saying so.' He smiled indulgently as though no other conclusion could have been reached.

'And your interview also went very well.'

'I left the meeting feeling very satisfied and, in fact, with the whole selection process.'

'Your referee reports were first-class and the reports from the headhunters outstanding.'

'Thank you.' Razer smiled smugly.

'But you were not the preferred candidate.'

'I'm sure you had a strong field,' suggested Razer as his smile faded. Sally decided to leave him ignorant on that.

'Frankly, I wanted a female President, and an Indigenous one.' Sally sat back, crossing her arms.

Razer failed to hide his surprise.

'I know, that sounds unlikely but I had a suitable candidate in mind.'

'Oh?'

'Professor Gladys Cherbourg. A senior Indigenous woman in north Queensland. Kurt Kropp managed to persuade her to apply and we interviewed her. She painted a real vision for BU. She understands the Australian higher education system and would have been warmly received by the local Indigenous community.'

'What was the problem?'

Sally's expression revealed her disappointment.

'Do you know anything about the man after whom this university is named?'

'Controversial chap, I gather.'

'Gladys said she couldn't work in a university named after a racist villain. That was the end of the matter. I agree with her, and that's why the university's always BU for me. The Batman heritage is deplorable.'

'So, I was runner-up to a woman who didn't want the role anyway?'

'I've said more than I should have already.' Sally could see she had wounded Razer, but knew he would not succumb to an existential crisis. She pressed on.

'A bit of advice, if I might, Nicholas. Get yourself a tough-minded deputy. A Vice President. Richardson never appointed one even though the funds are there. Best not to waste time and funds on searching for a person. I think there's someone here already.'

Razer's first inclination was to bristle at the suggestion. A woman running an antipodean university Board advising a senior professor from an elite British university? But, best not to disregard his acting Chairman, and perhaps her advice could be worth considering.

'One of the Deans, I suppose,' said Razer, trying to remember them. 'Haven't had much to do with them yet. Who'd you have in mind?'

'With one exception, that being Lexi Dunne who would run a mile, the Deans are a shower of shit,' Sally said with a saltiness that surprised Razer. 'You should have a chat with Barry Motherwell in the science faculty. Hasn't been here long enough to be dragged down by the ennui of the place. Ex-Sandstone, good researcher, seems to be the one running the faculty. The Dean, Pilgrim, is a bit of a nut case.'

Razer was starting to recognise Sally Sloane's tough-mindedness.

'What sort of fellow is he, this Motherwell?'

'Fairly humourless, even taciturn. That makes colleagues treat him with caution. Doesn't mind being unpopular.'

This is getting interesting, thought Razer.

'His disposition's probably been affected by events in his personal life,' Sally explained. 'His wife was seriously ill for some time and died about a year ago. Soon after that, he came to BU.'

Sally mistook Razer's furrowed brow for empathy towards Motherwell's grief, but his thoughts were elsewhere.

Just the sort of enforcer I need, he thought, without comment.

Sally nodded. Heartless bastard, she thought.

'I think he's keen to leave Science,' she continued. 'Had a few run-ins with Pilgrim who's trying to introduce faith-based material into all the courses in the faculty. As a good scientist, Motherwell's been pushing back on that. They'll be glad to see the end of each other.'

Sally rose to leave and pushed a sealed envelope across Razer's desk.

'Read this and see what you think,' she said.

Razer stood to walk Sally to the door.

'One more thing,' she said. 'Almost forgot. Open Day is our big showcase event. The last one was terrible, what with the pandemic and countless other problems. We rely on that day for enrolments. Keep an eye on the committee.'

And Sally intended to keep an eye on Razer.

Chapter 6

The President's Man

Razer returned to his desk and slit open the envelope Sally had left. He found – to his surprise – a recruitment consultant appraisal of Motherwell on GoodKropp letterhead. Attached to it was a post-it note from Sally with the words 'Read and burn!' Razer leafed through the report and discovered that Motherwell's academic qualifications were sound. A PhD from a prestigious US university, publications in top international journals, and some competitive research grants. Referee reports were glowing, and the GoodKropp report was very positive.

In summary, Professor Motherwell would be an ideal fit for Batman University. His academic standing is high, his speciality in animal genetics would serve him well as professor of veterinary genetics in the semi-rural environment of Batman. His research record is solid and his experience in research supervision also renders him very suitable for appointment as Research Dean in the Faculty of Science.

Professor Motherwell can present as rather taciturn and humourless. He does not suffer fools gladly. His strong personality has never caused problems at Sandstone; he enjoys the respect of his colleagues if not their affection. We have been assured he has a softer side, too, which he rarely allows to manifest. As a manager, he is likely to give unquestioning loyalty to his superior and expect the same from his subordinates.

OPEN DAY

Although he is the only candidate, he is recommended for short-listing.

I think I may have my enforcer, thought Razer.

ooo**O**oo

Razer looked up from his desk and leaned back fully in his office chair. He smiled a greeting, and pointed to the chair on the other side. He'd met Motherwell somewhere – was it as one of the tedious induction sessions? – but they'd never spoken.

'Have a seat, Barry,' said Razer with renewed interest in Motherwell. In front of him he saw a shortish, stout man with a florid complexion under a messy full head of black hair. He was dressed plainly with heavy agricultural boots, shapeless trousers and a featureless necktie dangling lopsidedly at the neck of a white short-sleeved shirt. Unlike Razer, he was not a man who made concessions to style or formality. His expression was dour. Razer liked what he saw. Looks like a country vet accustomed to shoving his arm up the rear end of cows, thought Razer.

Motherwell muttered a thank-you, and sat at the desk opposite his boss, wary as to why the President should have summoned him to a one-on-one meeting. 'Coffee, Barry?'

'No, thanks,' said Motherwell, whose sole and pressing interest was in ascertaining the purpose of the meeting.

'I wanted to have a chat with you about your career.'

Motherwell stiffened and, unable read Razer's expression, became even more anxious. Was his career about to be terminated for reasons he couldn't guess? Razer opened the GoodKropp file.

'Very good academic record you have,' he said without looking up. 'What's this about animal behaviour? One of your avocations?'

Motherwell hesitated. What had this to do with Batman?

'My wife and I ...'

'Bit of bad news there, I gather,' Razer interrupted. 'But go on.'

Motherwell was relieved that Razer didn't want to linger on the topic.

'Maureen was an animal behaviour specialist. We did dog obedience training as a business.'

'Fascinating,' Razer said as he stretched each arm in turn and tugged his shift cuffs. 'But down to business.' He smiled. 'Barry, it's time you spread your wings.'

Motherwell's eyes narrowed under his bushy eyebrows and he nodded guardedly.

'I think you'd make an excellent Vice President. I need a deputy to help me reform this directionless university. Make it into a real university, an international university.'

Motherwell gave a nod but remained silent. Razer knew from GoodKropp's assessment that he was dealing with a man of few words.

'You're not exactly jumping for joy, old chap,' suggested Razer.

'I'm just a bit stunned. I ...'

'Of course you are, but I think you're the man for the job,' Razer said, trying to enliven Motherwell.

'It's not something I'd ever ...'

'Understood. I'll get Board approval, retrospectively, at our first meeting. But you can start right away.'

'Right away?' Motherwell's mind was racing. 'Is there a position description?' he finally asked.

'I'll get HR to knock something up. But it's all very simple. All you've got to remember is that as President, I'm the Minister for good news and you're the Minister for bad news.' Nicholas Razer flashed a conspiratorial smile.

Motherwell let the President's words hang in the air for the briefest moment.

'That sounds like, ah, a good division of labour,' he agreed, finally appearing to relax. 'Mervyn Pilgrim mightn't be too happy to lose his Professor of veterinary genetics.'

'Pilgrim? Religious maniac, I'm told. You're better off out of there. I'll get Kurt Kropp to find him a replacement. That'll shut him up.'

Motherwell doubted a successor would be found, or that Pilgrim would ever be satisfied.

'There're a couple of tasks you can start on,' Razer said to change the topic.

'Happy to take on anything you want, Nicholas,' Motherwell said, uttering for the first time the words that would fall from his lips many more times.

Razer smiled his signature sudden-fade smile. 'It will fall to you to introduce the Deans to a new organisational structure.'

'What will it look like?'

'Still working on it. Batman University needs serious disturbance,' Razer asserted gravely.

Motherwell nodded in agreement, though he wasn't sure what he was agreeing to.

'I'm going to call a planning meeting soon to discuss this, and I want you and Roddy to attend too.'

'Roddy Rodman?' Motherwell's normally poker face showed the slightest sign of surprise.

'Strikes me as a reliable fellow with a good knowledge of the university. I'm also going to invite Kurt Kropp.'

'He was the one who approached me about switching to Batman. He was very helpful.'

'Good fellow. He knows about Deans and that's where the changes will start.'

Motherwell nodded in assent but already he was feeling torn. Apart from Pilgrim, the one Dean he'd had much to do with was Lexi Dunne, to whom he'd become surprisingly close. They'd met on an ethics committee and she'd been very supportive to the recently widowed professor of veterinary genetics. Sensing the depth of his loss, she'd even invited him to fun-filled dinners at her house.

'I'm determined to uplift this university one way or another. There's more than one way to flay a feline, eh, Barry?'

Motherwell nodded again as Razer flicked through the pages of the GoodKropp report.

'Here we are.' His eye fell on the page he was seeking. 'You're a Colonel in the Army Reserve?'

'Yes,' Motherwell confirmed, wondering how it was that Razer could have that report.

'And you've got good connections in Homeland Defence?' Razer asked without looking up.

'I regularly visit Canberra advising on dog breeding and animal behaviour.'

'The Minister persuaded cabinet to fund a range of initiatives to raise awareness of the threats to Australia's national security. University Presidents have been advised that he plans to fund the establishment of army regiments in Australian universities.'

'I can't see it working so well everywhere, but at Batman, it could be very successful.' opined Motherwell.

'And signing up with a university regiment will deliver a stipend which, surprise, surprise, will exactly match the student tuition fees. Now that domestic students pay the same fees as internationals, that will be pretty attractive here.'

'Here's the Ministerial Statement,' said Razer, tossing the document down in front of Motherwell. 'I want you to start planning for a Batman University Regiment. A BUR. The letter from the Minister gives us just three weeks to have a proposal to him. We need estimated numbers, a plan for campus developments – y'know – a parade ground somewhere in the Village Place, vehicles, uniforms, armoury, the whole lot. Think big.'

'I'll have a draft ready for you shortly.'

Motherwell had never before been given such a huge and important mission, and was not sure that he was equipped to think big. He was still reeling from the enormity of the task he'd been handed when Razer pushed a document across the desk.

'A first formality before you leave. I need your signature on this form. At the bottom there,' he pointed.

'Certainly.' Motherwell smiled, pleased to perform his first duty as Vice President. As he withdrew his Batman University ballpoint from his ink-stained shirt pocket, he glanced down at the Travel Approval Form, hesitated and looked at Razer.

'That's OK, is it? I can approve your application for travel?' Motherwell asked.

'I have to go overseas at the weekend.' Razer suddenly appeared peeved, unnerving Motherwell. 'Sally's nowhere near but I'll clear it with her when we next meet.'

'Not a problem,' said Motherwell, anxious to appease Razer.

'Splendid. I've asked Maintenance to fix up an office for you down the corridor. It'll be ready for a Monday morning start. Better get back to Science and pack up.' Razer smiled, and not even Motherwell could fail to recognise the sign that their meeting had been drawn to a close. Should he thank Razer or offer his hand? But Razer had already turned his attention to his desktop computer, so he made for the door.

'Barry,' Motherwell turned to see Razer looking over his rimless reading glasses. 'Sally's worried about the Open Day this year. Bit of a cock-up last time, I gather. Keep an eye on it, old chap.'

Motherwell passed by Razer's EA too stunned to acknowledge her and made his way to the elevator. His thoughts raced. Why had Razer singled him out to be his deputy? The two had barely met. Could it have been his Sandstone background? His solid academic record? Was Pilgrim trying to move him out?

Whatever it was, he left the meeting with thoughts of loyalty. He was struck by Razer's superior intellect and authoritative mien. He'd share and implement Razer's vision for Batman, whatever it might be. Like him, Razer had come from an elite institution, and he assumed they shared the same lofty goals for higher education.

But did a Vice President really have the authority to approve a President's travel?

Chapter 7

The Cocktail Party Phenomenon

At what he thought was the right moment, Razer nodded to Roddy Rodman, who called for the attention of his colleagues by tapping his glass with a spoon and turned, with a slight bow, to his President. Feigning surprise, Razer stepped up to the microphone, which had been set up in the dining area of Boy Wonder's, the campus restaurant. Roddy fell back behind the President and off to one side, the better to be able to view the assembled staff.

'Colleagues, friends, welcome to this little gathering to kick off our year.' He stooped and took a moment to place his glass of wine on a nearby table while a hush fell over the assembled senior staff. 'I haven't met many of you yet but all in good time. I'll be brief as I'm sure you've not come here to listen to me blather on.'

Some of the assembled senior staff of Batman University offered up polite laughter.

'I don't need to remind you that the new year will be upon us soon enough. I'd like to say a few words about our future. And to quote the great Yogi Berra once more: "If you don't know where you're going, you might not get there".'

'Oh, dear,' muttered Clive Goodenough, drawing hostile glances from several colleagues.

'So, where are we going?'

Razer spoke confidently, without notes, sprinkling his presentation with witty asides.

'I've already started work on my strategic plan for Batman. It will be a bold new vision. In due course, this university will rank with the best universities in the country,' Razer paused for effect.

'He obviously doesn't know where he is,' whispered Clive Goodenough to Lexi Dunne, standing beside him. 'Probably a form of spatial recognition disorder.' The Dean of Arts smiled and gently elbowed him.

'I can inform you,' Razer continued, 'that Batman is destined to become a high-ranking research university. One that pays due respect to the region in which it is so propitiously located, and to the community which will increasingly acknowledge its social and economic value.'

'Lexi,' whispered Goodenough out of the corner of his mouth, 'have you got your phone on you?'

'Why?' said Lexi, returning his whisper.

'Call an ambulance immediately. This man is dangerously deluded.'

'Shut up, Clive,' she glared and mouthed at him.

'I'll be leading a retreat of senior staff early in the new year to take us to the next step,' declared Razer.

'You should miss this one, Clive,' joked Lexi sotto voce.

'There've been other retreats at the Grand Hotel on the peninsular so let's keep this fine Batman tradition,' declared Razer, who continued with sage insights about higher education laced with amusing bon mots, amusing some of his audience and irritating others.

'And there we are. I've kept to the ten minutes I promised. Now, please enjoy the fine offerings of Boy Wonder's, and the service of our own hospitality students so expertly trained by Rajesh Sharma.'

With that, Razer picked up his drink from the side table and Roddy

Rodman moved to centre stage clapping with a vigour that suggested others should follow. With Roddy following, Razer left the stage to muted applause and some audible grumbling. Roddy moved to his side, shepherding Razer through the crowd. Razer headed to the rear of the function room where he'd spied the recently appointed Chairman of the Batman University Board.

Reg O'Toole had slipped into the back of the room during Razer's presentation, hoping to keep himself inconspicuous. He'd carefully observed this collection of senior university staff whom the fates and the Minister for Higher Education had decreed he should now govern. His assistance no longer required, Roddy picked up a beer from a passing tray and moved to the periphery of the gathering from where he could observe Razer and Reg, and be ready at any moment to save them from pesky interlopers.

Unacknowledged by Razer in his speech, Barry Motherwell cut a lonely figure standing alone by the door examining the glass of white wine in his hand. He might be the newly appointed Vice President but, apart from Henry Zimmer of the staff association, no-one approached him to offer congratulations, and Zimmer soon abandoned him when he noticed Razer and Reg at the rear of the room. Occasionally looking up from his wine, Motherwell could see Lexi Dunne, the Dean of Arts, chatting animatedly to two of her senior colleagues. If there was anyone in the room he'd want to be talking with it was Lexi. But he was too unsure of himself to approach her.

Over on the far wall, he saw Roddy Rodman holding court with Lexi's three fellow Deans. As moths are drawn to a light, he thought. Motherwell knew that Razer had enlisted Roddy as some sort of henchman, or factotum. Motherwell was beginning to sense at the meetings they both attended that Roddy was increasingly being invited by Razer to act as an informal chief of staff. He longed for an opportunity to silently slip away and get back to his farm.

Reg O'Toole had never before been in the presence of a group of academics en masse. A short, wiry man with a ruddy complexion, he stood unrecognised by most of those present. His anonymity had gifted him an opportunity to cast a careful eye over his new charges, including the university President. Higher education was unfamiliar territory but he felt comfortable that, as in business, a confident demeanour backed by enormous personal wealth engendered respect in most situations.

'Hello, Nick,' said O'Toole as Razer approached with his right hand extended.

'Reg, good of you to come. And thanks for the dinner the other night, too.'

'There'll be more of them, I can tell you,' Reg chuckled.

The two men had barely begun to speak when they heard an unmistakably sharp comment.

'He'd rather have a fight than a fuck.'

Razer and his Chairman both stiffened, and only the slightest of eye movements of either betrayed the fact that this assertion had pierced through the clatter of multiple conversations. Razer decided to ignore it.

'Reg, what about dropping in on our retreat?'

O'Toole screwed up his face and shook his bald head.

'Can't for the life of me understand this crap about retreats. Remember, Mother Church has been having retreats for centuries and where has it got her?'

The quick-witted Razer instantly composed a clever reply, but kept it to himself while adopting his practiced pained expression.

'I'm afraid retreats are just one of the crosses managers of universities have to bear these days,' he offered.

'Maybe. The Minister told me about the last retreat run by your predecessor. Bit of a train wreck, I heard,' said Reg, looking up at the much taller man.

'I'm told Richardson had a short fuse when he'd had a few drinks and one of the Deans kept needling him about something or other.'

'According to the Minister,' observed Reg with apparent approbation, 'he decked him at the final dinner.'

'Hardly what one expects …'

Reg cut him off.

'No, I'm not the retreating type. In business, you never retreat.'

O'Toole clicked a middle finger and thumb and pointed his forefinger at Razer.

'Hold on. Where did you say you'll be having your love-in?'

'The Grand.'

'How many people?'

'I suppose about a dozen or fifteen. Y'know, just senior staff. A few support staff.'

'Forget the Grand. The O'Toole Tavern at our vineyard would be very suitable. Not far from here and with enough accommodation, too. There's a cordon bleu chef and we serve local wines.'

'That's very generous of you, Reg.'

'Generous be buggered, Nick. But, it'll be mate's rates for Batman. I'm very passionate about this university.'

Razer had been snookered by an expert and seemed uncharacteristically lost for words.

'Just get your people to call my office tomorrow. I'll sort it out,' Reg instructed.

Nicholas Razer forced a smile and moved quickly to change the topic.

'Tell me more about your business, Reg. I understand you started it as a family thing and you're now the biggest employer in the region.'

Reg was about to respond when one of the waiting staff approached, offering canapés prepared by hospitality students. Another one offered wines grown in the region.

Probably Domaine O'Toole, thought Razer.

'The biggest. And that's despite the fact that I'm a university dropout.' Reg rocked on the balls of his feet, and allowed himself a self-congratulatory smile.

'You obviously were naturally gifted. Didn't need the benefits of higher education for success,' Razer felt forced to concede.

'Never a truer word. Got through matric at St Brian's, scholarship to Sandstone and started a commerce degree. My dad wasn't keen on me going to uni, said it would be a waste of my time. And theirs. He had no time for university people.'

'I'm sure he had his reasons,' Razer offered.

Reg looked away and squinted as though squeezing out of his brain a long-forgotten memory.

'Y'know, the night before I was to enrol, he tried to talk me out of it. Gave me a warning I've never forgotten. He said, "Son, if you're intent on going to university, just remember, some of those university people are scabs on society." Now how could he have known that, never having been near a uni?'

'Quite extraordinary.'

'I never forgot those words and I think it's what led me to drop out. Sandstone at that time, y'know, the early 70s, was full of real drongos. Staff and students alike. Maybe it's all changed now but my recent experience with Sandstone suggests not. As my dad used to say, wouldn't know if you were up 'em unless you tapped them on the shoulder.'

The Chairman broke into a wheezing cackle and slapped his thigh. Razer forced a smile.

'But that was all a long time ago,' Reg went on, 'and Simon Brady told me universities are different now. More focused on helping industry, more staff with real world experience, that sort of thing. He wants us to make sure Batman is one of the new breed of universities and I reckon I'm up for that challenge, Nick. How about you?'

Razer was about to assure his Chairman of his commitment to the new directions for Batman, which would be summarised in his forthcoming strategic plan, when they were approached by a scruffy man. O'Toole noted the threadbare cardigan, the sandals and a scrap of boiled egg in the man's unkempt beard.

'Hello, Mr O'Toole. Hello, professor,' the dishevelled man volunteered. Nicholas Razer thought he recognised him as a staff member about whom he had been warned. O'Toole's mind turned to scabs on society. Roddy Rodman decided against intervening, Zimmer being a lightweight nuisance, in his view. Razer could handle him.

'Sorry to interrupt, but I wanted to talk about the President's vision for Batman.'

'I'm not sure my comments amounted to a vision, as such,' replied Razer, while looking to O'Toole who had taken two steps back. 'There'll be a formal strategic plan in the new academic year.'

Reg diverted his attention to the academics gathered around the bar set up at the far end of the meeting room. While the interloper had started with a compliment, Razer knew there was at least one 'but' coming, maybe more.

As he feared, the shambolic presence was that of the head of the staff association, a notorious nuisance to management. Opinion among management was divided as to whether Zimmer was mad, bad or just sad.

Razer decided not to extend his hand but said coolly, 'You're Dr Zimmer of BUSA, aren't you? Senior lecturer in physics, if I'm not mistaken.'

'That's right,' replied Zimmer, flattered to have already entered the consciousness of the President.

'Chairman,' Razer turned to address Reg, 'BUSA is the Batman University Staff Association, and Dr Zimmer is its chair.'

O'Toole grunted and turned away.

'Professor Razer,' Zimmer continued, 'I note you made no reference to deteriorating staff workloads and the casualisation of the academic workforce. Or the increased fees for domestic students and the disappearance of Asian students. Or the changes to university governance. I would have thought these would be some of the big issues facing higher education in Australia.'

'Look, Dr Zimmer, thank you for the observations, but if I may say so, they are a little premature. We need to get the big picture right before we can attend to the important issues you raise.'

'Yes, but ...' continued Dr Zimmer.

'Sorry, but the Chairman and I were discussing some university matters and now, if you'd excuse me ...'

Roddy watched as Razer gestured for his Chairman to follow him to the locked exit, on the other side of which was a corridor to Razer's office with its well equipped bar. Before they could exit, however, one of the student waiters caught up with them. Roddy was ready to intervene when he noticed the formidable presence of the Head of Campus Security watching the same incident.

'Hey, boss. Boss, hold on a minute. I wanna speak with you,' and with this, the young waiter blocked their path with his lean, dark body. Nicholas Razer did not recognise him, but assumed he was an international hospitality student.

'Yes? The Chairman and I were just taking our leave. Is there a problem?'

'Yeah, yeah, there is, bro.'

'And you are?'

Yeah, I'm Michael White, the President of BUICK.'

Is it a campus car club, wondered Razer.

'BUICK?' repeated Razer, while O'Toole turned away again.

'Yeah, bro, BUICK. The Batman University Indigenous Cooperative of Kulin.'

'I understand most of that but what is Kulin?'

'Kulin? That's the nation of Indigenous peoples that lived around this area before the invasion. My mob.'

Some of the young man's language started to ring alarm bells for Reg O'Toole. He didn't want to be listening to an aggressive young black man he didn't know or want to know.

'You said there's a problem,' said Razer.

'Yeah, bro, a big problem, eh?'

'And that is?'

'I been servin' food an' stuff to all the important people and listnin' to your speech. You didn't have an Acknowledgement of Country, bro. This campus is on Indigenous land and you gotta do Acknowledgement. My Mum's gonna be pretty upset. She does all the Welcomes and Acknowledgments here and she wasn't invited. She's gonna be pissed off when she hears, I can tell ya.'

At this, Reg looked for the exit and saw the uniformed Head of Campus Security gesturing for him to come.

'Look,' said Razer, anxious not to cause any racial offence, 'call my office tomorrow and come and have a chat. I have to go now. And can I ask you not to mention this to your mother for now?'

He was relieved to see the imposing figure of the Head of Campus Security approaching. Kevin Burke stepped between Razer and Michael White and led Razer and O'Toole to the exit door, which he opened with a salute.

The glowering Chairman strode along the corridor to the President's office.

Chapter 8

Something about Reg

As he ushered his Chairman into his office, Razer sensed from Reg's simmering silence that he was vexed. He'd been warned that Reg could be crusty but, to date, he'd found him to be even-tempered, if somewhat forcefully gruff. He correctly guessed that Reg was not one to hide his displeasure.

'Gimme a double whiskey,' Reg demanded, as he prowled around Razer's office looking at, but hardly seeing, the paintings and sculptures Razer had selected from campus Barak Gallery.

'Of course, Reg. I'll join you,' Razer said, anxious to placate his Chairman.

'I don't care for being ambushed on campus.' Reg O'Toole's eyes flashed as he rocked forward on his toes.

'You're talking about ...'

'I'm talking about the beard and the Abo,' snapped O'Toole.

'Yeeees,' drawled Razer with a pained smile, 'Michael was a bit on the pushy side. At least his mother wasn't there. Apparently, she's worse. Afraid I'm unfamiliar with Welcome to Country.'

'That's all bullshit anyway,' declared Reg with a dismissive wave. 'If ever it was their country, it sure as hell isn't now.'

'As to Henry Zimmer ...' Razer started.

'The Heeb in the cardigan? Looked like he's from one of the

tribes of Israel. Mind you, I've got no problems with them. They know how to run businesses. And a country. Christ, the Israelites have got the bloody Ahabs under their thumbs. Turn the other cheek? I don't think so.'

'It's normal to include the head of the staff association in events such as that one.'

'I don't give a shiny shit about all that,' Reg said vehemently. 'I just don't expect to be put in a position like that when I attend university functions. It certainly doesn't happen in any of the businesses I run. Everyone knows that I expect respect. I establish that early on. I'll give you a bit of free advice, Nick, to help you find your feet in Australia. The standard you walk past is the standard you accept.'

Nicholas Razer had early on got the measure of his Chairman, and was already devising strategies for best handling him. There was no doubt that Reg was well-endowed with street smarts. But while the rough edges of his ego could scratch a diamond, between them would be cavities of vulnerability. He would need to discover these and play to them.

Reg drained his glass, chomped on several ice cubes, and held up his glass to Razer who hadn't been relaxed enough to sit. 'Same again, Nick.'

He stood to take his drink and walked to the floor-to-ceiling plate glass window, which, being on a corner of the building, afforded commanding views. In the foreground was the campus Village Place, with its man-made hillocks, scattered benches and tables, and intersecting footpaths. Surrounding this area for student socialising and meeting was a hodgepodge of modest, four-level buildings radiating, fan-like, from the O'Toole administration building.

O'Toole rocked on the balls of his feet as he took in the view. He loved what he saw. Just fifty years earlier, had there been such a lofty vantage point, all that would have been evident was the farmland with small cottages dotted here and there. The few roads were unmade tracks that local farmers used to get their produce to market. There were a couple of wooden churches and a one-teacher State school.

The land was clearly underdeveloped and would have seemed to be waiting – waiting for the inevitable, inexorable march of 1970s suburbia. The drama of land development and community creation still sent a surge of excitement through Reg's very being. For him, the conversion of rural land to urban purpose was akin to a sacrament. The outward and visible sign of a visible and invisible imperative, and that imperative was progress. This was as close as Reg ever got to understanding matters sacred.

'I was telling you that I dropped out of uni,' began Reg, still taking in the view.

'That's right,' said Razer, hoping a bout of reminiscing would divert Reg's attention from campus ambushes.

'The old man was farming in those days and he wanted a brighter future for me. In fact, Nick, come here.' Razer moved to join Reg. 'I'll show you just where the farm was. My dad was a good capitalist and he understood the basic rule about land: they're not making any more of it. Gradually, he bought up adjoining properties until the old boyo – he didn't even finish primary school, Nick – he was the major land holder in the whole bloody outer east.'

Reg paused and drew an imaginary arc to the east and north with his extended hand.

'And what you see from the highway over there on the left, right through the housing estates and past the shopping mall and civic centre over to the sporting complex, the hospital, was all owned by my dad. The whole bloody lot of it, Nick, up to and including this campus.'

Now I get it, thought Razer. The old man sold the government the land for the campus.

'And just down there on the outside of the Village Place,' Reg went on, 'is the farmhouse the old man built. O'Toole Cottage, where I grew up. I paid for it to be restored to its former glory.'

'I haven't got over there yet, Reg. Roddy has suggested it could accommodate various support operations.'

'Yeah, well, tell them not to get too settled. I'm thinking about making it an O'Toole family museum.'

'A very fitting display of filial respect, Reg.'

Reg turned at looked at Razer quizzically.

'Nothing to do with horses, Nick.'

'I meant …' began Razer before O'Toole cut him off. Is he deaf, thought Razer, or just rude?

'The statue's there now. They kept on desecrating it, the bastards.'

'The statue?' Razer asked. 'I'm not with you, Reg.'

'The statue of John Batman. The government gave it to us after the corrupt Laborites took it out of Collins Street. It was put in front of this very building, but they were constantly desecrating it.'

'They, Reg?' Razer asked innocently.

'You know who I mean, Nick.'

Razer nodded, meaning to check with Roddy as to who 'they' might be.

'Sally rang me and suggested putting it in front of the cottage. Said it would honour the family there, out of harm's way, too. Seems to have worked.'

Reg fell into a brief rueful silence.

'You know what our biggest failure out here was?' he began. 'We couldn't get a rail line to the mall via the campus. That would have been the clincher, but the politics were against us.'

'The politics?'

'Yes, the bloody Laborites got in and refused to support any of our initiatives. We showed them the population projections, the uni and school enrolments, the lot. Everything. But the bastards held firm. By the time we got back in, Labor had rooted the Budget on their crazy bloody socialist projects and we just couldn't manage it. Besides, we'd had to sell off some of the land set aside for the rail and it wasn't viable any longer.'

Reg shook his head and emitted the sigh of the unrecognised visionary.

'Anyway,' he continued, 'we've ended up with a good community and a good university. So all's well that ends well, eh?'

'Indeed, Reg, but we could probably increase our student numbers if we had a train anywhere near the campus.'

'Maybe. But the thing to remember is the example of my dad. Shows what you can do if you've got some vision and some get up and go, Nick.'

'That can't be gainsaid, Reg.'

'Gain what?'

'Gainsaid. Y'know, contradicted.'

'That's for sure. What I hope for, and I know what the Minister hopes for, is a bit more vision and get up and go at this university. And a lot less gainsaying,' said O'Toole raising his eyebrows at Razer.

'The old man got active in local politics, y'know, to protect community interests and make sure the region got the right development. He could see that the city was growing and the farmland would be required for higher value use.'

'He went into local government?' Razer took a clever guess.

'Ended up Mayor. The longest serving Mayor of the shire, which later was declared a city. The State government were Libs and he was thick with a number of them including the Premier. The Premier and the Minister for Higher Education agreed with him that the region was going to have a population boom and they established a new municipality. It was my dad who dreamed up a name for the city:

Robert Gordon. And that's the name, as you know, that it bears today. The City of Robert Gordon.'

'And who was Robert Gordon, Reg?' inquired Nick.

'Ah, Nick, it seems like your knowledge of Australian political history is sadly lacking. Robert Gordon as in Robert Gordon Menzies, Australia's greatest PM by a country mile.'

'Oh, of course I know who Robert Menzies was, Reg. I just didn't make that link. Fine tribute to a great Australian, no doubt.'

'The municipality couldn't be called Menzies because there was already an electorate of that name. So, Robert Gordon it is. Everyone knows who it refers to.'

'There's a Robert Gordon University back in Scotland, which I know pretty well. Had the name not already been in use since the eighteenth century, it might have served us better than the current name,' Razer observed, making idle conversation. O'Toole addressed him tersely.

'What's wrong with "Batman"?'

'Well, nothing really, I was just …'

'I can tell you, Nick, it was very bloody popular back in the early 70s. We've got Batmans all over the city. Batman was the founder of the city. He came over from Tassie in the 1830s, I think it was, did a deal with the local tribes to buy some of their land.'

'Wasn't there some controversy about that transaction? And a bit of a bad odour over his dealing with the Indigenous people?' ventured Razer.

'Bad odour? No, no, no, Nick. All wrong. Him and Fawkner were pioneers who gave us our beginning. He did a deal with the Abos. Beads, rugs, tobacco, you name it. Fair and square. No good going back over all that past history. John Batman's a hero and the name stays.'

'It's well established,' conceded Razer.

'Look down there,' said O'Toole gesturing. 'The Village Place. You won't know this but the word "village" is another tribute to the great man. Y'know, "this is the place for a village", as Batman famously said when he established Melbourne.'

'Oh, I see.'

'And you must have seen the sign over the main entrance to the campus. "This is the Place for a University".'

'It's arresting,' admitted Razer, who'd early on decided the campus needed a more traditional main entrance.

'So, you follow me? The old man had them call that open space down there the Village Place.'

'Unique among universities, I should think,' admitted Razer, indulging O'Toole.

'Would be,' declared Reg with pride. 'And as you must have noticed, Batman University's coat of arms is a picture of the great man and the words *"hic locus academia est"*.'

'I noticed the Latin. More traditional.' Though not quite what I would have chosen, thought Razer.

'Yeah, we're stuck with it now. But, whenever we could, the old man and I, we got them to use the English version. Less poncey.'

'More accessible,' conceded Razer.

Reg looked at Razer, confused.

'The campus is hardly accessible, Nick. That's why we wanted the rail.'

Razer conceded his error with a self-effacing shrug.

'And, that reminds me, there's something I've noticed that's been creeping in here that I don't welcome. I think it's disrespectful to the memory of John Batman. And the university.'

'What's that, Reg?'

'BU, Nick, BU. One of my goals as Chairman of the Board will be to ban the use of BU. I see it all the time in the local press. It's even on our letterhead, business cards and the rest. The name is Batman University and it should he used in full,' Reg declared issuing, in his mind, an instruction to the new President.

'Of course. But BU could add a little lustre to our name nationally and internationally. It could be very useful for our marketing.'

'How d'ya mean?'

'The highly regarded Boston University is also known as BU.'

'Can't see what that's got to do with us.'

Reg glanced at his watch. Nick noticed it was a Rolex, a GMT Master, one of Razer's own indulgences. The Chairman drained his glass and turned to leave.

'I've got to get to the club and it's at least an hour's drive into Collins Street. By the way, I've nominated you for accelerated membership. Have you heard from them?'

'Yes. Thanks very much, Reg. All fixed.'

'Good. I'll arrange for us to have lunch soon. I'm on my way there for a meeting of the 200 Club. We're trying to raise at least a mill for the next State election. If we get back in, I think we can expect a few goodies in the Budget. For Robert Gordon, I mean. And what's good for Robert Gordon is good for Batman University.'

The Chairman turned again to the window, and the very satisfying panorama that it offered. Suddenly he seemed struck by something approaching a revelation.

'Speaking of the great City of Robert Gordon, Nick,' continued O'Toole, 'it's a great place to live, y'know. As the marketing sign says, "You'll never be bored in Robert Gordon".'

Razer looked blankly.

'Gordon,' said O'Toole, slightly exasperated at Razer's slow wit. '"Gordon" and "bored in". They rhyme, Nick'.

'Ah! Yes.' Razer smiled at the revelation while wondering who could ever have thought that was a rhyme, much less an alluring one.

'Some of Jamie Jamieson's assistance to the City,' Reg observed.

'Jamie? I'm told he's one of our more creative staff members,' observed Razer.

'Y'know, Nick, you ought to think about buying out here. Very sound investment for the future. Close to the campus and to the community.'

'Yes, Reg, that's true. Sinn and I have been thinking very much along those lines,' lied Razer. 'We love the feel of this region.'

'I've not met Sinn yet. Did I get the name right? Is it short for something?'

'It's a traditional Thai name. "Sin" but an extra "n". It means "treasure".'

'I'm all in favour of treasure. And occasional sin,' Reg sniggered. 'Hope there'll be an opportunity to meet your little treasure soon.'

'We're planning on that. She's a bit shy about coming to university events, but she's keen to meet you.'

'Goodo. On housing, if ever you need some local advice, O'Toole's Real Estate stands ready to help. Just give me a bell, be glad to get my people onto it.'

'I'll bear that in mind, Reg, thank you.'

'And for the home handyman, you can't go past O'Toole's Tools in the mall,' Reg said earnestly.

'Must bear that in mind, too, Reg. I've always wanted to do a bit of DIY.'

'Oh, and one last thing, Nick. At the drinks session, I overheard a comment about somebody who'd prefer a fight to, y'know, the other. Hope that wasn't a comment about me.'

'I'm sure it wasn't, Reg. In fact, I was hoping it wasn't about me,' he laughed. 'No,' Razer continued, 'I think it was in reference to my pick of a new Vice President. He's an ex-Sandstone man. He's impressed me and he's not been at Batman long enough to have been contaminated by the general malaise here. Tough, too.'

'Sounds like a perfect deputy, Nick.' They laughed as they shook hands.

'Who's your enforcer, Nick?' inquired Reg as he moved to leave.

'Barry Motherwell, Reg. When I got here, he was a professor in the Science Faculty and their Dean for Research. His colleagues called him "Bazza" but soon his muscular approach to management eventually saw "Bazza" morph into "Basher".'

Nicholas Razer walked his Chairman to the elevator and returned to his office. He poured himself another whiskey, straight this time, and with a deep sigh, lowered his large frame onto the couch and loosened his tie. It would take all his considerable interpersonal skills to manage Reg O'Toole. He emptied his glass, rose, packed his satchel and went to the ante-chamber where Brian Phipps, his driver, waited. They drove to his rented house in silence.

Chapter 9

Pilgrim and the Headhunter

Kurt Kropp parked his car in the visitors' car park at Batman and made his way to the Science Building. His appointment was with the eccentric Dean of Science, Mervyn Pilgrim. He'd not seen Pilgrim since the selection interview that led to his appointment at Batman. Pilgrim was annoyed that Razer had highjacked his relatively new professor of veterinary genetics, Barry Motherwell, to become Vice President but had been somewhat placated when Razer had suggested he engage GoodKropp to find a successor.

'I'm Faith,' Pilgrim's EA greeted Kropp with pronounced politeness, and invited him to take a seat on one of the plastic chairs lined up along the wall facing her desk. She fixed him with a guileless expression and demure smile. 'The Dean will summon you soon.'

Faith returned her attention to what looked to Kropp like a Bible. He cast his gaze around the plainly furnished office, his attention drawn to a packed bookshelf behind the EA. He could easily have been back in his father's study, all those years ago in northern Tasmania. His family were members of the Plymouth Brethren and his father was a leader in the local congregation. Theirs was a God-fearing household where God's word was revealed in the Bible. His father's bookshelf was just like this one, with several copies of the Holy Book and numerous other titles devoted to scriptural exegesis.

From his childhood, Kropp had been thoroughly immersed in

fundamentalist Christian doctrine and had even contemplated a life as a preacher. He was deep in thought about his fundamentalist youth as he ran his eye over the bookshelf when Faith startled him.

'Are you interested in God's word, Mr Kropp?'

Startled, Kropp admitted to being familiar with many of the volumes.

'How wonderful!' Faith smiled warmly. 'And what about those in the other book shelf? The Dean is a scientist so they're more scientific.'

Kropp stood to survey the titles, which included 'Seeking God in Science', 'Evolution: a Theory in Crisis' and 'The Bridge between Science and Theology'.

'And,' Faith was becoming more animated, 'there are some of his own books, too! Did you see them?' She stood and went to stand beside him. She ran her forefinger across the books until she found the 'Ps'.

'You know he's a geologist?'

Kropp nodded. He well remembered how he'd recruited Pilgrim from North Western Mining.

'This one won several prizes,' she announced proudly. "You Must have Rocks in your Head: a Professor of Geology Explains Intelligent Design". And this one for first year students: "Faith Rocks: a Student Guide to Intelligent Design"'.

I imagine they're heavily promoted in the faculty, Kropp thought.

'Over here is the journal "Eye 99", Faith said proudly, seemingly moving Kropp to a higher level of publication. 'You know it?'

Kropp shook his head.

'Pity. It's devoted to intelligent design for scientists. You're not a scientist I take it, Mr Kropp?'

'No, but science is very important for our lives,' Kropp parried.

Faith received this statement with pleasure and was explaining to Kropp how he could take out a subscription when a man's voice filled the ante-room.

'Come up higher, friend,' boomed Pilgrim and Kropp, relieved to be able to escape Faith's attention, turned to greet his host. The Dean, however, was nowhere to be seen.

'Oh, that's just his recorded message to say he's ready, Mr Kropp,' said Faith, resuming her seat. 'Go into his courts with praise.'

'Beg your pardon?'

'Psalm 100. Just a tip.'

Kropp knocked and entered the Dean's office. He found Pilgrim seated at this desk, apparently busy with paperwork. Without any greeting, he looked up and gestured for Kropp to take a seat opposite him. Even before Kropp had sat down, he spoke.

'Tell me, Mr Kropp, what does the corporate world think of intelligent design?'

It's Mr Kropp now, thought Kropp. It was all Kurt when I was headhunting him. Maybe he doesn't remember me. Or perhaps putting me in my place.

'Intelligent design? I'm not sure I know what that is,' Kropp lied.

The bizarre start to the meeting reminded him of his earlier encounters with Pilgrim. But could he be getting even nuttier? Over a long career of headhunting, interviewing, recruiting and dealing with senior academics, he'd encountered many oddballs. Among academics, especially in the sciences, he'd rarely encountered men and women of faith. Not merely a man of faith, however; Pilgrim was a Christian fundamentalist. And a zealous one.

When Kropp had approached him as a potential candidate for the role of Dean of Science at Batman, Pilgrim surprised the search consultant by declaring that he felt God was calling him to the role. Then, when Kropp phoned him with the news that he was the selection committee's preferred candidate, Pilgrim told him he would need a few days of prayerful consideration before he could be certain this was God's plan for him.

Kropp had warned the selection committee that Pilgrim might harbour some 'unfashionable' religious beliefs. He was also suspicious about Pilgrim's glowing referee reports. He didn't trust written reports about candidates, always preferring to speak with referees. Kropp's referees could think of no good reason why Pilgrim would not be an excellent appointment as Dean at Batman. Kropp pointed out to the panel that one of them was a co-religionist and the others were his superiors in a geological company who, Kropp was certain, were trying to offload him.

But so barren was the field of applicants, the selection committee had dismissed Kropp's concerns. Pilgrim was, as too often the case at Batman, the best of the small bunch of applicants.

'Intelligent Design.' Pilgrim held his open hands up and smiled incredulously. 'You don't know it?'

Kropp shook his head.

'Sure?' Pilgrim probed.

'I'm afraid not,' Kropp lied again.

'It's a revolutionary way of thinking about our universe,' he smiled, as though addressing a child. 'It explains why our world is not some cosmic accident.'

'Would it involve God?' ventured Kropp.

Pilgrim's face lit up as he clasped his hands together as if in celebration.

'Precisely. It's a branch of science which allows us to definitively prove the existence of God.'

With that, Pilgrim opened a desk drawer and withdrew a small metal box, which he theatrically placed in front of Kropp.

'I want you to participate in a little experiment, Mr Kropp.'

'An experiment?' This was a very atypical meeting with a client.

'Open the box and examine the contents,' Pilgrim instructed.

Kropp flipped open the lid of the box and observed a jumble of tiny cogs, wheels and springs. He looked to Pilgrim, aware he was being drawn into some heuristic game.

'What you see is a deconstructed time piece.' He paused for effect, looking intently at Kropp. 'A watch.'

Kropp's mind raced. Where was this bizarre conversation going?

'Now, close the lid and give it a good shake,' Pilgrim ordered.

'Shake it?'

'We want to see how long it will take to assemble the parts in the box into a functioning watch.' Pilgrim smiled a 'get it?' smile.

'I think it would be safe to say, Professor Pilgrim,' Kropp decided to deliver the correct response, 'that will never happen.'

'You see my point,' Pilgrim smiled smugly.

'I believe I do.'

'You believe you do? Good choice of verb, if I may say so.'

Kropp forced smile. He'd played along and hoped the preliminaries were now at an end and he could get down to business.

'Wouldn't you agree, Mr Kropp, this simple experiment has demonstrated clear proof of intelligent design in the cosmos?'

'I'd have to agree that's so,' said Kropp anxious to end the mad exchange.

Pilgrim leaned forward and fixed Kropp with a zealous eye.

'I want to introduce programs of teaching and research based on the insights of intelligent design. First, in the Faculty of Science, then throughout the whole university. I'm getting some resistance from colleagues. In their ignorance, they oppose me. The Science Faculty Board voted it down. They say we can't afford it. Nonsense, I say. I thought you might be able to assist.'

'Me? How?' Kropp asked, perplexed.

'Yours is the corporate world. To be blunt, I can't get university funding, so I'm seeking corporate funding.'

Kropp resolved that the only way forward was to enter this

man's delusional world, and he knew exactly how to do that.

'I'd be honoured to look into that. As we are told in Proverbs, "Surely there is a future and your hope will not be cut off".'

'Bless you. You must know a lot of people in the corporate world.'

'I do, and I know that many of them are men of faith. A certain number of women, too.'

'Praise God!'

'And like them, Professor Pilgrim,' Kropp said, warming to his ploy, 'I believe in divine intervention.'

'Bless you,' said Pilgrim clasping both hands over his heart.

'I believe I've been sent,' Kropp declared. 'Sent to help you find your way out of the wilderness.'

'Prepare ye the way of the Lord!'

'I will lead you along the path you wish to go.'

'The horse is made ready for the day of battle, but the victory belongs to the Lord.'

'I have ears to hear.'

'And that servant who knew his master's will but did not get ready or act according to his will, will receive a severe beating.'

'His will be done.'

'Hallelujah!'

'Hallelujah!'

'Brother Kropp,' Pilgrim addressed Kropp earnestly, 'I believe with all my heart that you have indeed been sent to search so that we may find.'

'Brother Pilgrim. How exactly may I serve you?' Kropp felt he might have manoeuvred the mad Dean to the point of the meeting.

'I am obliged to find a replacement for my professor of veterinary genetics.'

At last, thought Kropp – but if he were to get this consultancy, he would have to enter the Dean's delusional world even further.

'But, Brother Pilgrim. I cannot do this alone. We must call upon the help of the Lord.'

'How, exactly, Brother Kropp?' Kropp had him nibbling at the baited hook. 'Shall we pray for divine guidance, Brother Pilgrim?' he said, playing his best card.

'Our Lord told us so to do.'

Finally hooked, thought Kropp.

Pilgrim rose and moved around his desk to sit beside Kropp, taking both his hands in his own.

Thank God, thought Kropp whose arthritic knee would likely have failed him had he been expected to kneel.

'Heavenly Father,' intoned Pilgrim, bowing his head, 'we ask your blessing on this search project. You have told us we must be fishers of men and we ask for your blessing on Brother Kropp as he fishes for men and, according to modern practice, women, for the role of professor of veterinary genetics. Amen.'

'Amen,' repeated Kropp.

Pilgrim raised his head and smiled at Kropp.

Let go of my hands, you creepy bastard, thought Kropp, forcing another smile.

'Brother Pilgrim, brother in Christ,' he intoned, earnestly bobbing their clasped hands. 'I feel in my bones that we share a sacred mission. I shall go now and prepare the way.'

'God bless you, Brother Kropp. Can I help you further?'

'Perhaps you could give me the information pack and letter of engagement,' suggested Kropp, hoping to end the encounter with that necessary formality. 'That would allow us to get on with the search.'

'All in God's good time, Brother Kropp.'

Kropp's hopes of leaving with a formal engagement were dashed.

The two men stood, Pilgrim's grip still firm. Kropp looked into the eyes of the madman, dreading the possibility of a kiss of peace.

Finally released from Pilgrim's grasp, he turned to leave with a faux pious bow.

Pilgrim raised his right hand as in blessing as Kropp left. He passed by Faith, who waved limply without lifting her attention from her Bible.

Chapter 10

Open Day Ideas

The Open Day for 2022 was always going to be Jamie Jamieson's most important project. After the debacle of 2020, he was now going to be tested. As well, this would be the new President's first Open Day at Batman, and failure this time could seriously damage Jamie's prospects of a comfortable career with a defined benefit pension upon retirement. He'd convened the first meeting for 2022 to 'capture', as he explained it to himself, 'the new buds of fun and creativity' that would shoot after the long summer break.

The first meeting of the committee had been disappointing, forcing him reluctantly to conclude that if there were to be fun and creativity, it would fall to him to deliver them. As he made his way to their second meeting, he reminded himself he needed patience with the marketing novices who comprised the committee. He must also, always, radiate positivity.

'Welcome back, everyone!' Jamie gushed as he entered the meeting room with the seated committee members. He flashed a welcoming smile at each of them, and led off.

'2022 is an auspicious year. Why? According to my Chinese calendar, this is the Year of the Tiger and we, this dynamic little committee, are going to work like tigers. Yeah? I often marvel at the wisdom of the East.'

'Pity there's not more wisdom in the outer east,' jibed Arso Kikavic.

'As I've been saying for months,' Jamie carried on, ignoring Arso, 'this is going to be an Open Day to remember. It is going to be fun. That's our mission.'

'Fun's all very well, Jamie, but it's the educational information and opportunities to showcase our academic programs that is the real purpose of Open Day,' said Marilyn Worthy.

'Of course, I quite agree. But, every university has that stuff. We have to differentiate. And fun, with a capital F, is what will differentiate Batman from the mob.'

'The mob, as you refer to them, Jamie, leave us for dead in all the university rankings,' observed Dr Economopoulos.

'I rest your case, Kon.' Jamie smiled indulgently. 'The fact is, those rankings never include the way a university presents itself to the world. How it markets itself.'

'Maybe good reason for that,' Arso sneered.

'Anyway, down to business. I believe we need an energy hit,' explained Jamie. 'Let's get into the dark chocolate of our business. Forget the minutes, the agenda, let's just let the dynamism of a powerful group dictate where we go today.'

'I go to lunch then,' joked Arso.

Jamie ignored the barb.

'Declan,' Jamie addressed the President of the Batman University Student Society, 'give us an insight, if you would, into what you and your guys have got in store for Open Day. How you're planning to attract and entertain whole families on our family fun day.'

'Cheers, Jamie.' The President of BUSS leaned back in his chair and gestured to the other student present. 'I'll ask Michael White from BUICK to kick off, in deference to the fact that we're on his mob's land.'

'Yeah, thanks, Mike. The Batman University Indigenous Club of Kulin, BUICK, are gunna start the day with a Welcome to Country by my mum, Aunty Thelma. If she's back by then. If not, Uncle Lionel will do it.'

'And that will be a one-off, Michael?' inquired Jamie.

'One-off? Like, what d'ya mean, one-off?'

'Just one welcome? Not welcomes in different places at different times?'

'Can't keep welcoming people all fuckin' day,' Michael cackled at his own joke.

'No, mustn't overdo it,' conceded Jamie.

'After the welcome, there's gunna be a traditional smokin' ceremony by Uncle Lionel. Right outside the main entrance to Village Place, where most people will come in. Apparently, there's some bullshit issue with fire safety if we do the smokin' inside the Village Place. As well as that, there'll be a bush tucker cookin' demonstration throughout the day and plenty to eat, too. Then, later on, there'll be a performance of *Coranderrk*.'

'What's that all about, Michael?' inquired Marilyn.

'It's a play about the hero of our mob in this area, William Barak.'

'Oh, yes, a great leader of your people,' acknowledged Marilyn.

'It's about his fight with the white settlers and the struggle for our land.'

'What's that to do with Batman University?' inquired Arso Kikavic.

'Mate,' said the head of BUICK, glaring at Kikavic, 'this land we're on right now was where William Barak and our mob lived, hunted, everything. Until white settlers ...'

'Just wondering,' Kikavic retreated.

'Wonder no more, mate,' said White. 'Consider yourself our guest here.'

'What other events are planned by BUSS?' Jamie intervened as Arso bristled. 'Declan, over to you.'

'Cheers, Jamie. BUSS has got a whole lot of fun organised for the big day. I'll just hand out this paper which lists everything we've organised. And cheers, Jamie, for the generous funding.'

'If the dollars bring us fun, Declan,' beamed Jamie, 'they're worth every cent.'

'Declan, this is an impressive list of activities and stalls,' observed Marilyn Worthy. 'I see face painting, novelty bikes, even a coconut shy. Haven't seen one of them in years. But there's a couple I'm not too sure about.'

'Like what?'

'Like "Feels on Wheels".'

'Shit, is that still there? Sorry, everyone, scratch that. Some girls from Business thought they had an idea for their entrepreneurship group project. Y'know, home service. But it was ruled out.'

'On moral grounds?' inquired Marilyn.

'Not really. They couldn't get enough volunteers.'

'At least some of them have some morals.'

'Nah, wasn't that. They wanted penalty rates for Sunday. Just didn't stack up in terms of cash flow.'

'Pure luck, Declan,' observed Marilyn. 'You could have been in hot water. And what about this entry "BatBet"?'

'Yeah, that's another Business student innovation. "Bat" as in "Batman".'

'Got the "Bat" bit, but the "Bet" bit?'

'Actually, it's not short for anything. It's just plain old "bet".'

'"Bet" as in wager, gamble. That "bet"?'

'Yeah! That "bet". Also part of another entrepreneurship group project.'

'And?'

'And the group will be demonstrating a new app that allows kids to bet on things.'

'Things?'

'Yeah, things. Like races, footy, y'know, things like that that kids like to bet on. It's gonna compete with the big guys. No other student body we know of has ever developed an app like this.'

'Sounds very exciting, Declan,' enthused Jamie.

'Jamie, are you serious?' exclaimed Marilyn. 'This is probably illegal. We'll have the cops on us.'

'Nah, it's just a game,' Declan said.

'No money involved? No bets placed with money?' Marilyn pursued the question.

'Nah. I don't think so. Like I said, it's just a game.'

'Frankly, Marilyn, I can't see the problem,' said Kon Economopoulos from Business.

'Correct me if I'm wrong, Kon,' said Marilyn, 'but you're the coordinator of the entrepreneurship project. Right?'

'That's so,' admitted Kon. 'But, I'm more interested in the Children's Jumping Castle. Tell us about that, Declan.'

'Oh, yeah, that'll be a big hit with the kids. Idea of the students in the Child Care diploma. Y'know, it's one of those inflatable thingos that kids jump around on.'

'Jamie, come on,' said Arso exasperated, 'we planning university Open Day or primary school fete?'

'It's just a bit of fun, Arso,' implored Jamie. 'Don't forget we are trying to get whole families on campus and give them a sense that this is a place for fun, fun, fun. Not a forbidding place.'

'Maybe we give them all degrees as they leave, too. Come on!' said Arso throwing his hands up in despair.

'Hey, chill, Ars,' suggested Declan. 'Students are taking a big role in Open Day this year, doin' all sorts of stuff.'

'That's right, Arso. And the one that always sets hearts racing is the BURCA demos,' enthused Jamie.

'Now we demonstrating burkas? Muslim fashion parade?' asked Kikavic.

'No, BURCA, the Batman University Rock Climbing Association,'

Declan corrected him. 'What they're gunna do is climb the O'Toole Building. They'll fire off some vouchers to the crowd below to be redeemed at Boy Wonder's. Then they'll abseil back down. It's gunna be very impressive.'

'More bread and circuses for the great unwashed,' sighed Kikavic.

'Anyway, Arso, you can ignore all the fun, if you want,' said Jamie, with a sly reference to the notoriously low science enrolments. 'Hopefully, you'll get plenty of interest in science courses.'

'I see there's plan to have a multi-faith marquee,' said Arso, perusing the program. 'Now religion is fun, too?' he sneered.

'We had a lot of pressure from Professor Pilgrim,' said Declan. 'He's some sort of Christian. So, we agreed but said they had to have other religions in with them.'

'And Declan,' said Kellie, 'what about the batmail from BUCA?'

'Yeah, the Batman University Collective of Atheists,' scoffed Declan. 'They're threatening to picket the multi-faith marquee. But we're not worried, they've only got three or four members.'

'The last thing we need on Open Day is some religious conflict,' Marilyn warned.

'Nah, forget 'em,' said Declan. 'All talk.'

'Now, absolutely rushing on, guys,' Jamie intervened, 'Kellie, I assume everything is under control over at Equine Studies? They're a bit out of sight, out of mind, yeah?'

'Miranda Callahan says everything is set up. They actually don't have to do much. Most of the visitors just want to be able to pat horses and watch them on the training track. There'll be a shuttle bus running between the main campus and the Equine Studies campus throughout the day.'

'Ta, Kellie.'

'And last of all, a huge innovation. There'll be a marque in the

Village Place for the new Centre for Red Studies,' Jamie announced proudly. 'Take a bow, Declan.'

'Cheers, Jamie,' said Declan proudly, as he leaned back and ran the fingers of both hands through his luxuriant red hair. 'I'm gunna be working on the marquee on Open Day.'

'What's it about?' inquired Arso sceptically.

'It's about us reds as a minority,' Declan said defensively. 'There's gunna be teaching and research about redheads. At last. To advocate for us.'

'A world first, Arso,' said Jamie, as if to remove any doubt about the significance of the initiative.

'No disrespect, Declan,' said Kon, 'but it sounds like bullshit to me.'

'Yeah, you might think so with your complexion. You just don't know … ah, forget it.' With that, Declan stood and left the meeting.

'Think of it this way, Kon,' Jamie moved to settle the atmosphere, 'Red Studies is going to bring heaps of dollars into Batman. Courtesy of the old redhead himself, Reg O'Toole. He's giving Batman big bucks for Red Studies. There's even going to be a professor.'

'Now I heard everything,' groaned Arso.

Chapter 11

Down Come the Silos

'Kurt, thank you for coming all this way.' Nicholas Razer emerged from his office and approached with his hand outstretched. Kropp rose, smiling, to take it. 'Come in, come in. You won't have seen the office since I remodelled it.'

Indeed, Kropp had not, and he was taken aback by the scale and value of the work, and the transformation of the space. The President's office and associated spaces now occupied the majority of Level 12. Kropp knew a little about art and guessed that the works on the wall were originals and of considerable value. The carpets alone would have cost tens of thousands of dollars. Kropp's eye was drawn in particular to the President's desk, which seemed to occupy a quarter of the space.

'You like that?' Razer asked with pride. 'Made in Denmark. I saw it in a London antique shop just before I left. Had to have it.'

Kropp had a predilection for expensive furnishings and art himself, but Nicholas Razer had the advantage of a university budget to indulge his desires.

'The office transformation is simply brilliant, Nicholas. Congratulations. You've achieved a great deal in a few short months.'

'Yes, it's been a challenging time setting things up. The office refurbishment took rather too much of my time and energy. Getting the car through Customs was a nightmare, too.'

'Setting up in a new role is always challenging, Nicholas,' Kropp observed.

Kropp watched as Razer opened a cupboard door on the rear of which Kropp could see a full-length mirror. Razer stood for a moment looking at his reflection, tugged the back of his suit jacket and adjusted his tie. He ran his hand through his thinning hair, which he'd grown long at the back. He leaned forward, smiling, to examine his teeth.

'Left the house in a bit of a hurry this morning,' he said by way of apology before sitting at his meeting table and gesturing for Kropp to do likewise. 'Let me explain why I wanted to see you,' he began. 'I understand you were involved in the hiring of the Deans when all the positions were spilled a couple of years ago. My predecessor apparently wanted a change of personnel. Not a bad idea in theory, not sure it worked so well in practice.'

'That's correct,' Kropp confirmed. 'We did all four of those searches. They were difficult roles to fill.'

'Why?'

Kropp chose not to add that it was damn near impossible to attract good staff to Batman at any time. It was as true for Deans as it had been for the President.

'It had a lot to do with the unfavourable publicity around Richardson's departure. Poor old Richardson wasn't a good appointment himself,' Kropp went on. 'As one wit remarked, there were four candidates for the job, Richardson, Johnnie Walker, Jack Daniels and Jim Beam. They all got it.'

'Very droll. I want to throw around some ideas with you about the organisational changes I'm about to introduce.'

Kropp retrieved his notebook to be briefed on four new searches for Batman.

'My first and only encounter with the four faculty Deans convinced me they lack vision. I'm going to abolish the faculties in favour of two colleges that will subsume the faculties and the other bits and pieces. And that, Kurt, presents me with a problem of what to do with the existing Deans.'

'It's common for them to be terminated and given a payout,' observed Kropp.

'There's the problem,' explained Razer. 'Sally Sloane tells me the Minister would not allow the payouts. There's also the problem of bad publicity in the media. It seems I've got to keep them, at least in the short-term, and find them new roles.'

'Two of the Deans will lead the two new colleges,' Razer want on. 'That should pretty quickly expose their limitations. We'll call them Executive Deans. And then I have to find some out-of-the way roles for two others.'

'But how can I help with this, Nicholas?' asked Kropp, hoping he was managing to conceal his disappointment at this proposal, which appeared to involve no new searches.

'You know all of the Deans, having been the search consultant,' said Razer.

There was a knock at the door. Barry Motherwell and Roddy Rodman entered.

'Kurt, I've invited these two to join us. Roddy seems to know everything about the Deans and, in fact, everybody else who matters on campus.'

Rodman bowed with false modesty.

'Barry's going to put the plan into practice.' Motherwell nodded a greeting at Kropp. 'Have a seat, you two. I'm just about to explain the new structure for Batman.'

Before he sat, Roddy went to the whiteboard and wiped off what looked to Kropp like a list of items to be procured for the President's liquor cabinet.

'We're going to have two new colleges. The current faculties of commerce and arts will merge to form the College of Business and Social Science,' began Razer. 'It's time to give at least the impression of a harder, scientific edge to the arts area, and calling them Social Science should sell well in the marketplace.'

'Other universities have gone down that path, Nicholas,' Kropp chimed in, 'and it worked pretty well.'

'And the current Faculties of Science and Engineering will merge to form a College of Technology. The label "technology" better represents our future directions and, from what I know of traditional engineering schools, ours is anything but. Hardly a laboratory or serious piece of engineering equipment anywhere. It's all IT and so on, isn't it?'

'That's pretty much the case, President,' said Roddy Rodman. 'They've never been able to get accreditation from the professional association.'

'My point precisely,' replied his President.

'There will be no additional remuneration, of course,' Razer declared. 'Their reward will be their elevated status. We'll call them Executive Deans.'

'What about the Departments of Health and Education?' asked Motherwell.

'Not sure,' replied Razer offhandedly. 'Health is mainly nursing and a few other odds and sods, isn't it? Not sure why they're even in a university. Maybe put them in with Technology? Teachers use technology, too, don't they?'

'I doubt that would be a good fit,' observed Motherwell cautiously. 'Both have very poor research standing.' Razer ignored the comment.

'Let's pool what you all know about the four Deans,' suggested Razer, 'and see who'd best fit the new roles.' The others nodded.

'First, the College of Technology,' Razer began. 'Who'd be the ideal Executive Dean of that College?'

No-one spoke.

'How would you all feel about the current Dean of Science, Mervyn Pilgrim?' asked Razer. 'He has a PhD in geology and has been involved in industry research. Mining, I think.'

Kropp recalled his recent encounter with Pilgrim but, alert to Razer's tactic, he chose to keep the encounter to himself.

'That's right,' said Kropp, 'we located him in the west working as a geologist with North Western Mining. The bottom had fallen out of mining and his prospects with the company were not good. From what I learned of Mervyn Pilgrim, he would be the man for the new Executive Dean of Science and Technology role.'

'Why do you say that?' inquired Razer.

'I recall that his research record is modest and is very much industry based, rather than academic. He's known to be sceptical about the value of research output metrics.'

'Anything else about him?' asked Razer.

'He's a born-again Christian. A bishop in one of those mega churches out here in Robert Gordon.'

'Would that be useful?' asked Razer.

'He's not taken seriously by science and technology types,' Kropp declared and, as if to settle the matter, added, 'He's a creationist.'

'You're getting my drift, Kurt,' smiled Razer approvingly. 'Let's put Mervyn Pilgrim's name alongside that college,' said Razer, motioning Roddy to the whiteboard.

'Now, who would do best with the College of Business and Social Science?'

'I think Dr Dunne is the standout there,' Motherwell led off. 'Her teaching assessments are first-rate. She's popular with her staff and students, and very much a public academic, which has been good for Batman. And she has an international reputation in her research field.'

'What field is that?' inquired Razer.

'It's North Korean film studies,' advised Motherwell.

'I have another plan for Dr Dunne that will capitalise on her expertise,' added Razer.

'If I might make a suggestion,' ventured Kropp, 'the candidate for Executive Dean of Business and Social Science chooses himself. I'd recommend the Dean of Business, Professor Morgan Freestone.'

Still convinced that Lexi Dunne deserved the role, Motherwell raised a forefinger as if to press her case, but thought better of it.

'Go on,' said Razer.

'We were under pressure from the then Vice-Chancellor to identify candidates from the corporate world. It was a difficult assignment. High-flying corporates don't typically have PhDs and publications. Likewise, business academics rarely have business experience. Professor Richardson wanted to appoint someone with real world business experience to teach and conduct research on business in Australia and internationally.'

'Then how did Dr Morgan Freestone get to be the Dean?' inquired Razer incredulously. 'He had no business experience as far as I can tell from his CV. Seems to have spent most of his career in government.'

'That's true, President,' volunteered Roddy, 'but the selection panel was impressed by his role in liaising with business on behalf of government. He had a good network of contacts in State government.'

'And I can confirm,' said Kropp, 'almost no university in this country has a Dean of Business with extensive business experience.'

'Splendid! He's our choice for Executive Dean of Business and Social Science. I assume he knows nothing about Humanities and Social Sciences?' inquired the President.

'President,' said Roddy, 'Professor Freestone is an arts buff in his private life. Y'know live theatre, ballet, opera. But I'm afraid,' he added with confected regret, 'his style of management is likely to alienate Arts staff.'

'Perfect,' declared Kropp and Razer in unison. Roddy moved again to the whiteboard.

'Now, what special role can we conjure for Professor Clive Goodenough, our feisty Dean of Engineering?' asked Razer.

'Professor Goodenough is an electrical engineer,' Roddy said.

'A rather prickly and ineffectual character, as I recall,' said Kropp.

'And a notorious and tiresome pedant,' added Roddy. 'I was once sitting next to his wife at a graduation dinner and she told us she had discovered some letters she'd sent him while they were courting. He'd corrected her grammar and punctuation in red biro. She's never let him forget it.'

'To be frank,' Kropp continued, 'I was truly amazed when he was appointed Dean. We didn't even recommend him for short-listing.'

'Sounds promising,' smiled Razer.

'Early on, he was a modestly successful researcher,' Kropp continued, 'but we were told he showed no evidence of being able to nurture junior researchers and engage in research teams. He has an awkward personality and his private life is dominated by a harridan of a wife.'

'You know,' Razer interrupted, 'I think it's time for Batman to build contacts with the community, with schools, the professions and so on. Wouldn't you agree that Clive Goodenough would be good enough to be the new Dean of Outreach and Engagement?'

They all did. Roddy stood again to make an entry on the whiteboard.

'Now, that leaves Professor Lexi Dunne,' Razer said, looking at Motherwell. 'Given her seminal work on North Korean film, I think she'd make an excellent Dean for International. Don't you, Barry?' Razer said, looking to Motherwell who, by this time, was looking at his shoes. 'Or do you think she'd prefer to be Dean for Equity?'

Motherwell looked up and shifted uncomfortably. 'I hardly think a few visits to North Korea would qualify her ...' but his voice trailed off when he realised the futility and indeed, the danger, of opposing the President's plan. He well knew the Dean for Equity role would be an unwelcome and career-limiting appointment for Lexi Dunne. She deserved a better prospect.

'Good. That's settled,' smiled Razer. 'All that remains now is to make the announcement. I've had HR do the position descriptions for each of the new roles. That's where you come in, Barry. We'll need some KPIs. Ones that will stretch our new Executive Deans.'

'Just one matter remaining,' suggested Roddy. 'What to do with Health and Teacher Education.'

'I think we all agree on that. Pop them into Technology,' Nicholas Razer ruled.

The small group of men agreed it had been a very productive meeting and Nicholas thanked Barry Motherwell and Roddy, signalling they should leave.

'Thanks for your input, Kurt,' said Razer. 'I hope you've left some time for lunch.'

'Indeed I have. I believe we're to dine at Boy Wonder's.'

'What!' exploded Razer. 'Who told you that? I only eat there when I have to. And only with my team. I don't need to encounter bloody academics at lunch. Brian's waiting to take us to the club. You can stagger back to your office from there.'

ooOOoo

Barry Motherwell left the meeting about restructuring a troubled and conflicted man. He knew he must be loyal to Nicholas Razer and had committed himself to implementing, without question, whatever Nicholas decided. On the other hand, he had strong feelings for Lexi Dunne, which he didn't fully understand. He felt very protective towards her, even though he knew no woman less in need of the support of a man. Her professional future under Razer's new structure was almost certainly not what she wanted or needed. He felt he should alert her to Razer's plan for her and counsel her on how best to react to the proposed restructure. He knew she would be devastated to lose her faculty, and to lose it to Morgan Freestone, for whom she had little regard. She'd once confided to Motherwell that Freestone was a sanctimonious bore.

Motherwell closed his office door and called her office number.

'Lexi, Barry here. Got a moment?'

'Shoot.'

'I'd like to have an off the record discussion with you,' Motherwell said softly, not that his EA could have heard him. 'Not now, not on the phone.'

'How about lunch at Boy Wonder's?' Lexi suggested.

'Ah, I'd prefer to meet off campus, and not in the mall, either,' he said, hesitating before revealing his preferred arrangement. 'Can I drop around to your place after work?'

'Super, Mother,' Lexi enthused. 'You'll stay for a bowl of pasta, I hope.'

'That'd be great,' he said, relieved.

No one had called him 'Mother' since school and university and for that he was glad. It was a taunt that had been used against him all his life. But, her way of saying it quite charmed him. The prospect of a quiet dinner with her excited him even though he was apprehensive about her likely reaction to what he had to reveal.

'OK. Come about seven,' she suggested. 'After I've supervised Vine's homework.'

oooOooo

Barry Motherwell had not been the only one to leave the meeting on a mission. Among Roddy Rodman's failings was that he was a gossip.

He returned to his office down the corridor and closed his office door, explaining to his EA that he needed to make a private call.

'Jamie, are you sitting down?'

'Of course I am, you donkey. Do you think I work standing up?'

'Have I got news for you!'

'Spill it, Pumpkin. I'm about to head off to a regional branding meeting with the worthies of the City of Robert Gordon. Mustn't be late for a very important date.'

'Want to know who your new boss is going to be?'

'Couldn't care less, my little carbuncle. Marketing is virtually autonomous. I report to the President and since he cares fuck-all about marketing, I report to myself.'

'Batman's going to have a restructure at the top. There's going to be a new post. Dean for Outreach and Engagement.'

'Oooh, I'm going to be a Dean?'

'It's not going to be you, Professor Brian Cox.'

'Why not?'

'Because it's going to be Clive Goodenough.'

'Clive fucking Goodenough? You're pulling my pud!'

'Unless he says no to it, he's going to engage for the university. And reach out.'

'Engage? Enrage, more likely.'

'So, marketing will be reporting to him. Congrats.'

'I'm going to resign,' Jamie huffed.

'Don't be a duffer. Do you really think Clive Goodenough will last more than five minutes in that space? Y'see, it's all part of Razer's master plan for dealing with the dopey Deans. Can't say any more now. Don't want to be indiscreet. It'll all be official soonish.'

'Gotta go. Thanks for nothing.'

'See you at home.'

Chapter 12

Bad News and Romance

Barry Motherwell eased his large university car down the narrow inner-suburban street and was lucky enough to find a park within walking distance of Lexi Dunne's house. He'd been there several times at Lexi's memorable dinner parties. He knew little and cared less about fancy food but Lexi's meals were invariably delicious. Her friends from the worlds of art and film were always lively and he didn't mind if he had little to contribute to the discussion. He enjoyed learning about a world that was as foreign to him as any he'd ever visited.

Best of all, none of the guests were associated with Batman. Now that he was her boss, he wondered if she might have a different point of view. This night, however, it would be just him and Lexi and although he was anxious about what he was about to reveal to her, he was excited at the prospect of time with her. His life since Maureen died had been lonely.

He jangled the dangling cow bells at the door of Lexi's terrace house, took a couple of steps back and looked up and down the street. He hoped she'd like the flowers he'd purchased on the way at the Robert Gordon mall.

It was a hot night and Lexi opened the door in t-shirt, shorts and bare feet. She looked wonderful and so relaxed. By contrast, he felt hot, sweaty and crumpled.

'Come in, Mother.' She pecked him on the cheek and squealed with delight. 'Are they for me?'

'I wasn't sure what you like ...'

'They're gorgeous. Come in. Vine's in her bedroom, no doubt on her device allegedly finishing homework. And take off that tie. Care for a beer?'

'That would be great,' he replied, so pleased that Lexi treated his being in her house as so unremarkable.

Motherwell watched as she found a vase, arranged the flowers in it and watered them while telling him to get 'a couple of cold ones' from the fridge. He liked that. Being put to work, not standing around unsure what to do.

'They're screw-tops. Take them outside and we'll sit in the courtyard under the spreading apricot tree.'

Barry Motherwell felt very much at home in this place and with this woman. His late wife had been a Minnesota woman of serious mind and sober habits. Lexi, a free-spirited Californian, could hardly have been more different. Even though she had risen to be a Dean at Batman, she somehow managed to retain a sunny, relaxed Californian style. Beneath that exterior, however, Motherwell recognised a tough-minded high achiever typical of the best of American academics.

Lexi Slutzkin had completed her undergraduate degree at the University of California on the laid-back, it-never-rains-in-southern California, hashish-fuelled, very cool Goleta campus of UC Santa Barbara. She had majored in film and her grades were sufficiently good to win a scholarship to UCLA.

It was at that illustrious professional school that she completed her doctoral dissertation on North Korean film, a topic about which little was known in the West. Many academic awards and invitations flowed her way following the publication of her highly acclaimed and pioneering work on Kim Jong-il, 'The Great Leader and his Movies'.

While at the Faculty of Movies, Lexi had fallen in love with an Australian whom she had encountered at an Australian film festival. 'Gazza' Dunne cultivated the persona of a stereotypical Aussie. He was garrulous, mischievous and matey. His approach to film-making was innovative and edgy, and both he and his work excited her. He had come to LA with the intention of becoming the most famous Australian film-maker in the US and Lexi believed in him.

When his hopes for fame and fortune turned to shit, as he put it, Gazza announced that he was fed up with Hollywood and intended to return to 'Terror Australis'. She was devastated. That is, until he proposed they get married and she come along. With her recently completed and award-winning thesis, she would easily get work in Melbourne, he promised. Lexi Slutzkin became Lexi Dunne and set off on a new adventure with her new husband to the land Down Under.

Marital bliss, however, soon faded as Lexi saw a new side of Gazza: a hard drinking, neglectful husband who soon realised he preferred the company of the girl he'd left behind when he ventured to the US. He moved out of their tiny inner-city terrace house and left Lexi with a few unfinished film scripts, a mortgage and a baby girl.

Lexi started to build a new life and her big break had come in the form of a successful application for a lectureship in film studies in the Faculty of Arts at Batman University.

Soon after his appointment to Batman, Motherwell encountered Lexi in a research committee and began contriving opportunities to speak with her on research matters after meetings. Her exotic background and free spirit dazzled him. For her part, Lexi welcomed Motherwell's attention and, in due course, she began to invite him to soirees at her home.

Motherwell sat in one of the easy chairs Lexi had in her tiny backyard and stretched his legs. Lexi soon appeared with a tray on which were two stubbies of beer and a bowl of nuts, which she placed on an upturned plastic carton within his reach.

'Before you do anything else, Mother, take those Farmer Brown boots off,' she ordered.

'Sure?' he asked.

She answered with an expression of gentle admonishment.

In silence, Motherwell unlaced his boots.

'I have to say I'm feeling a little uncomfortable,' he said, removing his socks.

'I've seen men's bare feet before,' she said.

Motherwell was about to correct her when he realised she'd been joking.

'Now that ordeal's over, cheers,' she said raising her stubby. He did the same and they took their first swigs of the chilled beer.

'Now you've wet your whistle, tell me what you wanted to speak to me about.'

Motherwell took a deep breath and repeated that he was uncomfortable about being there.

'Surely we've got past that stage. Or is this a last supper situation?' she inquired, suddenly anxious.

'Nothing like that,' Motherwell assured her. 'I just need to know that I can share something with you on a strictly confidential basis.'

'This is suddenly sounding ominous. Spill it.'

'Nicholas is planning a major reorganisation of the faculties,' he began. 'The Arts Faculty is going to be abolished,' he said apprehensively.

'What! He's going to eliminate a whole faculty?' Lexi slammed her beer on the carton. 'I can't believe it. He's a psychologist, but I didn't think he'd be that mad.'

'He's going to merge Arts and Business into one new entity. A

College of Business and Social Science. And the other faculties into a second college.'

'I can't believe what you're saying,' she leaned back as though she'd been shoved. Tell me it's a joke.'

'I'm afraid it's not. With the new powers of university Presidents, he can do pretty much what he likes.'

'What's his plan for the Deans?' Lexi stood and faced Motherwell, still sitting. 'Are we all to be made redundant?'

'He's going to offer new roles to all four of you. Morgan Freestone is going to head the College of Business and Social Science. He's going to offer you the role of Dean for International.'

'International!' she repeated. 'And if I don't want it?'

'He'll probably make one other offer. A career dead end. Dean for Equity. If you refuse it, he would declare you redundant.'

'I certainly wouldn't be prepared to work on equity,' she declared emphatically. 'I guess I could do international. I have that experience in North Korea. I dunno. What do you think?'

'I think you could do a good job and it would offer new challenges. You'd no longer be part of the executive team so you might have more time for your research. The fact is, I don't want you to leave Batman.'

'And I don't want to leave, either. I'm pretty pissed off.'

Lexi stood and walked off a few paces.

'I knew you would be,' he said to her back. 'But I thought I should alert you. Now you've got to pretend it's news when you hear it officially.'

'When does he plan to meet us?' she said, turning to look at him.

'He doesn't,' said Motherwell, getting to his feet.

'What! He's just going to announce it? The bastard!' Lexi moved back to the carton to get her beer.

'No, it's down to me. I'll be telling you and the other Deans on Monday. He instructed me to keep it close till then. So, I'm sticking my neck out being here and telling you this.'

'I realise that, Mother. I really appreciate you levelling with me but it's cast a bit of a shadow over tonight. Let's eat and drown my sorrows.'

'Will Vine be joining us?'

'No, I fed her earlier. I'm sure she's busy networking on her iPad.'

'I've always wondered,' said Motherwell, anxious to move the conversation to safer topics, 'how you chose that name? Vine? Very American, I'd say.'

'Her father chose it,' Lexi said offhandedly, still smouldering about Motherwell's bombshell. 'Gazza was delighted when she was born. He said his professional and personal lives were now complete. Here he was, an aspiring film-maker in Hollywood with a beautiful baby girl.'

'And?'

'You've heard of Hollywood and Vine?'

'Oh, I get it.'

But it was clear that changing the topic hadn't at all assuaged Lexi's anger and sense of loss.

'I'll get us some dinner,' she said, as she disappeared into the house.

Motherwell stood anxiously considering what he should do. Eventually, he followed her into the cramped kitchen, wondering whether he should leave.

'You OK?' he asked nervously.

'Yeah, I'm American. We're survivors,' she said as she added sauce to the bowls of pasta. 'This one's yours,' she said, handing him a bowl.

They returned to the courtyard and each did their best to put the earlier conversation out of their minds. But Lexi seemed flat and there were uncustomary lapses in their conversation. Not a gifted conversationalist, Motherwell struggled to lift her spirits. Whenever he mentioned Batman, she begged him to desist. When he told her about some of the problems he had on his farm, she feigned interest but her thoughts were elsewhere. Motherwell realised the evening had gone flat.

Lexi suddenly sat upright and slapped her hand on her thighs.

'I've decided that tonight's not going to be spoiled by bad news. I'm going to put this shitty stuff out of my mind and you and I can talk about more pleasant things.'

'For instance?'

'How nice it is to have you here. And what a good man you are. I know you've stuck your neck out for me coming here tonight.' She stood, went to him and pecked his on the cheek.

'That's as may be, but I feel I've just ruined our night,' he lamented.

'You haven't,' she reassured him.

'The other times I've been here, it's been fun. Non-stop lively conversation, lots of laughs. And tonight, I've made you sad,' said Motherwell.

'I have been rather flattened,' she admitted.

'I'm sorry about the bad news. I'm afraid there's nothing I can do.'

'Maybe there is,' said Lexi, bending to take his hand. 'Come to bed.'

Chapter 13

The Professor Goes to Canberra

Barry Motherwell left Lexi Dunne's house a troubled man. Everything about her excited him, her trim but voluptuous body, her long blond hair, her casual yet confident gait. She fascinated him with her penetrating analyses of films, literature, art and contemporary politics. Her sharp intellect was so superior to that of her fellow Deans in executive meetings and was matched by a vivacious, breezy style. He found her completely beguiling, and knew that he was falling inexorably under her spell.

He was concerned that the canny Nicholas Razer, who had a nose for intrigue, would sense his infatuation. Or maybe Roddy, with his extensive network of campus informants, would tumble to what was going on. All this uncertainly caused Motherwell to dread his Monday morning meetings with Razer who invariably led off with the same teasing inquisition.

'And what new naughtiness have you been up to over the weekend, Bazza?'

'Absolutely nothing,' Motherwell would reply, 'I lead a quiet farmer's life.'

If Razer ever caught the slightest clue about Motherwell and Lexi Dunne, he would be merciless in exploiting that knowledge against him. If he should ever know that Barry Motherwell revealed confidential discussions about the proposed reorganisation to the object of his growing infatuation, Razer would destroy him. He would have to be very careful. He was sure Lexi understood this, too. But she was disarmingly honest and a woman not given to dissembling.

These thoughts had raced through his mind when Lexi took his hand, coaxed him from his chair and led him down the narrow hall to her bedroom. Powerful and contradictory emotions competed with each other. Motherwell stopped outside her bedroom door.

'I'm really sorry, Lexi, I've got to go to Canberra first thing. It's a meeting with the Minister for Homeland Defence and I need to be fresh. I'd best be going.'

Lexi dropped his hand and turned to face him.

'Sure, Mother, I understand. What's on in Canberra?'

'It's a meeting about a new initiative by the government to form university regiments. We've made a submission and Nicholas wants me to go to a meeting of university leaders with the Minister. I'm going to …'

'Look, Mother,' said Lexi taking his hand again, 'I really appreciate you giving me a heads-up about the re-organisation. And for listening to my grumbling. It's very helpful to have some warning. I'll treat what you've told me in the strictest confidence.'

'I'd appreciate that. I'll see you at the meeting of Deans on Monday morning.'

'That could be interesting. I'll try to be on my best behaviour.'

'I'd appreciate that, too.'

'Good night, Mother,' and she hugged him.

ooOOoo

The long twilight was already melting away when Barry Motherwell left Lexi's house and walked, as though in a trance, to his car. He sat for several minutes with his hands on the steering wheel and thought,

What if? With a sigh of regret, he turned on the ignition and headed for the freeway.

Traffic on that Thursday night was light for the whole journey, and his thoughts turned again to Lexi and the opportunity for intimacy he'd foregone. He thought of Maureen and how he'd not been with another woman since she passed. Was it a residue of guilt that also nearly paralysed him at the critical moment? If so, would it ever end? Was he doomed never again to know the warm softness of a naked woman beside him? Had he been a fool to reject Lexi?

He slept fitfully that night and when deep sleep was finally about to engulf him, the first rays of the new day were invading his bedroom and his bedside alarm sounded. He threw off the summer sheets and dragged his weary body to the shower. He always took a cold shower, whatever the time of year. The shock of the water cascading over his body had the usual effect of engendering the first signs of wakefulness. A strong black coffee over breakfast would complete the process. But first, he had to give his dogs their breakfast.

Having tended to the dogs, he returned to the kitchen and sat at the island bench, sipping his coffee and eating his marmalade toast. He scanned the day's news on his iPad. There was still widespread consternation and hostility at the merging of the national Departments of Home Affairs and Defence. The Minister for Home Affairs had made a grab for Defence and his supine cabinet colleagues had capitulated to his demands for a mega Ministry of Homeland Defence. Such a ministry, he'd argued, would provide the optimal arrangement for the government to carry out its most sacred obligation, namely to defend the homeland and its citizens.

The news report noted that the Minister had already achieved significant success in enhancing homeland defence through increased spending and tighter immigration. The new, lavishly equipped and armed Coast Guard Australia patrolled the borders of the country, and had met with great success in intercepting numerous unseaworthy craft carrying illegal asylum seekers and drug runners.

The Minister had also signalled a major contribution to national defence while at the same time addressing the soaring youth unemployment problem. For those women and men aged 17 to 25 and not in education or employment, there was to be the reintroduction of national service.

Motherwell's eye fell on the next paragraph.

Today the Minister for Homeland Defence will meet senior university officials in Canberra. On the agenda will be the imminent establishment of university regiments. The Minister is expecting the cooperation of all Australian universities in this venture. Significant benefits will flow to participating universities, including new buildings, staffing and facilities.

Students who sign up for their campus regiment and who fulfil all obligations will receive a stipend equivalent to their tuition fees. Following basic military training, they will be eligible for vacation time active service in the form of international peacekeeping operations and community support projects within Australia. The expects regiments will be formed in the coming months.

Nicholas Razer had made several minor amendments to Motherwell's submission to the Minister for Homeland Defence before sending it to Canberra over his own name. Informal feedback from advisers in the Minister's office had been very positive and both Razer and Motherwell had every reason to expect a favourable outcome. To Barry Motherwell's surprise, Nicholas Razer had entrusted him to represent Batman at the meeting with the Minister.

'Never been there, never want to, Barry,' Razer had declared. 'More your kind of place, old chap.'

THE PROFESSOR GOES TO CANBERRA

ooOOoo

At the Russell Offices in Canberra, Presidents and Vice Presidents from most of the nation's universities greeted each other as they took their seats in the Homeland Defence auditorium.

Barry Motherwell sat alone at the rear of the auditorium betraying no emotion as the Minister singled out Batman's submission for special commendation. He heaped praise upon Batman and several other smaller and regional universities for their positive response to the government's initiative. With his customary deadpan yet menacing delivery, he held up to ridicule those universities who declined to submit a proposal or attend the meeting. He would be speaking with them further, he said, and expected that in due course, they would also sign up.

The meeting was brought to a conclusion without questions, and the Minister made his exit to host his next meeting. Most of the attendees left to return to their respective institutions via one of the excellent restaurants in the near vicinity of the department. There was time for a pre-lunch drink and a review of their meeting with the Minister before a good lunch.

As a new Vice President and unknown to most of the other attendees, Barry Motherwell waited for the auditorium to clear. As he rose to leave, he was approached by a young woman whom he had noticed taking notes and sitting toward the front of the auditorium during the Minister's address.

'Professor Motherwell?' She advanced with serious intent, extending her right hand.

'Yes?'

'I'm Karisma Jones, one of the Minster's advisers. Can you spare me a minute?'

'Ah, yes, of course, Miss Jones.'

'You can call my by my first name,' she said, more by way of direction than suggestion.

'I'm sorry, I didn't quite ...' Motherwell was stumbling into an awkward situation. He knew from his Meeting and Greeting tutorial that you must repeat a name when you're introduced. But he always forgot.

'Is it Carlotta?'

The young woman looked him reproachfully. It was on the long plane flight across the Pacific to her appointment Down Under that she'd decided to have a name makeover. She'd no longer be plain old Mary-Lou Jones from Ohio. That weak surname needed support. It demanded a name that spoke of who she wanted to be and what she aspired to do. Charisma had seemed popular with her politics professor but that 'ch' could be confusing. A 'k' would solve that.

'It's Karisma,' she said, urging the blushing Motherwell, who reminded her of a suntanned potato farmer back home in Idaho.

'Karisma,' he repeated. 'Karisma.'

'Awesome. There's a meeting room along here.' Karisma Jones stepped snappily ahead and, clicking noisily along in her hard-heel shoes, she opened the door of one of the breakout rooms gesturing to Motherwell to take a seat.

'Is that an American accent I detect?' inquired Motherwell. The Meet and Greet tutorial had also recommended trying to get people to talk about their favourite topic, themselves.

'It is. I'm just a month into a two-year secondment to the Minister's office from the US Defense Department. Have a seat. I'll have to be brief,' she explained as she closed the door, 'as I've got to get to the Minister's next meeting. It's with the US Secretary of Defense. I'm keen to meet my real boss.'

Karisma perched herself on the edge of the conference table as she'd seen powerful women do in movies and addressed Motherwell earnestly.

'The Minister wants to know how long it would take you to set up your regiment. He's keen to get a demonstration model up and running soon.'

'I'd need to speak with my President but the notional timetable in our proposal is realistic. It's a matter of about three months, based on the costings we provided.'

'Awesome. That would be around April?'

'Yes, I'd think so.' Motherwell hesitated as he began to realise the enormity of the task that lay before him.

'Cool. And if the Minister wanted to come and review a parade a couple of months later?'

'What does he have in mind?'

'Open Day.'

'Sorry, I can't recall just now when that will be.'

'It's Sunday, July 24.'

'I can't see why not.'

'Look, I've got to leave now. But I can assure the Minister that Batman will be ready for him to visit on that date, OK?'

'Ah, yes, I suppose you can.'

With that, Karisma Jones stood, shook Motherwell's hand and clip-clopped out of the room. Barry Motherwell was certain Nicholas Razer would endorse his decision. A massive injection of funds into Batman for a demonstration model of national significance would bolster the university's shaky budget. It would also bring great kudos to the university in the Robert Gordon region and even nationally.

Motherwell took a taxi to Canberra airport, passed through the newly heightened security checks and proceeded straight to the business class lounge. He noticed the small group of other Presidents and Vice Presidents in muffled discussion off in a far corner. He helped himself to a full strength beer and settled down to make some calls.

'Nicholas, Barry here, calling from Canberra.'

'Mission accomplished?'

'I'd say so.'

'Splendid. Where are you now? Out at Fyshwick, stocking up on sex toys?' joked Razer.

'I thought I'd give you quick update on the meeting.'

'Go on.'

'Good news. Batman's submission got a favourable mention. In fact, after the close of the meeting, one of the Minister's staffers asked me how quickly we could establish the regiment. The Minister wants to come to Batman to review a parade of the regiment. On Open Day.'

'Christ! When's that? Can we do it?'

'I've said we could.'

'Barry, I think we have an addition to your KPIs for the year.'

'I've sounded out the Sandstone regiment already and they'll help us.'

'I want an operational plan from you soon. Everything we need to do with clear time lines. If a Minister, especially this Minister, is going to be on campus, there's to be no fuck ups.'

'You'll have the plan soon.'

Motherwell had just minutes remaining before his flight would be called.

'Hello, Lexi. I'm about to fly back.'

'Hi, Mother, I've been thinking about you. How did it go?'

'Really well.'

'I'm pleased to hear it. I know you did the proposal so it's a real win for you. Nicholas knows that, doesn't he? I mean, he knows the work you've put in?'

'Not sure. Doesn't matter, he's the boss.'

Lexi let the comment pass.

'I wanted to thank you for dinner last night.' Motherwell lowered his voice in the crowded lounge. 'And for the company.'

'I was hoping you hadn't regretted coming.'

'Not at all,' replied Motherwell, 'far from it.'

'I've been worried that I may have been out of line. If so, I'm sorry. I didn't sleep too well last night.'

'Same here.'

'Maybe we just need …' Lexi faltered, 'I dunno, maybe just need to slow down a little. You know, work colleagues, male boss and female staff member, that sort of thing.'

'Whatever you say, Lexi,' Motherwell said, deflated. He heard the paging call for his flight.

Chapter 14

The Deans get a Surprise

A certain insouciance regarding punctuality was the only criticism colleagues could level at Lexi Dunne, the Dean of Arts. It had become something of a standing joke among them. Some would gently rib her as she sauntered late into a staff meeting, papers jammed under her arm and a coffee in the other hand. Other colleagues took each late arrival as a personal affront and would glare at her or refuse to establish eye contact. Senior students, accustomed to her casual style, often broke into applause as she arrived late for a class. Lexi would effect a grateful bow.

It came as no surprise to her fellow Deans, therefore, when she arrived late for their special meeting with the Vice President.

'Lexi,' offered the Dean of Business, Morgan Freestone, 'we've been expecting you. Hope you haven't had to leave anything more important to be with us.'

Lexi ignored Freestone's sarcasm and addressed the group as she flipped into her chair.

'Soooorry, everyone,' she drawled looking around at the group and Barry Motherwell. 'Had to drop off Vine for a school excursion. The traffic was appalling.'

'You're here now so we can begin,' said Barry Motherwell, without looking at her. 'As you know, Nicholas is overseas at the moment and he's asked me to convene this meeting.'

'Overseas? I don't think we did know,' said Clive Goodenough. 'I must have missed that email. Where is he, Barry?'

'Not sure,' said Motherwell. He could have said 'no idea' but didn't want to acknowledge that was the case. Razer came and went overseas often, and Motherwell had become accustomed to providing his signature without daring to read the details on the travel application form.

'Do you think he's being interviewed for a job?' Goodenough persisted.

'Of course not!' Motherwell snarled, becoming increasingly irritated.

'I'd have thought it's matter of professional courtesy among senior colleagues. Keeping us informed.' Clive Goodenough smiled around at his fellow Deans.

Motherwell pressed on, consoling himself with the thought that in a few minutes, he'd have the satisfaction of delivering Clive Goodenough some bad news.

'Nicholas is going to introduce an organisational change that can take us into the future and is more fit for purpose. He wants to do away with academic silos as far as possible and modernise the structure.'

Motherwell now had the undivided attention of the Deans.

'There'll be two new colleges replacing the faculties,' he continued, as he passed around a single page showing revised organisational structure, 'each headed by an Executive Dean appointed from among you. You'll see the names of the appointees on the diagram. There's also two new positions created for international education and outreach and engagement. Also named.'

'But,' objected Goodenough, 'we haven't had any discussion of this. I think it's foolhardy to just do away with a Faculty of Engineering. The profession will be up in arms.'

'There's no plan to do away with engineering, Clive,' said Motherwell tersely, 'it's simply going to be a restructure to allow efficiencies and to promote interdisciplinarity at Batman. No change to the engineering programs at all.'

'And in fairness, Clive,' ventured Mervyn Pilgrim, the Dean of Science, 'your faculty doesn't have professional accreditation and is unlikely to get it with the programs you offer. You have to admit the Faculty of Engineering doesn't look much like a traditional one.'

'But that's its strength,' protested Goodenough, looking around at his colleagues. 'Our engineering is the future of engineering. It's about big data, smart systems, IT, software. Cutting-edge stuff.'

'And, dare I say, Clive, those are the areas that would make it a good fit with Science,' countered Mervyn Pilgrim with a patronising smile.

'You would say that, Mervyn, since you're identified as the Executive Dean of the College,' snapped Goodenough, scrunching the page and tossing it on the table, 'and I am consigned to a nothing role.'

'That's not how Nicholas sees it, Clive,' said Motherwell. 'In fact, in many ways the university's future is all about outreach and engagement.'

'That's as may be. I just don't want to be involved. I plan to appeal.'

'The decision is final, no appeals,' said Motherwell. 'University Presidents now have absolute powers in these matters. End of story.'

'I have no choice then?' muttered Goodenough.

'Not if you want to stay at Batman.'

Clive Goodenough grimaced and fell silent.

'Any other comments?' asked Motherwell.

'Barry, this has come as something of a shock,' began Lexi Dunne. 'I can't say it looks like a good career move for me. One day to be a Dean of Arts, the next to be Dean for International. The International Office is already underfunded and has been banished from the

O'Toole Building to an old cottage on the edge of the campus. We have very few international students and the situation's unlikely to improve.'

Barry Motherwell couldn't believe his ears. He looked with barely disguised desperation at Lexi. Was this what she had in mind when she suggested they cool their relationship? He knew the articulate American was capable of mounting a forceful argument against the plan and arousing the support of the other Deans. That would make life very difficult for him in his relations with Razer. The President would brook no opposition and if Motherwell wasn't able to impose his will on the Deans, it would go very badly for him.

'However,' continued Lexi Dunne, 'in the interests of supporting the President's plan, I'm prepared to move into the international area. I've done a lot of work in China and North Korea. My contacts in Pyongyang have led to Batman having the first ever students from North Korea. I know the US scene very well. I suppose it's something of a logical move for me. I'll give it a go.'

Motherwell hoped his relief at hearing this declaration of support was not obvious.

'Thanks, Lexi,' he said, 'Nicholas will be pleased to hear that. I'm sure we can build up the International Office and get Jamie Jamieson and the media and marketing group more focused on international recruitment.'

'That's very encouraging,' said Lexi, surrendering to the inevitable.

'No other comments?' Motherwell looked in turn at each of the Deans, daring any to defy the President.

Morgan Freestone gave a characteristic clack of his tongue and head wobble. 'Barry, I think this is a pretty good model for Batman and I'm looking forward to learning more about the work of the Arts staff I'll have the honour of leading.'

Typically pompous crap, thought Lexi.

'One final matter,' said Motherwell. 'Due to the financial restrictions of the university, there'll be no alteration to the remuneration packages.'

'That'd be right,' muttered Goodenough. 'We labour for the love of Batman.'

'Nicholas will sign off the submission to the Board when he returns.'

'And when might that be?' inquired Goodenough, with barely disguised sarcasm.

'Not sure. But soon after that it will be implemented.'

With that, Motherwell gathered his papers, rose and left the Deans to consider their fates.

As it turned out, it was only Clive Goodenough who was seriously upset at the new structure. He slid his chair back from the table, slumped and glared at the ceiling. Lexi Dunne broke the awkward silence.

'I think we're left with no options, Clive,' she said solicitously. 'We know that under the new management arrangements, Nicholas can virtually do what he wants. At least we all have jobs. I guess things could be worse.'

'You may think so, Lexi,' muttered Goodenough, eyes still downcast, 'but I'm pretty pissed off. I am certainly going to consider my options.'

'You know, Clive,' began Mervyn Pilgrim with a patronising air, 'a wise reverend gentleman once said we should thank God for the jobs we don't get.'

'Wise and reverend, Mervyn? There's two adjectives you don't often see together,' snapped Goodenough.

Chapter 15

Weekend Warriors

Barry Motherwell left the meeting with a feeling as close to exultation as he ever expected. He'd had one of his first meetings with the Deans and he'd successfully imposed Nicholas's will. Not even Lexi's presence had swayed him from the surliness which was his default setting in vexed professional encounters. He realised things could have gone a lot worse with outright opposition to Razer's plan.

Arriving back at his office, he found the Head of Campus Security, chatting with Mez Carter, his EA. Motherwell had been so caught up thinking about his win with the Deans that he'd completely forgotten the 10 am appointment.

'Kevin, give me a minute. I have to make a quick call,' he explained. He wanted to report back to Razer with the news.

'Yessir!' Kevin threw a salute and winked at Mez Carter.

Motherwell pressed Jenny Partridge's extension on his desk phone.

'President's office,' trilled Jenny.

'Jenny, Barry here. I'd like a meeting with Nicholas as soon as you can organise it.'

'I'll make a diary note.'

'Thanks. When will that be?'

'Not sure.'

'You said you'd put it in the diary.'

'I said I'd make a note. I'm not sure when he returns. I think it will before the end of the week.'

'Ah, where is he now?' Motherwell had felt awkward when Goodenough challenged him on Razer's whereabouts, and he preferred to be in the know.

'It's not something I need to know,' Jenny said matter-of-factly. 'That's what he says.'

'Don't you organise his flights?' Motherwell persisted.

'He outsources his arrangements. I think it's someone at Sandstone in the Cephallus.'

Motherwell thought this a strange arrangement, but imagined Razer had some established service provider at the Institute.

'He says wherever he is,' Jenny went on, 'he's only a phone call away.'

'OK, let me know when he's back.'

'Bye,' chirped Jenny Partridge.

Motherwell was perplexed, and very glad he had taken the precaution of closing his office door before making the call. The Head of Campus Security might have been reminded of secret ops in which he'd been engaged in Afghanistan.

'Kevin,' he said, opening the door and interrupting Kevin as he was showing Mez Carter some photos of his dog, 'come in.'

'Thanks, Prof,' he said, glancing around as he entered the office for the first time.

A powerfully built man with sleeves rolled up to expose heavily tattooed forearms, Kevin Burke looked like the right man to head campus security. In his youth, he had been an interstate truck driver, but that failed to satisfy his need for a physically active life. A visit to an Army recruiting office in the regional city where he lived led to the most satisfying career he could have hoped for. He joined as a private soldier, serving with a mostly distinguished military record. He served three tours of duty in Afghanistan, the first two as a grunt.

His record of enemy kills was outstanding, and it was only when the civilian kills started to outnumber those of the jihadists that his superiors began to consider employing his talents in other ways. Army psychologists tested and interviewed him and recommended that he would be best suited for the role of military policeman. He served as sergeant with the MPs until a career-ending incident.

A court martial found that he had assaulted a senior Australian SAS officer. The captain had, Kevin explained at his court martial, been 'mouthing off' about the low intelligence, girliness and poor fighting capacity of regular Army soldiers. Kevin had countered this line of argument with his fists. However, given his distinguished record both as a rifleman and an MP, Army was reluctant to discharge him dishonourably. In the end, he was given an honourable discharge, a grateful send off and his record was without serious blemish. They also let him take his Army dog.

'Have a seat, Kev,' said Motherwell. Kevin hesitated, he wasn't accustomed to being offered a seat by his superiors in their offices. Mostly, he'd been instructed to remain standing at attention while he was bawled out or charged with some offence. Motherwell pointed at the chair on the other side of the desk, which Kevin eventually took. He'd never been invited to sit before being reprimanded.

'Kev,' Motherwell began, oblivious to Burke's discomfiture, 'I wanted to have a chat about a big development for Batman.'

Motherwell's manner seemed so benign that Kevin began to relax. He sat back in the seat.

'The government's announced they're going to establish university regiments.'

'Oh yeah. Weekend warriors,' said Burke disparagingly. 'No offence to yourself, Prof. Sorry.'

Motherwell waved away the apology.

'There'll certainly be weekend training, but there'll also be the usual reserve evening parades.'

'Hadn't heard that, Prof, but it's a bloody good thing. I 'spose Army'll set up a recruiting desk in the mall?'

'We'll be recruiting from our students.'

'Oh, no, Prof. It'll never work. You could never whip most of those slack-arsed kids into military discipline. Have you been out in the Village Place lately?'

'I'm going to be OC of the regiment, Kevin, and I rather hoped with all your experience, you'd like to help me. You'd get an allowance for regimental sergeant major.'

'Hold on, Prof. RSM is Warrant Officer Class 1. I was discharged as a sergeant.'

'Leave that to me, Kev.'

'Would I have to resign as Head of Campus Security?'

'It'd be an Army Reserve post and you'd stay on in your current role.'

'And I'd report to you?' asked Kevin, warming to the idea.

'On regimental matters.'

'Yeah. I get it.'

'The Minister for Homeland Defence ...'

'Now there's a good man, Prof,' Kevin cut in. 'If he says it's a goer, I'm in. Isn't he ex-Army?'

'I think it was police.'

'Yeah, but I reckon he knows a thing or two about defence and homeland security.'

'He's promised Batman significant funding for everything we'll need. A properly resourced regiment, here on campus.'

Burke shook his head in wonder at the idea.

'Here's a copy of our submission,' Motherwell said, sliding the document across the desk. 'Have a look at it and let's meet again soon to discuss how to go. We've got to have everything up and running by Open Day.'

'Open Day, Prof? That's July.'

'The Minister wants to come and inspect a parade.'

'Jeez, that's pretty soon.'

'We can do it, Kevin.'

'If you say so, Prof.'

'Have you still got your discharge papers?'

'All framed and on the wall of the pool room.'

'I'll need them to get Army to appoint you.'

'Yessir! Consider it done.'

'By the way, do you still have Micha?'

'Sure do.'

Micha was the brother of Richa, who won fame as an Army dog in Afghanistan. In temperament, he was unlike his famous sister, however. In the matter of psychological disposition, Micha more closely resembled his handler, Kevin Burke. Like him, he could be ill-disciplined when provoked. Like him, he was tough, carried himself well and oozed military bearing. Like him, he was easy to antagonise and quick to snarl.

When Kevin was reassigned to the military police, there was a sense of relief among operational soldiers who wished them both all the best and hoped they'd seen the last of both of them. When Burke was discharged from the Army, Micha went with him into well-earned retirement.

'I think there's a role for Micha, too. I have two retired Army dogs on the farm. I know Micha saw service with you in Afghanistan. So, that would give us three dogs with military experience to train for a regimental dog squad. Real military base style.'

'Now that would get me in, Prof. To be able to work with Micha in a military setting. I think he misses it as much as I do.'

'Music to my ears, Kevin. I'm planning for us to have the best university regiment in the country. And I believe it'll be the first of the new breed.'

Kevin Burke left the Vice President's office with a renewed interest in his work. Barry Motherwell also felt a new energy. He faced a daunting task in setting up a regiment in such a short space of time. But the challenge was one he would not shirk. He now had to think about implementation. How to recruit students to the regiment. How to organise campus planning for the new drill hall, parade ground, rifle range. So many issues. He would need to organise soon and well. He'd need to liaise closely with Roger Priestly, the Campus Manager, one of Razer's inner circle.

He called the head of Student Administration, Sarah Wells.

'Sarah, Barry Motherwell here.'

'Ooh, this is a pleasant surprise, Barry,' she oozed.

'Sarah, I want to be sure that you have up-to-date batmail addresses for all enrolled students.'

'We certainly do,' she confirmed proudly.

'Good. In the next little while, I'll need to contact all students concerning an important university development. It will go out over my name.'

'That won't be any problem at all, Barry. Just let me know and I'll ensure it all happens.'

'Thanks, I appreciate your assistance.'

'Barry, you did say all students, didn't you?' inquired Sarah. 'You know, undergrad, graduate. All faculties?'

'Yes, this announcement could be of interest to any of our students so I want them all to see it.'

'It sounds very important, Barry. Can't wait to see what it's all about. I'll get the batmail out just as soon as you let me have the text.'

What a nice woman, thought Barry Motherwell. If only all Batman staff were as efficient and pleasant as Sarah Wells.

Next, Motherwell called the head of media and marketing.

'Jamie Jamieson, marketing guru,' Jamie answered with his customary schtick. 'How can we help you and your enterprise?'

Motherwell cringed at Jamie's overblown style.

'Morning, Jamie, Barry Motherwell here.'

'Top of the morning, dude.'

'Jamie, don't call me "dude".'

'Roger that.'

'It's Barry.'

'Duh.'

'Did you call me "dude" again?'

'No.'

'So what did you call me?'

'I didn't call you anything.'

'What did you say?'

'I said I know it's you.'

'And what did you say before that?'

'I said "roger that". You know, message received.'

'What message?'

'The message that you don't like to be called "dude".'

'And you didn't call me that again?'

'I did not.'

Motherwell drew a deep breath.

'I need your help. We need to disseminate some news about a major development for the university.'

'Oh, yes, that would be the new college structure.'

'How the hell do you know about that?'

'I don't.'

'This place leaks like a bloody sieve,' snarled Motherwell. 'That is strictly confidential, Jamie, until the President announces it. Forget you ever heard it.'

'Roger that.'

'Thank you. I wanted you to organise a publicity campaign about the establishment of a university regiment on campus.'

'Ooh, yes, I saw the Minister's statement. Very exciting, having men in uniform on campus.'

'Settle down, there'll be women too.'

'Just joshing with you, Barry.'

'I'm going to batmail you our submission to the Minister for Homeland Defence and I'd like you to work up three media releases. One for the Gotham City News on campus, one for the Robert Gordon Bugle and one for the metropolitan and national press. And other media.'

'That covers the main players.'

'There'll be a notice sent to all students. Sarah Wells will distribute it via batmail. Let me have drafts of all of them within 48 hours. Clear?'

'Roger that.'

'Would you please stop saying that?'

Motherwell hung up abruptly and as Jamie pressed the end button on his desk phone, he poked his tongue at it.

'Copy that.'

Next, Barry Motherwell decided it was time to call Lexi Dunne.

'Lexi, it's me.'

'Hi, Vice, what's news?'

'First, thanks for being so helpful in the meeting with the Deans. Y'know, going along with the reorganisation without any fuss.'

'You looked so hell bent, I thought I'd better comply. That was your bad cop persona, I take it.'

'You could say that.'

'In any case, I'd given it a lot of thought. I've had a small taste of international work and I like it. Mind you, I'll be surprised if we ever recruit large numbers of international students to Batman. There aren't too many attracted to a life of rural idiocy.'

'Rural idiocy?'

'Sorry. Nothing personal. A Karl Marx reference.'

Karl Marx? She's read some odd stuff, thought Motherwell.

Chapter 16

Straplines

Jamie Jamieson was exasperated. The Open Day committee was supposed to be the engine room that would drive the Open Day's activities. Yet, Kellie told him, there were four apologies for the upcoming meeting. Didn't they understand this was the second last meeting before the big day? Did he have to do the whole bloody thing himself? Didn't they understand what Open Day and marketing meant for Batman University? To him it was inconceivable that Kon Economopoulos could give priority to an econometrics conference. Or Matthew Thistlethwaite could prefer to keep an appointment with his speech therapist.

As to the student reps, they – no doubt in collusion – had advised Jamie that they were resigning from the committee. Declan McGee said he'd be putting all his time and energy into the Red Studies Open Day marquee. Michael White preferred to spend his time organising the Indigenous students for their cultural activities on Open Day. He was also busy learning his lines for the part of William Barak in the play *Coranderrk*.

Kellie reported to the committee that she'd had no response to her calls and batmails to Professor Goodenough. 'His phone went to a voicemail message advising that he was "working off campus for some time",' Kellie said.

'His loss,' Jamie said dismissively. 'Cos I've got an exciting surprise for the committee today.'

'Early finish, Jamie?' suggested Arso.

'Hardly!' said Jamie, not taking the bait. 'I want us to devote our attention to the entries I've received for the Batman University strapline competition.'

'Strapline, Jamie?'

'Marketing 101, Marilyn. It's what we used to call in the profession a "tagline". There's been a conceptual breakthrough and we now use the term "strapline". It's the short, sharp statement that summarises what an enterprise is all about.'

'Not sure I follow about strapline,' said Arso. 'Give us example.'

'Easy peasy. There's the brilliant strapline from a few years ago that won Sandstone such acclaim. 'Get this. "Sandstone – Where Great Minds Collide." Hugely successful.'

'Sandstone? Huh! More like where great minds collude,' sneered Arso. 'Or where bigheads collide.'

'Jamie,' said Marilyn Worthy, 'I'm curious. You say the Sandstone campaign was very successful. In what sense?'

'Oh, it just won heaps of industry awards. That's all, Marilyn! Yeah?'

'But did it bring in any extra students? Or better students?' she countered.

'Oh, God, I wouldn't know about that,' Jamie retorted. 'I just know the industry absolutely loved it.'

'And the competition bit?' inquired Marilyn.

'It's a little competition I've been running in my office. All that marketing knowhow in one place. It was bound to deliver. I've asked the Vice President to invite the President himself to announce the winners in a gala ceremony at the end of Open Day.'

'Mustn't miss that,' muttered Arso.

'There's various categories. Like straplines for the whole uni and others for particular disciplines. That sort of thing.'

Jamie stood, walked to the whiteboard with marker pen in hand and addressed the two committee members animatedly.

'A little explanation to begin,' he said as he wrote 'Jamie's 3 Fs' on the whiteboard.

Marilyn and Arso steeled themselves for another dive into the arcane world of marketing.

'Any good strapline must display the following three Fs. Yeah? First, and foremost, fun,' he said as he wrote beside the first F. 'You know my thoughts on this matter. We have to have fun, in study, work and even in committees! Second, the entry must be fabulous,' and he wrote beside the second F. 'Every great strapline is a knockout. It just bowls you over and you want to hug the guy who came up with it. And, third, it must have a future focus.'

'That's four Fs,' Marilyn Worthy corrected.

'No, Marilyn,' Jamie corrected, '"focus" is just there in support of "future". Yeah? It doesn't have an existence outside of "future", does it?'

'It could. I don't think there's anything wrong with "focus", as such.'

Jamie cocked his head, closed one eye and paused to consider this suggestion.

'Hey!' he declared. '"Focus" might indeed be able to stand independently. Maybe it's Jamie's 4 Fs. Cheers, Marilyn.'

'It's nothing, really.'

'Back to the entries. I'm going to unveil each of the highly rated ones today and we'll vote for the winners. Yeah?' he said as he resumed his seat. 'I'm pretty excited, I can tell you.'

'Jamie, can we be brief? I got class in half hour,' said Arso.

'Let's get to it then,' urged Jamie. 'I want to present the best of the straplines submitted for the whole university, then I will go to some of the brilliant entries for specific disciplines, and so on. Trust me, you're about to be blown away!'

'Jamie, couldn't we leave the judging to you?' pleaded Marilyn.

'Not really,' Jamie replied. 'And think of this as a learning experience for you.'

Jamie produced his file marked 'Open Day Strapline Competition 2022'.

'I'm going to start with the entries for the university as a whole and then introduce the discipline entries. Yeah?'

'Jamie, couldn't we skip the duds?' asked Marilyn.

'Now, to help you think in a Jamie "3 Fs" kind of way, I'm going to start with some of the entries that would not qualify. Like this: "A University Like No Other". See what I'm looking for? No fun, no fabulous, no future focus.'

'I'd have thought its main deficiency was that it's open to more than one interpretation,' said Marilyn. 'Batman's main problem in attracting students and staff is just that. It's like no other.'

Jamie ignored her and continued.

'Another poor example is: "Start Here, Go Anywhere". See my point?'

'I think my point is still more relevant for that one, Jamie,' said Marilyn. 'It seems to suggest students might start at Batman but go elsewhere.'

'And what about "Victoria's No. 1 University Under 45 Years Old"? I think you'd all agree that's pretty weak in terms of Jamie's "3 Fs". Are you getting my drift?'

Arso and Marilyn remained silent.

'So, those were some of the dregs. Now, for my winning entry. It's fun. It's pithy, punchy, pregnant with meaning. And it meets Jamie's "3 Fs" criteria. Everyone ready?'

'More than ready,' muttered Arso.

Jamie moved to the whiteboard and wrote: 'BU@BU'.

'Drop the "at" symbol and it's "booboo",' said Arso, scoffing. 'That's *so* Batman.'

'Sorry, I don't get it,' said Marilyn.

'It's meant to be cryptic,' Jamie said, losing patience.

'Cryptic means mysterious or confusing,' Marilyn said.

'It's certainly not confusing,' Jamie replied defensively. 'It's cryptic for "Be You at Batman University". Yeah?'

'That the best you got?' inquired Arso.

'Hands down winner,' Jamie declared.

'I must go,' said Arso Kikavic, standing.

'Me too, Jamie,' said Marilyn, anxious not to be alone with Jamie and his 3 or 4 Fs.

'Hold on a minnie. Next, the winner for Business. Pity Kon Economopoulos isn't here. It's "Do Your Business at Batman University". Bit naughty but isn't that just so clever?'

Arso Kikavic made for the door.

'Hold on, Arso, here's the one I've chosen for Science: "Batman – We'll Blind You with Science".'

'We blind students with science?' Arso asked incredulously, heading for the door.

'With your heritage, perhaps you aren't familiar with the old metaphor "blind as a bat". Bat, Batman. Yeah?'

'Jamie, enough. You decide who wins. I go.'

'But we need a formal motion,' Jamie pleaded.

'Then,' said Arso, almost to the door, 'I move that ultimate decisions on straplines for Batman University be decided by Director of Media and Marketing.'

'Seconded,' said Marilyn as she followed Arso.

'No! Can't accept that,' Jamie called after them defiantly.

'Why not?' asked Marilyn wide-eyed.

'No quorum,' Jamie declared and folded his arms.

'Goodbye, Jamie.' Arso waved as he and Marilyn left the room.

Jamie leaned forward with an elbow on the table and clapped the back of his wrist to his forehead.

'Bitches! Sorry, Kellie, but they really don't respect me.'

oooOoo

Jamie gathered up his papers, instructed Kellie to remove 'Jamie's 3 Fs' from the whiteboard, and he returned to his office. He thought for a while as to what he should do given that he was getting no support from his committee. Open Day was racing towards him and he felt abandoned. He phoned the Vice President.

'Barry, it's Jamie here. I need to speak with you.'

'Yeah, go on.'

'I've had enough. I'm resigning as Convenor of the Open Day committee.'

'Geez, Jamie, slow down. That sounds like a bad idea,' said Motherwell. 'What's up?'

'The academics don't respect me. I've just chaired a meeting which some didn't attend, just didn't show up. Then, I had the Worthy-Kikavic alliance walk out early – in the very middle of the discussion about the entries for the strapline competition. I can't take it anymore.'

While Motherwell himself had no time for marketing, he knew any disruption to Open Day planning could be disastrous.

'I wouldn't worry about them, Jamie, but …'

'And there's all the problems with Clive Goodenough.'

'I thought he'd stopped attending.'

'He has. But I'm worried about the reputation of the Open Day committee. And the Open Day.'

'I'm sure you've got everything under control.'

'It's not me. It's Clive. I've been receiving reports from a number of high schools that he's failed to attend any of the events my office had arranged. I take it very personally, Barry.'

'Just not turning up, you say?' Motherwell was now getting more worried.

'And when I called him to ask, politely of course, what was going on, he was horrible to me. He became extremely aggressive and told me to butt out. He just said he'd "look after things".'

'Just keep an eye on him, Jamie, and keep me up to date with any developments.'

'But …'

'Frankly, we couldn't do Open Day if you pulled out now. You're the key to it all, Jamie. I'd be afraid we might have to cancel,' Motherwell lied.

'Really?' said Jamie, brightening.

'I'm serious. Batman really would be nowhere without your experience.'

'That's very kind, Barry. Thank you so much for listening to me. You've cheered me up no end.'

'That's the spirit.'

'Oh, did the President agree to give out the prizes for the straplines on Open Day?'

'Er, I've yet to have that discussion,' Motherwell stalled, having been loath to raise the topic with Razer.

'He's gonna be blown away.'

oooOooo

'Jenny, Barry here, I'd like a word with Nicholas, please.'

'I thought you were with him and the others. They went off to lunch at La Scala and I'm not expecting him back any time soon. You could try his mobile. They'd be in the car now.'

'Thanks.'

Motherwell was perplexed. He was accustomed to being in the President's lunch team at La Scala Italian restaurant in the Robert Gordon mall. He'd just glimpsed Brian Phipps at his desk eating sandwiches he'd brought from home. From this, Motherwell concluded that Roddy Rodman was driver for the day which, in turn, suggested that Razer was lunching with his inner circle. Why had he been excluded?

Motherwell called Razer's mobile number.

'Hallo, Bazza,' said Razer in jocular tone. 'We were just talking about you.' Motherwell was certain he could hear muffled laughter in the background.

'Nicholas, I thought you should know that Clive Goodenough seems to be acting up,' Motherwell said.

'How d'ya mean?'

'Apparently, he's not attending Open Day committee meetings. He's also not turning up to high school information sessions. I've heard from Lexi Dunne that he's more often absent from the office than not.'

'Yes, Lexi is always on the job, Barry.' More muffled laughter.

Motherwell tensed.

'Anyway,' Razer continued, 'I've been getting the same messages about your Professor Goodenough. Better keep an eye on him. He's been terrorising Sinn, and she's started saying she doesn't want to work in the cottage. I also asked Roddy to look into our friend and he confirms everything Jamie and Sinn say. Roddy thinks he's an eccentric, an oddball, and probably getting worse.'

'Maybe he has mental health issues,' suggested Motherwell.

'I think it's more than that.'

'Oh?'

'I had a call from Betty Allsop at Dame Pattie. Goodenough was the Batman representative at an information night at the College and he told the students and parents that Batman was undergoing some major changes which had disrupted university life and the teaching programs. He suggested some of the other universities were offering good academic programs which would be worth considering.'

'Christ. That's treachery.'

'Indeed it is. I think it's time you stepped in before he does any more damage to Batman. Anyway, we've arrived now so over to you, old chap.'

Chapter 17

Chairman Reg Gets Grumpy

It was a bright sunny morning as Brian Phipps drove into the President's driveway. His instructions for his daily pickup were to park and wait. The elaborate security system Razer had the university install when he took up residence allowed the Razers to view any arrivals or intrusions.

Brian waited, on edge, ready to leap out and open the car door for the President. It was never clear until Nicholas Razer pointed just which door was to be opened. On rare occasions, it would be the front passenger door, and Brian could expect a very jolly drive to campus where Nicholas would gossip and regale him with amusing anecdotes and discuss the staff he liked and those he didn't.

More commonly, Nicholas chose to occupy one of the rear seats. Should he choose to sit diagonally behind his driver, Brian could expect the President to ignore him, burying himself in the newspapers and making calls on his phone. Should Nicholas sit directly behind his driver, an uncomfortable silence lasted for the duration of the journey.

Brian Phipps watched as the front door of the White House, as Razer liked to call it, opened. Razer pecked Sinn perfunctorily on the cheek, stepped out and gestured to the front door. Phipps was relieved. Although he was no match for a conversationalist like Nicholas Razer, he understood his role for the next hour or so was to laugh at old jokes and tut-tut at the stories of workplace perfidy, stupidity and incompetence that his President had to endure. Brian Phipps understood that he himself was probably discussed in such terms with other audiences.

As they approached the O'Toole Building, Phipps pulled the car around the drive and raised a forefinger from the steering wheel to the Head of Campus Security who was waiting to open the car door. Kevin Burke's role was to ensure that Nicholas Razer's transit from the car into the foyer of the O'Toole Building passed without incident and without encountering bothersome staff or students.

Kevin saluted Nicholas as he alighted from the car and escorted him to the elevator, which Kevin had earlier locked into the Ground setting. The young women from Finance, clustered around the elevator with their takeaway coffees, stepped back as Kevin advanced ahead of the President. It would have been unclear to an observer whether the university President in the elegant suit or the muscular man in the campus security uniform was the more impressive.

Nicholas Razer exited on Level 12 and made his way to his office.

'Good morning, Professor Razer,' smiled Jenny Partridge.

'Morning, Jenny. Coffee and quickly, please,' Razer instructed as he passed his EA's desk.

'I've had a call from Mr O'Toole,' she called as he opened his office door. He stopped and half-turned, with pained expression, to face her. 'He'd like you to call him as soon as you arrive.'

'That's all?' he asked.

'He sounded a bit cranky,' she said, uncertain whether she should express such an opinion.

'Get him on the line then.' Razer sighed as he disappeared into his office. Cranky, eh? he thought. Perpetual state of mind, I'd say.

Jenny poured the strong brew of coffee into the President's mug and placed it on his desk before scurrying back to her own desk.

'Hello, Mr O'Toole. I'll pop you through to Professor Razer.'

Jenny strained to hear how her boss handled his vexed Chairman but Razer had closed his door.

'Morning, Reg,' Razer started off brightly.

'Nick, I'm not very happy,' began Reg O'Toole, forgoing any of the common niceties.

'What's on your mind, Reg?'

'What's on my mind is the fact that Batman seems to have dropped the ball on the O'Toole professor thing. The old man's approaching ninety and I want to have it all in place before he carks it.'

'Yes, of course, I completely understand. I'll get on to it right away. I'll come back to you later today.'

The Chairman grunted 'Right' and ended the call.

'Jenny!' shouted Razer through the closed door.

His EA sprang from her chair and opened the door to the President's office.

'What's the O'Toole professorship?'

'Sorry, Professor Razer, I don't know.'

'That's two of us,' snapped Razer.

'I think you'd best ask Roddy Rodman about that,' Jenny advised as she scurried back to her desk. 'I'll get him for you.'

Razer grunted and waited for the call.

'Good morning, President,' Roddy said warily.

'What the fuck is the O'Toole professorship?' Razer demanded.

'That's the one we haven't filled yet.'

'I just had an angry Chairman on the line. More information, please.'

'I'm sorry, President. I thought you would have been briefed on that,' said Roddy. He was aware that he bore no responsibility in the matter, but was anxious not to be collateral damage as Razer sought out a culprit. 'I think you'd best speak with Professor Sloane.

The O'Toole professorship was at Sandstone but now it's here.'

'What d'you mean, here? At Batman?'

'Yes but no-one's been appointed. Not yet, anyway. Or should I say, not again.'

'Not again?' snapped Razer, his patience running out.

'The incumbent resigned from Sandstone. Now the position is coming to Batman.'

Nicholas hung up and considered his next step.

'Jenny!' he barked again through the closed door. 'Try and set up a meeting with Professor Sloane and Kurt Kropp. As soon as both of them can be here. And have Roddy attend, too.'

'Yes, Professor Razer, right away.' Jenny opened the door and brought him a second cup of coffee.

'Professor Razer, would you like me to remind you which button on your handset you can use to call me?'

'No.'

Deflated, Jenny closed the door as she left Razer's office to find Brian Phipps hovering at her desk.

'I heard him shouting again, Jenny. Don't take it too hard.'

She beckoned him to the corridor.

'How do you cope with him so well? You seem to be so calm and cheerful all the time.'

'Easy. After many years driving for senior Army officers, I've developed my own method of dealing with the high and mighty ones.'

'And what's that?'

'I just imagine how they'd look in their underpants. Somehow that brings them down to my level. Like we're all humans underneath it all. They don't seem so different from anyone else then.'

'I've never thought of it like that before. Maybe I'll try that too. On second thought,' she started to giggle, 'I don't really want to imagine

Nicholas Razer in his undies, thank you very much! Got to get back and make some calls. Thanks Brian.'

oOoOoo

The meeting with Sally Sloane and Kurt Kropp was set for 3 pm that day in the President's office. They arrived early in the ante-room. Each admitted they had no idea why Razer had called them but Jenny had suggested the matter was urgent and confidential. They knew it must be both when Roddy Rodman joined them clutching a slim folder.

Roddy greeted them with a thin smile and approached Razer's office door. He knocked and, having heard a growled 'come in', beckoned the others to follow him. They found Razer at his desk looking decidedly liverish.

'Sally, Kurt, thanks to you both for coming at such short notice.' He gestured toward his meeting table where he joined them. 'There's a matter I'd like to discuss where there's some history I need. And some sensitivity, if the call from the Chairman this morning was any guide.'

'What's the itch in his undies this time?' inquired Sally.

'It's an unfilled professorial position about which apparently you and Roddy know.'

'That would be the O'Toole professorship,' volunteered, Sally now clear on why O'Toole and Razer were irritated in their own ways.

'He wants it filled, and quickly. That's why I've invited you, Kurt. Looks like there's a search coming for GoodKropp. I need a panel of names to shortlist. And soon.'

'Maybe I can give a little background,' suggested Sally.

'Go on,' Razer said coolly.

'Reg wanted some way to honour his Irish father, so after talking with some members at his club, he established a very large fund for a research centre and the O'Toole professorship in Celtic Studies.

He awarded the grant to Sandstone University. No doubt some old cronies persuaded him to give it to their alma mater.'

'The picture is becoming murkier rather than clearer,' Razer said.

'Actually, Nicholas,' offered Kropp, 'it's quite fortuitous that you've invited me along. Sandstone engaged GoodKropp to find the professor of Celtic Studies. We found a good candidate, but there were problems when he took up the post.'

'Celtic Studies? Rather specialised field,' observed Razer, himself a Celt. 'How many students in this city would be interested in Celtic Studies?'

You could count them on the fingers of an Irish butcher's hand, thought Roddy.

'The successful applicant was a fellow called O'Hare from Dublin,' Kropp reported. 'A specialist in Celtic history, well-published, good research grants, everything the university was looking for. We got the clear message from referees that Sandstone would be very fortunate to get him.'

'Unfortunately,' Sally took up the story, 'the idea was opposed by the History staff. There was already a small group of historians who believed they had things covered as far as Celtic history was concerned.'

'Surely they would welcome a colleague of presumably high standing?' inquired Nicholas.

'You might imagine so,' said Sally. 'But the professors saw a rival for scarce funding grants and they persuaded the junior ones that O'Hare would be a block to their promotion prospects. Mad, really.'

'We followed up O'Hare after a few months,' Kurt Kropp continued, 'and found that he was never accepted by his colleagues. He was increasingly ostracised and depressed. He was excluded from meetings, snubbed in the corridors and never invited to any social function with the other historians.'

'Within months,' said Sally, 'O'Hare was back in Ireland. Trinity College were glad to welcome him back.'

'So, the position was vacant again,' said Kurt. 'We knew we could go back to one or two of the unsuccessful candidates, but Reg O'Toole stepped in.'

'He was in a rage with Sandstone,' said Sally. 'He decided the grant would come in full to Batman. Sandstone agreed to refund the grant – and that would have hurt a lot – but they wanted some face-saving means of doing so.'

'So, we have the grant now?' inquired Nicholas.

'Not quite,' said Roddy. 'There are a few administrative matters to be sorted. But Reg has advanced enough funds to start the search process. For the professor.'

'Which hasn't yet started?' Razer asked with a note of sarcasm. Sally decided to admit some blame lay with her.

'That's correct,' she said. 'The compromise which Reg agreed with Sandstone was a change to the name of the O'Toole professorship. It's a pity, Nicholas, but there was some time lost in the inevitable settling on a suitable change of name. I think we're almost there with a name.'

'What is it?' demanded Razer.

'I'm working on an idea,' said Sally. 'I'm suggesting the O'Toole Professorship in Red Studies.'

Razer screwed up his face. 'And how was that particular name arrived at?' he asked.

'I read a book by a woman called Jacky Collis Harvey,' explained Sally. 'It's called "Red: A History of the Redhead". It's a serious piece of academic work on redheads.'

'I'm not getting the connection with Reg yet,' said Nicholas testily.

'That's a bit of a stretch but hear me out. Old man O'Toole was a stereotypical Irish redhead. Reg used to be, too. Harvey's concept of the red is one that includes Celts, like Reg. And a large number of other minorities, too. I've had a chat with Reg and I think he's come around to the name.'

'Red Studies? It's all about Rangas?' inquired Roddy incredulously.

'I think you're not getting it, Roddy,' said Sally reprovingly. 'We all need to be a little more cautious with our language. Everyone knows "Rangas" means "orangutan". It's OK to liken a person with red hair to an ape? I don't think so. Not in the third decade of the 21st century.'

Roddy shrugged, appearing to concede.

'I recall when I was visiting at the University of York,' said Razer, 'there was a bit of fuss about some kids at a local school who had a "kick a ginger day".'

'Harvey mentions it in her book,' said Sally. 'It was shocking.'

'Yes, shocking,' echoed Razer, nodding solemnly.

'Shocking,' repeated Kropp, becoming impatient at the descent into polemics. All this palaver about bloody redheads had only served to remind him of the song he and his friends loved to taunt Mickey Collins with in high school cadets. Parade drills each week were conducted to the marching song "Blaze Away" to which Kropp and his friends would lustily sing:

'Go home to your mother, you redheaded bugger, you don't belong to me.'

Fancy recalling that ditty after all these years, he thought.

Razer had more pressing issues to settle than the welfare of redheads. Reg was such an irascible character that unless there was some evidence of progress, and soon, he might well throw a paddy and withdraw his grant.

'What's the value of the grant?' inquired Razer.

'Five-and-a-half million,' said Roddy, poker-faced.

'What!' exclaimed Razer. 'Why wasn't I made aware of this?'

Sally Sloane knew that she should have briefed Razer but she was not going to admit any fault.

'I think part of the problem,' she said, 'is that the agreement with Sandstone is that there's to be no publicity. We felt that we shouldn't be seen to be crowing. I also felt that we shouldn't rush it. We should wait until we had a new President and …'

'You have a new President now,' Razer cut in, 'and I want action. Among the unsuccessful applicants for Sandstone,' Razer addressed Kropp. 'Were there any suitable for Batman?'

'There were two others interviewed. I'd have to go back and look at their CVs and our notes on them to be sure.'

'Please do that, and quickly,' Razer instructed.

Kropp nodded his agreement.

'Let's talk again at the end of the week and review where we stand with possible appointees. Since this appointment is to be made on the basis of a private grant from our own Chairman, I am prepared to make an appointment by Presidential diktat. If we can find a halfway decent candidate, of course. If we can't, we can probably kiss the grant goodbye.'

Kurt Kropp had his doubts about getting any suitable candidates. The field would be tiny, and Batman was an academic backwater.

'Let's get something underway immediately,' said Razer. 'We'll establish a Centre for Red Studies. At least I'll have something to tell Reg. Roddy, tell the Vice President to get a proposal together. Quickly.'

'I'd suggest proceeding with caution, Nicholas,' said Sally.

'Why?' inquired Razer.

'It's already been mooted. As acting President, I initiated confidential discussions with the Deans and a few others on how to implement the grant. The first difficulty was that the Centre would be established before the professor arrived. That seemed the wrong way to proceed.'

'I can see that,' said Razer, 'but I am thinking of a virtual centre. A shell, if you like, that'll have a name, a letterhead and so on. We can put it on the university website. I've got to be able to point to some developments to keep Reg happy.'

'All that's true,' said Sally, 'but how would it relate to the existing structures of the university?'

'It could be free-standing. It needn't relate to any of them.'

'Perhaps. But that will bring its own problems for the Centre. It'll be an orphan.'

'A redheaded stepchild, Sally?' asked Roddy mischievously.

'I get the feeling you might be catching on, Roddy. At least, I hope that was an informed attempt at humour,' said Sally.

'The second issue was academic avarice and territoriality,' she continued.

'I'm afraid I know where you're going with this,' said Razer.

'I found myself standing between four Deans and a wheelbarrow of dollars. The main shootout was between the Arts and Science Faculties. Both performed gold medal standard mental gymnastics in advancing their causes, too.'

Sally paused to recall the claims.

'O'Hare had been in History at Sandstone so Lexi Dunne assumed her faculty was a lay down misère. Her History staff had a reasonable claim but, after the Sandstone debacle, Reg had vetoed historians ever getting their hands on his money. Harvey's book dwelt on the depiction of redheads in European art, so the senior lecturer in Art History thought if there were to be a new Centre, it logically belonged with her discipline. The sociologists were confident that the concept of alterity assured them their place in the sun.'

'Alterity. That's new one on me,' said Razer.

'Otherness, Nicholas,' explained Sally. 'Alterity is the concept of otherness. Redheads are a minority so they are "the other". Minorities are often subject to prejudice and discrimination. Even superstition, such as the ancient notion that redheaded women on sailing ships would cause disasters at sea. This approach won the support of the Indigenous studies group who enlisted BUICK, the Indigenous students association. Media Studies proposed to investigate alterity as it occurs in the public media.'

'I'm getting the picture,' said Razer.

'But there's more. Health Studies is the home for Disability Studies. They proposed that redheadedness was a disability and the grant would be best located with them. The Science faculty were sure that Red Studies would sit best with them. Their main line of argument was via genetics.'

'Genetics?' inquired Razer.

'A British geneticist identified a gene for red hair. It's known as MC1R. It's a recessive gene that must be carried by both parents for a child to inherit red hair. The geneticists developed a proposal to conduct research into MC1R with a view to being able to switch it off. In other words, eliminate redheadedness for once and all.'

'I suppose it's within the realms of possibility,' mused Razer.

'It may well be but it was not without its critics. Our Ethics lecturer was enraged at this suggestion of interfering in the natural order. And the Social Work Department were up in arms, too. They rejected the notion that redheadedness was a disability that had to be corrected. Being a redhead was a legitimate self-concept which was important to retain. And unless the community of redheads embraced the suggestion, it would be a form of eugenics to proceed with it.

'The scientists also proposed the establishment of a dermatology research project. The argument went like this. Redheadedness is usually accompanied by fair skin and fair skin is prone to skin cancers, especially melanoma. The physicists proposed devising an app for mobile phones that would allow anyone to constantly monitor skin lesions on their bodies.

'There is no end to ingenuity flowing when millions of dollars are in the offing,' smiled Sally. 'Of course, when Morgan Freestone saw how divisive an issue it was, he actually proposed what he said was a sensible compromise. He said the best outcome would be to locate the Centre in the neutral territory of the Business Faculty.'

'Clive Goodenough countered by noting that the Engineering Faculty would have as much claim to neutrality as the Business Faculty.'

'I dare say, Sally,' remarked Roddy, 'Morgan then suggested that with their accounting and finance expertise, his faculty would be better stewards of the five-and-a-half million dollars.'

Razer returned the conversation to his main concern.

'I'm dubious about a Centre for Red Studies being a good idea,' Razer declared. 'I can tell Reg we're close to establishing it and issue a press release to that effect. Roddy, get Jamie working on that, will you? Let me see a draft asap.'

'I'll get on his back right way,' said Roddy, deadpan, but the mischievous comment wasn't missed by Sally, who frowned at him.

'We can say it's the prelude to the appointment of the O'Toole professor which is imminent,' said Razer. 'Which it probably isn't. Having a named Centre should also make the professorship more attractive to a potential appointee. All you have to do now, Kurt,' said Razer, 'is find us a Professor of Red Studies.'

ooOOoo

As Kurt Kropp drove back to his office, he ran through his mind the two unsuccessful candidates for the Sandstone position. He knew they'd be uninterested and unsuitable. Another thought was running through his mind. It was a long shot but it might just work. 'Siri, my office number.'

'Valerie. I'm on the way back to the office. Call that bookshop downstairs and see if they've got a book by someone called Harvey.

It's about redheads. If they've got it, take the corporate card and buy a copy. Right away.'

'Yes, Kurt, right away.'

As Kropp entered his office, his EA held up a copy of the book triumphantly.

'This was the last copy, Kurt,' she smiled, pleased with herself.

Kropp took the book without comment and turned to the dust jacket.

'Is that all, Kurt?'

'Wait. Yes, that's the name. Jacky Collis Harvey. Nothing here about how to contact her,' he muttered, leafing through the title pages and checking the dust jacket. 'Tell Megan to get me her contact details, and right away,' instructed Kropp, handing the book back to Valerie.

'Right away, Kurt. I was browsing through the book in the lift. I've got a redheaded brother. I'm sure he'd like to read it and so would I.'

'It's yours.'

'I'm happy to wait till you've finished it.'

'I've no intention of reading it. Chop, chop. Get Megan on the job.'

ooOOoo

Next morning, Kurt Kropp was in self-congratulatory mode. He'd been up late and, with all the luck that sometimes falls into the hands of the veteran headhunter, he'd managed to contact Harvey, and was feeling upbeat. As he drove to his office, he called Nicholas Razer who was being driven to the Batman campus.

'Take that call, would you?' Razer instructed Brian Phipps, not recognising the number on the screen. 'Don't say who you are and leave the loudspeaker on.'

'Hello,' answered Phipps.

'Brian?' It was 9.15 am and Kropp immediately assumed the scene. 'It's Kurt Kropp here. I take it the President is with you?'

Razer pressed the speak button.

'Morning, Kurt. What news?'

'Morning, Nicholas. I've looked at every application received for the Sandstone job. Nothing doing at all, I'm afraid.'

'So, how are you going to solve our problem?'

'I think I may have a solution for you. Even if short-term.'

'Go on.'

'You recall Sally Sloane spoke about the woman who'd written a book on redheads. That woman is Jacky Collis Harvey. I've had a look at the book and I think she'd be an ideal professor of Red Studies at Batman.'

'Go on.'

'I tracked her down in London where she lives some part of each year. The rest of the time she's in New York. We had a very interesting chat.'

'Yes?'

'I asked if she'd be interested in working in Australia. I told her about the proposed O'Toole professorship in Red Studies and that its name owed a great deal to her book. Of course, I played up Reg's generous grant. She became increasingly interested in the possibilities for research on Antipodean bloodnuts. She said she was aware of the high proportion of redheads in Australia.'

'Sounds interesting.'

'I liked her style, too.'

'How d'you mean?'

'She raised the possibility of a major research project which she suggested could be called "Redheads Down Under".'

'D'you think it's possible? Getting her?'

Kropp knew he had to remain positive.

'She would cost you a lot but you're going to get a lot. I may be wrong but, judging by my conversation with her and the photo of her on the dust jacket, I think she would charm the pants off Reg.'

'Are you sure you've explained Batman fully to her?'

'I did and she was quite positive. I think the idea of a spell in an out-of-the-way university with a big budget for her to play with would be quite attractive.'

This was a point of view that Razer himself understood well.

'There'd be two matters for you to consider,' Kropp continued.

'Go on.'

'She'd want a generous travel budget. Harvey has an international reputation and she's in great demand internationally as a speaker.'

'Can't see a problem there. And the other matter?' inquired Razer.

'She'd only commit to a year. At least, in the first instance. Who knows what will happen after that if she happens to like Batman and living here. But I thought it would be a prestigious appointment for Batman and would placate Reg for a time. And it would give you some breathing space. A little time for us to help find you a long-term incumbent.'

Razer ignored Kropp's hint at another search assignment for GoodKropp.

'When could I run my eye over her?'

'Her major commitment in the US winds up at the end of their academic year. She could be here in the second half of July.'

'Well done, Kurt. Just in time for Open Day.'

Chapter 18

The University Board Meets

When he came to Razer's office prior to his first Board meeting, Reg O'Toole seemed to Razer to be on edge. Razer assumed he was still annoyed about lack of progress on Red Studies, but he made no mention of it. Nor did Razer, who assumed the suburban businessman was anxious about chairing his first university board meeting. Razer's executive team was waiting in his ante-chamber and rose in respectful silence as the Chairman and President emerged from Razer's office.

The community members had taken their seats and were awaiting, with no little sense of excitement, the arrival of their new Chairman. They fell silent as the diminutive Reg entered the Boardroom alongside the towering Nicholas Razer, followed by Razer's executive team who peeled off silently to the observers' seats. As Razer showed Reg to his place, the members broke into applause when their local hero took his place at their head.

'Steady on you lot,' joked Reg with mock embarrassment, 'I'm new to this caper. Mightn't be much chop at it.'

The members all joined in the joke, offering various encouragements. Reg opened his Board papers and called the meeting to order.

'Roddy, hot to trot?' he asked Roddy, the secretary to the Board. 'Pen at the ready?'

'Yes, Chair, metaphorically speaking, anyway,' Roddy replied. 'I actually use my device.'

Reg expressed mock shock. 'I'll let that one go through to the keeper,' he laughed. 'First item. Any apologies?'

'No, Chair.'

'Thank you. Welcome everyone to your second meeting of the Board for 2022. My first, but your second. You've all met Nick and his team last time. Not forgetting the men in black in the observer seats.'

Razer's team acknowledged the members.

'Let's kick off with a get-to-know-you, eh? I'll start. I'm Reg O'Toole ...'

'Really, Chair,' interrupted Betty Allsop, with a cloying smile, 'I think we all know who you are. And everything you've done for our community.'

'As owner of the Robert Gordon Bugle, Bets, surely I can blow my own trumpet?' Reg laughed.

You certainly do, thought Razer.

'You're too modest,' Betty Allsop gently chided Reg.

Reg help up his hand in protest.

'As my old dad says, let your modesty become you. Whatever that means! So, on with the show,' Reg declared.

'No need for introduction for our President. Take a bow, Nick.'

Razer remained seated, bowing his head.

'Barry Motherwell,' Reg announced looking at the Vice President. 'Nick's new right-hand fella.'

Motherwell hated being the object of attention but forced a brief embarrassed smile.

'Professor Sally Sloane, the Deputy Chairman. Doesn't look much like a man, as you can all see. On my left. Where she belongs! She reckons everybody's to my left! Eh, Sal?'

'As you might say yourself, Chair, I'll let that one go through to the keeper,' Sally smiled indulgently. Reg lives in a world of clichés, she thought.

'Got me there, Sal. Now, a lady we all know, Mrs Betty Allsop. Making ladies out of girls at Dame Pattie College. Bets, good to have you here.'

'Thank you, Chair,' Betty Allsop blushed and smiled obsequiously.

'I'm just consulting some notes I had Jamie Jamieson put together for me. Where are they? He's our protocol man at Batman. Here we go.'

Reg looked up to find his man.

'Welcome to Dr Pieter Scheisser from the Outer Eastern Development Authority. Did I get that right, Pete?'

'Not quite, Chair. My surname rhymes with "leaser", not "licer".'

'I'll take that on board, Pete.'

'One more thing, Chair. To be perfectly precise, I may be addressed as Dr Dr Schiesser.'

'You're a double doctor?' Reg asked perplexed.

'Ja, but for here, single doctor vill be satisfactory. In ze minutes, of course, it should be Dr Dr. But for an introduction, one Dr is acceptable.'

Reg motioned for Roddy to ensure the minutes properly recorded the titles.

'Good on yer, Pete,' enthused O'Toole. 'That's the Aussie way. But it says here you're sometimes addressed as, hold on, it's spelt H-e-r-r.' Reg looked at Schiesser, puzzled.

'Chair, if I may, it's pronounced as is hair,' patting his bald pate, 'not her, as in her,' pointing at Betty Allsop.

'Think I'll stick to Dr,' joked Reg. 'Moving on, our next welcome is to my old mate, Sig … Signor Mario Tempeste. Jamie says here …'

'Hold on, Reg,' interjected Tempeste. 'It's not Sig. More Sin.'

'Didn't I get the pronunciation right?' Reg inquired.

'No, it should be in the Italian way: Signor. But, it's not the pronunciation. You can forget all that ethnic stuff. I'm Aussie through and through. "Mr" will be fine or just simple Mario.'

Simple Mario sounds right, thought Razer.

'Thanks Mars. I was just trying to be respectful of your race.'

The Chairman consulted his notes.

'Jamie also says here,' Reg looked up smiling, 'that Tempeste is a French baby girl's name. I never knew that. Did you? Baby girl. And French.'

'French? No way. I take offence to that. It's a traditional Italian name. And I'm proud of my Italian heritage. Proud to be called Tempeste.'

'Jamie says here it means stormy.'

'Sometimes it does.'

'And, last, but certainly not least, our very own solicitor-general, Prudence Wills. Welcome, Prudes.'

'Cheers, Chair, it's, like, an honour to be here,' Prudence responded demurely, swivelling from side to side in her chair.

'Welcome to you all. Let's get underway. I'll ask the President to present his report, first up.'

To the amusement of members, Nicholas Razer introduced his report with several Yogi Berra observations before turning to the serious issues facing the university. The financial position of Batman would improve thanks to his restructure and the salary savings resulting from abolition of administrative positions in the Deans' offices. The new college structure had been introduced and, Razer assured the Board without any evidence, was being enthusiastically embraced by staff.

A steady increase in international student enrolments was expected with the appointment of a Dean for International. The university's impact on the region would grow with the appointment of a Dean for Outreach and Engagement. Rival universities continued to prey upon prospective Batman students, and government cuts continued to threaten the university's viability.

'Of course, the most important event on the near horizon is next month's Open Day.' Razer wound up his presentation. 'As Open Day is rushing toward us, I asked the head of media and marketing to prepare some notes.' Razer slipped a sheet of paper in front of Motherwell. 'I'll pass over to the Vice President to update the Board.'

Motherwell attempted to conceal his shock at this unanticipated turn of events, and poured himself a glass of water while trying to assemble his thoughts. He cleared his throat and wiped his brow with a forefinger.

'Thank you, President, for the, ah, opportunity to advise the Board about the upcoming, um, Open Day. We are certainly hoping that this year's event will be the best ever.'

Motherwell kept his head down, desperately scanning the notes.

'The Village Place will be, as Jamie says here, chock-a-block with marquees, food and drink outlets and all the fun of the fair.'

'Fun? Vy fun, may I ask? Srough you, Chair. Batman's a university, not a kindergarten. Vich, by da vay, is a Cherman word.'

'Jamie feels, Dr Schiesser,' explained Motherwell, 'that fun will add to the overall experience. Make us different.'

'Ve not different enough already? Apology, srough you, Chair.'

Motherwell returned his attention to the notes.

'There'll also be a number of innovations in addition to the normal, ah, Open Day activities. In particular, Open Day this year will provide not only information for prospective students but, ah, also fun. Sorry, think I'm repeating myself.'

Motherwell looked up briefly at his audience and felt the weight of expectations with all eyes trained on him. He took another sip of water.

'We, ah, feel that a, ah, positive experience of the Batman campus for the whole family could only be of benefit to the, ah, university. BUSS will have an important role …'

'Vy a bus? Through you, Chair. We have plan for long vehicle parking?

'No, Dr Schiesser,' Motherwell explained, 'Jamie's referring to the Batman University Student Society, BUSS. They've agreed to take charge of the entertainment and fun aspects of Open Day and we've given them a generous grant to that, to that, ah, to that end.'

'Barry,' Reg O'Toole growled as Motherwell stiffened. 'Speak up, will you? I'm having trouble hearing what you're saying.'

'Sorry, Chair. I was speaking about buses. There will be, ah, regular buses from this campus to our satellite campus where Equine Studies are located.'

'Now you're shouting as though we're outside,' Reg protested.

'Sorry again, Chair.' Motherwell coughed. 'Equine Studies is always a popular destination for families and Dr Callahan and her staff will have all the horses and facilities on display.'

'That's wonderful news, Professor Motherwell,' enthused Betty Allsop. 'The Dame Pattie girls just love visiting Equine Studies. We always have a big contingent and we get them there on our college bus. The Pattie Wagon, the girls call it. Aren't they naughty?'

'As a part-time farmer myself,' Motherwell went on, 'I must say Equine Studies is a favourite of mine, too. If the students are coming on your own college bus, we can arrange bus parking on this campus, too.'

'Oh, that won't be necessary. It's Equine Studies the girls want to visit. It's a bit of an outing for the boarders.'

'The one, ah, topic I feel the Board would be very interested in, Chair, is the parade by our newly formed Batman University Regiment. One of my, ah, roles at Batman is officer in charge of the new regiment. The Board will know our Head of Campus Security, Kevin Burke. He is my assistant, being an ex-Army man himself. I'm a, ah, colonel in the Army Reserve and I am, ah, as I was saying, ah, commanding officer of the regiment.'

'You're getting hard to hear, again,' said Reg, who was beginning to tire of this formal meeting with its complex agenda. He glanced up at the wall clock and was annoyed with himself. He'd allowed the meeting to run over by four minutes.

'We have one minute left, Barry,' he warned Motherwell.

'I'll be quick then, Chair. I can inform the Board that the regiment will have a parade on the new parade ground on Open Day. And I'm pleased to advise the Board that the parade will be inspected by the Minister for Homeland Defence himself.'

'The Minister, you say? Coming on campus?' Reg asked.

'That's right, Chair. It's been confirmed. And we hope you will be able to officially welcome him.'

'That goes without saying, Barry! I'd say this is the highlight of the meeting.'

'He's very pleased with Batman and our adoption of his program of university regiments.'

'He's a man I know and respect. Well done, Barry, well done. His presence alone will ensure a memorable Open Day.'

Chapter 19

Taking Care of Business

Barry Motherwell arrived at the President's office for their Monday morning meeting. As the second most senior person at Batman, Motherwell was glad of these one-on-one meetings. In recent months, however, Razer had been cancelling some of them on the grounds that 'there's not much to report, is there?' Motherwell suspected Roddy Rodman, and perhaps some of members of Razer's team, had usurped his position as Razer's chief adviser. But why? he wondered.

Jenny told him to go in and he knocked and entered.

'Hallo,' sighed Razer, without looking up. 'Take a seat, old chap.'

'Morning, Nicholas,' responded Motherwell cautiously. He still wasn't completely comfortable in the presence of the President. Razer continued writing while Motherwell sat uneasily. Eventually, Razer spoke perfunctorily while continuing to write.

'Had a good weekend?' Razer smiled.

'Yes, thanks.'

Razer finally looked up.

'And what naughtiness did you get up to out there on the farm?' he inquired playfully.

'As you know Nicholas, I lead a quiet life.'

'So you say, Barry, so you say. Anyway, what have we to talk about?'

'A few things to catch up on,' Motherwell said, referring to his clipboard. 'Some since last week.'

'Yes?' Razer said, uninterestedly, returning his concentration to the documents on his desk.

'First, the university regiment. That seems to be going well but the timetable for recruitment and training is tight. Student Admin have sent out the invitation to all students by batmail.'

'How many warriors do you need?'

'Ideally, we'll have at least a hundred and more than two hundred have registered interest. Applications have gone direct to Sandstone University Regiment who'll assess them for us. I hear a few have had school cadet experience. There's also a handful of veterans, mature age students. They'll be helpful to Kevin and me in training and organising the whole show.'

'Splendid,' said Razer, checking his watch.

'We'd like to be ready for a parade on Anzac Day.' Motherwell gestured with open hands, 'But that might be too much of a stretch.'

'Pity. I imagine you were looking forward to a dawn service. You'd like a dawn service, eh?' said Razer, lasciviously raising his eyebrows.

'Yes, that would have been my ... oh, I get it,' Motherwell said, flustered.

'No need to wait for Anzac Day for that, eh, Barry?'

'As I said, I lead a quiet life, Nicholas.' Unsettled, Motherwell wondered yet again if Razer had discerned his growing affection for Lexi Dunne.

'And Roger Priestly is across all the campus planning issues the regiment will generate?'

'Yes, Campus Management's on board. Roger's got a firm of architects and landscape architects working on the depot buildings, the parade ground and other facilities that we have to construct.'

'We can't afford any mishaps with any Minister coming on campus. Least of all, that particular gentleman from what I've heard of him.'

'I think everything's under control.'

'Nothing else?' inquired Razer, clearly tiring of the meeting.

'Ah, Kurt Kropp has confirmed the dates for the visit by Ms Harvey for the O'Toole professorship process.'

'Yes, Jacky Collis Harvey,' Razer dragged out each name. 'Our potential head red. I'll call Reg when we've finished and let him know. Make sure there's an event where he can spend time with her. Amazingly, our pathetic little excuse for a university library happens to have a copy. I had a quick look. Load of old rubbish, of course.'

With that, Razer reached for the book on his desk.

'Take a look at her photo on the dust jacket. Good looker, eh? The blurb says she's been a life model.'

Motherwell looked blank.

'Life model, Barry. It means they take their clothes off. To be painted. By dirty old men posing as artists. What a caper!'

'Oh, I didn't know that …'

'But wait, there's more. It says here,' Razer flicked to the index, 'yes, page eleven. She herself writes "there's a century-long linkage" – listen to this, Bazza – "between red-haired women and sexual desirability".'

'Speaking as a geneticist …'

'Tell Jenny to organise for me to take her to dinner, would you, old chap?'

'I will.'

'That all?' inquired Razer.

'I've informed the former Deans of their new roles.'

'Any push back?'

'Only Clive Goodenough, of course.'

'Sally's warned me about him, Barry. Nutter. Keep a close eye on him.'

'And you'll have seen the all-staff batmail outlining the new academic structure. There's quite a bit of staff disquiet but no sign of any real opposition. I think the new powers given to Presidents are widely understood. Henry Zimmer is trying to whip up some opposition but only a dozen or so academics turned up to a meeting he called. I think it'll all happen without much fuss.'

'And the KPIs?'

'I've finished drafts for you to sign off on,' said Motherwell, offering a folder to Razer.

'You sign off. I don't need to see them. It's going to be very interesting to see who falls at the hurdle. Anything else?' inquired Razer.

Motherwell hesitated. He feared what Razer's reaction would be but Jamie Jamieson had pleaded with him to raise it.

'Just a minor matter. As part of our branding, Jamie Jamieson got his office staff to come up with a set of university straplines – things to put on our advertising for the new academic year.'

'Straplines?' said Razer quizzically.

'You know, the words that go with an organisation's logo.'

'I've no idea what you mean,' said Razer, checking his watch again.

'The one we have been using is: "Batman – Your Future Awaits".'

'Your future awaits? It hasn't left without you?' Razer scoffed.

'The marketers like them,' Motherwell said lamely.

'Fatuous nonsense if you ask me,' declared Razer.

'I'm afraid it's become common in Australian universities in recent years.'

'The triumph of the marketers, eh?' Razer shook his head. 'Any problems with having a competition?'

'Not really. Jamie proposes that the Open Day committee should collate the submissions, identify the better ones and that some prizes should be given for the best entries at the drinks session at the end of Open Day. Doesn't commit us to any particular one, of course.'

'Seems harmless enough. Why do I need to know?'

'He'd like you to present the strapline awards. At the drinks session after Open Day.'

'Straps? Sounds more like your kind of thing, Barry,' said Razer, returning to the papers on his desk.

Chapter 20

The Disgruntled Dean

Clive Goodenough was still smarting at the prospect of being demoted from Dean of Engineering to the marginalised role of Dean for Outreach and Engagement. It was a nothing role, and his demotion hurt him deeply. His options, however, were limited. There was no provision for appeal to the Board and even if there were, as Lexi Dunne had gently reminded him, the Board would be unlikely to overrule the President on a staffing matter.

While he'd been a Dean, he'd neglected his research. Indeed, he found being Dean a more satisfying role than that of teacher or researcher. As a consequence, his plan to see out his career as a Dean at Batman had rendered him unlikely to be able to find employment in another university.

If his own reaction to his loss of status had been extreme bitterness, his wife's was even more severe. She had berated him for allowing this situation to develop and even accused him of being spineless in not confronting Razer, dissenting from his decision and mobilising support. His attempts to explain the realities of modern day higher education management were fiercely dismissed. In one fiery attack, she went so far as to tell him he was 'as weak as piss.' Deirdre Goodenough had been humiliated by her husband's demotion – and it could be understood as nothing less – and she was unable to disguise her devastation among her women friends.

THE DISGRUNTLED DEAN

The new Dean for Outreach and Engagement had received an email from his Vice President, Barry Motherwell, setting out his new areas of responsibility. These included schools liaison, community engagement and planning for Open Day. The targets set in his KPIs were simply ridiculous, in his view. How could he visit every high school in the region and in the whole geographic sector from Robert Gordon to the inner suburbs? How was he to set up and attend a Batman University office in the mall at Robert Gordon? And given his antipathy to Open Days in general, why should he bother himself with the Open Day committee?

He concluded Razer and Motherwell had set him up to fail. Perhaps failure and a payout would not be such a bad outcome. Though how Deirdre might react to him being prematurely retired he dared not contemplate. His emotions were a roiling mix of negatives. He felt hurt, denigrated, embarrassed, regretful and angry. He was to spend the last few days as Dean with his actions subject to this tangle of emotions. It was a time when his emotional state might get the better of him and might cloud his judgement. It was a time fraught with danger. The expressions of commiseration and support he'd expected from his faculty staff never materialised. Colleagues had passed him in the car park or the corridors with a smile or an embarrassed nod, but none really offered words of comfort.

The exceptions were Henry Zimmer and the hotheads in BUSA, who urged him to take a stand against Razer and Motherwell. They promised their support but Goodenough, never a member of the staff association, rebuffed those with whom he never had much truck. He felt quite alone. Among the soon-to-be former Deans, only Lexi Dunne had offered any solace and for that he was grateful. Lexi was a woman he'd always secretly admired, even fancied. A woman so unlike Deirdre.

Perhaps it was his anger that led Clive Goodenough to conclude that he should attempt to sort out a few of his faculty's more egregious personnel problems, the ones to which hitherto he had found it easier to turn a blind eye.

On his watch, some Engineering staff had allowed their energies to be directed to lucrative extracurricular activities such as engineering consultancies. Their attentions had gradually turned from students and research to supplementing their university salaries with external earnings.

It was commonly believed around the faculty that these staff could double or treble their university salaries. A number of the better performing senior students had been drawn into these consultancies and, in more than one case, graduate theses had been abandoned to pursue the rich pickings of the consultancy world. The chief offender was Ian Potter in Civil Engineering. Dealing firmly with Potter might frighten the others away from their extracurricular pursuits.

Then there were those staff who rarely appeared on campus. Some were engaged in research projects off-campus, some preferred to work from home, but the majority found the campus lacked stimulation. And the drive to get there was long and through heavy traffic. In Goodenough's view, the most egregious offender was Dr Greg Milligan who was responsible for Advanced Studies in Electronics. These were notoriously difficult subjects which only the brightest students passed. Milligan was a hard taskmaster, too.

As a consequence, many years earlier, when Milligan had advised the faculty timetabler that the only time that suited him to offer the third year elective Advanced Electronics was at 8 am Mondays, it was no surprise that the subject was cancelled due to insufficient enrolments.

Clive Goodenough was angry enough about his impending demotion to decide that he would sort out these problems before he was forced to relinquish his role as Dean. He could have left the problems to Mervyn Pilgrim, but that might end up being embarrassing for him. Pilgrim would no doubt make a meal of them to Goodenough's embarrassment. No, he concluded that the better course would be to demonstrate that he was capable of a muscular approach to staff management.

Ian Potter was an associate professor whose practice it was to inveigle two or three more junior colleagues and several masters and honours students to join him in his private consulting business, Potter Engineering Partners. Potter had been a principal lecturer at Robert Gordon College when Batman took over that local technical institute. To the chagrin of his new colleagues in Engineering, he'd been made associate professor at Batman as part of the agreement for the College to join Batman.

It had always rankled with Goodenough that he had an associate professor on his staff who lacked a PhD and whose only written output were low-level consultants' reports. Goodenough dared to hope that his clipping of Potter's wings might even encourage him to resign from the university and pursue the life of a consultant, a life which Goodenough held in contempt.

Goodenough sat himself at his desk, took a deep breath and considered his tactics. He would take a forceful approach, demanding to see Potter in his office next morning. He would convey his authority in the matter by choosing the time for the meeting and allowing no other. With one final deep inhalation, his hand reached for the phone to call Ian Potter's university office extension.

'Good morning, Potter Engineering Partners. Our office is temporarily unattended. Please leave a message for Mr Potter or his EA. Your call is important to us and we will get back to you shortly.'

Clive Goodenough stood up enraged and slammed the phone down. He strode to his office door intent on marching to Potter's office to satisfy himself that it was unattended.

He paused. No, I'll leave a voice message and follow up with an email instructing Potter to report to his office.

His voicemail message left with Potter's EA was curt.

'It's the Dean. Advise Mr Potter he should be in my office at 9 am tomorrow.'

A follow-up email to Potter was equally brief and blunt.

The email reply from Potter's EA explained that Potter was out on site and that she had been absent from her desk on an errand for him. She apologised for missing the Dean's call. She'd conveyed Goodenough's message to Potter who was off campus. Although he was due at a site meeting next morning, he would rearrange this commitment to meet with the Dean as requested.

Now fired with a new-found reformist, if belated, staff management zeal, Goodenough decided to deal with the other malfeasant on his staff, Dr Greg Milligan, who was another 'lump under the rug'.

For as long as he could recall, Milligan, Senior Lecturer in Electronic Engineering and Mathematics, had been a parasite on his colleagues. One of the earliest appointments to Batman's Engineering faculty, he had long fashioned his professional persona as master of highly esoteric subject matter and an exacting assessor. He rarely bid for or won research grants and his record of publications was meagre. The few graduate students he was prepared to supervise were obliged to meet him at his home. He presented himself as a serious scholar whose mission was to read widely and make himself available to senior students on a strictly limited basis for advice on his obscure areas of expertise.

Most of his colleagues thought him 'work shy'. To a few, however, this seemed churlish because he was a charming and amusing, if only occasional, visitor to the staff room. He enjoyed a wide reputation as a bon vivant and his dinner parties, where he hosted senior colleagues from across the university, were lavish affairs.

In recognition of Milligan's somewhat protected status in the faculty, Goodenough chose to send a polite email inviting him to his office the next day for a chat. Within minutes, Milligan had returned an equally polite reply to the effect that, if it suited his Dean, he would pop in to the office at noon tomorrow. He was looking forward to their meeting and wondered if they might 'repair to Boy Wonder's for a chat over lunch'.

This suggestion reminded Goodenough of why he needed to confront Milligan. He responded that a meeting in his office at 10 am would be preferable. Milligan replied that he thought this a very good idea.

Goodenough thought for a while about these meetings and made some handwritten notes, setting out his requirements of each malfeasant. He would be calm but forceful.

Looking every bit the consultant engineer in a three-piece suit, a shirt and tie, Ian Potter arrived punctually at 9 am next day in the Dean's outer office. Goodenough heard him greet his PA Felicity in his usual garrulous, even flirtatious, fashion. Everything about Potter annoyed Goodenough: his sharp suits and ties, his ever-ready, toothy smile, his lame jokes, his top-of-the-range car, and his whole consultant demeanour.

Goodenough watched his digital clock click over to 9.04 am. Best not to let him stew for a few minutes, he reassured himself. With a final fidget of his tie, he moved to open his office door.

'Ian. Come in.'

Potter, who'd not been stewing but had been standing admiring Felicity Bell's ample breasts, turned to extend his right hand to Goodenough and flashed his hail-fellow-well-met consultant's smile.

'Clive, good to see you.'

Potter followed Goodenough into his office, observing 'I believe congratulations are in order.'

'Have a seat,' Goodenough said, ignoring Potter's fawning.

Goodenough retreated behind his desk, sat and shrugged, intending not to be congratulated for anything. But Potter was not to be derailed.

'A little bird tells me,' he said with a wink, 'that you've had a promotion. I've heard you're moving more into my area.'

'Your area? How d'you mean?' Goodenough said tersely.

'The big wide, exciting world of outreach and engagement,' declared Potter, extending both arms as if to encircle the globe.

'I can honestly say my O and E work is the most satisfying I've ever had. Working in the community on behalf of Batman. Providing expert advice on community projects and helping solve community problems. Winning respect for the university out there, beyond the walls of acadamia.'

Acadamia, thought Goodenough, rhymes with macadamia. Doesn't he even know the language of higher education?

'You're going to enjoy yourself, Clive,' Potter went on. 'And me and my team are looking forward to working with you.'

Ignoring these attempts at ingratiation, Goodenough leaned forward on his elbows, clasped his hands and looked directly at Potter.

'As it happens, I want to discuss the future of university outreach and engagement, too.'

'All ears, Clive,' he said, with a jaunty swivel of his shoulders.

'It's your consulting. I'm going to curtail it. This is a university and our core mission is teaching and research. In my opinion, you're not doing enough of either.'

Potter gasped. 'I have to say I'm kinda shocked, Clive, that you could say that. I'm out there in the real world. For Batman. I take grad students on site and teach them how to survive and prosper in a dynamic, entrepreneurial world. I write technical reports. I ...'

'Yes, I know all that. But my concern is that the students are acquiring only low-level skills and that they are nothing more than cheap labour for you.'

'Cheap labour? Low-level skills? I can't believe you're saying this.'

'Your technical reports are in no sense academic. They'd never be published in any reputable journal and have no impact or relevance beyond the setting in which you're working.'

Potter shook his head in disbelief.

'Worst of all,' Goodenough went on, 'you're earning multiples of your university salary through your consultancies. That's all going to come under control. From now on, consultancies will be limited to no more than a day a week, university resources will not be used on consultancies without reimbursement, my Office of Outreach and Engagement will take twenty per cent of all income, and I must approve all consultancies. Batman is a university, Ian, and not a platform for lucrative comsultancies.'

Goodenough folded his arms and sat back in his chair with an expression which said 'I have spoken'. Potter would now have to comply or leave.

'Clive, I must say I am surprised at your views which seem to be at odds with the Vice President's.'

'The Vice President's. What do you mean?'

'When I got your invitation to a meeting this morning, I was pretty excited. I thought you were going to offer me more support for my O and E work. That seems to be the thinking behind the Vice President's recent batmail to business units.'

'Batmail? What batmail?' demanded Goodenough.

'You know, the one headed "Rules of Engagement". I've got a hard copy with me. It's a ripper. It recognises the new directions for universities and basically opens the way for universities to engage even more with communities, government, the private sector, everybody, really. Look,' said Potter reaching into his satchel, 'here it is. You haven't seen it? I thought you were going to be in charge of O and E.'

Potter leaned forward and slid the document across Goodenough's desk.

'If you haven't seen it, keep that one, Clive. I just had it here to discuss with you. You'll see I've scrawled a few comments here and there. You'll see some rough financial estimates. That will give you some idea of what I was hoping to negotiate with you this morning. I thought we might be able to tweak it a bit to give a higher proportion of the earnings to Potter Engineering Partners. But, y'know, maybe that's something we could discuss some other time.'

Goodenough had scanned enough of the 'Rules of Engagement' to know that he'd been left out of an information loop in which he should have been included. Thoughts tumbled through his head and, confused, he stood and walked to his office window.

He looked out onto the grassy lawns that made up the Village Place but saw nothing. How could Motherwell have issued this document to, well, to whom? Was he the only person who hadn't received it? Was his omission from the distribution list simply an innocent oversight? He felt angry, gutted, humiliated.

'Clive?' ventured Potter, addressing Goodenough's back. 'Clive?'

Goodenough made no response.

Potter stood and, with a slight wave, said less effusively than was his custom 'Thank you, Clive,' and left closing the Dean's door gently behind him. He passed Felicity Bell, gave her a shrug and a baffled expression and headed back to the offices of Potter Engineering Partners.

Still standing at the window, Clive Goodenough flinched involuntarily, uncertain as to how to interpret the changes swirling around him. He punched his open hand. He was shaken and now felt he had to sit down, and did so resting his head on folded arms on his desk. How should he react?

He thought of calling Barry Motherwell for an explanation. But he had little confidence in the Vice President, the author of the policy. He picked up his desk phone.

'Hello, Clive,' said Razer's EA. 'How can I help you?'

Goodenough cleared his dry throat and spoke with measured delivery. 'I want to speak with Nicholas,' he said, pausing deliberately after each word.

'Can I tell him what it's about?' Jenny asked, sensing Goodenough was just managing to control his temper.

'It's about the "Rules of Engagement" document,' he said, again stressing each word.

'Shouldn't you speak with Professor Motherwell?' Jenny suggested, aware that Razer had told her that was the proper line of authority.

'I want to speak with the baker, not the dough.'

'Just a moment, please,' she said, sensing that Goodenough was highly agitated.

Goodenough paced around his desk while waiting for Nicholas Razer to take his call.

'Clive, how can I help, old chap?' said Razer cheerily.

'Nicholas, I was dismayed, quite frankly, distressed,' he blurted out, 'to be shown a document about so-called rules of engagement. Apparently it went out recently but I hadn't seen it. As Dean of Engineering and as Dean Designate for Outreach and Engagement, I thought this strange. In fact, I was insulted.'

'I don't think I can help you there. That's Barry Motherwell's bailiwick. Give him a call. I imagine there's some simple explanation.'

'But it's directly relevant to the new role you want me to take. I would have thought ...'

'I'm sure it's a simple oversight in Barry's office, old chap,' Razer cut him off. 'Thanks for the call.'

Goodenough fell into shock and despair again. He thought in

vain about whom he could consult about this slight, this insult, this undermining. There was no-one. His fellow Deans, with the possible exception of Lexi Dunne, would be useless. He was determined never to fall into the clutches of the staff association. No sympathy would be found in confiding in Deirdre. He was still in a trance-like state, staring at the ceiling almost prostrate in his office chair, when Felicity knocked gently on his door. Goodenough gathered his thoughts, sat upright at his desk, and contrived to be occupied with his desktop computer.

'Yes?'

Felicity entered, closing the door behind her.

'Is everything OK, Clive?' she inquired with concern. 'I buzzed you and when you didn't answer, I thought you might not be feeling well.'

'No, no,' he stammered, 'I'm fine.'

'Can I get you a coffee or water? I've just made a cappuccino for Dr Milligan. Would you like one?'

'Er, no thanks. Did you say Milligan?'

'Yes, Dr Milligan is your 10 am appointment, remember?'

'Of course, I remember,' he said angrily, though the truth was, in his distress, he had indeed forgotten.

'He's lovely, isn't he?' gushed Felicity, removing his empty coffee cup. 'I've been with you for two years now and I don't think I've ever met him. Very amusing. He was telling me about some things that he did on his last study leave in Cambridge ...'

'Tell him to come in now. No, wait, give me a minute.'

He consulted the notes he'd made for his meeting with the mercurial Dr Milligan, then buzzed Felicity and told her to send Milligan in.

Milligan entered somewhat diffidently. He was a man of short and trim stature, conservatively dressed in slacks and a heavy tweed jacket – surely too heavy for this time of year, thought Goodenough.

His shoes were highly polished and he wore a crisp, freshly ironed shirt with a brightly speckled cravat. His hair, like his speech, was clipped.

Still smarting from his earlier encounter, Clive Goodenough began hesitantly, with less fervour.

'Come in,' he said, gesturing to Milligan to sit.

'Thank you, Clive. Just here?'

The Dean nodded.

Milligan remained standing, casting his eyes around the office.

'That window behind you is spectacular. Wonderful views of the campus, I imagine.'

'The view is good.'

'And the light. It's really quite lovely, the southern light. Have you thought of angling your desk to capture the full benefit of the light and the view?'

'Not really. This is a work place, not an observatory or an art studio.'

'Oh, of course. I just thought ...'

Goodenough remained seated behind his desk waiting for Milligan to sit. His visitor, however, continued to stand and survey the office. Goodenough became increasingly irritated. What was Milligan's game? Was he stalling for time? Or was he, as so many of his close colleagues had opined, excessively fey? Whatever the fact of the matter, Clive Goodenough had run out of patience.

'I'd like you to sit down, please, Greg. There are some important matters I'd like to discuss.'

'Of course, Clive, of course. I hadn't imagined anything less. It's just that I'm fascinated by interior design and I can see so much potential with your office ...'

Goodenough cut him off with a gesture to the seat he wished him to occupy.

'Enough!'

Milligan approached the chair, brushing away some imaginary lint from it before slowly settling into it. He crossed his legs and glanced up at the ceiling. 'Have you ever thought of installing ...'

'Greg, I want to discuss your contribution to the faculty.'

'Ah, that's a matter close to my heart, Clive. I've been here for many years, from the very start actually, and hopefully played my role in building the faculty into the powerhouse that it is today.'

'Yes, but I think we need more of your expertise in the classroom. I intend to increase the number of subjects you teach and your teaching hours,' Goodenough announced.

'I'm afraid my material is very advanced, Clive. Students tend to struggle. I set very high standards.'

'That may be so. But if we were to offer your class at a more student-friendly time ...'

'It fits in with my other commitments, Clive. Surely I have some discretion in the matter?'

'Most of our students can't get out here by 8 am. Others don't choose to.'

'I really don't think the faculty should be ...'

'And then there's the matter of your graduate students.'

'My pride and joy. I know I don't have many but, again, they tend to shy away from the more challenging areas I specialise in.'

'That may be true, but you may have to compromise there. The fact that you require them to come to your home is also a problem.'

'No-one's ever mentioned that, Clive.'

'I'm going to require that you see graduate students on campus from now on. And that you post consultation hours on your office door. In short, Greg, I want to see you around the faculty more. A lot more.'

'I'm surprised to hear you say that, Clive. With all due respect, I'm on campus as often as required.'

'That's not my observation. Nor that of your colleagues. I'm your Dean and I never see you around the faculty.'

'I think we must come in on different days.'

'I'm here every day.'

'Exactly my point, Clive,' smiled Milligan, wickedly. Goodenough had heard enough.

'Get out!' he shouted, so loudly his EA stopped typing, alarmed at the ferocity of her boss's outburst.

'I beg your pardon?' said Milligan, looking startled.

His eyes flashing, his jaw firmly set and fists clenched, Goodenough stood, his thighs pressed against his desk.

'I'll write to you with explicit directions on what I expect. Now get out.' With that, he started to move toward Milligan.

In fear for his safety as his Dean advanced on him, Milligan got to his feet.

'I find your attitude very unprofessional, Clive,' he declared as he backed towards the office door. 'Unacademic, I might say.'

Shaken, he left Goodenough's office with the certain conviction that his Dean understood nothing about the life of the intellectual.

Clive Goodenough's heart was racing. Within a few days, he would no longer be Dean of Engineering, but a disgruntled and resentful Dean for Outreach and Engagement.

Chapter 21

The Pedant

Clive Goodenough was beginning to understand the awfulness of his situation. He'd considered jumping ship after his failed meetings with Potter and Milligan. But he was determined not to be ground down by Razer and Motherwell. He'd play along for a while, meet his commitments and plan his revenge on people who had brought him so low. With less than honourable intentions, he prepared himself for his first meeting of the Open Day committee which, he understood, was to be the only meaningful role left to him on the Batman campus. He had no intention of meeting any of his off-campus obligations.

He dawdled towards the appointed room to attend his first meeting. He'd deliberately planned a late arrival both to keep his new charges waiting and to signal his lack of interest in Open Day planning. He entered the room, looked around the small group of members and saw his former colleague in Engineering, the acerbic Serb, Arso Kikavic, look up. Goodenough found Jamie Jamieson sitting at the head of the oval conference table. He paused at the door, annoyed.

'I'm going to chair the Open Day meeting from now on, Jamie,' he declared haughtily, 'I should sit at the head of the table.'

Familiar with his former Dean's waspish nature, Arso was savouring the suddenly dramatic moment. He locked eyes with Marilyn Worthy and pouted his bottom lip as he knocked his knee against Kon's. Overawed by the arrival of an angry professor, the two students remained expressionless, eyes darting between the pretender and the incumbent.

'Good morning, Clive,' Jamie beamed at Goodenough. 'Everybody, I think you all know Professor Goodenough, our new Dean for Outreach and Engagement.'

Goodenough looked around, forcing a weak smile at the other members of the Open Day committee.

'Clive,' Jamie turned in his chair and looked up at Goodenough, 'according to the memo I've had from the Vice President ...'

'Th-th-that th-th-thug.'

'... I am to continue chairing the Open Day committee. You didn't see the memo?'

He hadn't. His jaw threatened to lock. Once again, he had been humiliatingly sidelined. Sullenly, he took the seat at the other end of the table and cast his eyes down at the agenda papers.

'Now, let's begin,' Jamie addressed the committee. 'We've been meeting all year and things are pretty much under control. So far, that is. Yeah?'

No-one broke the uncomfortable silence but Jamie was determined not to be diverted by Goodenough's simmering anger. He went on.

'I've written to all Deans, Heads of School and so on, asking them to let me have their plans for Open Day. They should of all replied but ...'

'Should have,' interjected Clive Goodenough forcefully, still with his eyes downcast.

'Sorry?' said Jamie, nonplussed.

Goodenough looked up with a forced superior smile. 'I said "should *have*". They should have replied, not should *of* replied,' said Goodenough.

'OK, they should *have* replied by last Friday,' said Jamie, resigning himself to correction. 'Apparently, that was a mistake on my behalf.'

'It was not on your behalf. You made the mistake yourself, no-one made it for you.'

'Huh?'

'I think you meant it was a mistake on your part. Not your behalf.'

Jamie began to realise that Goodenough would be using any excuse to unnerve him.

'According to my list of plans for the day,' Jamie gathered his thoughts, 'only one Dean hasn't yet replied. Sorry to say that's Engineering, Clive.' With raised eyebrows and a cocked head, he looked expectantly at Goodenough, who replied with equally hollow sincerity.

'I'm sorry to say you seem to be misinformed, Jamie,' returned Goodenough. 'It must *of* escaped your attention that I'm no longer Dean of Engineering. I suggest you speak with Professor Pilgrim.' Goodenough smiled as he began to enjoy unsettling Jamie.

'I guess one of the benefits of the new college structure,' Jamie struck back, 'is that I'll have less people to try to chase for replies.'

'Fewer,' corrected Goodenough.

'Huh?' said Jamie.

'I said "fewer". You said "less" people. You should have said "fewer".'

'Sorry, I don't get it. But if you say it should be "fewer", I'll try to remember that going forward,' conceded Jamie.

'Going forward? As opposed to going backward, Jamie?' inquired Goodenough.

'Sorry?' said Jamie.

'You said you'd try to remember something "going forward". Why did you add the phrase "going forward"? If you'd simply said "I'll try to remember that" and left it at that, your meaning would have been unambiguous. In other words, the phrase "going forward" was superfluous.'

The members of the committee shifted in their seats and Arso was alone in enjoying the heightened tension. The others, initially respectful of Goodenough's status, were losing patience with him.

'Clive, it's just one of those modern phrases,' ventured Marilyn Worthy. 'I know it's irritating but let's face it, it is in common usage.'

'As a lecturer in English, would you use it?' Goodenough challenged.

'Professor Goodenough,' began the head of the Batman University Student Society, Declan, hesitantly, 'I think you might be splitting hairs. After all, what Jamie said and what you said, well, frankly, I think they're both the same. If you get my drift.'

'Indeed, I do get your drift,' said Goodenough condescendingly. 'But why did you say that what Jamie and I said are "both the same"?'

'I really thought they were both the same.'

'Both the same as what?'

'Both the same as each other.'

'But you could have said they were "the same" without adding the word "both". By doing so, you potentially confuse the listener.'

'Not this listener,' muttered Jamie.

'Perhaps not,' Goodenough turned on Jamie, 'but precision in our language is important, and as Convenor or whatever I am of this committee – a university committee, need I remind you? – you should be ensuring we have precision of language and meaning!'

'Moving on, but not forward, then,' said Jamie brightly, 'I want to tell the committee about a new and very special event that will grace our Open Day this year. And it just could be the biggest and funnest event of the day. Ready? We're going to have a parade by the new regiment. They've been in intensive training, and the parade is to be inspected by the Minister for Homeland Defence.'

'Th-th-that th-th-thug.'

'There'll be demonstrations highlighting the skills of Army dogs. A dais will be set up in Village Place in front of a new parade ground for the Minister, the President and Mr O'Toole. The Minister will deliver a short speech.'

'I wonder which crap pot he'll dig into for that,' sneered Marilyn Worthy.

'Military parade is good idea,' said Arso. 'Create good atmosphere.'

'Our Chairman, Mr O'Toole, will be the presiding official for the university so he'll accompany the Minister on his inspection of the parade,' advised Jamie. 'They've had tons of rehearsals and that all seems tickety-boo.'

'Basher Motherwell is the chocolate soldier colonel of the regiment, is he?' inquired Kon. 'Does he get a starring role?'

'Indeed, Professor Motherwell does have an important role to play. He accompanies the Minister with his ceremonial sword and his Army dog.'

'So he can do two things at once?' remarked Goodenough, without looking up.

Jamie ignored the snipe.

'A pace or so behind them will be Mr O'Toole,' Jamie filled out the picture of the official inspection party. 'Kevin Burke will be at the head of the regiment with his dog and will salute the Minister as he begins his inspection.'

'Dogs saluting,' smirked Marilyn Worthy, 'maybe I'll come along after all. Wonder if Kevin could teach my Dachshund to salute.'

'I've spoken to both the Vice President …'

'Th-th-that th-th-thug.'

'… and the Head of Campus Security and the rehearsals have been going brilliantly and Mr O'Toole is comfortable with his role. Apparently, he knows the Minister quite well so that should make things a little easier all round.'

'I'll bet he knows him very well,' asserted Economopoulos. 'After all, he's one of the State's biggest donors to the Party.'

'Let's not bring politics into Open Day,' chided Jamie. 'Now if we can finish up with the matter of publicity, yeah? The brochures are in preparation and we'll get them out to you all for any final suggestions before unleashing them on an unsuspecting public.' He chuckled at his own joke. 'They'll go out to schools in the region in due course reminding them of the date and the importance of attending. We'll do the final work on the program in, say, early July to be ready for them to be distributed on campus on the day. Everyone OK with that? Yeah?'

There were no dissenters.

'Excellent. One last thing and I am looking to you now, Clive.'

Goodenough's mind had already left the meeting and he was surprised to hear his name. He looked up at Jamie, startled.

'I've asked Sharelle to send you a list of our target schools in the region. And a few others outside Robert Gordon that we have hopes of penetrating. If I could use that word,' he added with a naughty expression.

'And?' inquired Goodenough.

'The Veep has advised me ...'

'Th-th-that th-th-thug.'

'The Veep, Jamie? Do you mean the Vice President? Spare us the Americanisms.'

'Oh, beg your pardon, Clive. I'll try to do better. Going forward. As I was saying, the Vice President has advised me that he wants you to spearhead the assault on schools.'

'Spearhead the assault? Now we're at war with the schools? We're going to penetrate them? Honestly, Jamie, cut the crap.'

'What I mean is, you're to do the schools liaison for Open Day. Kellie and her team would normally do the visits, but Professor Motherwell feels we need a new approach with more senior representation. He wants you to do the school visits to excite the interest of students and staff alike. My office will supply the info kits, of course. Then, it's over to you to give us our best attended Open Day yet.'

oooOooo

Jamie drove his sports car rather faster than usual up the long drive to the house and screeched to a halt on the gravel drive. He snatched his satchel from the passenger seat, got out, pressed the lock button and made his way to the front door. He threw open the door, walked in and slammed the door behind him with his foot. His eyes were lashing with anger. He was in a stink and Roddy Rodman prepared for one of their difficult office workplace flair-up conversations.

'What. A. Bitch.' Jamie snapped, standing with one hand defiantly on his hip.

'What's that, my little drama queen?' Roddy inquired, looking up casually from his *New Yorker*.

Having got Roddy's attention, Jamie resumed his entry into the sitting room. 'What an arrogant fucking bitch,' he elaborated, throwing down his satchel and dropping onto the couch to face Roddy.

'Bad day at the office?' inquired Roddy. 'Sounds like my precious has spent too long in the hyperbolic chamber today. Who is the object of your ire, today, my mild-mannered mate?'

'I'll give you one guess,' said Jamie, holding up a forefinger. 'That's all it will take, believe me.'

'Let's see,' Roddy sat back and looked into the distance, stroking his chin. 'Could it be that cute, chubby Indian waiter at Boy Wonder's? The married one you think is gay but who won't return your lustful glances?'

'Wrong. And he is gay, believe me.'

'Hmmm,' said Roddy, surveying the ceiling. 'Could it be,' he lingered with the next thought, 'perhaps, Brian Phipps?'

'Brian Phipps? Why would it be Brian Phipps, for God's sake?' Jamie snarled.

'I just thought he might have refused again to drive you into town for your hair appointment.'

'That was ages ago. Wrong again.'

'Let me see, then,' he said, scratching his head. 'Who could today's arrogant, fucking bitch be? While I'm thinking, shall I get you a calming drink?' Roddy stood and moved to the drinks cabinet.

'The usual. Please,' Jamie said, tapping his foot.

'Hold on,' Roddy paused and turned dramatically to face Jamie. 'I think I've got it. It's Clive Goodenough! Tell me I'm right.'

'I can tell you you're slow. That should have been your first and only guess.'

'Oooh, that's your "dogshit-on-my-shoe, face", Roddy observed. 'It was always going to be your new boss.'

'If he smiled, his face would crack.'

'Not a jolly fellow, is he? Ice? He's pissed off at being made Dean for O and E and if he can inflict pain on anyone, he'll feel sooo much better. Public service announcement,' Roddy cupped his lips. 'You, Jamie Archibald Jamieson, will be in the firing line.'

'He burst in late to the Open Day committee today,' Jamie said, plonking himself down on an easy chair. 'He was horrible.'

'Hard to believe,' said Roddy, shaking his head, 'normally such a nice chap.'

'He thought he was to chair the meetings. But I had an email from Barry Motherwell himself to say I would be the chair.'

'Don't tell me!' Roddy guessed. 'Goodenough kept acting as though it was his meeting?'

'And he took every opportunity to criticise and correct me. He killed the meeting. No-one was game to speak for fear of being corrected.'

'Was he pedantic and frenetic?'

'He was like a fox terrier trying to fuck a billiard ball.'

'Ech. What an image.'

'My staff have taken an instant dislike to him. They all loathe him.'

'With a little encouragement from you, my dear?'

'Perhaps. Anyway,' he pouted, 'he's now known around the office as Farty McFartface.'

'Be careful with that one, my dear.'

'Why?'

'As you well know, farts can sometimes turn to shit.'

'And?'

'And the word is he's not very keen on you.'

'The feeling's mutual.'

Chapter 22

The Finer Points of Office Design

The Executive Deans of the two new colleges had refurbished their offices to reflect their new status. New business cards and other stationery had been printed. They'd met with their academic and support staffs, and were warming to their new roles. Both Morgan Freestone and Mervyn Pilgrim laboured under the mistaken belief that Razer held them in high esteem, having entrusted them to loftier heights of management responsibility. Neither suspected Razer's master plan for their ultimate failure; instead, each strode around among their augmented faculties with heightened self-confidence and enhanced estimation of their own talents.

Early reports finding their way back to Motherwell and Razer, however, indicated the early seeds of discontent and the gathering clouds of revolt in the colleges. Morgan Freestone received a frosty reception from the Arts staff in his 'getting to know you' meeting. He spoke at some length and without modesty of his distinguished career in government and of achievements that failed to impress them. To illustrate his tender-minded, arts-oriented side, he informed them he was an opera aficionado, unaware that most of them held that art form in low regard. His plan to take himself overseas on a learning tour of international education providers left them speechless.

Mervyn Pilgrim had an equally rocky start to his new role. He opened his first college Board with a prayer asking for the Lord's blessing on their deliberations. This was preceded by a novel variation on 'Welcome to Country', which Pilgrim laboured unsuccessfully to construe as a 'welcome to the promised land'. While his former charges in Engineering had suffered his faith in silence, the scientists new to his decanal care but well-schooled in meeting procedures, resolved by a show of hands that prayers be banned from college Board meetings. Even the long-suffering Engineering staff, emboldened by their new colleagues from Science, voted in support, much to Pilgrim's chagrin.

Clive Goodenough's resentment at being stripped of his deanship and put in charge of an activity that he held in contempt was clear. Being banished to a small timber cottage on the periphery of the campus was, for him, akin to being cast into outer darkness. He'd lost the comfort and prestige of a Dean's office and the services of a full-time EA; he now had to share an assistant. The only upside for him was his cottage mate, the ever-cheerful Lexi Dunne, the only person to offer any consolation.

For her part, Lexi Dunne had accepted her new role with grace. Even enthusiasm. She'd decided that developing Batman's international profile was a worthy challenge. She'd already made her mark three years ago in pulling off a stunning international deal, the envy of every Australian university. More or less single-handed, she'd reached a deal for Batman University to receive the first ever cohort of fee-paying North Korean students in Australia. With this stellar achievement behind her, making a big splash in intentional education seemed assured. She'd decided to give it her all.

In devising their respective KPIs, Barry Motherwell had done his best to lay the groundwork for Razer's unofficial but unambiguous goal: namely, the ultimate failure of each of them. Only one seemed to have any chance of survival, and Motherwell was intent upon giving Lexi Dunne every assistance towards that end. In his view, she was so smart she could succeed in any role. He'd designed her KPIs so that he'd virtually assured that she'd match or even better them.

Motherwell allowed a month to pass before setting up review meetings with the four Deans. He ensured that the first would be Lexi Dunne. His spirits rose as she breezed into his office radiating vigour and American charm. She looked so positively captivating that he could only manage a shy, boyish smile. Dressed stylishly on this late autumn day, Lexi closed the door with an exaggerated carefulness and mouthed 'Hello, Mother'.

He seemed incapable of speech until Lexi saved him.

'You know, Mother,' she said glancing around his office, 'you have one of the best offices on campus.' He remained seated as she moved past him to take in the view from the floor-to-ceiling window. 'I don't think you even realise it.'

'An office is an office,' replied Motherwell, finally finding his voice.

'You sit with your back to this marvellous window,' she enthused. 'Why don't you turn your desk ninety degrees so you can take in the view? It's quite something to be on the top floor of O'Toole.'

'All I'd see would be bloody students lazing around in the Village Place,' Motherwell grumbled.

'And what about the office itself?' she said, looking around his workspace. 'As a place to meet people, it's not great is it?'

'No one's ever complained,' he protested, thinking she was starting to sound like Maureen. Maybe it was a woman thing.

'In my not so humble view, it needs a little feminine softening.'

It *is* a woman thing, he thought to himself. He screwed up his face.

'Too many hard edges,' she suggested. 'The lighting's too harsh. It's all rather boring and functional. Dated.'

'I hadn't noticed,' said Motherwell, resigning himself to being lectured about his office's appearance.

'You have a lot of important people come through here. You want to make a good impression. When they're making movies, they pay a great deal of attention to managing impressions through clothes, perspectives, furnishings, that sort of stuff.'

'What needs to be done?' he asked, finally capitulating.

'I'll give you a list of suggestions.' Lexi said, more by way of instruction than suggestion. 'You need some soft furnishings, some strategically placed lighting, some art on the walls, a rug or two. I could go on. I presume you have a budget for your office?'

'I presume so.'

'For starters, this daggy couch has to go.'

'Why?'

'It's uncomfortable and it looks like crap. It's ex-government office furniture. You need a soft, welcoming couch, not one with vinyl seats on which people's bums slip. It shouldn't have hard wooden arm-rests,' she said, slapping the faux timber. 'There are stains from years of coffee mugs resting on them. You need a couple of stylish coffee tables. The arms of the couch should be soft like a pillow when you ever feel the need of an afternoon nap.'

'I never nap at work.'

'You should. It's scientifically proven to be good for you. Why do you think the Latins ...'

'OK, I get it,' he chuckled, knowing resistance was futile. 'Let's have your list of suggestions. I'll see what I can do.'

'That's more like it, Mother,' she said with a triumphant smile as she sat on the vinyl couch. 'Yuk! It's such an awful experience. Now,' she said adopting a businesslike demeanour, 'I believe you wanted a formal chat.'

'You're set up in the cottage?'

'I feel like a farmer's wife.'

'What have you been doing?'

'I've been reviewing the International Office and all our international activities. My early conclusions are that the office is underfunded. There's no strategic plan and our performance has been miserable.'

'I'm sure you can rectify that. As to funding, let me have a submission and I'll see what we can do.'

'And then,' Lexi said conspiratorially, 'there's the little issue of the President's wife, Sinn.'

'Haven't met her. What's the issue?'

'She doesn't add any value. Her English is poor, she's shy, and she doesn't seem to know much about international education.'

'She'd worked in the international office at Nicholas's former university.'

'Yeah, elite British university with scads of Thai students and she's Thai. Not exactly Batman, is it? I'd like to have her salary for a more appropriate appointment.'

'That's not going to happen. For obvious reasons,' Motherwell said, changing the topic. 'And what about Clive?'

'He's not in much.'

'Hmm.' Motherwell nodded. He'd decided to let the Dean for Outreach and Engagement determine his own future, so he didn't pursue the matter of Clive's activities.

'Anything else?'

'You know our biggest cohort of internationals are the North Koreans? And we're the first and only university bar China to have any students from there.'

'That's all down to you and your connections.'

'Their tuition fees are fully paid up front by the DPRK government. A river of gold for Batman. But things could always get tricky with Pyongyang. I think we've got to do more to make sure we keep the ones we've got and we keep the flow going. I've been thinking about extracurricular programs we could introduce.'

'To integrate them with Australian students?'

'Definitely not. That's not what Pyongyang wants. Why do you think the North Koreans built Kim Jong-un College on the other side of the creek and surrounded it with a high, electrified fence? Students get to and from class on buses. They travel as a group and classes are solely for them. No other Australian universities would come at that.'

'What then?'

'I dunno. Maybe give them opportunities to display their culture on campus. I'm thinking Open Day would be the ideal opportunity.'

'Better talk to Jamie,' Motherwell suggested. 'How many North Koreans are there?'

'Total of 62 across three years.'

'I can't say I've ever seen them around campus.'

'They look just like any other Asian students. Except, perhaps a little older. On average, the men are older, of course, having done three years of national service. In fact, they're probably still technically enlisted.'

'How did you get interested in North Korea movies?'

'The North Koreans have a history of making movies and lots of them. Kim Jong-il was a film fanatic.'

'And he or she is?'

'No-one in particular. He's just the dictator son of the founder of North Korea. And he was also the father of Kim Jong-un, the current dictator.'

'Got it.'

'Kim directed many movies himself. All designed to convince the North Koreans that they lived in a paradise on earth. The theme running through them all was 'nothing to envy'. And that the North Koreans led the world in science, education, culture, whatever. Above all, they certainly could outdo the hated United States in every respect.'

'Clearly mad.'

'I had to go to see for myself. At that time, UCLA had an international partnership with Dandong University in China.'

'Dandong?'

'It's a university in north-western China. They had an agreement with Kim il-Sung University in Pyongyang. I spent some time at Dandong and persuaded the international office to get me a permit to enter North Korea.'

'I knew you had skills in international education.'

'Smart-ass. I used my time in Pyongyang to get to know people, important people in the university and in the education ministry. I still have all those connections and I don't think any of them have been liquidated. I made quite few visits there when I was a doctoral student. I think the people I met both like and respect me.'

'I can understand that.'

'Since I've been at Batman, I've kept up my links with North Korea and have been back several times. And now I can go back as Batman's official rep. That should make things easier.'

'How did you arrange it all?'

'It was my connections with the authorities in Pyongyang. I'm indeed regarded as their Eomeoni, or mother. I'm the only non-Korean allowed to enter Kim Jong-un College.'

Motherwell's rambling discussion with Lexi Dunne was interrupted by an intercom call from his EA reminding him of his appointment with Clive Goodenough. He'd been waiting for fifteen minutes and Motherwell knew that would be annoying him.

'Clive,' Motherwell said to Lexi softly.

Lexi smiled conspiratorially, blew him a kiss and left. He heard her acknowledge Goodenough as she closed his door.

'Sorry, Clive, I'm afraid I chatted on a bit much. See you back at the cottage?'

OPEN DAY

ooOOoo

Motherwell gathered his thoughts as to what he needed to discuss with the new Dean for Outreach and Engagement. He'd had a report from Jamie Jamieson on Goodenough's first Open Day committee meeting, which seemed to have gone the way that Razer would have hoped. Lexi had reported that the former Dean of Engineering with whom she now shared office space in the cottage was not coming in often, and when he did, he was grumpy. His irascibility threw a blanket of gloom over the office.

His proclivity for pedantry and rigidity of thought became more pronounced as he raged against the wickedness of his superiors. The EA he shared with Lexi Dunne had already consulted Henry Zimmer about Clive's overbearing behaviour, and there'd been claims of bullying and harassment. Lexi began to notice that Sinn Razer would find she had errands to run whenever Goodenough entered the cottage.

Barry Motherwell allowed a few minutes to pass before opening his office door and fixing Goodenough with an expressionless face. With a slight nod, he turned and waved a 'follow me' gesture. Goodenough watched the Vice President's back retreating into his office and looked at Mez Carter who returned his glare with an indulgent smile.

'You wanted to see me, Barry,' he said abruptly, as he stood facing Motherwell, who'd sat at his desk.

'Just a catch-up on outreach and engagement,' said Motherwell, affecting indifference.

'First off, I want to register a complaint,' said Goodenough agitatedly and still standing.

Motherwell raised his eyebrows and remained silent, as he'd seen Razer do.

'I'm not really in charge of outreach and engagement.'

'You are.'

'So how is it you've decided that Master Jamieson, head of media and marketing or some such rubbish, is chairing the Open Day planning committee?'

'He's handled that role for the past few years and knows the ropes,' Motherwell countered.

'I'm an experienced chairman, more experienced than him. I know more about higher education than he'll ever know. And he shows no respect for me. He even called me "dude".'

'Don't worry about it.'

'And why am I meant to do all the high school visits for Open Day?'

'We need someone out there with many years of experience in higher education.'

'But I haven't been in a high school since I graduated from mine. What would I know about high school students?'

'You're a father of teenagers, aren't you?'

'Oh, please! I don't know if I can go on in this role.'

'You've hardly started it.'

'I'm warning you, Barry, I play hard ball.' Still standing, Goodenough rocked from side to side as his agitation grew. Motherwell wondered if he could become violent but knew that he had to maximise the pressure on Goodenough.

'It's the only role we have for you in the new structure,' he said flatly.

Goodenough dry spat in exasperation.

'After all the years I've given to Batman, that's all there is. You've been here five minutes. Same for Razer. Compared to me, you two have given nothing to this university.'

'I'm expecting to see your strategic plan soon,' Motherwell said, ramping up the pressure.

'Well, you won't,' Goodenough declared defiantly.

'Close the door as you leave, Clive,' Motherwell said, matching Goodenough's truculence.

Motherwell turned to his desktop computer and Clive Goodenough made an angry exit slamming the door. Startled, Mez Carter looked up and watched him, grim-faced, hurry past. She stood and knocked on Motherwell's door and entered to find him standing, apparently looking from his window down at the Village Square.

'Barry, can I get you a coffee or tea?'

When she got no reply from her boss, she closed the door quietly and left him to his private thoughts.

Motherwell stood for several minutes, looking but not taking anything in. His public persona was the tough manager, but being heavy-handed with colleagues didn't sit well with him. Was he too tough on Clive, too much Razer's man? He'd signed up to Razer's agenda and it was too late for doubts. Still at the window, he called Lexi Dunne's mobile number.

'Hello, Mother,' answered Lexi cheerfully, 'didn't I see you less than an hour ago?'

'Has Clive returned to the cottage?'

'No, in fact, he called Anne a few minutes ago and said he would be off campus for the rest of the day. Why?'

'No reason, just wondering.'

'Would his no-show have anything to do with his meeting with you?'

Ignoring this inquiry, Motherwell said, 'I've been thinking about my office. I think you're right. It needs a makeover.'

'Super! I'll email you my suggestions in a few days,' Lexi said, excited to have won him over to her thinking.

'Not too expensive though.'

'Damn it, Mother,' she rebuked him, 'think big.'

Chapter 23

Motherwell's Misstep

Motherwell smiled to himself, surprised again to find himself so captivated by this woman. He was still savouring the memory of Lexi when Mez Carter buzzed him to advise that Kevin Burke was with her and wanted to speak with him on a matter of some urgency. The Head of Campus Security entered the office looking troubled. Motherwell wasn't too concerned because he knew that even some minor unfamiliar problems would test Kevin's problem-solving abilities.

'Hallo, Kevin. What's up?' he greeted the Head of Campus Security.

'Prof, I mean, Colonel, we may have a problem.'

'What sort of a problem?'

'You know that notice that went out to all students about the regiment?'

'Yeah, inviting applications.'

'And you know how Captain Doubel at the Sandstone Regiment agreed to process the applications?'

'Yeah, Sandstone has all the expertise and experience. Is there a problem?'

'I've just had a call from the RSM at the Sandstone regiment and the Captain's, well, he's a bit unhappy.'

He now had Motherwell's complete attention.

'Get it out, Kev,' he urged.

'You know how you invited applications from Batman students?'

Motherwell was trying not to let Kevin see his growing impatience. 'We've already established that.'

'And you know how we had a pretty good response?'

'Over 200,' he agreed, waiting for Kevin to get to the issue.

'Did we expect a good response from the North Korean students?'

'The what!'

'Y'know, the North Korean students.'

'We have applications from North Koreans? For our regiment?' Motherwell exclaimed.

'Yes, sir,' Kevin said, taking a step back.

'What idiot allowed that to happen?' raged Motherwell.

'Not too sure, Sir. But all of the male North Korean students have sent in the forms and Captain Doubel has apparently got his knickers in a knot. Said they're from the axis of evil and ineligible for the regiment.'

'Of course they can't join the bloody regiment! How could they think they could?'

'They had the forms, downloaded from the batmail.'

'Sneaky bastards. Probably hacking our batmail system. Leave it with me, Kev. And tell the RSM to tell Captain Doubel we'll sort it out. And tell him I apologise for Batman's mistake. Keep it to yourself and ask him to do the same, for God's sake.'

Motherwell's mind was racing. What should he do next?

'And Prof, the RSM says that Captain Doubel says they all claimed prior military experience.'

Motherwell's gut knotted and he clapped his hands over his face. He dismissed the Head of Campus Security without looking up. 'Leave it with me,' he muttered.

How could this have happened? What idiot …? He decided to call Sarah Wells in student administration.

'Ooooh, Barry, this is a pleasant surprise. Getting to be a bit of a habit,' she giggled. 'How can I be of assistance?'

'The batmail I asked you to send out about the formation of the regiment,' he said testily. 'Did that go to international students?'

'Yes, Barry, it went to all students. As per your instruction,' Sarah confirmed, pleased with her efficiency.

'You're telling me it went to all international students?' he asked, his voice rising.

'My word, yes, all of them.'

'Including North Korean students?'

'They're internationals, aren't they?'

'How could you be so stupid?' he spluttered.

'I beg your pardon?'

'You sent that message to international students! That was just plain fucking stupid.'

'I beg your pardon! I don't think there's any need for vulgar language, Professor Motherwell. Your email said ...'

'But I didn't mean *all* students. I meant all Australian students.'

'Then you should have said so. Now you've really upset me,' she began to snivel. 'You're a very nasty man. It's not my fault, you know. I did exactly ...'

Motherwell ended the call. It was important to fix this issue before it got out of hand, before the North Koreans or Sandstone Regiment caused a fuss, before Nicholas Razer became aware of his carelessness. He was still cursing Sarah Wells as he tapped in Lexi Dunne's extension.

'Vice President,' Lexi answered. 'I hope you're not reconsidering the matter of your office modernisation 'cos I'm underway already.'

'Lexi, I'm in a spot of bother. Can you come up here right away? I hope you can help get me out of a tricky situation.'

ooOOoo

'Let me get this right, Mother,' Lexi stood facing Motherwell slumped in his chair, eyes downcast, 'you've sent an invitation to the North Korean students to join the Batman University Regiment.'

'Not exactly,' Motherwell winced. 'Strictly speaking, Sarah Wells sent it.'

'Over her name?'

Motherwell's head dropped.

'Over mine,' he admitted almost inaudibly. 'It's probably my fault. For not being quite clear enough.'

'Clear enough! I don't know what to say. Presumably it's also gone to all international students?'

'It has.'

'The Pacific Islanders, the Maldivians, the Indonesians, the Indians, God knows who else. This is a problem I didn't expect to have as Dean for International.'

'No,' Motherwell said lamely. 'I got Kevin to check with the Sandstone regiment. It's only the North Koreans who've applied.'

'You can be sure Mr Kim is behind this,' she said.

'Mr Kim?' Motherwell asked.

'The head of Kim Jong-un College,' she explained.

'And he's behind it, you say?' Motherwell asked feebly.

'You bet!' Lexi asserted. 'They'd love to get inside the Australian military. He'll have learned about your cock-up and then orchestrated the applications.'

'Oh, God!' Motherwell signed deeply.

'After he'd checked with his superiors, of course.'

'His superiors?'

'Probably the head of the North Korean Higher Education Ministry. And the RGB.'

'The RGB?'

'The Reconnaissance General Bureau. It's the North Korean spy agency. Our Mr Kim is undoubtedly one of their officials.'

'What!' exclaimed Motherwell. 'We have a North Korean spy on campus?'

'Of course the North Koreans have a spy at Batman, Mother! They're all spies, one way or another.'

Motherwell looked at Lexi with growing alarm.

'They have spies and informers all over their own country, so you can be sure they send spies with anyone they overseas.'

Motherwell sank further into his chair.

'What am I going to do, Lexi? I was hoping that with your connections with the North Koreans ...'

'Who else knows about this?' she demanded.

'Kevin Burke. The Captain in charge of the Sandstone regiment and his RSM. No one else. I hope.'

'I'll see what I can do,' she said, approaching Motherwell and laying a hand on his shoulder.

'Mother, don't worry. I'm sure it will all be fine.'

With that, she bent to peck him on the cheek and left. Lexi Dunne was not at all sure everything would turn out well. The North Koreans were experts at exploiting missteps such as Motherwell's and the artful Mr Kim would be plotting to turn this to his advantage in ways she couldn't imagine.

oooOoo

Barry Motherwell slipped out of his office early with the intention of distracting himself from his predicament. He also wanted to ensure that he didn't run into Nicolas Razer or any of his team. He intended to occupy himself with physical labour on the farm. There were fences to be repaired, cattle to be fed and crops to be tended. And Mena and Herbie, the dogs, to be exercised.

The last rays of autumn sunlight forced his labours to a halt as he made his way despondently to his house. Usually, he would lock the dogs in their compound but this night he needed their company. As if aware of this rare privilege, both dogs entered hesitantly and settled near the door, attending to every move he made and every word he spoke, as though they might at any moment be evicted.

Despite his physical labour, Motherwell had lost his appetite. Instead of microwaving his customary frozen dinner, he took a stubby of beer from the fridge. He flicked on the television but immediately turned it off when he saw the news report was about new North Korean hypersonic missiles. He was making his way to the sofa when his landline phone rang. He checked the screen and his gut tightened as he recognised Lexi Dunne's mobile number. He switched the TV to mute.

'Oh, hi, Lexi,' he answered, affecting nonchalance. 'I didn't know you had my home number.'

'I didn't. Mr Kim gave it to me.'

'What! How the hell did he …'

'I'm joking, Mother. I had to look you up in directories. Did you turn off your mobile?'

'Not sure where it is. Must have left it outside.'

'That's not like you. You sound awful. You OK?'

'I'm hoping you'll tell me,' he said anxiously.

'It took quite a while to find your number. I've no idea of the name of the town or place you live. All I could remember …'

'Lexi,' he pleaded, unable any longer to contain himself, 'this is killing me. Tell me you have some good news.'

'Maybe I do. The first thing is that you're going to have to replace two bottles of Soju.'

'Of what?'

'Soju. It's Mr Kim's favourite Korean tipple. He prefers the South Korean to the North and I happened to have two bottles left from my last trip to Seoul. I took them to a meeting this evening with Mr Kim. We finished one and I've left him the other. I've just left his suite in Kim Jong-un College. Now I've none left at home. The alcohol content is around 50 per cent.'

Motherwell was becoming impatient with the detail.

'I think I'm a little shickered,' she said.

'Doesn't matter,' he said. Except, he thought, it's slowing your ability to process your thoughts.

'And you'll also have to pay for my taxi home. I'm in no state to drive.'

'God, Lexi, get to the point,' he pleaded. 'I'll do whatever you want. Just tell me what happened!'

'There's good news and not so good.'

'Yes?'

'The good news is that Mr Kim has a sense of humour and he found your predicament very amusing. Hilarious, in fact. He threw back his head and laughed so hard I could see the gold fillings in his back teeth. He joked that if he'd bungled like this in North Korea he'd probably be shot with a missile launcher. He realised from the outset, of course, that it would be impossible for any of his students to join the regiment. But he thought it would be fun to try it on.'

'Funny idea of fun,' retorted Motherwell.

'By the time we'd emptied the first bottle, he agreed to write to the Sandstone regiment withdrawing the applications. He'll do it tomorrow and copy you in. I'll contact him early on to remind him. I don't think he'll forget but even he must have been pretty pissed by the time I left.'

'What about the bad news?'

'Being a North Korean, he was always going to exact some price for his act of mercy. But, I think you'll be able to cope.'

'For God's sake, tell me.'

'First, he wants a formal invitation for the new North Korean Consul to attend Open Day.'

'To do what? There can't be any speeches. Or formal events. And no meeting with the Minister.'

'None of those things. And his English wouldn't be up to making a speech. A low key visit to see the campus and mix with the North Korean students.'

'Why Open Day?'

'Why not? I told him about his students putting on cultural events.'

'If you're sure it's going to be low key, I won't bother Nicholas with it.'

'Your call. Second, Mr Kim wants to screen a North Korean movie in the cinema. Which he would attend. And he wants it to be on the program for Open Day.'

'What sort of a film? Propaganda?'

'Presumably. But, who cares?' she asked flightily. 'Probably only the North Korean students will attend. I've agreed to introduce him and the movie.'

'So that's it?'

'That's all. But you owe me big time now, Mother.'

'Lexi, you're wonderful,' Motherwell said, beginning to relax.

'I am.'

'I don't know how I can ever repay you.'

'I have a few ideas. Oh,' she stifled a yawn, 'there's just one loose end arising out of this mess.'

'What's that?'

'Sarah Wells.'

'From student admin?'

'She's been speaking with Henry Zimmer about abusive language you used to her on the phone. Is it true?'

'Lexi, I might need your help again. Right now, I have to get another stubby from the fridge.'

'Sweet dreams, Mother.

Chapter 24

Faith Marketing

It was a source of some annoyance, even hurt, to Jamie Jamieson that his work at Batman largely went unrecognised and uncelebrated. Lecturers might be brilliant, researchers might win acclaim in their narrow fields, but the world would remain ignorant of their achievements without marketing. Among his own staff, Jamie thought of himself as the intellectual leader, the equal of any professor, constantly urging them on to reach new heights, to break down barriers, to innovate. Theirs was at least as noble a calling in the university as any academic's.

When Jamie received a call inviting him to a meeting with the Executive Dean of the new college of technology, it struck him that this was the very first time he'd even been invited to such a meeting. This could portend a new era for marketing and communications at Batman. He phoned Roddy but he could throw no light on the matter, merely observing that a meeting with Pilgrim would involve a sacrifice of minutes or even hours he could never retrieve.

Still wondering why he'd been summoned, Jamie made his way across the Village Place to Pilgrim's office. The reception area was unattended so he knocked on Pilgrim's door and, believing he'd heard a grunt, entered.

'You wanted to see me, Mervyn?' he asked.

'Whoa! Stop right there.' Pilgrim looked up from his desk and raised a stop-sign hand. 'This is the office of "Professor Pilgrim". Let's try that entry again.'

Chastened, Jamie left the office, closed the door and knocked again.

'Come in,' Pilgrim grunted.

'You wanted to see me, Professor Pilgrim?'

'Jamie, come in. Did Faith offer you something to drink?'

'She's not there.'

'She is,' he declared. Jamie decided not to argue.

'I'd actually love a cup of tea,' Jamie said, hoping the initial awkwardness of his entry was forgotten.

'Did we bring our tea bag?' asked Pilgrim.

'Tea bag? I'm afraid not.'

'College rule. It was one of my first initiatives when I became Executive Dean of the College. It's part of my austerity campaign. Anyone who comes to see the Executive Dean and wants tea, brings a tea bag. The generous ones bring two or more. Or a sachet of coffee. We supply the boiling water and a clean cup.'

'I didn't know.'

'It's early days and word will get around. A case, Jamie, of the word not being in the beginning, eh?'

'I'm sorry, I …'

'In the beginning was the Word,' Pilgrim spoke as though to a child.

I'll be ensuring the word gets around, alright, Jamie promised himself.

'Luckily,' Pilgrim said reproachfully 'I keep a little horde of tea bags which various guests and well-wishers have provided.'

He reached into a bottom drawer of his desk and opened a plastic ice cream tub.

'Actually, Professor Pilgrim, I'll pass on the tea.'

'Quite sure?'

'Quite sure.'

'Swear on the Bible sure?'

'Yes, that sure.'

'Very well,' said Pilgrim returning the tub to the drawer. Pilgrim's expression now changed from gracious host to co-conspirator. 'I wanted to have a chat about tag lines.'

'Straplines, actually. It's a conceptual development.'

'Dr Kikavic told me. I've been thinking about a strapline for Batman University.'

'We already have some good ones for the university from the competition,' Jamie offered.

'I'm not interested in the competition,' Pilgrim fixed Jamie with an intense expression. 'I'm looking for a fresh approach.'

'Fresh I have,' Jamie began to enthuse. 'What about "Batman University – the Evolution Starts Here"?'

'Evolution? Wrong message.'

'Batman – World Ready.'

'World ready is hardly what I'm after. "Do not love the world or anything in the world." 1 John Chapter 2.'

'Batman – Be What You Want to Be.'

'It's a matter of being what Heavenly Father wants us to be.'

'Batman – Own the unknown.'

'Preposterous.'

'Batman – Dream large.'

'Ridiculous.'

'Chase your calling.'

'Getting warmer.'

'There are oodles of others, Professor Pilgrim,' said Jamie plaintively.

'I want one that sums up what Batman is all about. One that can be used all over the campus on the day.'

'I don't have a budget for that.'

'Take no thought for the morrow, Jamie. God will provide.'

'God?'

'Metaphorically speaking, Jamie.'

'I love a metaphor. But I'm not sure …'

'I'm saying I will pay.'

'What did you have in mind?'

'I understand from Dr Kikavic that you're expert at workshopping straplines, vision statements, mission statements and the like.'

'That's my passion,' said Jamie with undisguised pride.

'Let's workshop it, shall we? I'm looking for a noun. What would you say is the essence, the very essence, of teaching and research in a university? In any discipline.'

Jamie squirmed, realising he was caught in a bizarre exercise. 'That's not exactly my beat.'

'Give it a go,' Pilgrim smiled benignly. 'I'll give you a clue. It starts with "d",' he said as he traced the capital D in the air.

'Hmmmm. The essence … dialectic?'

'Communist. Second letter "e". Two syllables.'

'Ah, "demand"? What students demand?'

'Students don't demand, Jamie. Not in the College of Technology. Starts with "de", two syllables, rhymes with "define".'

'Got it!' Jamie exclaimed. "Decline". Decline of standards in all disciplines. Standards of entry, standards of learning, standards of results.'

Pilgrim regarded Jamie with disappointment.

'The word we're looking for, Jamie, is "design". Think of it,' he challenged. 'Name one discipline where design is not of the essence. Just one.'

'Can't think of a single one.'

'Exactly!' Pilgrim crowed.

'I see your point, Professor Pilgrim. It's been an interesting exercise and I want to thank you,' said Jamie, rising from his chair.

'Wait, sit down, we're not there yet. "Design" is only half the story.' Pilgrim stood in front of Jamie, looking down at him.

'Only half?' Jamie asked, trying to conjure up an excuse to leave.

'Design could be good or bad. Agree?'

'I agree.' Jamie felt increasingly as though he were in the hands of a torturer determined to extract a confession from an innocent man.

'Effective or ineffective. For noble purposes or evil. Godly or ungodly,' Pilgrim said with excitement. 'What I'm looking for is an adjective, Jamie. What would be the ultimate adjective to sit with "design"? Eh?'

'Could it be "good" or "effective", "noble". Or "godly"?'

'Close. I'll give you a clue. Universities are centres of intelligence.' Pilgrim's eyes lit up in anticipation.

'Would the adjective we're looking for be "intelligent"?' ventured Jamie. 'As in "intelligent design"?'

'Exactly!' Pilgrim gave his hands a single clap. 'Have you ever heard of intelligent design, Jamie?'

'I haven't.'

'Never heard the phrase?' Pilgrim was now becoming excited.

'Don't think so.'

'Don't you think it would be the foundation of a wonderful strapline? "Batman University for Intelligent Design".'

'It's perhaps not in the same league as the best of our entries for the strapline competition.'

'You surprise me. In any case, it has the ring of truth. Agree?'

'I guess I do,' Jamie resigned himself to the inevitable.

'And truth is what it's all about, isn't it Jamie?'

'It is.' Please release me, he thought.

'And wouldn't any university be proud to be famous for intelligent design?'

'It would.'

'Wouldn't this set Batman apart?'

'It would.'

'So, what's our next step, Jamie?' asked Pilgrim

'I think you'll have to tell me that, too.' Is this nearly over? he thought.

'Saturation.'

'Saturation?'

'For I will saturate the thirst of the weary and every person who languishes I will replenish.'

'Sorry?'

'Jeremiah.'

'Oh.'

'We need saturation coverage of the tagline …'

'Strapline …' Jamie muttered, beaten.

'… on Open Day. I want to be sure everyone here on Open Day gets at least one prod about intelligent design.'

'Poke,' Jamie ventured.

'I beg your pardon?' Pilgrim said, upper lip curled.

'Poke. You want everyone to get a poke.'

'Prod will do for our purposes. We want a prod for every man, woman and child.'

'We do,' conceded Jamie, worn down.

'I need your help. I have a handful of young men and women in the college who believe in the cause of intelligent design. My soldiers of the Lord. I want you to design – there's that word again – a flyer that they can distribute on Open Day. You know, an attractive, eye-catching thing. That's what you do, isn't it?'

'It is.'

'And I'll need a banner. Ten metres wide and, say, one metre high.'

'That's pretty big. For the interfaith marquee?'

'Don't worry yourself about that. My Soldiers for the Lord will fix all that.'

Jamie nodded submissively.

'One more thing. Have the following message prominently displayed on the flyers and the banner. "Inquiries to Professor Pilgrim at the Multi-faith Marquee".'

'Will that be OK with them? The people in the marquee?'

'They're ID people, Jamie.'

'ID?'

'Intelligent design.'

Jamie decided he must rally and take the initiative. He stood, inhaling deeply, and moved to the whiteboard.

'May I?'

'Of course.'

Jamie wrote and stood back to admire his efforts.

'ID@BU. Might just work. Sharp, to the point,' he suggested. 'Missing fun, perhaps.'

'We won't be using that.'

'BU4ID?' he wrote.

'Or that.'

'Just playing with ideas. Looking for the fun angle.'

'Send me some mock-ups and I'll decide which suits us best. I'll organise my Soldiers to distribute.'

'Are the soldiers part of the university regiment?'

'They're Christian soldiers.'

'As in Onward …'

'Exactly.'

'Different from the university regiment, then.'

'Very. Think of my idea, Jamie, as some fun for Open Day.'

'Fun? That's my basic design for Open Day, you might say.'

'There you go. Design. What did I tell you? Everywhere.'

'You're right, Professor Pilgrim,' Jamie brightened as he sensed his ordeal was coming to an end, 'design is in everything we do! And it might as well be intelligent.'

'One final matter,' said Pilgrim with serous intent. 'You'll send all invoices to me and me only. Are my words acceptable in thy sight?'

'Do I agree, you mean? I guess I do.'

'Praise, God. Now, depart in peace, Jamie.'

'That's how I came.'

'It's a blessing, Jamie.'

'Thank you, Professor Pilgrim. It's been a fun meeting.'

Chapter 25

Weighty Matters for the Board

Nicholas Razer had raised his idea for Batman Board meetings with Sally Sloane, but she had politely told him to check it with Reg O'Toole. Her own view was that it wasn't such a good idea to serve a full dinner to the members prior to the meeting. It may have been a kind thought to busy members, she conceded, but it was unnecessary, expensive and, if alcohol were served with the meal, might well affect the tone and efficiency of proceedings. That, of course, was Razer's intention.

When he raised the idea with Reg O'Toole, he found his Chairman enthusiastic. Not only did Reg prefer an early dinner, he liked to wash it down with a stout. Razer clinched the deal and it was agreed that from now on, members would arrive an hour before the Board's starting time to enjoy a fine dinner served by Rajesh and his staff from Boy Wonder's. Their instructions were to keep members' glasses full throughout the meeting.

By way of making a small, silent protest at this innovation, Sally Sloane chose to arrive just in time for the meeting start. Reg saw her arrive as he shuffled his papers and waved her in.

'Sally missed the meal,' Reg said to Razer, miffed.

'A pity,' said Razer who cared not at all.

'Another stout, Mr O'Toole?' asked the head of Boy Wonder's.

'Thanks, Rastus.'

'Certainly, Mr O'Toole. Actually, it's Rajesh.'

'Eh?'

'My name, Sir, is Rajesh.'

'I was close, though!'

'Very close, Sir.'

'And, you'll do the bikkies and cheese when we're under way?'

'Yes, Mr O'Toole.'

'Top up for me, too, Rajesh.'

'Certainly, Professor Razer.'

'What's that you're drinking, Nick?' inquired O'Toole.

'It's a red from South Australia,' said Razer, swirling the wine in its glass. 'Very acceptable.'

'As a rule, I drink O'Toole,' smiled Reg.

'I didn't think you drank wine, Reg.'

Reg was annoyed that yet again he had to explain to Razer something all citizens of Robert Gordon understood.

'It's the O'Toole vineyard motto.'

'I think you'll find it's a strapline.'

'Eh?'

'Quite an agenda tonight, Reg,' Razer changed the topic. 'The usual plus, of course, a preview of next month's Open Day. That reminds me,' said Razer, lowering his voice and gesturing Motherwell to move closer, 'these are some more notes Jamie prepared about Open Day. All very self-explanatory. I'll get you to update the Board.'

Motherwell froze. He'd stumbled through speaking to the Board last meeting and hoped that would be the last time. Flustered, he opened the folder. With a sense of dread, he found one sheet of paper with several dot points in a sea of white space. It was headed 'Batman Open Day 2022 – The Evolution Continues: Fun, Funner, Funnest'.

Reg hurried the Board through the general business which, even though this was just his second meeting, already bored him.

He moved that the Board note the reports in the agenda papers and endorse all recommendation. The motion was carried with a show of hands. Reg was keen to hear about the impending Open Day, and especially his funded initiative in Red Studies and the Ministerial visit. He invited the Vice President to address the Board.

Barry Motherwell made his way through Jamie's notes, desperately hoping no one would interrupt with questions.

'I see from Jamie's list,' he droned on, 'we won't be overlooking Indigenous students on Open Day. The Board will know,' he lifted his eyes to his audience again and extemporised, 'there has been a pleasing growth of Indigenous student enrolments. There'll be a, ah, smoking ceremony at the main entrance to Village Place at the beginning of the Open Day and, ah, a, ah, range of cultural events throughout the, ah, the day. There'll be an Indigenous play, I see. Not sure how to pronounce it but to be performed, it says here, by our Indigenous theatre group.'

He paused to sip from a glass of water.

'And, ah, here's one Jamie has highlighted. A very special event, one that's the result of the, ah, generosity of our Chairman.'

Reg looked down at his papers and waved a hand in mock embarrassment.

'There'll be a marquee to showcase a new area of, ah, I suppose you'd call it cultural studies. It's the new discipline, that is, field or perhaps area, of Red Studies.'

'Red?' repeated Pieter Schiesser, 'Kein Weg! Unmöglich. Ich kann das nicht …'

'Hey, Pete, English, please,' Reg admonished the city planner.

'Apology, Chairman,' said Schiesser. But teaching Communist studies at Batman? I cannot accept zat after vot ve in za former East Chermany suffered viz za Red Army hammer to our heads and za sickle up our arses.'

'Chair, if I may,' intervened Sally Sloane, 'the area of Red Studies is an emerging one and it has nothing to do with communism. It's an area of study to do with red-headed people as a minority social group. It is very respectable, I can assure the Board of that.'

'If I may add my tuppence,' said Reg O'Toole, 'I had the same initial reaction as Dr Scheister ...'

'Schiesser.'

'Thank you. Pete. But Professor Sloane convinced me, a lifelong anti-communist, that Red Studies is Kosher.'

'So, it's Chewish Red Studies?' asked Schiesser, incredulously.

'Settle down, Pete,' O'Toole was becoming irritated, 'it's just a turn of phrase.'

Schiesser looked sceptical but held his peace.

'What's more,' O'Toole continued, 'I'm prepared, personally, to fund the appointment and a new Centre for Red Studies.'

'Vell, I haff to accept the decision in zat case, Chair. But, certainly, there muz be a better name zan Red Studies. My English is not good enough. Maybe anuzzer member can help?'

'What about "Auburn Studies",' suggested Betty Allsop. 'Auburn is a lovely word, very expressive and without other connotations. Best of all, it's hard to find words that rhyme with "auburn".'

'Rhyme?' said Sally Sloane, perplexed. 'I'm not quite sure I get your point.'

'Oh, you know what young people are like. We have to put up with it all the time at Dame Pattie. If we had Red Studies, it would soon be Dead Studies, Bed Studies, Head Studies, Fred Studies, Zed Studies. That sort of thing. But what can you do with "auburn"?'

Prudence Wills had her iPad on her lap, which she'd been surreptitiously using during the meeting.

'If you, like, give me a moment,' she said, 'I think I can help. Yes, here we are. According to the online rhyming dictionary, there's, like, only "corban" that rhymes with auburn. It says that's the chemical element of atomic number six. Whatever that may mean. Oh, and maybe bourbon. Doesn't really rhyme, I think. So, like, I think Mrs Allsop is correct.'

'Auburn's not quite what we had in mind,' said Sally Sloane.

'If you don't like "auburn",' said Betty Allsop, 'what about "sandy"? There's another nice word. And with pleasant connotations – beach, lazy summer days, warmth, family holidays.'

'But Betty,' offered Sally, 'it rhymes with bandy, brandy, candy, dandy, handy, just to name the few at the beginning of the alphabet.'

'And randy,' Razer whispered, straight-faced, to Roddy.

'Yes, I see your point,' conceded Betty Allsop, already running other possibilities through her mind.

Prudence Wills was still googling while Razer sat passively, feigning interest. The more time the village idiots ramble on, the happier I am, he thought.

'Hey, I've looked at the thesaurus. What about '"Tawny Studies"?' offered Prudence. 'Or, better still, I think this could be it, "Russet Studies".'

'I am not liking any of zose,' observed Schiesser. 'Srough you, Chair.'

'No, they're not really very good,' agreed Betty.

'There's also "Copper Studies",' offered Prudence.

'Can't see that working,' said Mario Tempeste, chuckling. 'Sounds like metal work or maybe police studies. Nah, not a goer.'

'Here's one that sounds rather academic,' offered Prudence. '"Rufous Studies". How about that? Says here it means reddish brown. That's close, isn't it?'

'It sounds very much like a Latin word, too,' enthused Betty. 'That seems appropriate for a university. I think it would pass the rhyming test, too.'

'Hold on,' said Prudence. 'I'll check that.'

Betty Allsop looked to Prudence Wills with a smile of expectation.

'No!' she declared. 'Nothing rhymes with "rufous" according to the rhyming dic.'

Betty Allsop's smile turned from anxious expectant to bashful triumphant, while Sally Sloane could barely disguise her obvious frustration.

'We've had some very intelligent discussion on this topic,' observed O'Toole. 'I thank the Board for their contributions. Professor of Rufous Studies is sounding good to me but I suppose Red Studies is still possible. Let's take a vote!'

Razer was wondering how this weighty issue of nomenclature might be resolved when Sally Sloane spoke.

'Chairman, you'll soon be meeting the person we hope to have in the role of head of the new area. Perhaps we could seek her advice and get back to the Board?'

'Good thinking, Sal. Let's agree then, I'll get back to the Board after I've met the lady herself. See what she says.'

'One more thing, Chair,' said Betty, 'can we know the name of the person for the Professor in Rufous Studies? Or whatever it may be.'

'If I may,' Sally interjected, 'discussions are at a delicate stage and any university would be pleased to have this person on their staff. What I will say is she'll join us on Open Day. There's to be a marquee for Red Studies. Or, of course, Rufous Studies, whichever is our final decision.'

'Think that's the last word on that,' Reg ruled. 'Now, Barry, we all want to hear about the parade. The Minister's still locked in?'

'I can confirm that, Chair. He'll inspect the parade and it would be normal for you to accompany him on his inspection. I hope you'll agree to that.'

'I certainly do, Barry.'

'And, Barry, you must tell the Board about the dog squad,' intervened Razer.

'Thank you, President,' said Motherwell, turning to a topic with which he was more comfortable. 'That's another innovation at Batman which will add to the spectacle on Open Day. Board members will all know Kevin Burke, the Head of Campus Security. Kevin's ex-Army, and he and I have retired Army dogs, three between us, but only two are fit for service. We've been retraining them to support the regiment. They are older dogs but were well trained and have overseas combat experience.'

'That is vonderful, Professor Muzzervell,' said Pieter Schiesser. 'Through you, Chair. Zey are Cherman Shepherds, of course.'

'Actually, Belgian Shepherds,' Motherwell said.

'Ach, I sink you vill find zey are Cherman,' he declared.

'Malinoise, actually.'

'Cherman, actually.'

'I'll check on that, Dr Schiesser.'

'Sank you. You haff my contact details?'

'Of course. Ah, we will be putting on a display of their combat, detection and surveillance exercises right before the parade. We believe it'll be a real crowd pleaser.'

'Vun uzzer sing, Chair, if I may,' Pieter Schiesser returned to his theme.

'Go on, Dr, ah ...' said O'Toole.

'Schiesser ... If za Minister is coming on za campus, it vill be necessary to do a lot of cleaning up.'

'Cleaning up?'

'Ja. Cleaning up. If zere are plenty of za public here on Open Day, za Village Place vill be very messy. Ve must haff extra cleaning staff before za people come and all during za day. Going around everyvere, picking up, sveeping, zat sort of sing. But not wiz za noisy blowing machines.'

'Thank you for the suggestion, Dr Schiesser ...' began Razer.

'But, it's not all.'

'It's not?'

'No, za trees along za drivevay from za road.'

'The eucalypts?' said O'Toole. 'What about them?'

'Zey represent danger to za public. And, of course, to za Minister.'

'Zey do? I mean, they do?'

'Ja, as Director of Planning, I haff recommended to za Board of za Outer Eastern Development Ausority, a program in za region for za eradication of gum trees. Excuse me, I can't say za uzzer vord.'

'Eucalypt?' said O'Toole.

'Ja, dat vun. Za Board gave me permission to say gum tree ven talking but ven writing, I must say za uzzer name.'

'Eucalypt.'

'Ja. Za gum trees, zey keep dropping branches to damage za cars. Or efen people. It is my solution.' Schiesser crossed his thin arms across his narrow chest and looked for approbation from the Board.

'Yeah,' offered Mario Tempeste, 'the Robert Gordon Council have seen Pieter's report and we're considering it. Makes a lotta sense.'

'A lot of sense? I can't believe what I'm hearing,' said Betty Allsop. 'You're planning for the removal of all the eucalypts in the region? Am I hearing right?'

'No, not all of zem. Only za vuns along motor vays. Vere za cars go. And, of course, around houses, vere za people are liffing. Za rest, zey stay concentrated in special protection zones.'

Exasperated by the trivial discussion, Sally Sloane brought the time to the attention of the Chairman.

'Thank you, Sally. Time to draw stumps, ladies and gents. Thank you for your attendance. See you for the August meeting and we'll do a post mortem on our Open Day.'

'Oh, Chair,' giggled Betty Alsop, 'here's hoping there's no need for a post-mortem!'

'Over my dead body, Bets!' joked Reg.

Chapter 26

A Day in the Country

Motherwell arrived early at Boy Wonder's and ordered a coffee, which he took to a table ideally placed to allow a private conversation without appearing to be conducting a secret meeting. He'd invited Lexi to have a coffee with him on the pretext that their earlier meeting had ended prematurely. He brought a file of papers which he placed conspicuously on the table. He feigned preoccupation with one of his files, looking up with a business-like expression as Lexi announced her arrival.

'Morning, Vice President,' she offered as she sat down opposite.

'Hi.' Motherwell looked up, trying to portray formality. 'Just wanted to catch up on a few international matters. Though we might as well have a coffee at the same time. What can I get you?'

'I'm good, thanks.'

'About Open Day, how are plans going for the North Koreans?'

'Excellent. Mr Kim is very enthusiastic and has appointed one of the senior students, Kang, to organise it all.'

'The consul's coming?'

'Yep. All fixed. He's bringing a couple of staff and wants it all to be low key.'

'That's a relief.'

Lexi thought Motherwell looked uncomfortable, as though he'd decided meeting in public hadn't been such a good idea.

'You OK, Mother?' she inquired, troubled at the discomfort he appeared to be enduring.

'I was wondering if you and Vine would like to see my farm. I realise it may not be your thing …'

Ah, that's it, she thought. Poor Barry.

'I'm a city gal through and through, Mother. All that open space and fresh air makes me anxious.'

Motherwell looked crestfallen.

'Am I to understand that this is an invitation to your country estate?' she asked coyly.

'That's the general idea.' Motherwell was starting to regret raising the topic.

'And I have to bring Vine?'

'I just thought …'

'Just kidding,' she laughed, and Motherwell was immediately relieved. 'Of course, we'd love to come. Do you happen to have horses?'

'Afraid not. But I have a neighbour with horses. You even know her.'

'I do?'

'Miranda Callahan.'

'The Head of Equine Studies?'

'That's her. I'm sure she'd be happy to take Vine for a ride.'

Lexi smiled, pleased at the prospect of satisfying one of her daughter's loves.

'When did you have in mind?'

'How about this Sunday?' Motherwell ventured hopefully.

'We could do that.'

'Come for lunch. I'll barbecue some steaks.'

'Oh, oh. Problem. You probably don't know that Vine is a vegetarian. It goes with the gender and the age. Like horse riding.'

'There'll be lots of salad. And spuds.'

'Super! I'll bring wine.'

Motherwell returned her smile and inwardly sighed with relief. It had been a long time since he had invited a woman to do anything. He felt rather pleased with himself.

'Now, we really do need to do some business,' said Motherwell as he checked out the other patrons and turned to some files he'd brought.

'I believe that's why I'm here, Vice President,' she said, with a dutiful smile.

'I've had a look at your strategic plan. You want to go to North Korea?'

'I've gotta maintain those links, especially now as they loosen up travel for students and consider alternative destinations.'

'We're ahead of the field, aren't we?'

'We are. But what I didn't reveal in my plan, Mother,' Lexi checked the neighbouring tables and lowered her voice, 'is my idea for Batman to establish a campus in Pyongyang. We'd be the first Western university in the world to do it.'

'That would please Nicholas. The first Australian university President to make an official visit to North Korea. He'd be over the moon. He's got a strong interest in matters Asian.'

'So I hear,' said Lexi, with a serious expression. 'What's that all about, Mother? Razer and Asia?'

'No idea,' he said, deadpan.

Lexi decided against pushing the topic. Maybe he hasn't heard the campus gossip, she wondered.

ooOOoo

Vine Dunne displayed little interest in spending a Sunday visiting a farm and it wasn't until her mother told her of the plan for her to ride a horse that her reluctance showed signs of abating. Even so, she annoyed her mother with complaints and questions.

'How far is it?' she moaned 'And who's this farmer, anyway?'

'He's my boss, honey. Barry Motherwell. You've met him at our house when he's been to dinner a few times.'

'Which one was he?'

'He's a bit chubby, tanned, good head of hair, going a bit grey. He doesn't say much, softly spoken, more of a listener.'

'The one who doesn't smile much?'

Lexi sighed, saddened that her daughter couldn't see the real Barry Motherwell.

About mid-morning on Sunday, they strapped themselves into their seat belts in Lexi's tiny car and headed for the freeway. In order to keep the peace, Lexi allowed her daughter to use her headset to listen to her music while she kept her head down on her iPad to remain in constant contact with her school friends.

Barry Motherwell was waiting for them in his car at the turnoff that heralded the end of the bitumen road and the commencement of the long, unmade track to his property. With a wave from his car, he led them along the four kilometres of dusty track to the farm gates. Lexi kept a safe distance behind hoping, in vain, to avoid a film of dust over her car. She followed along the gravel drive to the entrance to the house and gasped. Her idea of a farm house was a tumbling down, shabby shack. Instead, she beheld a bold architectural statement surrounded by a neat lawn and carefully tended gardens.

'Welcome,' said Barry Motherwell approaching Lexi and Vine as they exited their car. 'Hello, Vine. I'm glad you could make it.'

Vine smiled hello as she slipped an arm through her mother's. Lexi stepped forward, extending her hand, which Motherwell shook.

'Thanks for inviting us, Barry. Look at this place! It's magnificent,' remarked Lexi, genuinely impressed.

'Come and I'll make us a cup of bushman's tea, then show you around.'

'Come on Vine,' she said cheerily as she took her daughter's hand.

As they sat around Motherwell's kitchen table with their tea and some packet biscuits, there was a knock at the door and a trim, middle-aged woman dressed for riding entered.

'I see your guests beat me here. Hallo, Lexi. And you,' she said smiling 'must be Vine. Pleased to meet you. I'm Miranda.'

'Hello,' Vine replied shyly.

'I understand you're interested in horses. If you'd like a ride now, I've got a perfect horse for you. If you're ready, I've got a helmet that should fit you.'

Vine looked to her mother who nodded her approval and with that, she excitedly followed Miranda out of the door.

'See you in about three hours,' Miranda called over her shoulder, and Vine gave her mother an excited wave.

'Do you mind if I have a look around?' asked Lexi.

'Come with me,' said Motherwell.

They stood and Lexi walked from the kitchen to the large living room.

'Mother, this is superb. The house has a cosiness and there's stylish decor. It's wonderful. I thought you said you had no interest in the finer things.'

'You're talking about my office?'

'Funnily enough, it crossed my mind.'

'Maureen designed the house and everything in it. And all the landscaping. The whole place is a monument to her, really.'

'You must miss her, and everything here must remind you of her.'

'True.'

'Are you sure you feel comfortable having me here?'

'Very sure. Let's have a tour, then I'll fire up the barbecue.'

Lexi followed Motherwell to the rear door, from which there was a commanding view of the property with gentle hills in the distance and neat lawns surrounding freshly painted sheds in the foreground. Behind a high wire fence, Lexi spotted two large dogs that stood rigidly, ears pricked with their alert eyes fixed on Motherwell and the stranger, tails wagging slowly.

'Sit!' instructed Motherwell as he raised and sharply dropped his hand. The two dogs obeyed, their eyes never leaving him. Motherwell unlocked their gate and the dogs, trembling with excitement, remained sitting.

'Here!' He instructed, pointing at his feet and with that, they bounded toward him and sat at his feet looking from him to Lexi who flinched as the dogs vied with each other to sniff at her.

'Stop!' Motherwell instructed, holding up his hand. 'Sorry about that. They're just getting to know you,' Motherwell said as he pushed their heads away.

'They're Belgian Shepherds, so-called Malinois. Army uses them and Kevin Burke has one, too, which will also be working on Open Day.'

'What's so good about the Belgians?'

'They're super intelligent and they like to dominate. Very protective of their handlers. Ideal for military and police work. I adopted them when they were retired by Army.'

Lexi admired these two large canines but couldn't help feeling nervous.

'Mena's trained in assault.'

'By the way,' Lexi joked, 'I don't want to be assaulted today,'

'On instruction, she'll disable a person. Even if they're armed.'

'You mean like when they chase and bring down some guy in a protective suit? Like in the movies?'

'Exactly. But, in Afghanistan, the bad guys had no protective suits, just weapons. So, Mena had to be ready to attack despite the risk of being shot or blown up. She won several combat awards.'

'I'm in the presence of a hero?'

'You could say that.'

'Why has she got an eye closed up?' asked Lexi, while the dog's other eye fixed on her with an intensity that suggested deadly force.

'She was bringing down a Jihadist and he managed to stab her in the eye,' he said, patting the dog.

'That's awful. Poor Mena,' she said still with her hands behind her back. 'I guess it cured her of attacking.'

'Army told me it only made her more ferocious. That's when they changed her name. She used to be Nina.' Motherwell always enjoyed relating the story, 'Now she's Mena.'

Lexi looked confused.

'Mena,' Motherwell repeated, 'as in "meaner than a junk yard dog".'

'I see,' Lexi said, wanting to take a step back but afraid to move.

'And she ensured that Jihadist would never use a knife again.'

'She's a trained killer? Damn it, Mother, now I'm not feeling safe.'

Lexi flinched and, as if on cue, Mena sniffed at her crotch.

'They decided to retire her just in case …'

Lexi's body froze while her eyes widened.

'Mena! Down,' Motherwell instructed, sharply pointing down and both dogs prostrated themselves. 'See how I have complete voice control?' Motherwell said, desperate to demonstrate that his guest should have no fears for her safety.

'So, why gesticulate wildly when you give a command?'

'Oh, that. Mena was exposed to a lot of explosions in Afghanistan and she's as deaf as a post. I say voice control but I mean voice and gesture control. Not sure whether she's learned the signals or just copies Herbie.'

'Not what's usually understood by the term voice control,' Lexi giggled nervously.

'It seems to work,' Motherwell said.

'Who's Mena's buddy?' inquired Lexi, still conscious of the two dogs at her feet, mouths agape exposing rows of large teeth.

'Herbie. His speciality is explosives detection and he saved soldiers' lives in Afghanistan. He's showing his age these days,' Motherwell said, bending down to pat Herbie's head.

'On Open Day you'll be able to see Mena do her stuff. We plan to showcase her skills as part of the parade. Kevin Burke and I are preparing Mena and his dog Micha for the performance. Micha is another assault dog.'

'And what will Herbie do on Open Day?'

'He's a little old now and performance might be a bit much for him.' Motherwell slapped his thigh and commanded 'stand' and both dogs leapt up, tails wagging. Lexi noticed that the dogs' heads were as big as her own and disconcertingly near her chest.

'OK, let's go,' commanded Motherwell and turned to walk. 'Heel!' he pointed down and behind.

'Just walk on the other side of me and ignore them,' he instructed Lexi. 'And don't make any sudden moves. Mena could mistake your intentions.'

Lexi Dunne needed no counsel on that. A little way off, she could see a number of cattle grazing in a fenced off paddock.

'Are they your hobby, Mother?'

'More my retirement. I have a breeding program underway which I hope will provide me with a comfortable and fulfilling retirement.'

Lexi allowed herself for the first time to take in the expanse of Motherwell's property.

'Geez, cowboy, this is quite a ranch.'

'I'm no cowboy but I'm glad you like it.'

'It's very pretty countryside.'

Barry Motherwell draped his arm around Lexi's shoulders as if to orient her and pointed out the boundaries of his property. Mena emitted a low growl.

'Shaddup, Mena!' ordered Motherwell raising his hand as though to slap her.

'My protector,' smiled Lexi, as she slipped her arm through Motherwell's.

ooOOoo

Both Lexi and Vine left Motherwell's farm with some regret. Vine had throughly enjoyed her riding tutorial with Miranda and found the older woman easy company. Missing Barry's barbecue was not a disappointment and Miranda had brought sandwiches for them.

For her part, Lexi Dunne felt even closer to Barry Motherwell. Despite his reputation on campus as Razer's surly enforcer, she found him gentle, and even shy. She could identify with his sense of loss, and she saw more clearly than ever his vulnerabilities. The sun was close to setting as mother and daughter left Motherwell's property, each with a sense of a day well spent. They drove for some time in silence. Vine was already searching on her iPad for the local riding school that Miranda had mentioned.

'Mum,' said Vine without looking up from her iPad, 'I thought you said Barry was your boss.'

'I did. Why?'

'So, why were you cuddling him?'

'Cuddling him?'

'Yeah, Miranda and I were resting the horses on the hill. We saw you cuddling down at the creek.'

'Oh, I just felt sorry for him. His wife died and he's very sad.'

Chapter 27

The Prickly Ex-Dean

Barry Motherwell arrived early at his office the next day, still allowing himself to recall the moments of pleasure he'd enjoyed with Lexi Dunne at his farm. His plan for Vine to accompany Miranda for horse riding had worked very well, even better than he'd hoped. He'd been wondering how long he should wait before inviting them again. He was deep in this reverie when his mobile phone broke the silence. It was an unidentified number.

'Motherwell,' he said formally.

'It's me,' Lexi said, slightly thrown by his tone.

'Sorry, I didn't recognise the number.'

"I'm calling from home. Are you alone?'

'Everything alright?' Motherwell was slightly thrown by a call from Lexi so early in the day.

'Yeah, sure. I wanted to call you now to thank you for a wonderful day yesterday.'

He sighed silently.

'I'm glad you enjoyed it. I think Vine did, too.'

'You can shout that from the roof tops. She's already planning to enrol in your local riding school. I'm afraid we might be in your neighbourhood more often some time soon.'

'I'm pleased to hear it.'

'Miranda gave Vine a great time. I must see if I can take her for coffee next time she's in from the Equine Centre.'

'She's a special person.'

'Mother, I think I have to tell you that she and Vine saw us at the creek.' Lexi tensed, waiting for Motherwell to vent his annoyance.

'There really wasn't much to see, was there?'

'I think I passed it off alright. But I wonder if Miranda …'

'No problem there,' Motherwell asserted.

'Do you mean to say,' said Lexi mock accusingly, 'you arranged for her to take Vine away all that time?'

'You could say that.'

'Mother, you are a man of mystery!'

'I like to think so.'

'Anyway, I want you to know I'm glad you did. It was a wonderful day. I think I said that already.'

'I believe you did. Can't hear it too often.'

'My hero,' she mock-sighed.

Pleased with Lexi's praise, Motherwell changed the topic.

'Since we're talking, have you seen much of Clive lately?'

'He hasn't been in the office at all and there's a pile of Batman Open Day stuff cluttering up our reception area. I called him on Friday to see that he's OK.'

'And is he?' asked Motherwell, indifferently.

'Funny. He sounded decidedly odd. I asked if he'd like to have a coffee next time he was in the office.'

'And?'

'He just said he didn't know when that might be. He was too busy reaching out and engaging for universities.'

'He said "universities". Plural?'

'I think so. He's very stressed. Be gentle with him. I'm worried about his mental stability and don't think he should be pushed too hard.'

'Maybe not,' replied Motherwell, Razer's ultimatum forcing itself into his mind.

'I knew you'd understand,' said Lexi gratefully. 'Got to get Vine off to school now. Bye.'

Not for the first time, Barry Motherwell felt conflicted. Should he follow Lexi's advice and handle Goodenough gently? Nicholas Razer's instruction was clear. But what did he want? Should he call Goodenough in and give him a dressing down? Should he give him a warning? Was he supposed to sack him? Motherwell knew the perils of making precipitous management decisions. A careless handling of Goodenough could have calamitous implications for his own career. And he perfectly understood that any repercussions from a poor decision would rebound on him, not on Nicholas Razer.

He went to his office window and looked down on the Village Place. There, far below, young men and women lazed around in the summer sunshine on the grassy mounds, chatted and drank coffees, played music, read, talked. At this moment he envied them.

He gathered up his meeting papers, left his office and made his way along the corridor to the President's suite for the Monday morning executive team meeting.

'Morning Barry, good weekend?' inquired Roger Priestly.

He's picking up Razer's line, thought Motherwell. Why would he do that?

'Just a quiet weekend on the farm. The usual.'

'Lucky you. I had the pleasure of spending the whole weekend working on budget planning for Nicholas.'

'You've been here a while,' said Motherwell, 'how well do you know Clive Goodenough?'

'Not very well at all, really. A very mediocre Dean and rather a tedious person. And very brittle kind of personality. Why d'you ask?'

'He's a difficult person to understand,' Motherwell admitted. 'And manage.'

'I wouldn't feed him, frankly. Nicholas wants rid of him.'

Motherwell winced silently.

After Nicholas had led off with the customary gossip and frivolous chit-chat, the executive team meeting ranged over the usual matters concerning the university. It was obvious to them all, though they never confessed it to each other that, by and large, Razer had little interest in Batman University. Occasionally, he would indulge himself with an acerbic attack on one or other troublesome professor or student. Having endorsed his attacks and all his views, the members would depart feeling their time would have been better spent attending to their various responsibilities.

Motherwell waited till the other members had left the brief meeting.

'Nicholas, a quick word about Clive Goodenough?'

'Have you administered the coup de grâce yet?' he addressed Motherwell icily.

'I've been thinking about how best to handle him. And ...'

'He's a Judas in our midst,' Razer declared, glaring at Motherwell.

'That's true. But I ran into Lexi Dunne ...'

'More likely slipped into her, eh, Bazza?' said Razer, suddenly switching to one of his other personas.

'... and as you know,' Motherwell went on discomfited, 'she shares the cottage with him. She's a bit emotional about his mental health.'

'Emotion is a waste of time,' said Razer, waving with a dismissive gesture.

'It's just that he's been absent from the office a lot and is acting a bit strangely. Handling him could be a bit tricky.'

'I'll leave the management of Professor Goodenough to you and your personal HR advisor, Barry.' Razer bared teeth with his signature sudden-fade smile.

'Maybe we could give him a little more time,' suggested Motherwell. 'See how Open Day goes for him?'

'Your decision, old chap. I hope it works out for you both.'

Both? What did that mean, Motherwell pondered as he walked down the corridor and into his office. He was still struggling with this when Mez buzzed him.

'Barry, call for you. It's Karisma from the Minister for Homeland Defence's office.'

'Put her through.'

'Barry, it's Karisma. I'll come straight to the point. I need to tell you there's a change for your Open Day on Sunday.'

'A change?'

'I'm calling from the Western Hospital. The Minister's been injured.'

'Hope it's not serious.'

'We were at Western Metro Uni this morning where he was to give a speech promoting the university regiment program.'

'I've heard the students there are pretty solidly opposed to it.'

'That's the problem. They were blocking the main entrance to the campus and our driver was directed to an alternative. But they had that covered, too. We got past them with some help from campus security and made it to the entrance to the lecture theatre. Campus security then cleared a path for him to get into the theatre. He told me to stay in the car but I saw what happened.'

'What?'

'It was horrific, believe me. Security couldn't hold them back and they began to jostle him and were yelling at him all the time.' Her voice trembled. 'He just kept going and got to the first step up to the lecture theatre. I didn't see what happened next but suddenly, the mob dispersed in all directions and I saw him sprawled face down on the steps.'

'Good God!'

'He's a big strong man and used to being in hostile crowds. He fell heavily and he's badly damaged his elbow and has other abrasions. His face is badly bruised. We're at emergency at Western General now. He's had X-rays and scans and it's pretty serious. A Mason III fracture of the elbow, they say.'

Motherwell and Kevin Burke had based all their planning on having the Minister inspect the parade. Now he'd have to rethink it all.

'That's very disappointing,' he said, 'and I can understand he won't be able to get here on Sunday.'

'That's why I'm calling. He instructed me to tell you he won't be intimated by thugs. He intends to be at your Open Day.'

'That's great news.' Motherwell was genuinely relieved.

'There's a couple of matters, though. He's got a cast on his right arm. Wrist to bicep. And he's right-handed.'

'No returning salute, then.'

'Excuse me?'

'Sorry, just a silly attempt at humour.'

'Oh, I get it. No, no saluting. And he won't be able to accept the President's invitation for lunch prior to the parade. His media advisors think it would be infra dig if he was seen having someone cutting up his food. Bad look in the press and on TV news. But he wants plenty of coverage of himself, arm in a cast, doing his job regardless of pain and any possible student action.'

'I understand. But will he still be able to inspect the parade?'

'He's determined to keep the commitment.'

'I doubt Batman students are going to cause any problems.'

'Nonetheless, we're not taking any chances. We'll arrange some extra security on the day. Our security people will coordinate with yours.'

'When you say extra security, what kind of security?'

'The usual. Plus snipers.'

'Snipers! Jesus! Snipers on campus?' exclaimed Motherwell.

'Sorry, just a silly attempt at humour.'

oooOooo

Motherwell's thoughts raced as he called Razer's number.

'Barry,' answered Razer, 'good timing. Just off to lunch. It's Monday smorgasbord at the Auld Scotland. Doesn't get much better than that to start the working week.'

Motherwell knew well what that routine was. Razer would have his inner circle with him. A couple of beers to start, a dozen oysters as entree and then the special of the day, fried flake and tubs of potato chips for the table, washed down with heavy reds. And then the cleansing ales before returning mid-afternoon to deal with the issues confronting higher education in general and Batman in particular. All on the university entertainment fund, too.

Motherwell was at a loss to understand why he seemed no longer to be a member of that inner circle.

'Nicholas, I've had word that the Minister has been injured in some sort of fracas at Western Met.'

'Roddy was just telling us it's on the morning news. Nasty business. It's why I take precautions, Barry. You can never trust students. It's bad enough we've got those idiots in BUSS without the black radicals in BUICK.'

'His office has told me even though he's injured, he's still going to be coming for Open Day on Sunday.'

'Oh?' Razer sounded deflated. 'I'm going to have to host the Ministerial lunch after all,' said Razer.

'No, he won't be doing the lunch.'

'That's a relief. What sort of sensible discussion can you have with a Minister for Homeland Defence? Too late to cancel the lunch so I'll have it with the executive team. Sorry you can't join us, Barry, but you have your military duties to attend to.'

'Roddy,' Motherwell heard Razer say, 'pop out and tell Jenny to let Reg know he won't have to worry about lunch with the Minister. We wouldn't want to waste Reg's time.' Razer smiled with feigned disappointment.

'Anyway, Barry,' Razer went on, 'I'm glad I can watch the parade from the distance of the dais. I'm looking forward to seeing you and Kevin do your doggy tricks.'

Motherwell pictured Razer's inner circle smirking and winking to each other.

Chapter 28

The Arrival of the Red

On Razer's instructions, Kurt Kropp had done his best to arrange for Jacky Collis Harvey to visit Batman at her earliest convenience. He'd tried to persuade her to come before the onset of the Melbourne winter when the city and the campus, vulnerable to icy blasts, could look rather bleak. He knew he not only had to sell her on the role at Batman, and the attractions of the campus and the university, but also on the city and its environs. He called it place marketing. However, he worried that the lure he had held out to Harvey of visiting the world's most liveable city at that time of year might lead her to conclude she'd been a victim of misleading advertising.

Harvey's hectic schedule, however, would keep her occupied until the end of the northern hemisphere academic year. It was agreed she would visit in late July and specifically to attend the Batman Open Day, a suggestion from Kropp to which she readily agreed.

It was agreed that Kropp himself would meet their visitor at the airport and convey her to her hotel in the city. Next morning, there would be a preliminary meeting with Kurt Kropp at his city office where he would explain the program for the visit and address any inquiries she might have. This meeting would then be followed by a get-to-know-you lunch with Nicholas Razer and Reg O'Toole at their club, a short walk from Kropp's office. Kropp would plan a path that took Harvey past busy arcades, cafes thronging with city workers and chic fashion stores.

Razer had been concerned about Kropp's suggestion that their first meeting with Harvey should be at his club. He'd had many encounters with high-flying British women and his intuition was that the club could be the wrong environment for their meeting. While it boasted old world charm and fine dining, this could be a risky step if Harvey, like many of the senior professional women he knew, was a hard-line feminist. The club permitted female guests but not female members.

'She could be another humourless, vegetarian feminist,' he told Kropp.

Kropp gave Razer some comfort on this issue. In his discussions with Harvey, he'd become convinced that she was unlikely to be troubled by the club's antediluvian policies. She was in fact very worldly and, while being an unapologetic feminist, she was neither vegetarian nor humourless.

Kropp's suggestion that Sally Sloane should join them for a working lunch at the club was another master-stroke by the crafty search consultant. He gambled that the two women would relate well and the presence of the Deputy Chairman of the Board, herself an impressive and confident woman, would strike the right note. Kropp was confident that Sally Sloane would set aside her own loathing of the traditional club in the interests of the university.

Kurt Kropp waited with great anticipation at the international arrivals area. He was confident he'd recognise Harvey and she was one of the first to emerge through the sliding doors. She looked remarkably fresh after such a long flight and, having spotted her name on the iPad held by Megan Egan, strode smiling toward Kropp. The wily search consultant took her hand with both of his and was momentarily stunned by her natural beauty. Her handshake was warm and firm and Kropp's welcome was characteristically faux mannerly.

'Jacky, welcome. I hope you won't mind a touch of Australian familiarity.' He smiled. 'It's very good to meet you at last.'

'It's good to be here, Kurt. It's been no time since we first spoke and here I am. A brief stay but I'm used to making the most of brief encounters.'

Kropp hoped that was the case.

'The limo is just outside. Megan, just take Ms Harvey's suitcase, if you would. We'll take you to your hotel and let you have the afternoon to rest. I'll collect you tomorrow morning and we can go to my office nearby and have a coffee and chat.'

'Super. Lead on.'

ooOOoo

Next morning, Kurt Kropp met Harvey in the reception area of her hotel and walked her to his office on a brisk but sunny morning. He ordered a pot of coffee as they passed by his EA and he opened his office door to allow Harvey to enter his grand office.

'Kurt, it's huge,' she said. 'Do you play indoor tennis here?'

'Perhaps it's more than I actually need but it's a matter of impression management.'

'You've managed to impress me,' she said as she went to the full-length glass wall where she stood taking in the commanding view of the bay. Kropp exhaled silently as he admired her shapely silhouetted figure. Easy to see why she was a life model, he thought to himself. Harvey moved to one of the armchairs while Kropp poured their coffees.

'Tell me about the President and the fellow who gave money for Red Studies. What are they looking for?'

'Nicholas Razer, the President, is fairly new to the job. UK academic, a Scot by birth but very much the high-flying British academic. Very capable man, good academic standing, you know the type.'

'I do know the type.'

Kropp let the observation pass without comment.

'Nicholas is working towards international standing for Batman and believes you'd add to that.'

'That reminds me,' Harvey said 'this fellow Batman. He was a villainous figure, wasn't he? I mean, his dealings with the Aborigines were scandalous.'

'We're learning more about him these days,' Kropp explained, hoping Batman's emerging reputation would not be a deal breaker. 'His name's to be found throughout the city and, until a little while ago, a statue in his honour was on this street not far from here. Ironically, it's now on the Batman campus.'

'Isn't it rather curious to have a university named after him?'

Kropp knew Harvey was straying into dangerous territory.

'The problem is, you see,' he said apprehensively, 'the benefactor, Reg O'Toole, is a bit of a fan of John Batman. So, if you don't mind …'

'I understand.'

That's one hurdle leapt, thought Kropp with relief.

'Reg O'Toole is a fairly new Chairman of the Board. Nice guy, bit of a rough diamond, a self-made man, very rich. So rich, in fact, that he can fund the Professor in Red Studies from his small change.'

'You've never mentioned the quantum, but I assume it's substantial.'

'North of five million.' Kropp raised his eyebrows as though he was hearing this for the first time himself.

'Phew!' Harvey shared his sentiment. 'Did he come by his wealth honestly?'

'Please don't ask him!' said Kropp, only half joking.

'I'm not against men with wealth,' she assured him, 'particularly if they put it to good use. And especially,' she laughed, 'if it's my good use!'

Kropp was becoming increasingly confident that Harvey would strike the right note with Reg.

'You'll meet Reg at lunch today. A bit of a man's man. Surprisingly unworldly, in some ways. He speaks with a gravelly, working man's voice and a strong Australian accent.'

'What do they want to hear from me?'

She understands the game, Kropp thought. Good start.

'Nicholas will want a sense of what you'd do in the role. Sorry to introduce the V word but it wouldn't hurt if you said something about your vision for Red Studies at Batman.'

'That's easy,' Harvey declared. 'I've been waiting for an academic opportunity like this.'

'And could you mention the phrase "make a difference"? A couple of times?'

'If you say I should.' Harvey smiled, and Kropp was increasingly confident about her ability to deliver.

'And Mr O'Toole, what will he want to hear?'

'Nothing much, I suspect. He'll just want to be sure he likes you,' Kropp predicted. And I'm pretty sure he'll like what he sees, thought Kropp.

Kropp continued to tutor Harvey until he noticed it was time for them to leave for lunch at the Club.

oooOooo

Razer, O'Toole and Sally were already seated when Kurt Kropp ushered Jacky Harvey towards their table. All three rose to be introduced in order of rank. Reg O'Toole appeared to be dumbstruck and hardly able to look up at this strikingly attractive woman.

'Mrs Harvey,' was all he could manage as he fleetingly took her extended hand.

'Jacky, the President of Batman, Professor Nicholas Razer,' said Kropp.

'Welcome, Ms Harvey,' said Razer, warmly deploying his considerable charm.

'And the Board's Deputy Chair, Professor Sally Sloane.'

'Hello, Jacky,' smiled Sally easily, 'good to meet you. So glad you can make it to our Open Day this weekend.'

'I understand I'm to be on duty at a Red Studies marquee. That'll be a first for me.'

'Please have a seat.' Razer gestured to a seat beside himself and opposite Reg O'Toole. Razer prided himself in being able to sum up any person within the first five minutes of meeting. He was immediately impressed, even dazzled, by Harvey's vivaciousness. He knew instantly she would add great lustre to Batman, and that it would be a coup for him if she were appointed.

Harvey proved to be a comfortable and animated lunch companion. Kropp watched and was impressed as, at times, she led the conversation and, at others, deferred to Razer and thoughtfully answered questions and offered opinions. Reg seemed to melt whenever she turned her beguiling attention to him, which she did frequently. It was obvious that she established an instant rapport with Sally Sloane.

Kropp grew increasingly confident that his find, Jacky Collis Harvey, was the woman Batman needed for the O'Toole professorship. Her intellect was sharp, her style relaxed. His only concern, however, was the fact that Reg had barely spoken. While he appeared to hang on her every utterance, perhaps, Kropp worried, he didn't see her as a suitable appointment. When, as the lunch drew to a close, she asked if he had any questions, Reg paused as though lost for words, and then cleared his throat nervously.

'One important question, Mrs Harvey,' he said, looking at Harvey earnestly.

Harvey leaned forward and smiled a smile that Reg felt engulfed him.

'In your own personal opinion, is "Red Studies" the best name for us to use? The Board had been considering other names. Just wondering what you, yourself, think.'

'I can't think of a better name, Mr O'Toole,' Harvey declared confidently. 'After all "Red" is the title of my book. By the way,' she continued, reaching into her satchel, 'I've brought you a signed copy.'

Reg blushed as he accepted the gift, and opened it to take in Harvey's warm, personal message to him. Razer and Sally were certain Harvey would be an ideal academic appointment for Batman and Reg seemed completely won over by her personality and looks. But there was a detail Razer wanted to pursue.

'One final thing from me, if I may,' he ventured with a certain solemnity.

Harvey smiled at him with guarded curiosity.

'If we were able to offer you a professorship, when do you think …'

'If?' Reg interjected, suddenly assertive, fixing his eyes on Razer, 'There's no bloody if about it, Nick. It's my money and I want Mrs Harvey in the job. End of story. And the Board can forget any other name. It's the O'Toole Professor in Red Studies.'

'Well, that's settled then,' Razer declared, both surprised and relieved. 'I'll look forward to seeing you on Sunday at our Open Day, Jacky.'

The Last Marquee

Jamie had become increasingly edgy as Open Day approached. He'd tried to nail down every detail to ensure Batman's funnest Open Day, but he knew that things always go awry when you least expect it. The Open Day committee was at its last meeting before the big day and had dealt with preliminaries when Jamie turned the meeting's attention to Jamie's Fun Checklist. He had to satisfy himself that no stone had been left unturned.

'OK, boys and girls, let's do one last check. Yeah?' began Jamie.

'Jamie, I really object to you addressing us as boys and girls,' Marilyn Worthy protested.

'Just some fun, Marilyn. I always think the best committees are those that get the job done but also have fun.'

'Can we just get the job done,' she pleaded, 'and not worry about the fun?'

Jamie was tiring of academics questioning his style, so he decided not to respond to Dr Worthy, who was starting to annoy him.

'Open Day is just forty-eight hours away. Any outstanding issues? Any problems? No? That's what I was hoping. Now in breaking news, we have some exciting last-minute events to add to the program.'

'The Vice President …'

'Th-that th-thug.'

'… has advised me, and I'm very excited to announce, that the newly arrived Consul for North Korea will be a special visitor on campus for Open Day.'

'That's big news?'

'It certainly is, Kon. He'll host a North Korean film in the cinema. And our very own Dean for International, Professor Lexi Dunne, will deliver an introductory talk about the movie. At the end, there'll be a Q and A which she'll also host.'

'Sensational news,' said Arso with undisguised sarcasm. 'International news, even! Big media presence, Jamie?'

'No need for sarcasm, Arso. And, as a kind of brilliant curtain raiser to the movie, the North Korean lady students are going to perform fan dances in traditional North Korean costume. Kellie, you checked with the techs, yeah?'

'I have, indeed,' said Jamie's deputy dutifully. 'The public address system will set up for the dance music and will later be used for the parade and the speeches.'

'Gomapseumnida, Kellie. That's North Korean for thank you. Now, according to my spreadsheet,' Jamie went on, 'all disciplines have in hand arrangements for staffing on the day. Yeah? They all have plenty of brochures and registration of interest forms, Kellie? And, of course, sufficient provisional enrolment forms.'

'Yes, I can confirm that, Jamie,' replied his assistant perkily.

'Merci beaucoup, Kellie.'

'The marquee for the entrance to Village Place is organised?' he asked.

'Yes, Jamie,' smiled Kellie, 'it will be set up tomorrow afternoon. There'll be absolutely oodles of tables, chairs, notice boards and so on. Video screens will advise visitors on the various locations and there'll be plenty of campus maps.'

'Grazie, Kellie,' said Jamie.

'All the usual stalls and food, drinks and coffee outlets have been allocated their spots on the Village Place,' Kellie advised.

'Danke schön.'

'Jamie, why you bother us academics with details like this?' complained Arso. Jamie was about to pointedly ignore this intervention when Michael White introduced his own complaint.

'Hey, Jamie,' he said, 'I jus' noticed. Accordin' to this timetable, the *Coranderrk* play is on at 2 pm. When the regiment parade's on.'

'At 1400 hours as they say in the regiment,' Jamie confirmed.

'Why's that?' Michael pressed him.

'I think it's to do with the 24-hour clock.'

'No!' the Indigenous student snapped. 'Why's the parade on at the same time as the play about William Barak?'

'Professor – or should I say, Colonel – Motherwell …'

'Th-th-that thug.'

'… thought the parade wouldn't be of much interest to your people,' Jamie replied with a shrug.

'Well, he can think again. Me and my mob wanna see the parade. I'm gunna talk with 'im.'

'That's your perogative, Michael,' Jamie said offhandedly.

'Actually, it's *pre*rogative, Jamie,' said Marilyn.'

'Whatever. "Pre", "per" – what's the diff?'

'The difference is … it doesn't matter,' she sighed.

'What about weather, Kellie?' Jamie changed the topic. 'That's the one thing we can never control and in past years, it's sometimes been absolutely poopy.'

'All good there, it seems,' reported Kellie. 'I checked with the Bureau just before the meeting and Sunday will be warm with clear skies. Maximum of 17.'

'Spasibo, Kellie,' said Jamie, 'Remember the year before last, the skies opened, the Village Place was the village bog. Very poor roll up on the day but little kids loved it.'

'Never seen rain like it,' ventured Michael White. 'Sure buggered up the smoking ceremony. Uncle Lionel couldn't get the fire goin'! Geez, we laughed ourselves shitless.'

Michael was still laughing at his own story when the door flew open to reveal Clive Goodenough. He stood glaring at Jamie. He was barely recognisable. Gone were the suit and tie in favour of a heavy coat over a lumberjack shirt. He wore work boots and now sported a shaggy head of hair and a thick, unkempt beard.

'Clive. Hardly recognised you,' ventured Jamie. 'Would you like to join us? This is our last meeting before Open Day.'

'I know this is the bloody last meeting and I know Open Day is on Sunday.' Clive's eyes flashed. 'Have you forgotten I'm the Dean for Outreach and Engagement?'

'Not at all, it's just that we hadn't seen you for a while …'

'Of course you haven't seen me for a while,' Goodenough raised his voice. 'I've been busy reaching out and engaging!'

'Would you like to take a seat? We're nearly done and we …'

'No, I would not like to take a seat,' he replied curtly. 'I've already wasted too much time on this hopeless committee.'

Sensing Goodenough's emotional state, the members left it to Jamie to deal with him.

'I'm sorry you feel that way, Clive.'

'There's a giant bloody gap in your wonderful Open Day plans.'

'Oh?' said Jamie.

'There's no provision for a marquee for outreach and engagement. I intend to be on duty on Open Day and I need a proper base to work from.'

'But, Clive, all the plans …' began Jamie.

'I've seen the fucking plans, Jamie,' said Goodenough, advancing on him, 'and I'm telling you there's no Outreach and Engagement marquee. I want one and I want it in a prominent location.'

'At this late stage, Clive …'

'Don't mess around with me, Jamie. I play hardball. Fix it or else,' he snarled as he raised a clenched fist, turned and left, slamming the door behind him.

'Phew,' said the shaken Jamie. 'I think we can call it a day unless anyone has any burning issue?'

'Jamie, aren't you going to say anything about Professor Goodenough? Bursting in like that. It was really upsetting,' said Marilyn.

'I'm not sure.' Jamie was clearly befuddled by Goodenough's intervention.

'Are you sure he's not a bit dotty?' she asked. 'What if he's like that on Open Day?'

'Typical when he gets angry,' observed Arso.

'Yes, Open Day could be a problem. I'll talk to campus security. I wouldn't like to be Clive Goodenough if he crosses Kevin Burke on Open Day.'

He glanced up at the wall clock.

'I think that wraps up everything for now. See you all Sunday. No later than 8 am please for a 10 am opening. And don't forget, drinky poos and nibbles at Boy Wonder's from 5 pm. And the announcements of the Batman strapline competition winners. Don't miss it!'

oooOooo

Jamie was troubled by Goodenough's disruption of the meeting, and fretting about what he should do. He was also upset and close to tears when he phoned Roddy for advice. Roddy was unequivocal. He must report Goodenough immediately to Motherwell, and pass responsibility to him.

'That's what he's paid for, my darlin', Roddy advised, 'let fat Bazza earn his fat salary.'

Attempting to regain his composure, Jamie dialled Motherwell's number and his EA put the call straight through, alerting the Vice President to Jamie's distressed state.

'Barry? Jamie here. I need to talk,' Jamie snivelled.

'What's up, Jamie?' Motherwell did his best to sound consoling to the distraught marketer.

'It's just that … we just had our final Open Day committee meeting. And, ah …'

'Problem?'

'It's a bit upsetting,' he sniffed. 'It's just that … we hadn't seen Clive Goodenough at any meeting for weeks.'

I hope you're not complaining, thought Motherwell.

'He burst into our final meeting – I've just left it – and demanded a marquee in a prominent location on Open Day. For Outreach and Engagement, he said.'

'What does that mean?'

'He didn't say. I mean, we've supplied him with stacks of information pamphlets and so on. The ones he didn't use 'cos he didn't visit schools. Maybe he wants to distribute those. It was scary, Barry. He was very emotional.'

'Emotion's a waste of time,' declared Motherwell, who'd been waiting for an opportunity to reprise Razer's line.

'But what am I to do?' pleaded Jamie.

Motherwell agonised. Razer would no doubt want him to come down on Goodenough, rejecting his demand. Lexi would be more conciliatory, asking what harm it could do to placate him.

'Give him a marquee.'

'Give him a marquee?' Jamie repeated, incredulous.

'Yeah. He's going through some problems at the moment. Get maintenance to set up a marquee by the main entrance to the Village Place away from the other marquees. Outside, near where we have the main welcoming marquee.'

'If you say so, Barry,' said Jamie, making a note of the conversation.

Barry Motherwell exhaled a long breath. Had he made the correct decision about Goodenough? What else could he have done? The man was clearly unhinged and could be a risk for Open Day. Better to humour him.

Chapter 30

The Big Day

Barry Motherwell rose early on Open Day and flicked the switch on the coffee machine before shedding his T-shirt and shorts and heading for the bathroom. He ran his shower longer than his self-mandated four minutes as he thought through his tasks for the day. Corduroy slacks and lumberjack shirt would do for getting to the campus and he'd not wear a tie. He'd change later into his regimental ceremonial dress including Army necktie. One tie per day was quite enough.

He poured himself a mug of hot black coffee as he gathered up his regimental gear. He held high the suit bag containing his uniform and slipped on his garden clogs as he left the house for the garage. The suit bag was carefully hung from the hook behind the driver's seat. Herbie began barking and prancing for his breakfast and Mena followed his example.

'Shaddup the two of ya!' he bawled over his shoulder as he walked back to the house. He fetched his slouch hat and boots and returned to the car, placing the former carefully on the back seat and the boots on the floor of the 4WD. Herbie and Mena renewed their demands for breakfast.

'I told you two to shut up!' He released the dogs from their enclosure and they followed him to the back door of the house where he had set up their breakfast. He went indoors and took a first sip of the coffee and, still standing at the kitchen table, skimmed the Sunday newspaper online. The forecast was for a warm, clear day. Not too bad for an Open Day in late July, he thought.

Motherwell went to the shed and pulled out the dog trailer and attached it to the 4WD. The dogs looked up from their bowls to observe this manoeuvre intently, standing very still, alert with their tails up and moving slowly. Over the last several months they'd become accustomed to riding in the trailer to the Batman campus. They seemed to enjoy their time with the regiment, so persuading them into the dog trailer had become easy. Herbie started the barking and prancing of excitement and Mena followed suit.

With the dogs loaded on board the trailer and the house secure, Motherwell eased his generous body into the driver's seat and set off for the campus. There was little traffic early on this cool Sunday morning so he made good time. He took the slipway off the highway and turned onto the driveway leading to the campus entrance.

'Christ almighty!' He brought the car to a sudden halt and his dogs lurched forward in their wagon. He reached for his phone to call the Head of Campus Security.

'Kevin, did you drive through the main gate this morning?'

'About 0700 hours, sir.'

'Was there a banner over the gate?'

'Yeah. For Open Day, I guess.'

'It says "Batman University for Intelligent Design".' Motherwell was getting angrier.

'Yeah. Is there a problem?'

'Too right there's problem. It's not authorised. What's more, it's proselytising.'

'Geez, I didn't notice. Should I call the CFA?'

'The CFA?' Motherwell bellowed.

'That sheet would be highly flammable especially. And if it's pros … what did you say it's doing?'

Motherwell was becoming exasperated.

'It's gotta come down right away,' he ordered.

'I've got no gear that could get up that high, Sir,' Kevin advised, realising that he was failing the first test Motherwell had thrown him on Open Day.

'Shit!' Motherwell pressed hard on the accelerator and the dogs reeled back in their cage. He drove at speed to the regiment depot and slowed to reverse the 4WD up to the dog enclosure to unload his charges. He heard Micha barking excitedly as she anticipated the arrival of her buddies.

In his rear vision mirror, he saw the uniformed Kevin Burke and members of the Batman regiment busying themselves with preparations for Open Day. Alongside them, other uniformed soldiers were setting up a marquee under the direction of a lieutenant from the Sandstone regiment. Seeing his boss arrive and certain he was in a surly mood, Kevin hastened to Motherwell's vehicle, throwing a sharp salute as he drew near. Motherwell was still clearly annoyed.

'I'm looking into that sign on the gate, sir,' Kevin said, 'but not too hopeful of being able to get it down.'

'Bastards. I bet Pilgrim's up to his clerical collar in this,' Motherwell said. 'If Nicholas sees it, there'll be hell to pay.'

Motherwell took his dogs out of the wagon and walked them up to the enclosure where Micha scurried to and fro in excitement. Kevin opened the gate, and Motherwell's dogs and Micha greeted each other according to the evolved ritual of canines.

Realising the sign would not be removed, Motherwell turned his thoughts to other matters. Kevin was relieved his boss seemed to have put the matter out of his mind.

'Kev, with the Minister coming today, tell your guys to keep an eye out for anything out of the ordinary.'

'Yessir!' May was reluctant to reignite his boss's ire and hesitated before seeking clarification. 'Er, how do you mean, Sir?'

'I dunno. Just be prepared for anything and everything.'

'There was that business with the Minister at Western Uni a few days ago,' Kevin said. 'You thinking of something like that?'

'Don't think our students will give any trouble. But keep an eye out for any sign of foreigners on campus.'

'Foreigners? Like Muslims?'

'No, I mean people …' Motherwell was becoming exasperated again. 'Just use your common sense. Call me if you need to but I'm sure you and your guys can handle anything.'

'Thanks for the vote of confidence, Sir.'

'I'm going to my office for a while. I'll be back for regiment lunch.'

Kevin Burke threw another salute as his commanding officer left. Motherwell drove up to the rear entrance to O'Toole, retrieved his regimental uniform, hat and boots, swiped his security fob and rode the elevator to Level 12. As he anticipated, he was alone there. He was confident Razer and his team would go straight to lunch in the Batcave, commissioned by Razer as a VIP extension to Boy Wonder's.

He unlocked his office door, switched on the lights and carefully hung his uniform in the office wardrobe, placed his slouch hat onto the shelf above and slipped his boots in beneath. He turned to cast his eye over his office and allowed himself a satisfied smile as he picked up his desk phone and called Lexi Dunne's office number.

'Morning, Mother,' Lexi answered cheerily. 'Looks like we've got clement end-of-July weather for Open Day.'

'You on campus?' he inquired.

'In the cottage, all alone. Vine's father picked her up early for a day at the museum and I've been here a good half hour.'

'Any sign of Clive?'

'Haven't seen him but I think he's been in.'

'Oh?'

'Looking good,' she said. 'The piles of Batman brochures have gone. I reckon he's setting up the O and E marquee.'

'That's a good sign,' Motherwell agreed.

'Y'know, Mother, I think he might be quite good at Outreach and Engagement. He really is passionate about higher education.'

'Hope so. Where will you be later in the morning?'

'Like when?'

'About eleven.'

'I have to get to the cinema for the Korean film at noon. Why?"

Motherwell steeled himself. 'Thought we'd have a coffee. In my office. There's something I'd like to show you.'

'Ah, something you'd like to show me?' Ever the man of mystery.'

'You OK for that?'

'Sure.'

'The building's locked so text me when you're close and I'll come down and let you in.'

Chapter 31

The Troubles Begin

Motherwell went to his window and looked down on the now busy Village Place. Far below, staff and students gathered around the numerous colourful marquees, the food and coffee outlets, the family fun features and the temporary stage that would seat the Minister, the Chairman, the President and other dignitaries. A few families had already made their way onto the Village Place and were wandering about waiting for the marquees and academic buildings to be opened.

Just outside the buildings that enclosed the Village Place and which obscured his view was the new regimental depot where the regiment would line up for their rehearsal. Kevin Burke would be barking orders and he and the NCOs from the Sandstone regiment would be conducting final inspections of the dress of the regiment members.

Kevin Burke's Open Day was certain to be demanding. His regimental duties would require his presence at the depot and yet, as Head of Campus Security, he had a responsibility for ensuring good order on a day when large numbers of the public would be on the campus. Concerned by the events during the Minister's recent visit to Western Uni, Kevin Burke had given his staff strict instructions to be alert for any possible disruptions.

Motherwell satisfied himself that all appeared to be going well on the Village Place when his mobile rang.

'Colonel, Warrant Officer May here, Sir. We might have a problem.'

'What kind of a problem?'

'Suspected foreigners.'

'Where?'

'On campus.'

'I guessed that much, Kev. Where on campus?'

'Just outside the main entrance to the Village Place. There's a marquee there, the one set up outside the entrance for Prof Goodenough and he seems to be in charge of some foreigners.'

'Slow down, Kev. What's this about foreigners? They'll be Batman students there to help him.'

'I'm sure they're not, Sir.'

'How can you tell?'

'They're all wearing T shirts and baseball caps for their own unis. Y'know, Sandstone, Western Met, City Uni and others. Two or three at each table and they've got their own information day stuff.'

'What do you mean, their own stuff?' Motherwell asked rising from his chair.

'Brochures, pre-enrolment forms, that sort of stuff. From their own unis. They'd be foreigners, wouldn't they?'

'Damn right they are,' Motherwell exploded. 'Goodenough's a treacherous bastard.'

'My blokes asked him what it was all about and he said he's reaching out to other universities. Thinks Batman should be engaging with them more.'

'Get over there right away and take as many of your blokes as you can. Put the frighteners on him. Tell Goodenough that you've spoken with me and that the marquee is closed for the day. He's to leave the campus immediately. You instruct all the people from other universities to leave and confiscate their material. Any resistance, call the police and have them removed. Let me know what happens. It's nearly 8.30 and I want this settled within half an hour.'

Motherwell was now pacing around his office.

'I'm on the way, Sir.'

It took little time before Kevin Burke called Motherwell again.

'Colonel, it's me, Kev. Me and a few of my blokes have paid a little visit to the marquee.'

'And?'

'Scared the shit out of 'em. Never seen such a bunch of pussies. I'd say some of them were marketing staff, some students. They looked shit scared when me in uniform and my blokes came in with Micha. He damn near pulled me over barking and lunging at 'em. Made me real proud.'

'Problem solved?' Motherwell asked.

'The last of 'em is leaving now,' Burke proudly reported.

'And Goodenough?'

'Yeah, nah, that's a different story. He went kinda crazy, shouting at us and making threats.'

'What kind of threats?'

'Ah, all piss weak stuff, Prof. He's gonna get even with Motherwell … you haven't heard the last of him … you've shown him no respect. That sort of stuff.'

'What happened then?'

'Yeah, that was interesting. He eventually calmed right down and said he'd leave the campus. He just wanted some time to collect things from the cottage and then he'd be gone. Didn't even have to mention police.'

Motherwell sat at his desk and wondered about Goodenough's mental stability and whether he should share this incident with Lexi. Typical of women, though, she'd be upset for Goodenough and worried that he might be at a tipping point. Best not to worry her. He decided to have it out with Goodenough but his calls to the mobile number went unanswered. He picked up his Open Day program and perused it, marking events he might show up for after the parade. For now, he would do some paperwork and try to settle his nerves before his rendezvous with Lexi Dunne.

He'd agreed to represent the President at the drinks at Boy Wonder's at the end of the day to formally thank the Open Day team for their work and congratulate them on a successful day. There was also the awards event for the best straplines. Not comfortable with impromptu speeches, Motherwell was preparing notes for his thank you speech when his phone rang again.

'Sir, Warrant Officer May again. Think we've got a problem.'

'Another one?'

'Yeah. Prof Goodenough has caused some more trouble.'

'What is it this time?'

'We've got a couple of fire units here from Robert Gordon CFA.'

'There's a fire on campus?'

'Right where the O and E marquee was.'

'Was? You say was?'

'Yeah, she's burned down.'

'Christ. Everyone alright?'

'Yeah, no injuries and the fireys have got it under control.'

'You mentioned Goodenough. What's it got to do with him?'

'I think he's kinda gaga. Looks like he piled up the all the Batman information booklets and stuff inside the marquee and threw some petrol on them put a match to it all. Up she went.'

'What's happened to him?'

'The fireys called the cops. They came and took him away. I talked with them after they put him in the wagon.'

'What'd they say?'

'They reckon he told them he was having a smoking ceremony to welcome visitors to the campus.'

'He's mad.'

'Yeah, but now there's another problem.'

'What!'

'Yeah, the Indigenous students and Uncle Lionel were there preparing their stuff. Y'know, Uncle Lionel was to do the official smoking ceremony. He's said his mob have been disrespected on their own land. He's not gonna do the Welcome, either. I'm worried there could be some trouble on campus during the day, Sir.'

'Oh, Christ.'

'And, Sir, about the banner on the gates. I asked the fireys if they could help but they said it's against their rules. Just fires and cats up trees, that's what the bloke in charge said.'

It was dawning on Motherwell that the idea of a relaxed tête à tête with Lexi Dunne at 11 am seemed increasingly problematic. For a start, she would be upset if she'd learned about Clive Goodenough's actions. And he would personally have to be prepared to act should there be some disturbance by Indigenous students.

He called Nicholas Razer's number but there was no answer. At the recorded message by Jenny inviting the caller to leave a message for Professor Razer, Motherwell stammered: 'Er, good morning, Nicholas, it's, ah, Barry here and it's about 8.30 am on, on, ah, Open Day. We've had a, ah, minor incident with, ah, Clive Goodenough. Nothing to worry about, of course, and, ah, I'll fill you in if you, ah, have time to call me back. Otherwise, see you after the parade.'

But, should he come clean with Lexi? He decided to call her.

'Lexi, Barry.'

'Oh, hello, Professor Motherwell,' Lexi replied guardedly. 'Can I call you back?'

'Er, sure.' He hung up, confused by Lexi's formal tone.

At least 20 minutes passed before Lexi called.

'Mother, sorry 'bout that but I had an issue here at the cottage.'

'Don't tell me there was a fire!'

'No, but I know why you're asking.'

'You heard about Clive?'

'I've spoken with him.'

'I thought he was on his way to the Robert Gordon police station.'

'I think I've averted that. He'd asked the cops if he could collect a few things from his office and they rolled up here with him in the back of a wagon. I sat the cops all down for a cuppa and we had a chat.'

'Clive was still in the paddy wagon?'

'Yes. I explained to them that he was one of our most senior professors. They rolled their eyes. That he'd been under a lot of stress. I suggested I'd call his wife to collect him and I was sure he'd be no further trouble. They said it was Batman's marquee so if we could forget about it, so could they. And, being mid-winter, there's no danger of a bush fire so they weren't worried on that score.'

'Pure luck.'

'They were a couple of nice young guys on Sunday duty, hoping for a quiet shift, I'd say. They extracted an assurance from Clive that he'd go home and stay there and be no further trouble. Deirdre arrived pretty promptly and took him away.'

'I understand she's a bit of an ogre.'

'She certainly gave a very convincing portrayal. I think Clive might be in for a rough time when she gets him home.'

'So,' ventured Motherwell, deciding not to mention the possibility of Clive's aberrant behaviour causing an Indigenous uprising on campus, 'see you at eleven?'

'I assume there's more than coffee.'

Her question threw him.

'How d'you mean?'

'After all this, I think I deserve a treat,' she suggested.

'Er, sure.' Motherwell rang off and considered his next move. He hurried to Boy Wonder's where he purchased two muffins, one with chocolate chips and the other with apple and walnut.

Chapter 32

Cowgirl Wants

Having received her text indicating Lexi was approaching the O'Toole building, Motherwell had shuddered in anticipation. He took a deep breath as he took the lift to the ground level. He was still anxious lest Razer or one of his inner circle could happen along and draw the wrong conclusion. They'd no doubt report to Razer that Motherwell and Lexi Dunne were meeting surreptitiously in his office on Open Day.

But why should he be feeling anxious? There were any number of reasons, he argued to himself, why he might need to speak with the Dean for International on Open Day. But what? Of course! The momentous events of this morning with her colleague and office mate being detained after such bizarre behaviour! And the temerity to invite representatives from rival universities onto the Batman campus.

These were grave matters indeed. And, to her credit, Lexi Dunne had played a key role in resolving issues with minimum fuss and without damage to the university's reputation. Why would Motherwell not be within his rights, even be obliged, to invite Professor Dunne for a coffee to show official gratitude for her intervention? So, he convinced himself that his behaviour should arouse not the slightest suspicion. He rehearsed his lines as the lift descended.

Notwithstanding this reasoned stance of moral rectitude, Motherwell glanced nervously out for any witnesses as he punched – rather too forcefully – the green button to allow Lexi through the main entrance door. And, when she did enter, he turned and conspicuously walked a couple of paces ahead.

'Sure you're feeling comfortable with me being here, Mother?' inquired Lexi as she followed him to the elevator.

'Oh, sure, not at all,' he threw over his shoulder.

'You're not feeling comfortable?' Lexi asked, confused.

'I mean I'm not at all uncomfortable.'

'That's a strange way to put it,' she observed.

'I've had a bad morning,' he pleaded.

'I heard,' she said, following him into the lift. 'And I've come to your rescue again.'

'You have?' he asked surprised.

'Before I came here – it's OK, relax, and why don't you press the lift button? – I decided to take a look at the mess Clive's little conflagration had left. I ran into Uncle Lionel there.'

'I heard he's not happy.'

'We're on the committee of the William Barak Gallery on campus. I could see he was upset and he told me he wouldn't do the official smoking ceremony. Or the Welcome.'

The lift door opened on Level 12 and Motherwell exited ahead of Lexi, maintaining the distance he hoped would convince any observer that there was nothing to see here.

'I took him over to Boy Wonder's for a cuppa and I persuaded him to reconsider. So, it's on again,' she declared as the lift doors closed.

'That's good to hear,' said Motherwell as Lexi followed him along the corridor.

He opened his office door, desperate to get into the safety of his office and stood back to allow Lexi to enter.

'Mother,' she squealed with delight, 'you've done it. It's wonderful.'

He closed the door behind them and stood watching as Lexi surveyed his refurbished office.

'I told you I had a surprise for you,' he boasted.

'When did all this happen?' she asked as she slowly took in the major upgrade of the office.

'The painters and electricians were here early in the week and the furniture and appliances arrived on Thursday. The paintings were hung on Friday.'

'Why didn't you tell me?' she squealed with delight.

'Wanted to surprise you.'

'You sure did!' Lexi exclaimed. 'Next project is your clothes.' She looked at him with mock admonishment.

'Not you, too. Maureen was always at me about that.'

'I didn't mean to open old wounds, Mother,' Lexi said apologetically.

'Not a problem. Now, how about a coffee?'

'So, you were planning coffee, too?'

'Sure. You'll see over there the coffee machine which you recommended.'

'I didn't think you'd have the balls.'

'In for a penny … only problem is, I haven't mastered the instructions. But I reckon you'll know how to operate it.'

'Damn right, I do,' exclaimed Lexi. 'Stand aside, cowboy.'

'Coffee's by the machine. If you want milk, it's in the new bar fridge at the far end of the new cabinet.'

'Thanks, cowboy. Cowgirls need their cow juice.'

Cowboy? Motherwell loved the Americanisms Lexi resorted to when she was in a playful frame of mind.

'Mother, you haven't commented on my footwear. Look,' she said as she lifted her skirt high above her knees. 'I bought them after I'd been to your farm. Wadda ya think?'

'Spectacular,' said Motherwell, catching sight of Lexi's upper legs.

'They're my cowgirl boots. For my next visit to the farm. If I'm invited, that is.'

Lexi poured their coffees and placed them on the new coffee table. With a dramatic flourish she allowed herself to fall back onto the plush new couch. She wriggled on it, pleased with the sensation.

'This is even better than when I tried it in the showroom. It's so comfortable. Easy to remove stains, too.'

'Are you thinking you might spill coffee on it?'

'Just a woman's point of view.'

Motherwell remained standing, pleased with Lexi's fulsome assessment of his restyled office. She swivelled, lifted her feet and stretched out on the couch.

'Don't screw up your face like that,' she gently chided. 'The cowgirl boots are new and clean.'

'Sorry. Force of habit,' he admitted.

Lexi sipped at her coffee. 'Say, Mother, why are you Professor Motherwell today?'

'How d'you mean?' asked Motherwell, still standing.

'You're in your daggy civvies – oops, there I go again. I thought today you were going to be Colonel Motherwell.'

'I'll change into uniform later. The later the better for keeping the creases.'

'I've never seen you in uniform,' she pouted. 'Why don't you change now?'

Motherwell checked his watch.

'OK, guess it's not too soon.'

Lexi watched as he retrieved his suit bag and boots from the wardrobe and headed for the office door.

'Whoa there, cowboy, I meant for you to get into your gear here.'

Motherwell turned to face her. 'Here?' he asked, confused.

'Right here,' smiled Lexi coyly, her head on the soft moulded armrest.

Motherwell looked around desperately.

'I forgot to serve the muffins,' he stammered.

'Fuck the muffins,' Lexi said forcefully.

Would Nicholas Razer change his plans and arrive at his office along the corridor with his entourage early? Motherwell weighed up the possibilities of that and dismissed it. Would Kevin Burke call him to report yet another Open Day calamity? He laid his suit bag across his desk, placed his boots on the floor, turned off his mobile phone and disengaged the landline.

As he removed each item of clothing, Lexi demanded the next until Motherwell stood naked before her.

'I don't recall instructing you to stand to attention,' she teased, 'but I'm pleased to see you remember how, Colonel. With bar.'

Motherwell smiled sheepishly.

'Now, giddy-up your ass over here, cowboy. Cowgirl wants a ride.'

Chapter 33

Administrative Heights

Colonel Barry Motherwell, in full dress uniform, stepped smartly out of the entrance to O'Toole and made his way to the car park. It was a short walk to the regiment but he would have felt self-conscious walking though the growing crowd in full Army dress. He allowed himself a smile of satisfaction at the secret he now held as he drove along the campus ring road. Uncharacteristically, he found himself whistling.

Professor Lexi Dunne had left the O'Toole building before him, she too with a sense of accomplishment. She broke into a girlish skip as she crossed the little lawn in front of the cottage. Open Day was so far meeting all her expectations and if it kept her as happy as she was then, a perfect day lay ahead.

Now, however, the sated lovers had to put aside pleasant reveries and attend to their personal Open Day responsibilities.

Motherwell parked at the regiment depot where the members were enjoying a sandwich lunch provided by Rajesh Sharma. As he approached the depot, Kevin Burke strode out to meet him in an agitated state.

'Prof …'

'Warrant Officer May,' Motherwell interrupted in rebuke.

'Sorry, Sir,' May saluted without breaking stride. 'It's just that we've got a couple of problems.'

Motherwell resented the possibility that his post-coital musings were going to be interrupted.

'I've been trying to call you on the mobile and at your office for half an hour.'

'I had to go off the air for a while. What's up?'

'There's police on campus again.'

'Why?'

'A complaint about the jumping castle.'

'Was there an accident?'

'Kinda. Well, BUSS reckons it was an accident, anyway.'

'Yes?'

'You know we had the amusements over in one area of the Village Place? Seems someone either made a mistake or wanted to cause trouble. The jumping castle was an adult entertainment one.'

'What!'

'Yeah, they're hired out for stags' parties, things like that. The entrance was pink and shaped like, y'know, a woman's … you know, down there. Apparently inside there was a rodeo penis and something called the "Ride of Your Life". One for men and one for women. Look, here's the brochure.'

Motherwell snatched the glossy publication, opened it and froze.

'Oh, Christ!' Motherwell was aghast as he read "Randy Rod for Rent" and "Raunchy Rebecca for Rent". "Rebecca and Rod are mechanical rides with three speeds." "Rod has unique love handles." Shit. "Rebecca is designed to go the distance like no other." Oh, God!'

'Yeah, Prof, I've seen them when we've been on R&R but I never thought I'd see them in Oz. Professor Pilgrim rang the cops and they were here quick smart.'

'Oh, Christ!' How did he know about it. Him, of all people.'

'Couldn't miss it, sir. It was right next door to the multi-faith marquee.'

'Oh, great.'

'Anyway, the cops rolled up, booked some students and it was pretty soon closed down.'

'So much for wholesome family fun on Open Day,' Motherwell muttered.

'Media were here, too, sir,' Kevin said, aware that this would only add to his boss's anger.

'Oh my God.'

'Yeah, and they filmed the other raid, too.'

'What other raid?'

'The BatBet marquee was next to the jumping castle. They closed that, too, for illegal gambling. Booked some Business students working there. And Prof Pilgrim.'

'Pilgrim? Pilgrim got booked?' Motherwell spluttered.

'Yeah, the cops caught him and a group of his soldiers of the lord slashing at the jumping castle with car keys and stuff, trying to deflate it. Wilful property damage, they said.'

Motherwell sighed, his mind racing. Should he call Razer? What if Razer asked where was he when the cops arrived?

'Sir, there's something even more worrying, too.'

With that, Kevin called out two members of the regiment and beckoned them to approach. They marched up, stamped right feet to a halt and saluted.

'Sir, this is Privates Jaydn and Mia.'

Motherwell returned their salute and braced himself.

'Stand easy!' Kevin ordered.

'These soldiers are members of BURCA, the university rock climbing club and they do the annual scaling of O'Toole. Tell the colonel what you told me.'

'Well, sir, we each have a rope and we scale up the front of O'Toole. The people love it.'

'We have some fake rifles,' Jaydn took up the story, 'and when we get on the top of the building we fire off vouchers for a free drink or ice creams at Mario Tempeste's van. They flutter down for the kids to gather them up. Each one's numbered and when we come down, we announce the lucky number.'

'But we got a real fright, Sir. About half an hour ago.'

'That's right, Sir,' agreed Jaydn. 'We're still pretty shaken up.'

'Get to the point,' urged Kevin Burke.

'Sorry,' said Mia. 'So, today, I get to the top of O'Toole first, haul myself onto the roof. And there's two guys sitting there having a smoke. They're both, like, all in black, with balaclavas.'

Motherwell's eyes narrowed, his brown furrowed and he nodded for them to continue.

'Yeah, and there's real rifles,' added Jaydn. 'According to what we've learned in the firearms classes, they were sharp shooter rifles. Y'know, with telescopic lenses.'

'And they weren't up there when we set up the ropes this morning,' added Mia.

'That's correct, sir,' Kevin confirmed. 'Couple of my guys accompanied them up there. That's when they encountered Michael White and some Indigenous students.'

'What were they doing there?'

'They had one of those Indigenous flags and they were about to run it up the flagpole. Said it was to acknowledge Invasion Day.'

'And?'

'My boys escorted them down and out of the building. End of story.'

'I wouldn't be counting on that, Warrant Officer. I want your blokes to be watching out for any more Invasion Day nonsense. And especially while the Minister is here. Keep an eye on Michael White. He's trouble.'

'Will do, sir.'

'Back to your story,' Motherwell said, turning back to the recruits.

'Yeah, as Mia was saying, Sir, we were near the top of O'Toole and I was right behind her,' said Jaydn wide-eyed, 'and as I was hauling myself onto the roof, one of these guys, real tough looking guys, too, says to Mia "Who the fuck are you? And what's so fuckin' funny?"'

'Sorry for the language, Sir,' apologised Mia, 'but that's what he said.'

'What was so funny?' asked Motherwell.

'Oh, just a little joke we had on the way up.'

'Go on,' said Motherwell.

'Then, without even standing up,' Jaydn went on, 'the other one looks up at us, very aggressively, and pointing at Mia says "Fuck off, hairy legs". Then he looks at me and says "You too, Spider Man."'

'What happened then?' asked Motherwell.

'We fucked off, Sir,' said Jaydn. 'We left the fake rifles and were down the ropes at the double. The kids below were pretty disappointed but we got a good round of applause.'

'And Sir, we recorded the whole thing on video,' said Mia.

'How come?' inquired Motherwell.

'This year, for regiment training purposes,' said Kevin, 'we fitted the helmets with cameras.'

'Where are they now?' asked Motherwell.

'In the depot, Sir' replied Jaydn.

'Get them immediately and give them to Warrant Officer May,' said Motherwell.

'Yes, Sir,' said the recruits.

'Who've you told about this?' asked Motherwell.

'Only Warrant Office May.'

'Keep it to yourselves,' Motherwell instructed. 'It's all part of the Open Day fun.'

'Anything else?'

The privates looked at each other.

'No Sir,' said Private Mia.

'Tenshun!' ordered May. 'About turn! Bugger off!'

Motherwell and May watched the young recruits march off.

'Waddya reckon, Sir?' inquired May. 'Want me to get some of my boys to have a gander?'

'Nah, leave it, Kev,' said Motherwell. 'I know the Minister's people are worried about security everywhere he goes these days. Those guys on O'Toole will be surveillance. I doubt they are armed with anything more than high-powered binocs and communications. I think your climber kids were just spooked.'

'That may be, Sir, but I know they're liars.'

'How come?'

'They told you no-one else had seen the videos. Fact is, I saw them showing them to other regiment members out the back of the depot. Lots of raucous laughing.'

'All very well to be laughing now but they were shit scared up there,' said Motherwell.

Chapter 34

Reds and Koreans

Lexi Dunne had left the O'Toole building with a sense of elation. Through force of will, she'd finally broken through the defensive emotional wall that surrounded Barry Motherwell. So often she'd attempted to breach that barrier but each time, he had baulked. All it took was a degree of firmness on her part coupled with her natural playfulness.

Lexi was certain that their intimacy in his office had taken their relationship to a new level. And although she'd appeared audacious in her come-on to him, Lexi had been, like Motherwell, anxious. To the surprise of both of them, their love-making, though furtive and urgent, had been what Lexi had long wanted and what Motherwell had dared not contemplate. But each understood that need for discretion. Their professional relationship would now be trickier, and exposure of their secret relationship would spell disaster for them both.

If these thoughts were troubling Lexi Dunne as, with a spring in her step, she headed into the Village Place, no-one who knew her would have discerned it. As she meandered through the marquees and food and drink outlets, she greeted Open Day visitors, charming and disarming students and parents alike. It was approaching noon and, as arranged, Jamie Jamieson called Lexi Dunne to confirm that the cinema was open and the technician had the movie ready for the North Korean film.

'Thanks Jamie, we don't want any stuff-ups with this. Especially with the Consul in attendance. I'm slowly making my way there now. Who's there?'

'The Korean girls are here in the cinema in their traditional dance costume. They look really lovely,' said Jamie.

That's Jamie, loves colour and movement, thought Lexi as she continued across the Village Place, stopping at various marquees and cheerily wishing the staff on duty a successful day. Noticing the marquee for Red Studies, she approached it, pleased to see that Jacky Harvey was there. They'd met at a drinks session to welcome her on Friday.

'Good morning, Jacky. Great to have you here. How's business?'

'Hello, Lexi. We're going gang busters.'

'You're very well set up, I see.'

'Yes, I've got Declan and Catherine to help. Both what I believe Australians would call dinky-di reds.'

The reds smiled at Lexi.

'They're here signing up people for subscriptions to MC1R,' said Harvey.

'MC1R?'

'MC1R is the gene for redheadedness.'

'You can subscribe to a gene?'

Harvey laughed.

'It's the name of an international magazine for redheads. The first and maybe only one in the world.'

'We also have the Cancer Council just next door and we'll have a dermatology nurse giving talks and advice on skin care and protection. That's doing very well.'

'Could they give me some advice on reversing the effects of ageing on a once glowing Californian epidermis?' joked Lexi.

'I was thinking the same! But how about some face painting with colourful sunscreens? Catherine's a brilliant face artist.'

'Thanks, but no. I'm heading over to the cinema to meet some North Koreans and I wouldn't want to frighten anybody.'

'You're going to the movies?'

'I have to introduce the film being put on by the North Korean students. Actually, by the consulate. I'm to welcome the new North Korean Consul and say a few words about the North Korean film industry.'

'I mustn't keep you from your fun,' joked Harvey.

Lexi had missed out on her muffin at Motherwell's office so she paused to look at the possibilities at a donut stall. She was weighing up whether she had time to treat herself when her mobile phone rang.

'Hi, Jamie,' she answered.

'Are you nearly here, Lexi?' he asked. 'Cos we've got a problem.'

Lexi recognised the near hysteria in Jamie's voice. Jamie's such a drama queen, she thought.

'At the cinema?'

'Yes, and it's turning ugly.' This was extreme language, even for Jamie.

'What do you mean, ugly?'

'Lexi, I'm scared,' his said, his voice trembling. 'There's about, I dunno, twenty or two dozen Asians have arrived and they're aggressive and rowdy. I'm peeking out one of the windows. They're waving placards and blocking the entrance to the cinema. The dancers and I are locked in the cinema. I've been trying to call Roddy but he's not answering.'

'What do the placards say?'

'I can see one that says "ROK students against dictator Kim".'

'Goddamn, Jamie, they'll be South Koreans. Look, call the cops immediately. I'll call Kevin and try to get him to stop the Consul arriving. Last thing we need is a diplomatic incident.'

'Oh, shit!' Jamie exclaimed.

'What now?'

'There's another group of Asian men just arrived. I think they must be our North Korean students. Now there's a lot of shoving and yelling. I'm scared, Lexi.'

Lexi could hear the screams of the dancers, screams of abuse rather than fear, she concluded.

'Keep the doors locked. I'll get help.'

'I don't know if I can keep the doors locked,' Jamie wailed. 'The dancers are very angry. They're trying to unlock the door. They want to get out.'

Lexi found Kevin Burke's number in her contacts list.

'Kevin Burke, Head of Campus Security. Sorry, I mean Warrant Officer Burke, Batman University Regiment.'

'Kevin, I don't care which you are. It's Lexi Dunne. I think we've got a problem.'

'I been saying that all day, Prof.'

'You'd better get over to the cinema and fast. There's some scuffling between some North and South Koreans.'

'Stay right there, I'll have someone there soon, Prof.'

'I'm not there yet. Jamie Jamieson is though and he's wetting his pants locked inside with a bunch of North Korean dancers.'

Couldn't happen to a nicer little prick, thought Kevin Burke.

'I can't come myself,' explained Kevin. 'I'm trying to whip a bunch of dopey kids into line for the parade. To make matters worse, I've just had to send a couple of my blokes to the Red Studies Marquee.'

'Red Studies? I've just left there not long ago. There's trouble there?'

'Yeah. Something to do with a Consul.'

'That would be the North Korean Consul,' said Lexi alarmed. 'I'd better get there.'

REDS AND KOREANS

ooOOoo

Led by Mr Kim from Kim Jong-un College, the North Korean Consul and his two consular colleagues had been taking in the sights of the Open Day en route to the cinema. The North Korean men were still enjoying their double scoops of ice cream from one of Mario Tempeste's mobile ice cream vans when they happened upon the Red Studies marquee. Declan smiled warmly as suited men approached.

The Consul, however, looked past Declan to Catherine, a tall, fair-skinned young beauty with flaming red hair. He addressed her in Korean.

'This is Consul for Democratic People's Republic of Korea,' the interpreter explained to Catherine. 'Consul very pleased to learn that the university teaches about communism. He asks, however, if the university also teaches about Juche, the advanced ideology of the Democratic Peoples' Republic of Korea.'

'Declan,' said Catherine. 'I'm a nursing student and I've no idea what he's talking about. You're doing sociology. Can you help?'

Glad at last to be called on, Declan stepped forward while the Ambassador looked crestfallen as Catherine retreated and sat down with Jacky Harvey at her book display desk.

'Prof Jacky,' whispered Catherine, 'I didn't like the way those men were leering at me. That older one made me feel quite uncomfortable.'

'I'm keeping a close eye on them myself.'

'Nah, mate,' Declan replied, 'you can tell him that red has nothing to do with communism. It's all about redheads, like all of us here. See, we all have reddish hair,' he said touching his ginger mop and beard. 'And we're a persecuted minority. Tell him that. Might ring a bell.'

Whatever the interpreter conveyed to the Consul caused howls of derisive laughter among the visitors. Declan smiled along though it occurred to him he could be the subject of the joke.

He didn't flinch when the ambassador reached out and ran his hand through his long red hair and stroked his lush beard. He didn't baulk when the ambassador's two colleagues stepped up to do the same. He even refrained from reacting when the third man recoiled with a look of horror after touching his beard. This was followed by gales of belly laughing from the North Koreans.

Pointing at Harvey signing copies of her book, the Consul spoke again.

'Consul asks who is she,' the interpreter explained pointing at Harvey.

'That's Professor Harvey,' explained Declan, 'one of the most famous redheads in the world.'

This revelation was conveyed to the Consul who, looking again at Harvey, ooh'd earnestly and spoke again.

'Wad 'e say?' inquired Declan.

'Consul would like to meet the old woman.'

Declan flushed and looked around to Jacky who wore an indulgent smile.

'It's OK, Declan, I've been to Asia quite a lot and I'm used to it. He wants to touch my hair. I'll let him have a feel, give him a tube of Cancer Council block-out and hope he goes away.'

With that, Harvey stood and moved around the table to stand facing the four Korean men. Declan stood beside her as the Consul passed his ice cream to Kang, the North Korean student leader.

'Now, Mr Kim or whatever your name is,' said Harvey, taking his hand and placing it on her head, 'have a good feel.'

'Ooooh,' the Consul expressed his wonder at the sensation. He spoke to Jacky.

'And what's His Excellency's verdict?' smiled Harvey with concocted regard for the consul's opinion.

'Consul like the hair. Very soft. Colourful, too,' came the translation.

'Tell the Consul I thank him for his kind comment. Now he can piss off.'

'Sorry, can you repeat, please?' asked the interpreter.

'I wish the Consul a happy visit to Batman University.'

The Consul took Harvey's hand, holding it firmly and resisting her attempt to terminate what she took to be his prolonged farewell handshake. With his other hand, he pushed up the sleeve of her jacket, slid his spectacles onto his head and lifted her hand the better to examine her forearm.

'Hey, hold on, mate,' Declan remonstrated.

'It's OK, Declan,' Harvey said, 'I know this line, too. He's obviously never encountered a red in his life and he's curious about my skin.'

The Consul examined her arm closely, touching several points with his forefinger while speaking to his comrades in the style of a hospital dermatology consultant instructing students during a patient examination.

'Consul want to know what are these?' said the interpreter.

'Those, you can tell His Nosiness, are called freckles,' smiled Harvey.

'Freckers,' the interpreter repeated.

'No, freckles', repeated Declan 'Rhymes with heckles, but I doubt there's a word for that in North Korean.'

'Freckers,' Mr Kim repeated.

'If that makes the Consul happy, then, yes, they are indeed freckers,' smiled Harvey.

The Consul ran a forefinger along Harvey's forearm and spoke again to the amusement of his comrades.

'You know, Declan, in medieval Germany,' said Harvey while the Consul and then his comrades took turns in examining her forearm, 'freckles were known as Judasdreck. Judas-shit.'

'Trust the Krauts,' said Michael. 'Oh, sorry, that's racist.'

'And what, may I ask,' inquired Harvey of the interpreter 'is so amusing?'

The man guffawed. 'Consul say your skin look like boiled crab.'

Declan's patience expired. In defence of Harvey's honour and indeed the honour of all reds, he gave the Consul a shove which sent him reeling back into the arms of one of his colleagues. Incensed by this act of insolence toward his honoured compatriot, Kang pushed Declan who found himself sitting on the ground. Harvey and Catherine retreated to the Cancer Council marquee while Open Day visitors began to linger to watch the unfolding drama.

Declan was still on his backside when the two campus security officers forced their way through the growing crowd of incredulous Open Day visitors. Mr Kim approached the men and explained that Consul of the DPKR had been assaulted by a red man and that this was a grave insult to the people of his country.

'What's the Consul's business on campus?' inquired one of the security men.

'His excellency is here to attend North Korean film,' replied Mr Kim.

'Oh, yeah, over at the cinema,' said the security man. 'According to the program, the official opening by Professor Dunne is in a few minutes. Please tell the Consul that my colleague will escort him to the cinema now.'

'Yes, but what about assault on Consul by red ruffians?' demanded Mr Kim. 'He very angry. All North Korean people very angry.'

'Please tell the Consul I'll take a statement from him, perhaps after the film if he'd like to meet me then.'

Mr Kim informed the Consul and, after a final stream of Korean invective at the reds accompanied by clenched fists, the Consul and his contingent followed the security officer through the stunned onlookers.

'Now, Ginger Meggs,' said the security officer to Declan, who'd regained his feet, 'you're in deep shit. ID, please.'

The by now large crowd of parents and high school children who had stood dumbfounded to witness the affray went their several ways to take in some of the other highlights of Open Day.

As they departed, Lexi Dunne arrived at the Red Studies marquee and saw Jacky Harvey and her reds as they stood, shaken, at the entrance to the Cancer Council marquee.

'Oh, I am so sorry about this. Are you OK?'

'I'm alright. But this Open Day is one out of the box, Lexi.'

ooOOoo

The North Korean contingent and their campus escort made their way across the Village Place through the various marquees and commercial outlets. The North Koreans quickened their pace as they heard the insults flying. When the cinema came into view, they saw that a serious confrontation between two groups of Koreans was under way. The North Korean students were attempting to grab and destroy the placards that had been brought by the South Koreans who, in turn, were employing the placards as weapons. Among the combatants were the North Korean dancers who, despite his pleas for them to stay, had left Jamie alone and terrified in the cinema. They screamed shrill abuse and flayed at the interlopers.

Mr Kim broke from the Consul's group, shouting, and ventured in among the flying fists in a futile attempt to calm the situation. The two groups had separated and were continuing to jeer at each other, gesticulating and hurling insults, when a squad of uniformed police arrived. A sergeant addressed the South Koreans invaders.

'You've made your point,' he announced. 'You must now leave immediately or you'll be arrested and charged. This would throw your visa status into question and you would almost certainly be deported.'

The group spoke angrily among themselves and he wondered if they might defy him.

'What's more,' he lied, 'a strong force of armed riot police is about to arrive. I suggest you leave now.' Their mood changed and they laughed with bravado, throwing their arms around each other's shoulders as they returned to the buses they had hired for their political protest.

Mr Kim moved to the top step at the entrance to the cinema and announced the arrival of the Consul to the cheering applause of his compatriots. He addressed them in a fist-clenched, bellicose tone, his speech punctuated by more applause and cheers. At the conclusion of his brief but animated address, he gestured the students to follow him. Lexi Dunne had arrived in time to observe Mr Kim leading the North Korean students, the Consul and his staff away. At the rear of the group was the student leader, Kang, whom Lexi had befriended.

'Kang,' she called after him. He turned to face her. 'Oh, Kang, your face. It's bleeding,' she said, passing him a tissue.

'I bleed for Supreme Leader,' he announced as he slid the unused tissue in his pocket.

'We had no idea South Korean students might pull this stunt,' she said apologetically.

'We too strong for them. They soft Southerners.'

'We can still have the film, Kang,' she pleaded. 'It's all set up in the cinema and ready to go. Oh, shit.'

'Shit? Why shit?'

'I just remembered. One of our staff is still in the cinema.'

'Hope he enjoy film alone,' Kang declared.

'Alone? What do you mean?'

'Professor Lexi, Mr Kim say we not have film now or any time. Also, no traditional dancing. We very angry with this insult to Consul of DPRK. And invasion of South Korean thugs.'

'That's such a pity.'

'Too bad, I say. We all go now to Kim Jung-un College for meeting with consul. Many things to discuss there.'

With that, he left to catch up with his departing compatriots.

Troubled by the bitter reaction of Kang and the whole North Korean student cohort, Lexi hastened back to the cinema to liberate Jamie. She found the head of marketing and media sitting on the top of the cinema steps. Above him, half torn down by the South Korean students, was the banner which had been fixed above the entrance:

North Korean Film – Aim High in Creation

'Jamie, you OK?' she inquired, looking down on the forlorn figure.

'I'll be OK,' he snuffled. 'I was terrified they might invade the cinema.'

'Would you like to have a coffee? The film's been cancelled so I have some time.'

'That might be nice. I've got to get myself together. I'm master of ceremonies for the parade. Then at 5 pm, we've got the prize-giving for the straplines competition. It's the big event of the day and I look a fright, I imagine. Tell me honestly, Lexi, how do I look?'

'You look gorgeous. As usual.'

'Thanks. That means a lot to me.'

'Have you spoken with Roddy?'

'No, I couldn't get him.'

'Oh?'

'It's lunch time, isn't it? He'll be with the Razer gang in the Batcave. Stuffing their fat faces.'

Lexi's day had started on such a joyful high and her thoughts had often returned to the intimacy she'd shared with Barry Motherwell. Now her Batman world felt as though it could come crashing down around her. This seemed a cruel possibility given the enormous time and energy she had invested in the North Korean student program.

She'd not met the Consul as planned and that now seemed unlikely after the fracas at the Red Studies marquee. He, no doubt, would report to his superiors about the assault and would have no interest in dealing with her. Worse, the incident could jeopardise the future of the North Korean student program at Batman. She felt powerless.

Chapter 35

The President's Open Day Lunch

Nicholas Razer was grumpy from the moment he woke. He resented having to spend a good part of his Sunday at the campus on Open Day. Sinn would have to go to dim sum in Chinatown with their Thai friends without him. The highlight of his day instead would have to be the lunch in the Batcave. Roddy Rodman had vetted Rajesh's menu and wine list to ensure that Razer would enjoy a superior experience as compensation for sacrificing his Sunday.

Roddy had arranged to drive Razer to the campus. Despite his best efforts to lift his boss's spirits, however, Razer remained sullenly silent the whole journey. Roddy heard him sigh deeply as he drew the car to a halt at the entrance to the Batcave.

'Alright, let's get on with it,' said Razer in an effort to enthuse himself. 'With a bit of luck, there'll be an invasion of Martians or the outbreak of World War Three and we can all go home. After lunch, of course.'

Razer's mood improved markedly when he found his high-spirited and fawning acolytes waiting inside the Batcave. They were soon gathered around him and the group stood chatting and laughing at Razer's mordant take on the world, the university and their colleagues. Rajesh and his staff, under Roddy's instructions, ensured that the canapés were plentiful and no glass remained empty for long.

'Nicholas,' began the CFO, 'I heard there was a bit of trouble on campus earlier on.'

'What kind of trouble?' Razer snarled. The last thing he wanted to hear about was trouble.

'Clive Goodenough kind of trouble.'

'I warned Bazza about that looney. Told him to get rid of him. What's our deranged colleague been up to this time?'

When given a full account, Razer declared 'That's enough evidence for me. He's got to go. Roddy, make sure the Vice President gets on with it.'

'Will do, President,' Roddy obeyed.

'There was also some kind of incident at Equine Studies,' the CFO continued.

'Goodenough's been there, too?' asked Razer.

'No, they were spared that. It was a four-legged animal behaving badly this time.'

'That's correct, President,' Roddy advised. 'The Head of Equine Studies has been taken to Robert Gordon General Hospital. Crushed ribs, smashed knee, broken foot, bruising.'

'Awfully bad luck,' said Razer without interest, taking his place at the head of the table. 'Where's Rajesh? I've ordered a dozen oysters each. The bad news is I've only allowed a choice of three mains. My new austerity campaign. However, I've tried to compensate by providing you with a selection of imported cheeses and wines.'

'Nothing from Reg O'Toole's winery, Nicholas?' joked the Head of HR.

'I think I mentioned quality wines,' said Razer to the amusement of his inner circle.

'Someone mentioned the horse woman,' said Razer, casually inspecting the wine list. 'Face like a horse, too.'

'You met her at the stud?'

'Good God, no. At my beginning of year drinks. I remember her neighing at one of my anecdotes.'

His colleagues enjoyed the joke.

'Anyway,' Razer went on, sipping at his red wine, 'what actually happened to Horse Lady?'

'A frisky mare played up. Kicked her in the knee, stood on her foot, then crushed her against a fence. She might cause us some trouble,' said the head of HR.

'The mare?' Razer exclaimed with open-mouthed, wide-eyed, feigned shock.

They all laughed.

'Trouble?' said Razer. 'She'll be covered by workplace insurance, won't she?'

'It's not so much the injury claim,' said the head of HR, 'I fear there might be some repercussions with Dame Pattie College. You might get a call from Betty Allsop.'

'She's not coming today, thank God. What happened?'

'Standing rule at the stud is that visits are not allowed when there's to be a covering,' explained Roddy.

'What do you mean, a covering? A roof?'

'More like a root, President,' joked Roddy drolly. 'A mare that's in season is brought to a covering area and a stallion is introduced. A very randy stallion who checks her out with a bit of sniffing at the tail end.'

'Maybe I should get out to the stud to see the show, after all,' harrumphed Razer to the further amusement of his lunch companions. 'Go on, this is starting to get interesting.'

'Each horse is held by a handler and Dr Callahan was handling the mare. Sadly, the mare wasn't hobbled.'

'Hobbled? Is that a euphemism?' joked Razer. 'Tied a few mares up meself over the years.'

'The hobbles are kind of bedroom slippers strapped on her hooves,' advised Roddy. 'She could kick a lot when the stallion is on the job or when he bites her on the neck.'

'I know that move,' chortled Razer.

'Things can get a bit wild during his dangerous duty, and the hobbling protects him from getting a good kicking.'

'I'd never thought of hobbling,' joked Razer. 'Suffered a few kicks in my time, though!'

The lunchers guffawed.

'Long story short,' Roddy went on, 'the mare kicked Miranda Callahan and jammed her against one of the rails.'

'Very unfortunate, I'm sure. But what's that got to do with Dame Patti College?'

'There was a group of young ladies from DPC who witnessed the whole business,' reported Roddy. 'The sights and sounds of two 500 kilo horses romping in the passion pit was a bit too much for some of them. It can be very noisy and very violent. When they saw the Horse Lady crushed against the fence, screaming, they were very upset.'

'High drama, indeed,' observed Razer, sipping at a glass of red wine.

'That was bad enough,' Roddy continued, 'but was even more hysteria when they spotted the stallion's blood-engorged member. I don't think the girls had ever really … y'know, seen a show like that.'

The lunchers laughed and offered various amusing observations.

'Hope it hasn't put any of the little lassies off bedroom frolics for life!' Razer delivered his line deadpan but to much hilarity.

'How is it this unfortunate event happened on Open Day?' he demanded.

'I understand,' Roddy offered, 'Dr Callahan warned Barry Motherwell that there was to be a covering this morning. He said he thought it would be good for the Open Day visitors to see what farm life is like.'

'Bloody Motherwell, again,' said Razer. 'Anyway, now we're all seated, enjoy your entree, gentlemen. We'll worry about all this when we meet tomorrow.'

THE PRESIDENT'S OPEN DAY LUNCH

ooOOoo

The mains and desserts having been served by Rajesh and his staff, platters of cheese were served to round out the lunch. Roddy Rodman's mobile rang and he moved away from the table to take a call from the Head of Campus Security. He addressed the President gravely.

'President, there's been an incident on campus involving the North Korean Consul.'

'The North Korean Consul? On campus? First I've heard of it,' said Razer, vexed.

'One of our students has assaulted the Consul. TV cameras caught it all, too.'

'Who knew about the visit?' said Razer with growing irritation.

'The Vice President,' Roddy replied.

'Bloody Bazza again. He failed to advise me!' said Razer, annoyed. 'Tell him he's to be in my office 10 am tomorrow. You're all to come and we'll have it out with him.'

'President,' interjected Roddy, 'it's only 15 minutes before you have to rendezvous with the Chairman. According to Jamie's running sheet, you'll both wait at the main arch entry to the Village Place to meet the Minister and his entourage.'

'Last drinks,' Razer announced 'and don't forget to empty your bladders. We might be there a long time, more's the pity.'

'You'll see the seats for guests at the rear of the dais,' noted Roddy. 'Your names will be on your seat. Everyone to be seated by 13:45, thank you.'

'And after it's all over, you're all invited back here for a snack and a cleansing ale,' said Razer. 'Roddy, who's in the Minister's entourage?'

Roddy drew Jamie's running sheet from his jacket.

'Apart from the Minister himself, there's a senior officer from his department and an assistant, a Ms Karisma Jones. I believe Professor Motherwell's been handling her.'

281

'I'll bet he has!' joked Razer. 'Randy old Bazza. And incompetent. What that name again?'

'Jones. Karisma Jones.' Roddy knew Razer wouldn't let it pass without comment.

'American, I assume?' sneered Razer. 'What is it about Americans and names? Why can't they just have normal names?'

There was a collective shaking of heads.

'Who's the departmental officer?' Razer pressed on.

'A Mr Pat Miller, President. Not sure what he's about. Another free loader from Canberra, probably. Apparently, he's to sit on the dais with the Minister.'

'What about security? After that business at Western?'

'There'll be one officer with the Minister and there'll be undercover security.'

'No chance of the Minister breaking the other arm at Batman, eh?' joked Razer.

'And, President,' said Roddy, 'Ms Jones has said the Minister has asked that Mr Miller sits next to you on the dais. I gather he has a kid who wants some advice about university study or some such. Probably wants to pick your brains.'

'Bureaucrats are the same self-serving, opportunistic bastards the world over,' opined Razer as he led his team from the VIP room.

Chapter 36

The Distinguished Guest at Open Day

The regiment's dogs, Mena and Micha, were about to conclude the demonstration, climbing over obstacles, detecting imitation mines in hidden locations and drugs on volunteer regiment members. The crowds standing around were enthralled by the discipline of the dogs and their detection skills.

'Ladies and gentlemen, boys and girls,' Jamie Jamieson bellowed into the microphone to the Open Day crowd, 'wasn't that an amazing display by our Batman University Regiment dogs, Mena and Micha? Please put your hands together for them and their handlers, Colonel Barry Motherwell and Warrant Officer Kevin Burke. Don't go away 'cos they'll all be back soon for the impressive Batman University Regiment parade.'

A ripple of applause arose from the crowd as the two officers and their dogs marched out of the Village Place.

'There they go!' Jamie's attention was focused on the departing men and their dogs, so he was taken by surprise when Michael White leapt from behind onto the dais and snatched the microphone from his grip.

'Attention!' called Michael. 'This is Batman University Invasion Day,' he shouted at the stunned crowd. 'You're all here on the stolen land of the people of the Kulin nation and ….'

The first security officer pinned Michael's arms to his side while his colleague wrenched the microphone back and thrust it at Jamie who stood, mouth agape, still trying to grasp what had happened. The campus security men each took an arm and frogmarched the Indigenous student leader from the dais.

'Invasion! Invasion! Invasion!' Michael yelled. 'Let me go you racist bastards!'

He continued to shout as he was bundled away to the jubilant whistles and whoops of the large group of Indigenous students assembled to observe the stunt.

'Always was, always will be!' Michael bellowed as the security duo led him off to their campus office. The jubilant Indigenous students joined in the chant as they followed Michael, still struggling against his captors. Ever the showman, Jamie rallied to restore calm.

'Ladies and gentlemen, boys and girls, let's give it up for Michael White, our very own Indigenous student leader. Michael is one of the university's best-known pranksters. C'mon, join with me in giving Michael a huge round of applause as he leaves us with our amazing security staff. Let's show our appreciation for the fun he's added to our fun-filled Open Day.'

Still largely confused by what they'd just witnessed, the crowd obliged with varying degrees of enthusiasm.

'Thank you. I'm sure Michael and all our wonderful Indigenous students really appreciate that. There they go!'

Jamie clapped again in a vain attempt to elicit applause from his audience.

'Hey, what a surprise for you all on this special Batman University Open Day. Yeah? We planned to give you lots of fun and we've delivered. Yeah?' a shaken Jamie addressed the bemused crowd. 'I think all of us know about undergraduate pranks.'

Jamie prattled on, attempting to refocus the growing crowd on the fun of Open Day.

'I'm just waiting on a message from our people at the main entrance to Village Place … and, yes, I am delighted to tell you that the fabulous Commonwealth limousine carrying our very special guest, the Minister for Homeland Defence, is about to enter the campus. He'll soon join us on the dais. With his entourage. And that, of course, includes our region's very own Reg O'Toole, Chairman of the University Board, no stranger to residents of this part of this city.'

oOoOoo

'Reg, very good to see you,' said Razer, offering his large, limp hand to Reg O'Toole.

'Hello, Nick, we've got quite a fine day for our Open Day,' Reg observed. Razer noticed that Reg seemed as excited as a small boy waiting for the arrival of a football hero.

'Very auspicious, Reg. It promises to be a memorable Open Day. I've just finished a light working lunch with the executive team over in the Batcave. Bit of a dry run for our new VIP facility.'

'I doubt it would have been dry, Nick. Eh?' Reg said, looking up at Razer with a sly grin.

'Had to wet the baby's head, Reg.'

'Bloody near drowned the baby, I'll bet,' Reg chortled at his own joke.

'There's the Minister's limo coming up the drive now. Y'know, Nick, this Minister is someone I really admire. He's got integrity, courage, the lot. Speaks his mind and doesn't care if he's unpopular. We need more like him, Nick. In government. And universities.'

'Never a truer word, Reg,' Razer dissembled. The limo drew to a halt and a security officer left the front seat and moved to open the rear door to reveal the Minister. O'Toole stepped forward, smiling broadly.

'Reg, you keep turning up in the most unlikely places,' said the

Minister, looking up with a thin mile of recognition. O'Toole beamed.

'Welcome to Batman University, Minister.'

Still sitting, the Minister grimaced, turned gingerly to get his legs onto the ground and eased himself with pained difficulty from his car. Karisma Jones appeared from the other side of the limo to supervise her boss's struggle.

'Minister, careful now. Take it slowly.' Reg O'Toole moved to assist his injured hero.

Reg looked aghast at the cast on the Minister's right arm. He was without a jacket but wore a sleeveless vest against the July cold.

Slowly the Minister drew himself to his full height which Razer noticed was about his own. Two piercing, coal black eyes sat menacingly in pasty face and an immense bald head. His pugilist's nose seemed ideally matched to the combative personality presented in the media. The Minister's driver appeared with an overcoat and draped it over his shoulders, ensuring, as instructed, that it concealed the cast on his arm.

'Minster, let me introduce our President, Professor Razer.'

'Professor,' the Minister nodded. 'Congratulations on the intelligent design initiative I saw the banner over the entrance.'

Razer had been infuriated to see the sign as he arrived and had instructed Roddy that it must be gone before the Minister arrived. Roddy, however, had been given the same advice as had Motherwell. Surely, he thought, the Minister was being disingenuous.

'That's the sort of academic direction the government wants to see in our universities,' the Minister said approvingly.

'Er, thank you, Minister,' Razer said. 'It's an essential element of our vision statement.'

Or soon will be, he thought.

'Pat Miller from my department,' he introduced his suited companion. 'And my assistant, Karisma Jones. She's been working with your people on this visit. And Fred Ferrett, my security escort.'

With Reg O'Toole proudly escorting the Minister, the party made their way through the milling crowds of Open Day visitors into the Village Place. There, they were met by Jamie Jamieson, who directed them to their seats on the dais.

Reg O'Toole stood watching with concern as the Minister lowered himself into his seat before taking his own seat beside him. On the Minister's other side was Nicholas Razer and beside him, the departmental official, Pat Miller. Ferrett sat immediately behind the Minister, eyes darting, constantly scanning the crowds and the buildings enclosing the Village Place. He was speaking so softly into his mobile phone that no-one, even on the dais, could have heard his conversation.

O'Toole leaned toward the Minister.

'Minister, I really appreciate you coming today. In view of last week's disgraceful events at WMU.'

'I'll never give in to thuggery, Reg' the Minister affirmed.

'You've paid a heavy price.'

'Goes with the territory, Reg.'

'And all the criticism in the media, just for doing your job. They've got a lot to answer for.'

'They're dead to me, Reg. I just do what I know is right for the country.'

'But, your family, you've got little kids and a wife. What's it like for her every day and the kids at school?'

'I allow no newspapers into the house and we don't have TV. And my wife's always home-schooled the kids'.

'Brilliant,' enthused Reg.

Meanwhile, Pat Miller engaged Nicholas Razer.

'Since we've got a few moments before the parade, Professor Razer, I wonder if I could raise a personal matter with you?'

'Of course. I understand you have a son looking for some educational advice.'

'It's actually a colleague's son. Jason's got a first class honours degree. He's interested in post-grad study.'

'What's his field?'

'That's why I'd be grateful for your advice. It's neuropsychology. His interest is in men's sexual health.'

'I know a little about that area,' Razer said with false modesty.

'Jason's been looking at the Cephallus Institute at Sandstone.'

'That's a good start,' offered Razer.

'You retain some connection with the Institute, I believe.'

'In a very limited way. With the demands of this role, y'know …'

'I see from the website you're still a visiting research professor with Cephallus.'

'That's honorific, of course.'

'And that you chair their advisory Board.'

'Oh, that. Yes, occasional meetings. But I'm really fully committed here.'

'The Institute's work is to do with improving men's psychosexual health. Men with problems. Did I get that right?'

'Broadly, yes.'

'And Cephallus conducts residential programs for men.'

'That's so.'

'And the programs are operated offshore?'

'Ah, in part, yes. After some weeks of theory in the home country.'

'There are clinics in various Asian cities.'

'Working in our region is what the government urges us to do.'

'Of course.'

'You know, Mr Miller', Razer said, seizing an opportunity, 'we still have some difficulties attracting international students to Batman.

Would you have any advice for us there? Perhaps your department could assist us?'

'Perhaps we could. But, back to Cephallus, if I may. I understand it was established by you in the UK.'

'I couldn't take all the credit. It was a team effort. Usual thing in universities. Teams.'

Razer looked out at the parade ground and saw the campus security clearing the way for the impending regimental parade. He longed for the parade to start.

'The problem for Jason is,' Miller turned to look directly at Razer, 'we've heard that Sandstone will be closing the Cephallus Institute.'

Razer's jaw stiffened. He looked across and saw Reg, animated, addressing the expressionless Minister.

'I hadn't heard that. Times are tough in universities, these days, even Sandstone, I should think.'

'It wasn't a matter of funding as I heard it. I gather the cash flow through Cephallus is very heathy. More a question about their mission. And methodology.'

'That is surprising, I must say,' said Razer. 'But, with my heavy commitments here, I'm afraid I couldn't offer your son ...'

'My colleague's son.'

'Of course. But I wouldn't be able to help him out at Batman, I'm afraid.'

'I understand. Anyway, Professor Razer, I imagine you'll hear about the developments at Sandstone very soon.'

'Soon?'

'That's what we're hearing. In Canberra.'

'I'm afraid I haven't been much help to you, Mr Miller.'

'On the contrary, you've been very helpful.'

Where is the bloody regiment? thought Razer.

Chapter 37

Open Day Calamities

'Ladies and gents, boys and girls,' Jamie began, 'once again, welcome to the Batman University Open Day for 2022. As you can see, our official guests are now with us so we can commence the next part of Batman's fun-filled Open Day.

'I am very excited and it's my distinct pleasure to invite to the microphone the Chairman of the Batman University Board, a local identity, Mr Reg O'Toole, who'll introduce our very special guest today. Thank you, Mr O'Toole.'

Not accustomed to public speaking, Reg O'Toole kept his remarks brief, though no-one who heard him could be in any doubt that he held the Minister in the highest esteem. They were indeed long-standing political comrades. So enthused was Reg to have the Minister at Batman that he departed from the script prepared by Jamie and inevitably found himself fumbling for words. Reg finally began to round out his speech.

'And so, ladies and gentlemen, and all the youngsters here, this Open Day for Batman University in 2022 is one which affords us the opportunity of celebrating the lives of two Australian heroes. Two great men. One, the hero of this city's founding is John Batman, after whom this great university is named. The other,' said Reg turning to face the Minister, 'is our Minister for Homeland Defence, a true hero for modern Australia. Minister, I invite you to speak.'

The Minister rose and as he did so, Ferrett removed the overcoat revealing the plaster cast on his arm. Some in the crowd gasped. He moved to the lectern and with a practiced pause, surveyed his audience. They fell silent.

'Chairman O'Toole, President Razer, distinguished guests, friends,' he boomed. 'I thank my old friend Reg O'Toole for the invitation to Batman University in this lovely region of the city. And I thank him for putting me in the company of one of our great historical figures, John Batman. I am humbled.'

Here, he appeared to flinch with pain. Some in the crowd winced with him.

'As you've no doubt heard, I recently sustained injuries in the performance of my Ministerial duties on another university campus. You can see the result for yourselves. But no injury, no assault, no raging mob will ever intimidate me or the government,' he declared to scattered applause.

'Thank you. I'll keep my remarks brief and start by acknowledging the leadership of Chairman Reg O'Toole. As most of you will know, Reg has dedicated himself tirelessly to development of the Robert Gordon community. Batman University is just one of the many successes of the O'Toole family. And if ever there were a rags-to-riches story of immigrants to this country, it is the O'Toole family story. The O'Tooles are a model for all immigrants to our great country. I wish more would follow their example of loyalty, hard work and community involvement.'

Reg hated being singled out, but from this Minister, it was an honour. He gazed at his hero with undisguised admiration.

'I want to congratulate Mr O'Toole, President Razer and Batman University on taking up a challenge I threw down to all Australian universities just a few short months ago. Sadly, not all have yet risen to the challenge.'

The Minister paused for effect and ran his eyes around the crowd.

'Though all will. Eventually. That challenge was to establish university regiments to support the government's strong stance against growing threats in our region. In this city, I don't have to elaborate on those threats. We must prepare our country for the dangers which undoubtedly lie ahead.

'Friends, I am here today to celebrate the formation of the Batman University Regiment and to inspect their parade. As we admire these fine young people this afternoon, I want to remind you that the price of freedom is eternal vigilance. Thank you.'

With that, the Minister resumed his seat. Ferrett rose again to drape his overcoat over his shoulders but the Minister waved him away.

'Ladies and gentleman, boys and girls,' urged Jamie now back at the microphone, 'let's thank the Minister for a great speech and for honouring us with his presence today. Thank you, Minister,' said Jamie, turning to face him with his own gesture of applause. He turned back to face the crowd.

'We're waiting now to see that the main arch entry is clear.' Jamie looked for the signal from the campus securer officer. 'Yes, we're now ready to go. Make sure you all stay back behind the ropes security have set up. Thank you.'

The crowd could hear the distant sound of military orders being barked, followed by the unmistakable stomp of troops marching to a familiar military marching song.

'I now invite the official party and guests to be upstanding. The regiment will march in and the Minister will take the salute.'

Atop the O'Toole Building, two men in black, wearing balaclavas, scanned the scene below, one through a telescopic sight on a rifle.

'Now,' announced Jamie to the crowd with all the dramatic affect he could master, 'I invite you to welcome the proud Batman University Regiment as they march into the Village Place. Let's hear it for the regiment!'

With that, the stirring sounds of a military march blared out over the public address system and all eyes in Village Place turned to the main arch to see the regiment in three platoons marching in, led by Warrant Officer Burke with Richa at his side. At the rear of the regiment marched Colonel Barry Motherwell, with ceremonial sword held high. On her lead, Mena trotted along at his side.

Kitted out in ceremonial dress, the recruits marched into the Village Place in perfect formation. For this ceremony, they bore no weapons. All arms and feet moved in perfect synchronicity. They wore olive shirts and brown ties behind khaki tunics and matching pants. Their R.M. Williams black boots were highly polished and their heads topped by the traditional slouch hats with upturned right side brim bearing the gleaming rising sun badge.

So awed by this impressive entrance and stirring military music were the Open Day visitors that they broke into enthusiastic applause. Mistaken by some of the Open Day crowd for veterans, there were many spontaneous cries of 'good on yer' and 'thank you for your service'.

'By the right, change direction, right wheel' shouted Kevin Burke, and the regiment executed a manoeuvre to the right and marched towards the parade ground in front of the dais.

'Parade halt!' The shiny black boots on a hundred right feet stomped down in unison.

'Parade, right turn!' The regiment pivoted as one to face the dais and tight boots stomped down in unison again.

'Right dress!' Shuffling into line, eyes to the right, arms outstretched to the left, lining up from the right, the regiment executed the command.

'Stand at ease!' Left arms snapped down and heads turned sharply to the front.

'Parade, general salute!'

OPEN DAY

With his left arm, the Minister returned the salute. Confused, Reg O'Toole hesitated, shot a glance at his hero before emulating the left-handed salute.

Motherwell then marched to the dais to face the Minister and saluted again with his ceremonial sword, its hilt in front of his face. He held Mena's leash in the other. At this signal, the Minister stepped down from the dais, followed by Reg O'Toole who fell in behind him and Motherwell for the inspection.

So loud and stirring had been the military music and so arresting the sight of the well-drilled regiment in the enclosed Village Place that a respectful hush had fallen over the assembly as the Minister commenced his walk of inspection along the front row of the regiment. Proud parents of regiment members whispered to each other pointing with forefingers in front of their faces at their son or daughter.

All were caught up in the excitement of the occasion when the near reverential mood was pierced by the blare over the loud speaker of jarring, unfamiliar military music. All eyes were drawn to the main arch by the unmistakable sound of sharp, loudly issued military parade commands. A contingent of soldiers in olive green uniforms marched into Village Place with rifles shouldered.

Their bouncing, robotic goose-stepping march was unmistakably that of the army of the Democratic Peoples' Republic of Korea. The angry North Korean students intended to make a patriotic disruption to the Batman University Open Day. The Consul, his colleagues and Mr Kim, together with the women in traditional dress, followed on behind clapping in time to the martial music.

On top of the O'Toole building a telescopic lens was trained on the abdomen of Kang as, with appropriately severe countenance, he led in the North Korean troops. The Minister stopped, causing Motherwell to do likewise. They looked behind to see North Korean soldiers marching toward them. Motherwell decided to act.

'Minister,' he said, 'I'll deal with this.'

The Minister said nothing, unsure of how he should react. He looked to the dais for Ferrett.

'Hold this,' Motherwell said thrusting Mena's lead at the Reg O'Toole. 'She's too temperamental to take.'

Taken by surprise, Reg stood speechless, in charge of the regimental dog.

With his ceremonial sword still aloft, Motherwell strode toward the North Koreans. Stunned Open Day visitors fell back while the official party rose to their feet alarmed as the North Koreans advanced.

Reg O'Toole, hesitated, confused, and looked to the Minister who'd put his left hand to his ear to hear Fred Ferrett's instruction.

'Minister, those are North Korean military and they're armed. You must return to the dais immediately,' instructed Ferrett, checking his holster. 'Leave now!'

'In the confusion of the moment, the Minister set off at a trot after Motherwell. The hapless Reg O'Toole stood motionless, uncertain as to how he should respond. Mena became increasingly agitated, straining at her lead, as she watched Motherwell striding away from her.

For Mena, the practiced procedure of the parade inspection had been interrupted and Motherwell had abandoned her to a stranger. She had been trained over many years to sense danger and to respond. Her ears stood erect but she heard little. She saw a man chasing Motherwell and that man was wearing a protective arm shield. She knew her duty.

With a thrust of her ageing but still powerful legs, her sharp paws dug deep into the parade ground, scattering gravel onto the front line of regiment members, still at attention, as she propelled her huge body forward. The flummoxed Reg O'Toole was still clinging to her lead. It took no more than two metres before he tumbled heavily face forward onto the parade ground. Now free and with the lead flapping behind her, Mena accelerated away from her fallen charge.

Realising his error in following Motherwell, the Minister propped and turned to see Ferrett waving and calling to him. This was the very moment that, with all the lethal efficiency acquired over years of training and combat, Mena leapt at the cast on his arm. She took it firmly in her jaws, the impact of her leap causing the Minister to stumble. In a trice, he was face down on the parade ground. He struggled against her powerful grip, but Mena executed her years of training to disable a victim and, to the gasps of the Open Day officials and the crowd, she began dragging the Minister, face down, over the gravel surface.

In dismay, Reg O'Toole scrambled to his feet and rushed to the scene, yelling for the savaging dog to desist, vainly waving his arms and attempting to distract her from her prey. Mena, however, was intent upon disabling her victim and was deaf to his bawling. Finding the medical cast too firm for her ageing teeth, she deftly switched her savage attention to the Minister's left arm, dragging him across the parade ground again.

'Somebody do something,' Reg stopped and cried out but the horrified onlookers were paralysed as they watched the unfolding catastrophe. Finally, Mena looked up at Reg with one angry eye as he tried to grab her lead. She growled as if to warn him off while never releasing her grip on her victim.

Ferrett drew his handgun and cautiously advanced on the two men and the dog, locked in a fearful struggle. There was a collective gasp as he adopted the shoot-to-kill stance. His attempts to get a line of sight on Mena were, however, thwarted by the flailing Reg O'Toole.

Now wide-eyed in disbelief, Kang needed no intervention by an apparently armed Colonel Motherwell to order a retreat. The martial music continued to blare like a fitting musical score to a horror movie.

Hearing Reg's primal screams behind him, Motherwell turned, horrified, to see Mena in full attack and disable mode, still pulling at the Minister.

'Oh, Christ, no,' he shouted. 'Mena. Stop! Drop!' he instructed as he ran toward her, but the noise of war had taken its toll on her hearing.

Micha had watched this unfolding drama from the front row of the regiment, where Kevin Burke, stunned into inaction, remained at attention with his flummoxed troops. Micha observed intently and with increasing agitation as a man with a gun aimed at Mena advanced on her. He recognised danger. With all his considerable strength, Micha broke away from the befuddled handler and charged at the weapon holder, leaping to artfully disarm Ferrett and topple him.

Ferrett was also soon on his stomach on the parade ground. Micha was still standing triumphantly over him as Kevin Burke came running up to rescue him. Micha looked up, tail wagging in anticipation of his master's approbation.

'Micha! Get away! Here!' Micha obeyed, backed slowly away, never taking his eyes from his victim.

'Oh, mate,' Burke addressed Ferrett as he got to his feet, 'sorry about that. He was spooked seeing you with your weapon drawn. You OK?' he inquired. Ignoring Burke's apology, the shaken security officer swore and moved to pick up his revolver from where Micha had forced it from his grasp.

'Mate,' yelled Burke, 'don't go near that weapon! Or he'll attack you again. Leave it there and I'll get it for you later. Just back off slowly, don't run and stand well clear.'

With an eye on the still unfolding drama involving Reg O'Toole and the Minister, Kevin shouted desperately to O'Toole to back away from Mena. By now, the breathless Motherwell was approaching and gesticulating wildly but in vain at Mena. He approached cautiously, pleading with O'Toole.

'Reg, Mr O'Toole, you're in danger,' he called. 'Please move away from the dog.' Ignoring this plea, Reg readied himself to lunge once more at Mena's leash as it flew wildly around. Having completely disabled her prey, who now lay inert before her, Mena now turned her ferocious attention to the bothersome Reg O'Toole.

She leapt up at the Chairman who found himself face to face with the assault dog. Mena's large paws were on his shoulders, her teeth bared and a single flashing eye locked on his. Then began a strange dance, a dance of man and dog, with Reg forced to dance to the dog's choreography as she executed her learned manoeuvre to push him down.

A black-clad man on top of the O'Toole building had been looking down at the unfolding drama through the telescopic sight of his Blaser long-range rifle. He hesitated, unable to get clear sight of the dog as it savaged the Minister. Now the dog was attacking a lesser human and he had to intervene. He took aim at his target.

It was clear that Reg O'Toole could not last much longer in this interspecies struggle and ultimately succumbed, emitting a fearful cry as he collapsed backward. A collective gasp arose from the Open Day crowd as the Batman University Chairman fell heavily, his head sounding a dull thud as it smashed into the hard parade ground. Mena stood proudly with her forepaws on his chest. Some in the Open Day crowd gasped, others screamed. Razer and others in the official party rose from their seats but were powerless to intervene.

A drama was also unfolding on the top of the O'Toole Building.

'Suit down! Oh, shit!' blurted out the man in black. 'Ben!'

'What!' exclaimed his comrade.

'I was trying to bring down the dog.'

'What have you done, you dumbfuck.' he roared as he raised his binoculars to his eyes. 'Oh, shit. I leave for two minutes to take a piss and you knock a civilian.'

'Sorry, Ben, I …'

Mena bent her massive head and sniffed Reg's contorted face before returning her attention to the Minister who, groaning, was attempting to get to his knees. She threw her whole weight on his back, forcing him down once more, in her frenzy grabbing at the back of his neck.

'Mena! Leave it!' Motherwell instructed in vain. He circled around, wildly gesticulating the instruction, but her focus was on the struggling assailant she had pinned down.

'What are we gunna do, Ben?' pleaded the shooter in black. 'Oh, shit.'

'Drop the dog.'

'The dog?'

'The dog that's standing on the Minister's back, you dopey shit. Then we're outta here.'

The impact of the second shot from the Blaser saw Mena slump between the savaged, exhausted body of the Minister and the inert body of Reg O'Toole. The Minister's shirt on his upper left arm was torn and his face bloodied from its rough passage across the gravelled parade ground.

Ferrett limped toward his fallen Minister, face down on the parade ground, and crouched beside him.

'Sir, it's Ferrett. The situation is now under control. Let me help you up,' he offered as Pat Miller arrived from the dais. Together, they assisted their boss to his feet. His left arm was still bleeding and one side of his face was impregnated with bloodied gravel.

'Aaagh,' he groaned in pain. 'That hurts. Get me to a hospital,' he instructed. 'I need a rabies shot. And turn off that fucking music.'

The Minister paused as he and his entourage came upon an unconscious Reg O'Toole being attended by Kevin Burke.

'Thanks for trying, Reg,' he muttered and, supported by Ferrett and Miller, he moved on without comment past a distraught Barry Motherwell who was kneeling beside the lifeless Mena.

The sudden collapse to the ground of an old man clutching his chest and the renewed attack by a large savage dog on a Minister of the Crown lying on the parade ground stunned the Open Day crowd. Many watched in horror, waiting for an intervention, while most decided Open Day was now over.

Nicholas Razer and Roddy Rodman approached the Minister as he limped with the assistance of Miller and Ferrett toward his car. The usually composed Razer was clearly unsettled.

'Minister, I am very sorry about these awful events and I ...'

The Minister grimaced, halted and fixed Razer through bruised eyes.

'You're going to be sorrier yet, Razer. You're fucked now. Of that you can be certain,' he snarled as he limped off.

Clutching the Minister's coat, Karisma Jones approached the Ministerial limo, trembling with shock. It had been the second violent attack on her boss in a week.

'I think it's time I went home. This could never happen on a college campus in the States,' she whimpered to the driver.

Razer and Roddy followed and watched as the driver assisted the Minister into his vehicle. He was pale and clearly in shock. As the Commonwealth car pulled away, he managed a final vengeful scowl at Razer. Somewhere out on the highway, Razer could hear the wailing siren of an ambulance, probably two, with police escorts speeding toward his campus.

'What a fuckup, Roddy,' he said ruefully.

'President,' he suggested, 'the Chairman ...'

'Oh, yes, Reg. How is he?'

'It's serious.'

'Staring down the maw of a rampaging dog probably brought on a cardiac attack. Or he's concussed himself when his skull hit the parade ground.'

'Kevin says he's been shot,' said Roddy.

'Shot? How on earth could he have been shot?'

'Kevin thinks it might have been a sniper on top of O'Toole. Part of the Minister's security. Probably trying to hit the dog and with all the pirouetting, hit Reg instead.'

'Quite the marksman,' muttered Razer.

'Kevin sent a couple of his guys up there to have a look but they found no-one. Just a few fresh cigarette butts and a pool of urine. Kevin tried giving first aid until the ambulance arrived. They've taken Reg to Robert Gordon General.'

'Bugger of a role, university Board Chairman. You can get shot,' mused Razer.

'If Reg's position is as dire as Kevin believes, we may have another problem,' said Roddy.

'As if there aren't enough already,' muttered Razer.

'We don't yet have the five-and-a-half million from Reg. Just ten grand to cover the Harvey visit. Now we might never see the full grant.'

Roddy followed as Razer shrugged, turned and walked slowly away. 'Oh, well, easy come ...' he muttered.

'President,' Roddy caught up with him, 'the team are planning to retreat to the Auld Scotland. Should I take you there?'

'No, best take me home. I imagine the media will be after me tonight and I think I'll lie low for a while. Tell Jamie he can field the media inquiries and that I won't be available for comment so they needn't try.'

'Anything else you need me to do?'

'Nearly forgot. You've got Jacky Harvey's mobile number. Give her a call. Tell her I'm sorry we won't be able to have dinner tonight. Bugger it!'

Roddy walked with Razer toward the O'Toole car park as the last of the Open Day visitors made their way to their cars to which had been attached flyers declaring 'Batman University for Intelligent Design'.

The campus was now eerily silent. Stunned by the sight of the savage dog attacks on suited dignitaries, the North Korean troop had returned to Kim Jong-un College. Their attempt to disrupt and intimidate the Batman Regiment had been bettered in ways they could not have anticipated. Back at the college, the Consul spoke of revenge for the honour of the Motherland and said they would soon receive important orders from the Supreme Leader.

Lexi Dunne had decided to skip the regimental parade. She regretted abandoning Motherwell on this momentous day for him, but supporting the Indigenous cause seemed a higher duty. She'd attended the performance of the Indigenous play, *Coranderrk*, in the grounds of the cottage, and found it very moving. Batman's statue had been graffitied again but she understood why. It had been a day of mixed emotions and she wanted some quiet time.

As she'd sipped on a cup of green tea in the cottage, she heard the unmistakable sound of North Korean military music across the campus. Alarmed, she made her way to the Village Square in time to witness the violent scenes unfold. She stood, shaken, by Mena's savage attacks, by the sight of two men lying bloodied on the parade ground, a gun drawn on campus and Barry Motherwell possibly in danger. She stood rooted to the spot as the silent crowd dispersed, Kevin Burke marched the regiment and the dogs away, and the North Koreans departed.

On the dais, Jamie Jamieson sat alone, head in his hands, quietly sobbing. Again. A little distance off, beside the lifeless body of Mena, Motherwell stood, arms limp at his side, eyes downcast, expressionless. Lexi was torn. She mounted the dais and sat beside Jamie. He looked up at her through his tears and she draped an arm around his heaving shoulders.

'I'm sorry you had such a horrible experience, Jamie. So close to those terrible scenes, so close to danger.'

'It's shocking, so distressing, Lexi. I'm just so upset for them,' he wept.

'I know. We can just hope that Reg and the Minister are OK.'

'No, not them. I mean the entrants. Now we won't be able to have the prize giving for the strapline competition. All that work, for nothing. It's very upsetting.'

Lexi resisted the urge to slap him.

'Get over it, Jamie,' she snapped. With that she moved to Motherwell and slipped her arm through his.

'You OK, Mother?'

He bit his upper lip.

'Poor Mena. She was such a lovely dog,' she said.

'Yeah,' Motherwell managed to say, choking up.

'Mother,' she took his hand, 'let's just sit down here for a few minutes with her before they take her away.'

'Yeah. That would be nice.'

They sat on the rough parade ground and Motherwell stroked Mena tenderly for the last time.

oooOoo

The Open Day visitors had almost completely dispersed by the time three State police squad cars with uniformed officers arrived, followed by a carload of plain clothes detectives. Some academic and other staff had remained to clear up and some other university staff and students were soberly going about dismantling the stalls in the Village Place. The operators of the various food, drink and fun outlets were also closing up.

Kevin Burke had dismissed the regiment and ordered them to leave the campus. He locked Micha away in the regiment kennel with Herbie and returned to the parade ground to find Barry Motherwell. He was passing by the main arch as four plain clothes detectives accompanied by uniformed police approached.

'G'day,' he hailed the senior detective wearily. 'I'm Kevin Burke, Head of Campus Security. I'm glad to see you, we've had quite a day.'

'So we've heard. How are enrolments going?'

Kevin Burke forced a smile.

'This is now a crime scene, mate,' he informed Burke. 'Everybody has to leave. The uniforms are going to clear everyone out while the boys and I have a look around.'

'I can tell you what I saw happen.'

'No need, mate. We're federal police and we've been fully informed,' he replied.

'OK, understood,' said Kevin. 'Anything I can do?'

'Yeah, before you piss off, tell that fat bloke in the fancy dress,' he gestured toward Motherwell 'and Annie Oakley to leave. And take the dog.'

'That's Colonel Motherwell and Professor Dunne. His dog is dead,' said Kevin defensively.

'I don't care if it's Colonel Sanders and Professor Henrietta Higgins sharing a hot dog, mate. The campus is now closed.'

Chapter 38

Open Day: the Aftermath

Kurt Kropp sat at his desk on the following Monday morning, poring over the day's online metropolitan and national newspapers. They gave full accounts of the events at the university Open Day, highlighting the shocking assault upon the Minister and the Chairman of the university Board. There were file photographs of the Minister, Reg O'Toole and Nicholas Razer. Each newspaper reported again on the assault on the Minister at WMU just days earlier and injuries he had sustained. Coverage was extensive, even being picked up in international news outlets.

Occasionally, his attention was drawn to his office television where various channels showed graphic footage of the events with warnings about scenes that some viewers would find distressing. There was even footage of the arrests of Pilgrim and others vandalising a jumping castle and reports of assaults by a student on a Consul and fist fights between factions of Korean students. The images went viral on the internet, and Batman University joined the growing list of educational institutions whose names would forever be linked to violence. Batman had never before been so prominent, nationally and even internationally.

Kropp could scarcely believe the little-known Batman University was now so newsworthy.

'Poor old Reg,' he mused, 'must send a card.' His attempts to call

Nicholas Razer's mobile number had gone to message bank. Huh, he thought, Nicholas is lying low. Kropp had moved to the couch to watch the television coverage of the events at Batman when his EA buzzed him.

'Kurt, just had a call from Jenny, Professor Razer's EA at Batman. You're to attend a meeting in the President's office at 10 am Friday.'

Must be important for Nicholas to summon me, just like that, he thought.

'What it's about?'

'She didn't say.'

'I thought the campus was closed,' he said, based on a report he'd seen in all the media.

'You'll be met by security and you're to bring ID.'

No doubt about Nicholas, thought Kropp, looks like business as usual for Nicholas Razer and GoodKropp. He dashed off an email to Razer expressing his dismay at the awful events of Open Day and wishing him well in the difficult days ahead. 'Until Friday,' he signed off.

Kropp arrived at the campus that Friday and turned his Mercedes through the main entrance where a tattered banner fluttered in the breeze. He halted at the boom gate as a campus security approached.

'Can I help you, Sir?' the security officer asked.

'Kurt Kropp for a 10 am meeting with the President.'

Kropp passed him both his driver's licence and passport, noting the absence of vehicles and pedestrians along the long drive to the entrance to the campus buildings.

'All good, Sir. You know how to find the car park for the O'Toole building? You'll be met there.'

As Kropp entered the O'Toole car park, he sighted the Head of Campus Security waiting. Kropp's was one of just three vehicles in the car park save for a couple of police vehicles. Burke approached, dispensing with his traditional salute.

'Morning, Mr Kropp,' Kevin said formally. 'This way, please.'

Kropp followed him up the path to the entrance of the locked O'Toole building. Glancing up, he noticed the Australian and university flags at half mast. Village Place, usually thronging with students, was an empty, desolate space. Kropp cast his eye around the buildings that bordered Village Place and they were clearly unoccupied, adding to the sense that this was a ghost campus.

'There you are, Mr Kropp,' said Kevin pressing the elevator button. 'I'll meet you here at the conclusion of your meeting.'

The elevator made its way to Level 12 where Kropp was met by Jenny Partridge who escorted him in silence along the eerily quiet corridor to the President's office.

'Just knock and go in,' she said rather stiffly, Kropp thought, as she sat at her desk and stared at her black desktop screen.

To his surprise, he found Sally Sloane sitting at the President's office table. She looked up, gave a half smile, and invited him to take a seat.

'Thanks for coming,' Sally said. 'I presume you heard about Reg.'

'I hadn't in fact,' admitted Kropp, 'but I saw the flag on top of O'Toole.'

'He didn't make it,' she said softly.

'I'm sorry to hear that,' Kropp said.

'Never thought I'd say it, but I'm going to miss him,' she admitted.

'He was in a class of his own,' said Kropp.

'Y'know, during one of his moments of consciousness,' Sally said, reminiscing, 'the specialists told him his situation was grim and that they were proposing to airlift him to the ICU at Sandstone University Hospital. Reg said he'd rather die right there in the O'Toole Wing at Robert Gordon General than go anywhere near Sandstone.'

The old curmudgeon was an idiot, too, thought Kropp. Why am I here? Am I a bereavement counsellor?

'He never forgot or forgave,' said Kropp. 'Will Nicholas be joining us?' Kropp looked around as though Razer might walk in at any moment.

'Afraid not.' Sally's demeanour changed as she looked intently at him.

'Can't say I'm surprised,' said Kropp. 'I presume he's still in a state of shock.'

'We don't know what state he's in,' she asserted darkly, her eyes narrowing, 'but it's not the State of Victoria.'

Kropp struggled to comprehend what he was hearing.

'Brian Phipps turned up at the house at the usual time on Monday,' Sally continued. 'Sinn came to the car, highly distressed. She said she hadn't seen him since she'd gone to yum cha on Open Day.'

'Good God! He's in hospital, too?' Kropp speculated.

'When she returned from the city later in the day, she saw he'd been in the house. His study was in some disarray and, when she checked his bedroom, she found clothes had been removed along with a suitcase and all his toiletries.'

'What's going on?' asked Kropp dumbfounded.

'We think he's abandoned his employment. The Minister has appointed me interim President and I'm also going to be acting Chairman of the Board. Again.'

Kropp was still incredulous. Razer was a psychopath and a narcissist. But a quitter? Kropp found it hard to believe.

'I picked him as a proud man,' Kropp said still stunned. 'I suppose it was the shame of the Open Day debacle.'

'That's not what going on,' said Sally with a resigned shrug. 'I was called to a meeting with the Premier and the Minister earlier this week. The federal police had advised that Nicholas flew to Bangkok Sunday night.'

Surely not, thought Kropp.

'It turns out the Cephallus Institute was a cover for an international sex tourism operation.'

Even the worldly Kropp found it hard to comprehend what he was hearing.

'Cephallus was set up to capitalise on male sexual problems,' Sally went on. 'To exploit men with problems such as erectile dysfunction, impotence, performance anxiety, any kind of problem with sex. After a couple of weeks of theory here then came the off-shore therapy.'

Kropp's expression changed as his mind jumped to the correct conclusion.

'Yes, patients were sent to "clinics".' Sally employed the double inverted commas gesture. 'In various Asian cities for so-called therapy.'

'And the clinics were …'

'Modern buildings in good neighbourhoods, with pseudo-medical fit outs, professional medical signage and so on. The treatments were given by prostitutes trained by Cephallus to pose as therapists.'

'So what led Nicholas to take to his heels just now?'

'The head of the federal police vice squad, a fellow called Pat Miller, was part of the Minister's entourage on Open Day. He wanted to meet Nicholas and they had a conversation. Nicholas's flight seems suspicious, to say the least.'

'But … why?' Kropp found himself uncharacteristically struggling for words.

'Maybe the police took the view that if they signalled that they knew what he was up to, he'd flee. Then he's the problem of other jurisdictions. Turns out Scotland Yard are pursuing him, too.'

Kropp shook his head in disbelief but his mind had already turned to more pressing issues.

'All very unfortunate, Sally. What a pickle! I presume you want a search for another President.'

'Ever the opportunistic consultant, aren't you, Kurt? Sorry, but no.'

Perhaps he finally understood the purpose of the meeting. Sally wanted to remind him that she'd had serious reservations about Razer. He had been summoned for an 'I told you so' meeting.

'So, you're staying on as President?' Kropp asked, already planning his exit from the pointless meeting.

'Not on your Nellie! I'm completely and permanently over universities, especially since Open Day. I'll come back to the matter of the President later. However, there are some other appointments with which you might be able to help.'

Kropp's mood improved immediately.

'BU has taken a serious hit,' Sally went on. 'The Premier and the Minister are concerned that the university could become unviable.'

'There was international coverage on the TV this morning,' observed Kropp.

'Yes, and our international student business is looking as though it's on the ropes. You heard there were problems on Open Day with the North Koreans?'

'They were armed,' Kropp said.

'The rifles were purely ceremonial. The real problem was an incident with the North Korean Consul who was on campus. A student on the Red Studies marquee assaulted him.'

'I heard.' Typical blood nut, thought Kropp.

'The North Korean government's ordered their students home. They've already gone and with them our best income stream.'

'That will hurt.'

'The government fears starting some sort of contagion among international students, not only at BU but more widely. What's more, all this happened in front of Jacky Harvey. And there's another piece of bad news.'

Could there be more? thought Kropp.

'She's also left, never to return.'

After all the work I put in on her, thought Kropp, annoyed.

'She's left because of the minor Open Day incident?'

'More serious than that. The problem is the shooting of Reg.'

'I imagine she was pretty upset. I got the distinct impression that she really liked the old boy.'

'Reg hadn't yet signed off on the full grant to BU for Red Studies. Now, he never will.'

Is that all there is? Kropp thought. She wants me to find another professor of Red Studies? I'm going to decline.

'I could go on with lots more of the fall-out from Open Day,' said Sally, 'but back to BU's future. The Premier and the Minister want me to take some drastic steps to change the image of the university. If BU goes down, there'll be political fallout in the region. They've promised me funding and I pretty well have carte blanche.'

Perhaps this is the gold at the end of the rainbow, thought Kropp.

'What are you thinking, Sally?'

'BU needs an image makeover.' Sally seemed suddenly energised at the prospect. 'You'll need to know what's planned to have a good story for prospective candidates.'

So get on with it, thought Kropp.

'By the way, you should know that I had to work hard to persuade the Minister to let me use you again. He remembered that you were involved in the appointment of Nicholas.'

'Thanks, Sally. I appreciate your support.' Kurt Kropp knew that having been involved in Razer's appointment, his stocks would be low in government and other universities.

'I'm going to reinstate the former structure with the four faculties. So, we'll need four Deans.'

Now we're getting somewhere, thought Kropp.

'So, the former Deans will be able to apply for their old jobs, but you want me to find other candidates?'

'The former Deans have already gone,' Sally declared.

'All of them?' Kropp asked, bewildered. He hadn't had to run searches for a whole university senior management since the last time at Batman. The prospect was mouthwatering.

'Mervyn Pilgrim was humiliated at being booked by the police,' Sally smiled a knowing smile. 'He's heading to theology college and will become a university chaplain.'

To save souls on campuses, thought Kropp. Poor souls!

'And Morgan Freestone?' Kropp asked. 'Always a poor appointment.'

'The Minister's made a role for him in the Department of Higher Education. To do with international education and requiring him to travel overseas a great deal.'

'Something to keep him away from the Department?' smiled Kropp.

Sally confirmed this with a nod.

'What about the prickly Clive Goodenough?' he inquired, genuinely interested in the fate of the malcontent Dean.

'His actions on Open Day were serious misdemeanours.'

'So, you sacked him?'

'I didn't have to. His psychiatrist recommended he resign and he did. He's now in some program of therapy and isn't likely to work again. He's destined to spend his days at home being harassed by his notorious ogress of a wife.'

'And Lexi Dunne? She always struck me as being a great asset for Batman.'

'She was. The loss of the North Koreans was a big blow for her. But there was a more serious issue which meant she'd have no future at BU.'

OPEN DAY: THE AFTERMATH

Kropp could hardly imagine the intelligent, vivacious Lexi Dunne giving any grounds for dismissal.

'On that coffee table beside you,' said Sally as she pushed back her chair, 'is a remote for the TV over there. I'm stepping out for a few minutes while you look at a couple of short videos from Open Day.'

With that, Sally Sloane left Kropp with the television remote and a quizzical expression on his face. He watched each videos twice, pausing them occasionally, each pause accompanied by a gasp. Some minutes later, Sally reappeared, glass of water for each of them in hand. Kropp looked up at her, slumped in his chair.

Kropp gratefully took the glass and exhaled loudly. Sally resumed her seat with an expression that invited his comment.

'I could half see a woman. With what looked like cowgirl boots …' he ventured.

'None other than Professor Lexi Dunne,' Sally said, with a sigh of resignation.

'Oh dear. I can't imagine those boots have ever been so far from each other,' Kropp joked.

'Lexi Dunne's fate was sealed,' Sally observed.

'As was Barry Motherwell's,' Kropp observed.

'You recognised the thrusting buttocks?'

'Hardly. But, there's no mistaking the body shape. Amazing footage, if you'll excuse the pun.'

Sally suppressed a smile.

'You said the video's from Open Day?' inquired Kropp.

Sally nodded.

'Filmed on campus. But where?'

'In the Vice President's recently refurbished office.'

'But, how on earth …?'

'I got it from the Head of Campus Security.'

No wonder Kevin looked so awkward today, thought Kropp.

'Kevin Burke had a surveillance camera in the Vice President's office?' Kropp was aghast.

'He was merely the delivery man. A couple of his recruits in the regiment were doing a demonstration climb of the O'Toole building. For instructional purposes, Kevin had issued them with helmet cameras. When they reached Level 12, they found themselves looking in at an amazing scene in Barry's office. The cameras were operating and all they had to do was direct them. As you can see, their directions were a bit hit and miss, but the actors are easily recognisable.'

They weren't acting, thought Kropp.

'By the time the climbers heaved themselves onto the roof of O'Toole, they were laughing hysterically. That soon stopped when they encountered the guys on the roof. They were pretty quickly down and sharing the videos with the regiment. Kevin eventually got them but wasn't sure what to do with them. Nicholas wasn't contactable so he brought them to me.'

Kropp took a deep breath. 'So, both Lexi Dunne and Barry Motherwell have left?' he asked.

Searches for four Deans and a Vice President, thought Kropp. Four becomes five! Throw in a search for a President and it's six. Oh, happy days!

'I imagine the videos have been circulated by now among students,' Sally said. 'It's only a matter of time before they reach the staff. Then the internet. Lexi and Barry are going to be famous.'

'They're lucky their faces aren't shown.'

'They'd still find it very difficult to come on campus again.'

They'll have to come elsewhere, Kropp thought. 'What'll they do now?'

'There's going to be another happy ending. Lexi and her daughter are moving to the farm with Barry to develop his farming interests. He's a top rate animal geneticist and has plans for cattle breeding. And horse breeding with Miranda Callahan from Equine Studies. When she's walking again.'

'Phew. This is big news, Sally.'

'There's four big searches for you.'

Isn't it six? thought Kropp.

'Wonderful! Now, are you quite sure we can't help you to find you a President? And a Vice President?'

'Quite sure,' Sally declared. 'The new President has already been identified and will be joining us soon.'

Six becomes five, thought Kropp.

'She'll decide on her Vice President.'

Five becomes four, he conceded.

'No advertisement for President, no search, no short-listing, no interview, no referee reports, no security checks, no qualification checks, no psychometric testing, no presentations, no meet and greet ...'

'And no headhunter,' smiled Sally Sloane. 'I think you'll do quite well out of our Open Day debacle.'

'OK, but I'm intrigued,' admitted Kropp. 'Who's going to be the next President?'

'You probably need to know. But any loose lips and GoodKropp would soon be Damaged Kropp in every university in the country.'

Kropp acknowledged he understood with a nod.

'The higher education sector badly needs differentiation. BU is going to become Australia's first Indigenous university.'

'An Indigenous university?' Once more, Kropp could hardly believe his ears. 'Really?'

'There's not another Indigenous university in the country.'

That's all very well, he thought. It's going to make it much harder for me to sell the place, thought Kropp.

'Come on Sally,' his curiosity was at breaking point, 'who's the new President?'

'Surely you've worked that out, Kurt. It's going to be Gladys Cherbourg, of course.'

'But she's already said no.'

'As soon as I realised Nicholas was gone, I sounded her out and she was enthusiastic. The premier spoke to the PM and got a very positive response and promise of additional funding. Gladys will be with us in two or three months.'

'Astounding. I suppose I should congratulate you, Sally. As a headhunter, though, I wouldn't like to see this recruiting method becoming common.'

'It's your lucky day, Kurt. There'll be one other search for you.'

Not Vice President, Kropp already knew. Maybe he'd have to take on Red Studies, after all.

'I had an in-confidence chat with Jamie Jamieson about marketing and straplines for a new indigenous university. You can add a search for his successor to your list.'

'He baulked at it?'

'Not at all. He went at it with characteristic enthusiasm. His options for straplines for the nation's first Indigenous university were "Batman University – Making Blacks Whole". Then there was "Batman University – Where Dark Matters" and his favourite, "Batman University – Your Aboregional University".'

'He's gone?'

'And that meant losing Roddy Rodman, too. Going to retire to their country estate.'

So maybe Sally needs a new éminence grise for Gladys, hoped Kropp.

'There's something else you'll need to know. The government has approved a change of name for the university.'

Looks like no search for a henchman, he conceded.

'There's a rather obvious but very alluring name,' ventured Kropp. 'O'Toole University in honour of Reg. In a very real way, he gave his life for this university.'

'We'll be doing something to acknowledge Reg,' said Sally, 'but we won't be naming the university after him. We have to get over the ignominy of a university named after one of the villains of our colonial history. And the catastrophe that was the 2022 Open Day. We're going to be Barak University.'

'After the Aboriginal painter? Some of whose work I understand adorns the walls of Nicholas's house.'

'Not any longer. I had Brian retrieve them. The paintings will be returned to the Barak Gallery on campus.'

Barak University? mused Kropp. Might even work well in parts of the US.

'And our new name will bring another little benefit.'

'How so?'

'We'll save on letterhead. We'll still be BU.'

Postscript:
The Other Batman University

https://www.batman.edu.tr/En

From: president@barak.edu.au

Subject: Down Under Update

Date: 22 December 2022

To: rector@batman.edu.tr

Dear Musta,

Many thanks again for your email in July offering your commiserations after the debacle of our Open Day. Yes, it was a truly shocking day. The media coverage as far away as Turkey was astonishing. Sorry I didn't respond more fully at the time but, as you can imagine, as President and Chairman, I've been busy! There have been exciting developments here over the past months, which I'd like to bring you up to date on.

First, as you'll have noticed, my university is now known as Barak University, named after a nineteenth century Indigenous leader in this region. At last, the fourteen-year verbal feud between our Ministers over naming is over. Now, there's only one Batman University, so mission accomplished! Keep it to yourself for now because my Minister will write to yours very soon. That should make your guy happy, at last.

Second, my preferred candidate for President has taken up duty. You'll remember Gladys Cherbourg from when she and I visited your campus a couple of years ago. She's a first-rate academic and an experienced manager. More than that, she's the most important person in my life. I'll be replaced as chair of the Board in the new year and, after a respectable period when I've severed my links with Barak Uni, we'll move in together.

So, as we say, every cloud has a silver lining.

Sally

Wakefield Press is an independent publishing and
distribution company based in Adelaide, South Australia.
We love good stories and publish beautiful books.
To see our full range of books, please visit our website at
www.wakefieldpress.com.au
where all titles are available for purchase.
To keep up with our latest releases, news and events,
subscribe to our monthly newsletter.

Find us!

Facebook: www.facebook.com/wakefield.press
Twitter: www.twitter.com/wakefieldpress
Instagram: www.instagram.com/wakefieldpress